The PROMISE BRIDE

Also by Gina Welborn and Becca Whitham

Come Fly With Me (e-novella)

Published by Kensington Publishing Corporation

The PROMISE BRIDE

Gina Welborn
and
Becca Whitham

ZEBRA BOOKS
KENSINGTON PUBLISHING CORP.
http://www.kensingtonbooks.com

ZEBRA BOOKS are published by

Kensington Publishing Corp.
119 West 40th Street
New York, NY 10018

First Printing: September 2017
ISBN-13: 978-1-4201-4397-3
ISBN-10: 1-4201-4397-2

eISBN-13: 978-1-4201-4398-0
eISBN-10: 1-4201-4398-0

10 9 8 7 6 5 4 3 2 1

Printed in the United States of America

To the baristas of Starbucks
on Cache Road in Lawton, Oklahoma.
You've been with this project from the beginning,
fueling our creativity with sugar and caffeine.
Thank you from the bottom of our cups.

ACKNOWLEDGMENTS

There are a huge number of people to thank for their help and support while we worked on this project. Unfortunately, we couldn't name everyone and their contributions, or this section would be longer than the book itself. We would, however, be negligent if we didn't mention a few people who have contributed greatly to this story.

First, we are grateful to Dr. Ellen Baumler of the Montana Historical Society for her help with maps and articles about Helena during this time period. Much of the history we incorporated comes from what she sent, including information refuting what we found online. It's been great to have a dedicated historian working with us. Any factual errors are ours. Second, our agents, Karen Ball and Tamela Hancock Murray, worked hard to find a home for this series. We're glad it landed with Kensington Publishing in the hands of Selena James and the rest of the team there. Third, we've benefited from fabulous critique partners who have helped us hone our writing skills, specifically (for Becca) Kim Woodhouse, Kayla Woodhouse, and Darcie Gudger. Fourth, we want to thank Kelly Long for the offhand conversation she had with Gina that put the idea in her mind to submit to Kensington.

Our families deserve special thanks for putting up with the writing craziness. Our husbands, Jeremy Welborn and

Nathan Whitham, will be receiving special jewels in their eternal crowns because, let's face it, being married to a writer is probably the world's toughest job. Finally, thank You to our Lord for instilling in us the desire to write, for arranging our life circumstances so we would meet one day at a Starbucks, and for assuring us in both big and small ways that He is with us.

The vision is always solid and reliable;
the vision is always a fact.
It is the reality that is often a fraud.

—G. K. CHESTERTON

Let no debt remain outstanding, except the
continuing debt to love one another.

—ROMANS 13:8a (NIV)

Chapter One

Chicago, Illinois
Saturday, April 2, 1887

Fortune favored the persistent.

Emilia Stanek smiled, climbed into the cable car, and found her usual spot on the second bench on the left. As she adjusted her father's old leather army haversack from her side onto her lap, she noticed a brass button on the blue woolen coat she wore over her Spiegel uniform was, literally, hanging by a thread. She tugged it off. Rolled the tarnished metal with her fingers. The balls of her feet throbbed from so many hours managing the customer-service counter, and her fingers ached from filling out complaint forms and bill-paid receipts. She'd lost too much sleep, spent too little time with her siblings during the last nine months. And her cheeks were cold from the wind. Still . . .

She smiled.

The extra dollar a day she'd earned from volunteering for a Saturday shift made the inconveniences all worth it.

The cable car bumped up and down as people continued to load.

Emilia lifted the haversack's top flap and dropped the

button inside, where it came to rest against her week's wages. She settled against the seat. With what she'd saved since she'd begun corresponding with Finn, in three short months more, she would have the rest of the funds needed to purchase train fare for Roch, Luci, and Da to move with her to Montana. *Montana.* Her heart warmed at the thought of the heavenly word. Once they were settled, her dear Finn would spend a month courting her properly before he proposed. His last letter had mentioned how perfectly he believed they were suited. Oh, she agreed.

Mrs. Phineas Collins.

Emilia Stanek Collins.

Emilia Collins.

She closed her eyes. How perfect her name sounded with his. Finn's soon-to-be proposal would be more than she'd ever dreamed. More than a mail-order bride could ever hope for. She adored him. She relished knowing God had answered her prayer for a good man. She loved the future they'd have together on his ranch. Luci needed time to enjoy the remaining years of her childhood. Roch needed to escape the gang he was running with. Da's lungs needed fresh, healing air, the kind found out west.

Montana Territory was the land of many opportunities.

Chicago—

Her upper lip curled. Chicago wasn't the land of any opportunity, despite the buildings rising along the streets. The noisy city smelled of industry, sewage, and slaughtered pigs. If only they could leave now, before the summer heat blanketed the area with the stench that gave her headaches, made her nauseated, and interfered with her sleep. No sense bemoaning her circumstances, though. Finances and Da's health dictated they wait until the dry air of July to leave. She could endure three and a half more months in Chicago.

Mrs. Phineas Collins.

Emilia Stanek—

The cable car bell rang.

“Hold the car!” two familiar voices called out.

Emilia looked to her left. Jonny and Harv, two of Spiegel’s weekend stockmen and her self-appointed guardians, shoved their way through the pedestrian traffic, waving their newsboy caps. They jumped onto the car next to her. As they did every Saturday. Harv scrambled over Emilia’s legs to take a spot to her left, while Jonny sat on her right. The pair smelled of bratwurst, beer, and sweat. The packed cable car gathered speed, leaving the State Street stop and heading west toward the gold-and-pink sunset.

West. She sighed. *Thank You, God, thank You for bringing Finn into my life.*

With each bump and turn, the wooden slats of the bench pressed into Emilia’s back. Jonny and Harv squashed her shoulders. The chilly, late-afternoon breeze caused by the car’s twelve-mile-per-hour speed blew wisps of hair onto Emilia’s face, despite the black bonnet she wore. She shivered yet continued to smile. Hope warmed her soul. Joy flooded her heart.

Someday soon . . .

“Anything exciting arrive today?” Emilia asked after giving Jonny and Harv time to catch their breath.

Harv shifted to face her. “Teak tables from Burma.”

Now *that* was interesting. Emilia scrambled through her haversack for a pencil and her historical research journal. She’d already investigated Venice, but Burma was an unknown. “Burma”—she printed the letters—“as in B-u-r-m-a?”

Harv nodded. “It was what were stamped on the crates.”

The car stopped, and passengers unloaded and loaded.

Emilia swayed her shoulders, nudging the male bookends to give her space. Just because she barely weighed a hundred pounds, was a good twelve inches shorter than they were, and looked more fifteen than twenty-one, it didn't mean she had less of a right to equal space on the bench.

Jonny bumped her shoulder. "What'd ya learn about the fifth King Henry?"

"One of these days," she warned, "I won't be around to do the studying for you."

Harv eased up the tip of his cap. "You don't look like yer dying." For all the disbelief in his tone, concern flickered in his blue eyes.

Emilia patted his arm. "I'm not dying." And because she couldn't contain the joy she felt, she grinned. "I'm moving to Montana this summer."

Silence.

The cable car's bell rang.

Harv's laughter began a split-second before Jonny's.

Emilia pursed her lips to hold back a retort. Whether they believed her or not, she *was* leaving Chicago on July 16, once the public school's summer term ended. She and her family were moving to a cattle ranch on the magnificent grasslands of Montana. Where the air smelled of wildflowers and sunshine, where she could sing at the top of her lungs. Where Roch would learn to smile again. Responding to Finn's mail-order bride advertisement had been the best decision of her life.

As their laughter mellowed, and because she had sunlight, she flipped several pages back in her history journal. "Henry of Monmouth became king of England in 1413 . . ."

By the time the cable car reached the tenement stop, she'd given them a decent lecture on the young medieval monarch and his nine-year reign. They debarked the cable car and continued to talk as they headed down the uneven sidewalk, passing decrepit two- and three-story wood-frame and brick buildings that lined the unpaved streets. Clothes hung from windows. Dogs barked incessantly. Family fights were neighborhood fodder. Compliments of the factories within walking distance and the slaughterhouses farther south, not even the smells of roasted pork and fresh-baked bread could cover the stench of the neighborhood sewage.

Soon, though, this would all be a distant memory.

Emilia refocused on her notes. "In 1599 William Shakespeare wrote his play about King Henry's—"

"Ah, Miss Stanek," a craggy voice called out.

Emilia looked ahead. Her stride slowed, Jonny and Harv matching her pace. Her landlord descended the outside steps to the wooden tenement's second floor, where her family lived. For all Mr. Deegan's three-piece suits and oiled mustache, the man who owned the entire block was as grimy as Chicago. The only times he visited were when he came to collect the rent, which wasn't due for another month. But he'd clearly been upstairs. In the last year, from the moment Da returned home from the cotton mill on Friday, he never left the house, save for attending Sunday worship. Deegan had to know Da's pattern. This could only mean the two had talked. For how long?

Emilia shoved her journal inside the haversack. Her grip tightened on the bag's strap across her chest. Her pulse skittered.

Mr. Deegan's chestnut mare, tied at the post, looked fairly rested. Thirty minutes? An hour?

Heartbeat pounding, Emilia met Mr. Deegan at the bottom of the stairs. "Can I help you with something?"

Jonny and Harv towered behind her like the archangels they weren't.

Mr. Deegan's narrowed gaze shifted from her to Jonny and Harv, then back to her. "I expect you can." He withdrew a folded sheet of paper from inside his suit coat and held it out to her.

Jonny and Harv didn't move.

Emilia nodded to the four-story brownstone across the street, where Mr. Bello, standing on a ladder, had begun his round of lighting the tenement streetlamps. "Go on," she ordered. "Please. Mama Bello has dinner waiting for you two." She paused until her erstwhile guardians crossed the street to their boardinghouse before she turned back to Mr. Deegan's beady gaze. She took the paper he offered. "What's this?"

"List of repairs needed."

Emilia scanned the words from the Health Department compiled after their latest—and humiliating—round of inspections of heating, lighting, ventilation, plumbing, and drainage. *How can you live in this?* had been the inspector's silent question each time he'd glanced her way. It wasn't as if anyone in the tenements had a choice . . . as long as they stayed in Chicago. Both hands on the letter, she crumpled the sides, her mouth sour over the inspector's findings.

Disease is not a moral but a sanitary problem.

Not something she needed any health inspector to tell her. Diphtheria, typhoid, cholera, smallpox, yellow fever—most of the tenement deaths in the last decade had been from one of those diseases. Including her mother's. Showing her the official letter from the Health Department made no sense. Mr. Deegan was as literate as she. If anything, this was for show. To remind those in the tenements of his power and control.

"According to this, *you*"—she fixed him with a pointed look—"have been issued citations for multiple offenses."

"Offenses for which I am not at fault."

Did he think she was stupid? Despite their repeated requests for repairs, not a shingle had been replaced or window resealed. One of the walls of the privy they shared with the Jaegers still had bullet holes from the last street fight.

She glanced around to see a growing crowd on the street despite the chill in the air. "Sir, our monthly rent, which has been doubled from three years ago, is sufficient to cover the cost for repairs."

"Au contraire, my dear." He whisked the paper from her hand and read, "'Remedies for violations include repairing defective plumbing, construction of new sewers and drains, ventilation applied to waste and soil pipes, cleaning privy vaults, and lime-washing rooms. Thirty dollars will do.'" Mr. Deegan refolded the paper. "To be fair, I've divided the cost of repairs equally among each tenement. You have until this time Monday."

"You expect me to come up with thirty dollars *in two days*?"

He nodded. "I'm a generous man. Considering this is the fourth notification in the last two months, I could evict you instead."

Emilia flinched. Fourth? Her heart pounded against her rib cage. For all Deegan's sleaziness, he didn't look to be lying. Da had to know about the inspection report and extortion demand and had kept the truth from her. But why? She had the travel money from Finn, plus what she'd saved by working an extra shift. They needed every penny for train fare. She couldn't leave her family. She wouldn't.

She swallowed to ease her tight throat. "We don't have the money."

"How strange." His left eye twitched; the corner of his mouth curved. "I know that wealthy rancher of yours wired train fare for you to come to Montana. Thirty dollars, I hear. Enough to buy his mail-order bride a first-class ticket in the ladies' car. He must think highly of you."

Emilia gritted her teeth.

At her silence, he smirked. "Miss Stanek, unlike you, your sister is quite the hostess. Cordial, inviting, talkative." He stepped closer, close enough for her to smell the bitter coffee on his breath. "You'd be wise to stop thinking you're better than everyone else in these parts. You ain't going nowhere. This, dearie, is your lot in life." He tipped his hat to her—"Until this time Monday"—and then to the crowd, which began to disperse with mumbles and backward glances.

Without another word, Mr. Deegan mounted his horse and rode off.

Emilia gasped for air. She dashed up the stairs to their two-room tenement and jerked the door open; the smell of coffee and stew hit her. "Da!" She closed the door hard. He exited the bedroom Emilia and Roch shared with their twelve-year-old younger sister, Luci, who followed. Before either could speak, Emilia pulled the haversack's strap over her head. "Were you watching through the window? Did you hear everything? When were you going to tell me Deegan's extortion attempt?"

Da and Luci exchanged glances, their dark eyes wide.

"I'll set the table," Luci muttered. As she went to work, Da stroked his salt-and-pepper beard as he always did when pondering what to say.

Emilia hung her bag and coat on an empty wall hook next to the door. Roch's coat was missing. If he wasn't home soon, he'd break the curfew she'd insisted Da give him. Someday he wouldn't need a curfew. Someday Roch would have his own room and not have to sleep on the floor. Da would have one, too. No more sleeping on the couch for him. No more living in cramped spaces with grimy, paper-thin walls and sharing a privy with another family. This was *not* their lot in life. Once she married Finn, they would have privacy. Their lives would be better. Once they moved to Montana.

If they moved to Montana.

She clasped her hands together to contain the shaking. Took several deep breaths. She had to regain control. She had to be calm. She had to find a way to solve this problem. She would find a way. She always found a way. If she—

"Emilia, I know what you are doing." Da's Polish accent sounded like he'd immigrated to America recently instead of twenty-six years ago.

She stared at him. What was he talking about?

"You think you will find a way to solve this." He frowned. "Stop! We are doing it my way this time." Da motioned to the table, where Luci was placing bowls of stew. "We eat."

His way? Emilia found her seat next to Luci. Something odd had come over her father. His face held more color than she'd seen in months, and his shoulders seemed straighter. And he wasn't coughing. Though his clothes hung on his lithe frame, Da looked like he had renewed purpose, determination. A plan. How could this be? Da believed in living in the here and now, not dreaming of the future—an odd belief considering the years he'd fought in the War Between the States to prove his loyalty to his new country.

They bowed their heads.

Emilia stared absently at her lap as her father asked for the blessing. If Da were well enough to travel, they could leave for Montana sooner. All they needed was—

"Amen," Emilia blurted the moment the prayer ended. "I will write to Finn, explain the situation, and—"

Da groaned, then looked up. "This I did already."

"What?"

"Keep your voice down." His voice lowered. "The walls have ears."

Emilia fingered her spoon but didn't pick it up. "When did you do this?"

"Two months ago, after Deegan made the first demand." He took a bite of stew and then another. "Eat." The moment she obeyed, he spoke barely loud enough for her to hear. "Finn has agreed to marry you by proxy."

She collapsed against the back of her chair. "What?"

Luci grabbed the loaf of rye bread. "It means he marries a girl who is pretending to be you, and then, when you arrive in Helena, you'll already be his wife. He must really love you to agree to a proxy." She tore off a chunk, then handed the loaf to Da. "Right?"

"My girl listens well." He broke off a section of bread, then gave the remainder to Emilia, his brown eyes narrowing on her. "Listening is as much a virtue as persistence."

Emilia straightened. *She* listened quite well, despite what he thought. She ate several bites of the bland, meatless stew and the hard bread to keep from blurting out the myriad of questions flooding her mind. Once she had all the information Da was withholding, she'd be able to figure out what to do next. No one could make a plan like she could. No one could solve a problem like she could.

His bowl empty, Da left the table. He slid a box out from under the couch. He withdrew a buff-colored, paper-sized envelope, then walked back to the table.

Da sat next to Emilia, in Roch's empty chair. He spoke in a hushed tone. "This is a power of attorney granting a woman named Yancey Palmer permission to stand in for you as Finn's proxy bride. Monday morning you will take it to a notary, who will watch you sign." He handed her the envelope. "Keep it safe because you must file it once you reach Helena to make the marriage official. Usually, it must be in the judge's hands before he will agree to perform the proxy, but we don't have time to mail it, and Finn has arranged for the judge to act based on our word that it has been signed."

Emilia stared at her father, overwhelmed at the news.

"After it is notarized," Da continued, "you will then meet us at Dearborn Station. Once the judge in Helena telegrams that the marriage has taken place, you, Roch, and Luci will buy train fare to St. Paul, and then on to Helena. I will move into the Old Soldiers' Home. I will take odd jobs over the next three months to earn my train fare."

"No, our plan has always been—"

"Listen!" Da barked in a tone he usually reserved for Roch. "The plan has to change."

Emilia squirmed as she sat under his chilling gaze. She didn't like this change. Da needed to trust her to do what she did best: find a solution and make it work. *She* had found Finn's mail-order bride advertisement. *She* had convinced Da to move to Montana. *She* had taken the extra job. She had even figured out a timeline for leaving that accounted for Da's health and Roch and Luci's school schedule. Changing plans based on a frantic response to a crisis wasn't wise.

Luci moved around the small table and crawled onto Da's lap, laying her head against his chest. By the look on her face, Emilia knew her sister was close to tears.

Da kissed the top of Luci's head. "We have to be practical, Emme. You don't have enough to pay my fare, too."

"I'll buy tickets for the emigrant car." Better to have her father with them, even if it meant the unpleasant prospect of riding in an open train car for three days.

"You know my lungs can't—"

"But ours can! You can stay in second class."

"There isn't enough money for us all. You need money for food. You have to pay the lawyer for the power of attorney."

Luci broke into tears. Da held her tight.

"Please, Da." Emilia leaned forward, stretching her hands out to grip his arm. This wasn't happening. It couldn't be. "We have to stay together. I can find a way to buy us all tickets. Give me time."

He shook his head. "There's no time left."

The front door opened. Roch, his face red and chest heaving, dark hair tussled by the wind, stepped inside. He closed the door. "I returned her books."

Emilia straightened in her chair. Why were they making plans and not including her in decisions? She glanced between her father and brother. "What books?"

Roch shrugged off his woolen coat. "The library ones."

"I wasn't finished researching—"

"Shh," said Da and Luci in unison.

"Someone had to," Roch groused, "so you have nothing to keep you here."

"And I bet you happily volunteered to take them," Emilia snapped.

"If it gets you outta here quicker . . ." He shrugged. "Good riddance, I say."

His hateful words ripped into Emilia's heart. She held his gaze, waiting for a flicker of remorse, waiting for some sign he didn't mean what he'd said. Something in the last year had caused him to hate her, but once they were all in Montana and life was good again, he would appreciate what she'd sacrificed for him to have a better life. He would remember he loved her.

Roch tossed his coat onto a wall hook, then headed to the stove. "I'm starving."

Emilia stared at her brother. His words—*if it gets you outta here quicker*—resonated in her mind.

She gave Da a questioning look. "Doesn't he know he's—"

Da shook his head, cutting off the rest of her question. "You have to trust me, even with what doesn't make sense."

Luci managed a smile. Weak though it was, it seemed to say, *it will all work out, Emilia; just trust Da*.

Emilia clenched her hands together, lips pursed tight. Too much of his plan didn't make sense. Roch would not get on the train without Da. She knew it. Da knew it. This new plan was destined to fail, at Dearborn Station to be precise, and then where would they be? Stuck in Chicago for another year, maybe longer? Or, worse, their family divided and living three states apart? Da's lungs couldn't take another year of working in the cotton mill. The family was stronger when they stayed together. She had to find another solution.

Roch filled a bowl with the last of the stew. He sat in Da's usual seat and began eating.

Da patted Roch's back. Then his knowing gaze settled on Emilia. "Emme, if you can't trust your father, whom you can see, to do what's best for you, how can you trust God, whom you can't see?"

How dare he—!

Emilia snatched the envelope and walked to her bedroom without another word. Da's question was a slap in the face. This had nothing to do with God or her faith or even trust; it was about doing whatever was necessary to keep their family together.

She'd lost Mama.

She wasn't about to lose another person she loved.

Chapter Two

Circle C Ranch, Montana Territory
Saturday, 5:43 P.M.

He was running out of time.

Finn Collins scratched his chin, his black winter beard hot and itchy. If only he could relieve the prickle in his soul as easily. He laid the yellow telegram announcing Emilia's imminent arrival on the kitchen table, hoping the added weight wouldn't be the proverbial straw to break the rickety legs. "Thanks for comin' all the way out here to deliver this telegram, Miss Palmer, but it wasn't necessary. I could have picked it up myself next time I was in town."

Yancey Palmer grinned and scolded him with a glance. "Seeing as how I'm about to marry you, you can call me Yancey."

The joke was getting old. Two months ago, when Emilia's father first proposed the proxy marriage, Finn had asked Yancey if she'd be willing to secretly stand in as his bride. Though she'd kept the news quiet, every time she'd seen him at church, she'd wanted to pretend they had more of a friendship than they did. Because she was doing him a favor, he'd put up with it.

He winced when Yancey took off her leather gloves and added their weight to the table. It wobbled, and he grabbed the edge to keep it steady. He needed Yancey out of his house and fast, but she looked to be settling in for a cozy chat.

She took in the kitchen and the rest of his log cabin in one sweeping look. A small kitchen melded into a small sitting area, where a pine ladder led to a small bedroom loft.

Nose wrinkled, Yancey sniffed the air. "What's that smell?" Without waiting for him to answer, she took two steps to the cast-iron stove and, after grabbing a stained towel, lifted the lid from the pot. A wooden spoon lay on the countertop. She picked it up, stirred the beans, and took a small taste. "Awful. Where's your salt?" She reached over to open the yellow cupboard door nearest the stove.

He raced to block her from opening the next one. "What do you think you're doing?"

Yancey jerked her hand away from the handle and spun to face him. "Really, Finn, I'm just looking for salt. Must you yell?"

If it would keep her out of his business, he'd not only yell, he'd pick her up and toss her out the door. The brown of her suit would match the dirt outside, so it wouldn't even damage the wool. He took a deep breath to calm his galloping pulse. "Sorry, but proxy bride privileges don't extend to rummaging through my kitchen." He opened the cupboard with the salt and handed it to her.

She raised her blond eyebrows, her blue eyes twinkling. "May I? I wouldn't want to be accused of seasoning your beans uninvited."

Her saucy humor broke some of the tension in his chest. "Because you asked so nicely, of course."

Finn peered across the cramped room at the clock over his rock fireplace. In two more minutes, three at the most, he needed to be out the door, disguise in hand, to meet Madame Lestraude's new girls. Madame was already upset with him. He couldn't afford to make her unhappy by missing the rendezvous point. She might demand her four hundred dollars back, at which point his ranch would shrivel and die.

The brutal winter blizzards had left thousands upon thousands of cattle all across Montana dead. For weeks on end, he'd worked with fellow ranchers to clear their swollen bodies from creek beds, hollows, and anywhere else the landscape was littered with their carcasses. His twelve remaining cattle were emaciated things hardly worth nursing back to health. But they were all he had left of his dream to run the finest ranch in Helena. A dream so close to death he was choking on the decay.

Madame Lestraude's money had already been spent on alfalfa, fencing, a plow, and some new cattle. Though no one expected another hard winter like this last one, Finn wasn't taking any chances. Never again would he be caught unprepared.

At least not by weather. Yancey Palmer was another matter.

Tapping his toes inside his boots, Finn waited while she salted his beans, tasted, added more salt, tasted again, and repeated the process twice more before replacing the lid. He didn't want to raise her suspicions by asking her to leave—plus, being rude to a woman you needed to help you reach your dreams wasn't wise—but he needed her gone. Now!

"Much better." She looked around the room. "You could use some nice yellow curtains and a colorful rag rug."

Finn checked the clock again, irritation rising at her dillydallying. "Don't you think I should leave decorating to my actual bride, as opposed to the proxy one?"

She snickered. "Maybe, but it might make the actual

bride—as opposed to the proxy one—feel welcome." She cast another critical look around the room.

Would the woman never leave? Finn stuffed his hands inside his jeans pockets and squeezed them into fists. He was out of time. If she took offense and decided not to stand in for Emilia at the proxy wedding, he'd find someone else. He'd have to. "Sorry. I have someplace I need to be and I'm already running late."

Yancey cocked her head, studying him for a moment, then raised her eyes to the ceiling and shook her head. "Honestly, Finn. Stop being so secretive. I understand why you wanted to keep your mail-order bride and wedding hush-hush in case things went sour, but there's no reason to hide how you need to be somewhere."

The reason she thought he wanted to keep his mail-order bride a secret was far from being true, but he didn't disabuse her. She was leaving. That was all that mattered.

"Who are you meeting? Is it Hale?" Her eyes lit up and her voice went airy. "Is he going to be your best man?"

"Can I give you a bit of advice, Miss Palmer?" Finn pulled one hand from his pocket and tugged at the neckline of his green plaid shirt. "Stop chasing Hale Adams. You're never going to catch him."

Yancey gave him the exact shrug he'd seen her give his best friend, Mac—who was not only the county sheriff but a close friend of Hale's—when he'd offered the same advice. How a woman said, *That's what you think,* with the lift of her shoulders was a mystery. But pretty much everything women did was a mystery to him.

Yancey picked her gloves off the shuddering table. "What time do you want me to meet you at City Hall?"

Thank heaven she was still planning to help him! Finn walked to the door and held it open for her. "I imagine it will be somewhere around ten or eleven on Monday morning. Will you be working in the telegraph office then?"

"Of course." She tugged the end of her glove and came toward him. "Do you think the ceremony will take much longer than fifteen minutes?"

He shook his head. The less he said, the faster she would leave.

"Then I'm sure my father will be able to take my place for a bit."

They walked outside into the sunshine. Finn inhaled. The house, though solidly built, was too small, the walls too close together. The feeling too much like prison had been.

When they got to where Yancey's horse was tied against a tree, Finn leaned down and cupped his hands to help her mount. She stepped into them with a little more force than necessary. Maybe his warning about Hale hadn't been shrugged off after all.

She swung into the sidesaddle and adjusted her skirts. "Until Monday, Finn."

"Until Monday, Miss Palmer." He untied the horse and handed her the reins.

She slapped the leather strips and rode out so fast her straw hat fell back and her blond hair whipped in the wind.

Finn rubbed at his beard as he watched her ride out. The moment she disappeared, he raced back to the house, grabbed his greasepaint and bandanna, and ran for the barn. He prayed he wasn't too late. If he missed getting those girls, Madame Lestraude was going to kill him.

Chicago
Monday, 8:16 A.M.

Emilia tapped her fingers on the office chair's wooden armrests. Nipped at her bottom lip. Tapped her heels against the wooden floor. What would warrant Mr. Spiegel's insistence that she wait here in his office to talk while he spoke to his father? Notify them she was quitting, turn in her uniform, and leave the building—that was the plan Da had agreed to if she was going to do this his way. Spiegel first, notary second, then meet at Dearborn Station by ten to telegram Finn that the power of attorney was signed so the proxy marriage could commence. She smoothed the pink fabric of her skirt. Tugged on the cuffed sleeves.

The wall clock ticked.

She glanced around Mr. Spiegel's empty-save-for-her office. What was taking him so long? They didn't owe her any back pay. She owed them nothing. More than one salesgirl had up and quit, leaving the others to work her shift. Emilia wasn't a salesgirl, though. The customer service manager before her had spent a week training her before he moved on to managing the warehouse. She couldn't stay here another week. Or another day.

She gripped the haversack's leather shoulder strap across the bodice of her Sunday dress, drawing what comfort she could from it. After three years serving in the U.S. Calvary, Da had earned the promotion of being courier. Not a bullet or cinder had scarred the leather bag while he'd carried it. It had survived a war. Da had survived a war. He'd honored his commitment in the face of death and had not run. Nor would she run. Ever.

Emilia Stanek soon-to-be Collins did not run from a battle.

But she *was* running. Fleeing Chicago and their landlord's greed. Emilia shifted in the chair. Da said they had no choice. Deegan could keep their month's rent and everything in the tenement, save for their clothes and a few personal items. He could sell what they'd left behind, find new renters tomorrow. What he believed was their *debt* to him would be settled. It would all work out. She could trust Da to know what was best for his children.

She could. Would.

She gripped her bag close. Her heels tapped against the floor. She worried her bottom lip. Despite the cool breeze through the partially open window, perspiration beaded at her temples. Maybe she should remove her black straw bonnet, but that would imply she was willing to stay for a while. She needed to leave. Good gracious, this was taking too long.

The minutes passed.

And passed.

The clock ticked.

And ticked.

The door opened. "And bring me the working samples of next month's advertisements," the voice behind her said. "We need to begin the summer with an explosion, metaphorically speaking."

Emilia looked over her shoulder. Mr. Spiegel closed the door with his foot, his pudgy hands holding two steaming mugs, a folder under one arm.

He handed her a mug. "Sorry for the delay." He moved around his cluttered desk and tossed the file in the clearing between mounds of papers and what looked to be past-edition catalogs. His metal chair squeaked yet held his bulk. "Dad and I have given your resignation some thought and we've decided not to accept. We need you to continue managing our customer service department."

Emilia blinked. "But—but—"

He waved her to silence. "Relax, Miss Stanek. I have an offer for you." He sipped from his mug, then motioned for her to do the same.

Emilia pretended to drink the bitter brew. How anyone could enjoy coffee was beyond her. After a pretend swallow, she forced a grin. "I am not interested."

He set down his mug. “Don’t rush to judgment. I’ve reviewed your employee file. In the thirty-one months you’ve been working for Spiegel, you’ve arrived at work every day a minimum of five minutes early, never missed a day due to illness, your cash drawer has never come up short, and you have received one hundred and eight letters of praise from customers.” He leaned forward, his gray-eyed gaze intent on hers. “We receive complaints all the time. You are the only employee to ever earn such a plethora of compliments. Our business grows because customers like you.”

“Thank you.” Emilia stared into her coffee mug. Her cheeks warmed at his commendation. Knowing she’d put in an honorable day’s work was all the praise she needed. She couldn’t help glancing again at the Bavarian cuckoo clock on the side wall. Almost nine. She needed to leave. She took another pretend sip of coffee, then looked around for somewhere to put the mug. No empty space.

“Spiegel needs you,” Mr. Spiegel continued. “It’s why we are willing to increase your pay an additional twenty cents a day.”

Emilia nodded in gratitude. “I appreciate your generosity, sir. I have been honored to work for Spiegel, but—”

“Fifty cents.”

She stared at him. Hard. Was he serious? They would pay her a dollar *plus* fifty cents a day? At that rate she could save enough for Da’s train fare in one month instead of three. But if they stayed, they would have to pay Deegan. Finn—her dear, precious Finn, who had done the work to secure a proxy marriage—was expecting her. She’d give anything to see Finn in person. To hear him finally profess his love. To touch his cheek. To hold his hand. Leaving her father for three months—could she? What was she to do?

Emme, if you can’t trust your father, whom you can see,

to do what's best for you, how can you trust God, whom you can't see? Da's words scraped at her conscience.

The power of attorney weighed down her bag.

She knew what Da would say: *It's time to start your future in Helena.*

Finn would agree.

She released a weary breath. "Thank you, sir, but I have accepted the marriage proposal of a wonderful man in Montana." She stood. Shook his hand. Gave him her still-full mug. "It's been my honor to work for Spiegel. I wish the company all my best."

He offered a crooked grin. "Two dollars a day?"

That would make her one of the highest-paid employees, yet somehow it wasn't a temptation. This was not her lot in life.

She shook her head. "Good-bye, Mr. Spiegel."

Emilia was at the door when he called out, "Things in Montana may not be what you expect. If things don't work out, you always have a job at Spiegel."

She looked over her shoulder. "I know what I will find there, sir." She grinned. "It'll all work out."

Dearborn Station

Emilia rechecked her haversack's front latch to ensure it was buckled and the contents—signed power of attorney, telegrams and letters from Finn, money for meals, pencil, fountain pen, and her three journals—were safe. Her heart thumped against her chest. Never had she felt so small, so out of sorts. Even the busiest day at Spiegel had nowhere near the hundreds and hundreds of travelers and workers in Chicago's newest and most charming (according to the *Tribune*) station. She didn't see anything charming about it.

The marble floor bespoke an opulence unfitting for the Chicago she knew. Baggage handlers yelled. Customers bickered at the ticket counters. Harried travelers pushed through the crowds. Newsstands beckoned with papers from across the country. From other states. From other towns. From places Emilia had only read about. Because she'd never stepped outside the Chicago city limits before. She'd never ridden anything more than a cable car.

When she moved to Montana, she'd have to ride a horse. A horse!

Her mouth went dry. Beads of sweat trickled down her temple. *I'm not doing this alone. You are with me, Lord, and You will keep us safe—this I know.* She struggled for breath. "It will be all right . . ." she muttered because she needed to hear the words. She needed the encouragement and the reminder. With any luck, she'd soon feel what she knew.

Emilia stopped to give a man pushing a luggage cart room to pass. Ahead of her, Luci carried a basket of fruit. Da, dressed in his only suit, held Luci's other hand and their tickets. Roch carried two carpetbags filled with what little clothing they had and the family Bible. For one with only a year's schooling left, he was pretty dense not to realize the bags contained far more than what belonged to Emilia. Perhaps his exuberance to be rid of her clouded his thinking.

She released a nervous chuckle, yet her pulse continued to throb with each step she took closer to the boarding platform. Her stomach churned. She gripped the leather strap across her chest. She was choosing to trust Da. She should feel peace and calm, not as if she was about to lose what little lunch she'd eaten.

She wiped her moist forehead, then glanced around for Mr. Deegan, despite having no reason to be suspicious.

"Emilia, this way!" Da called out, waving at her.

She dashed over. Together they walked through an arched

German Romanesque entrance, as elaborate as all the other moldings and pillars, the crowd worse than frantic shoppers at a sale. After maneuvering through the station, they made their way to the next train leaving for St. Paul. First-class passengers were already boarding when they arrived.

"Boarding for St. Paul!" the conductor bellowed.

Da released Luci's hand. She moved next to Emilia and gripped her sleeve.

Da rested both hands behind Roch's neck. "Son, I need—" He stared at him for a long moment. Then he cleared his throat. "I need you to take care of your sisters for me until I can join you."

Roch's eyes widened. "No," he said, dropping the bags. The more he struggled to get free, the tighter Da held him.

"Stop, Roch."

Roch's forehead rested against Da's chest. "I won't leave you."

Da met Emilia's gaze. Tears welled in his eyes. "Being a man means sacrificing yourself for the good of your family." He looked at Roch. "Your choice is to stay here and keep running with these boys you think are tough, or you can do the tough thing and give up what you want in order to protect your sisters."

"Emilia has Finn. She doesn't need me."

Emilia flinched. She opened her mouth to respond, but Da spoke first.

"Oh, Roch." He sighed. "The world is a dangerous place. That Emilia now has Finn doesn't mean she doesn't need you, too. That Luci has Finn doesn't mean she doesn't need you. A father's job is to look out for his girls no matter where they are." Da stepped back and looked Roch in the eye. "Can I entrust this responsibility to you?"

Roch didn't move.

Luci gripped Emilia's hand. Emilia held tight.

Roch stared at the ground. His chin trembled. He sniffed, then nodded.

Da pulled the tickets out of his suit pocket. "Here."

Roch held the tickets tight.

Luci dashed into Da's open arms. Whatever he said to her, Emilia didn't hear, not over the noise of the train and her own heartbeat. After several minutes, Da released Luci. She stepped to Roch, who immediately gripped her hand.

Emilia didn't move.

Da stood there, staring at her, waiting, as if he knew she needed a moment to accept the finality of his plan. This wasn't how it was supposed to be. They were supposed to leave Chicago together. They were to step on the train full of joy and hope and anticipation. Emilia felt no joy, no hope, no anticipation. How could she?

She couldn't leave without him.

"Trust me, Emme."

Emilia struggled for breath. Her throat tightened, ached. This was not why she'd taken a Saturday shift. This was not why she'd sacrificed nine months working instead of spending time with Roch and Luci. She'd worked so hard, gotten so close, and now she had to trust someone else's plan.

Trust meant taking a step forward. In faith.

Hot tears streamed down her cheeks. She could trust God and Da—her heart told her so. Her mind did, too. She could trust the agony on Da's face. He would not choose to endure such pain without believing that sending them ahead without him was the best thing for them all. Emilia squeezed her eyes closed, ridding them of more tears.

She looked at Da. Pursed her lips and shifted her jaw as she fought for control of her emotions. "It will only be three months, right?"

He nodded, and she stepped into his embrace. Da held tight. She held tighter.

The train whistled.

Da kissed her forehead. With the pads of his thumbs, he wiped away her tears. "Let Roch help."

Emilia drew in a deep breath. She nodded. "I love you."

"I love—" His voice cracked. He rested her palm against his cheek, then placed a kiss in the center. "Three months."

"Three months," Emilia repeated.

The train whistled again.

"We've gotta go," Roch said.

Emilia looked over her shoulder. With one carpetbag under his arm, Roch gripped the second with one hand and Luci with his other, walking to the boarding ramp and the second-class porter motioning them forward. Roch was right; they had to go. Finn was waiting. Their new life was waiting.

Emilia stepped out of Da's hold and, without looking back, ran after them.

Chapter Three

Wednesday morning, 9:23 A.M.

"Next stop—Helena!"

The porter's call interrupted Emilia's discourse to Luci on what Finn had shared in his letters. As the train slowed, the porter strolled down the aisle, clearly at ease with the jerky motion of the car. Passengers in the three-quarter-filled car put away their papers and craned their necks to look out the windows. Like Emilia, they all seemed anxious to get off the train for more than a fifteen-minute stop.

Emilia laid the hairbrush in the lap of her pink skirt, then divided Luci's dark tresses into three strands. As her sister bit into their last apple, she began the braid. "You'll love Finn's cabin. He built it himself from trees he chopped off his land. It's two stories tall and has a hand-carved mantel. We can roast chestnuts in the hearth like we used to when Mama was alive. You and Roch can have your own rooms. Finn has two goats, a henhouse with five chickens, and—"

"We don't know anything about chickens," Luci interjected.

"—a garden we can help cultivate."

Luci yawned.

"Stop," Emilia warned. "You're going to make me—" She raised her hand to her mouth just in time to cover her yawn. "See, I told you."

Luci didn't look the least bit ashamed of having yawned. Her brow furrowed. "Emme, we don't know anything about milking goats or cultivating gardens."

The older couple on the bench behind them snickered.

Ignoring the pair, Emilia pulled the braid tight. "If Finn can't teach us, I am sure the library will have a book on the subject." She took the ribbon Luci offered and tied it around the braid's end, releasing it to hang to the middle of Luci's back. "The *Farmers' Almanac* is a wealth of information. We just have to learn when the first and last frost is. Gardening doesn't seem difficult. Nor cattle ranching or animal birthing, which I will probably have to learn, being a rancher's wife and all."

Luci looked over her shoulder, her droopy eyes red from lack of sleep. "Are you nervous?"

"Why do you ask?"

"Da says you talk a lot when you're nervous."

Emilia opened her mouth to defend herself. She was meeting her husband for the first time. She was *excited*, not nervous.

"It's all right." Luci yawned again, then blinked rapidly, the action doing nothing to lessen how tired she looked. "I'm nervous, too."

"Did you sleep any last night?"

Luci shrugged, took another bite of her apple, and stared out the window. "Helena looks bigger than I thought it would. And prettier. I bet it smells better than Chicago."

"More than ten thousand people live here." And Emilia knew only one.

Phineas Collins.

Finn.

Her husband.

"Finn says most of the brick and stone buildings were constructed since he moved here five years ago. In October there's to be their second annual Harvest Festival. Finn says he will take us for a ride in a hot-air balloon. Won't it be fun?" When Luci didn't respond, Emilia shifted to look at Roch on the wooden bench across the aisle from the one she and Luci had shared since boarding. His back rested against the window, his legs stretched out, his eyes closed. Since leaving Chicago, he'd done nothing but sleep.

She tapped the toe of his shoe. "We're here."

His eyes opened to a slit. A low grumble came from his throat.

Emilia smiled. She could enjoy mornings even if he didn't. Besides, this was the best kind of morning—one on which she'd see her husband. True, her heart missed Da. But the separation was only temporary, something she'd finally accepted after spending all her tears on the ride from Chicago to St. Paul.

"After we meet Finn, I have to file the power of attorney with the city clerk. Then we can get something to eat." She paused, checking to see if the mention of food improved Roch's mood. He continued to look uninterested. "Or we could go straight to the ranch. Finn said he's looking forward to teaching you how to shoot, fish, and ride. Wouldn't you like to?"

Roch glared. Why she expected a different response than the one he'd given her all trip she didn't know. He knew how much she'd had to spend on their meals and how much she'd had to pay for the power of attorney. He knew she had seven dollars to her name. Yet he couldn't show the least bit of gratitude.

Her shoulders slumped. "Three months, Roch, and then Da will join us. You're going to love Montana."

He scowled at her.

The train's brakes squealed. Emilia reached under the wooden bench for her black straw bonnet. She put it on. After two-and-a-half days' travel, this was the best she was going to look. She tied the black ribbon against the side of her jaw.

As the train came to a stop, Emilia leaned against Luci's back to look through the dusty window. A crowd of forty or fifty people stood near the boarding platform. Whether waiting for loved ones or ready to board themselves, she couldn't tell.

"Do you see him?" Emilia whispered.

Luci shook her head. "I don't know what he looks like."

"He's . . ." Emilia released a nervous laugh. "Actually, neither do I." Finn hadn't sent a photograph and had spent few words describing his appearance. About as tall as most men. Average-looking. From her view, everyone looked to be the same height. "Oh! He said his hair and eyes are brown."

"Now *that's* helpful."

Emilia chuckled. "Are you smarting me?"

Luci chuckled, too, then took another bite of her apple. "If you subtract the women, children, and old men, it looks like you may have a dozen husbands. Hmm . . . is that him?"

Emilia leaned closer to the dusty pane, her heartbeat increasing. "Which one?"

"The one with the black hat."

Her tired gaze settled on a man wearing a knee-length black coat, a tan pinstriped vest, and guns strapped to both thighs. Based on the heavy bristles on his cheeks and his rumpled appearance, one might guess he'd slept in his clothes. She knew the feeling. *Average-looking* would certainly not describe him. Good heavens, he was attractive. Considering the way he was straining his neck as he looked from train car to train car, she'd wager he was here to meet someone.

"You're staring at Mr. Romeo," came Luci's soft voice.

Emilia's cheeks warmed. She never should have read Shakespeare to her sister. "Yes, I am . . . at the badge on his left lapel. Finn is a rancher, not a lawman."

"Your loss." Luci bit into her apple.

"Excuse me, miss."

Emilia turned to the couple sitting behind them. Considering the older man's fine suit and the woman's large feathered hat, full-skirted dress, and ornate lace collar, the pair looked more first-class than second. Unlike everyone else who'd boarded the train in St. Paul, she vaguely remembered these two boarding earlier that morning, in Butte, when almost everyone in the car, except herself and Luci, had been sleeping.

She gave them a friendly smile. "Can I help you?"

The plump woman eased forward with a concerned expression on her face. "We couldn't help overhearing." Her voice softened to a whisper. "Are you a mail-order bride?"

Luci swiveled on the bench to face them, too.

Emilia rested her arm on the back of the wooden bench, giving them her full attention. "What makes you ask?"

The mustached gentleman gripped his wife's hand. "Little things you said. We've heard of men sending for brides but with the real intention of conscripting them into"—his gravelly voice lowered—"the sisterhood."

A nunnery? Why would—? Emilia gasped as another realization struck. He meant *prostitution.*

"What's the sisterhood?" Luci put in.

The couple looked from Luci to Emilia. *Are you going to tell her or should we?* was their unspoken yet obvious question.

She swallowed, despite the dryness of her throat. "It—uh, I'll tell you later."

"You and your sister looking like you do . . ." The woman squeezed Emilia's shoulder. "Be careful, dearie."

The man withdrew a card from inside his suit coat. He handed it to her. "In case things don't turn out as you expected," he said, then tipped his hat.

Out of the corner of her eyes, she could see Roch's smirk. The couple's words had affirmed his oft-stated critical opinion of Finn: *He's not going to be what you expect.*

Emilia offered the couple a polite smile. "Thank you for your concern."

As the man and his wife moved down the aisle to the opened vestibule door, Emilia looked at the card. She brushed her thumb across the raised print.

Mr. and Mrs. Alfred Deal
Deal's Boardinghouse

Doubt nibbled at her confidence. What if they were right and Finn wasn't who he'd claimed to be in his letters? What if he had lured her to Helena? What if—

No. The way he'd described being the son of a prostitute and told about years spent in an orphanage and running with thieves had been too raw and sincere not to be true. The way he'd answered when she'd asked why he'd placed the mail-order bride advertisement had almost insulted her. Why confess he'd placed the ad because he'd felt God telling him to rescue someone as he'd been rescued? Why say that if he didn't believe it? On more than one occasion, Finn had written that his overwhelming gratitude to God for his salvation had motivated him to look for any opportunity to extend the same saving hand to others.

One thing she knew for certain: She could trust Finn Collins. She didn't need this couple—or anyone—to rescue her from him.

Seeing nowhere to dispose of the card, Emilia slid it inside her haversack. "Luci, Roch, it's time to go."

She and Luci pulled on their winter coats as they waited for the other passengers wanting to disembark. Luci grabbed the empty food basket. Emilia stepped into the narrow aisle to let Luci go before her. She then checked the bench to see if they'd left anything behind. Finding nothing, she muttered, "Roch, come on," then followed her sister past the passengers traveling on to Idaho and California. As she glanced over her shoulder, Roch slapped the back of the bench. He jerked on his coat, then collected their three bags from under his seat. Emilia stopped at the vestibule steps, waiting for him to catch up.

Luci tugged on Emilia's sleeve.

"Just a minute." Emilia watched Roch trudge down the aisle. "Be careful with—"

A bag hit the back of an empty bench. With a grunt, Roch freed it. He looked like a prisoner on his way to his execution.

Luci tugged again. "Are you sure he's not Finn?"

Emilia looked at her sister as they stood at the top of the steps. "Who?"

"Mr. Romeo."

"Of course not. Why do you ask?"

"Because he's walking this way."

Roch reached her side at the same moment the man with the badge stopped at the base of the steps, blocking their exit.

"You Emilia Stanek?" His voice was gruff, and now, as he stood close, she could see the redness in his heavily lashed brown eyes. He didn't smell of liquor, so perhaps he'd stayed up all night, as Luci had.

"Ah, yes." A nervous queasiness grew in her stomach. Where was Finn? She moistened her lips and in a firmer voice said, "Yes, I am. Why do you ask?"

He climbed two steps, putting them on eye level. He

withdrew tickets from his inner coat pocket and a leather coin pouch from his trouser pocket and thrust them at her. "Take these."

Emilia drew back, bumping into Roch. He shoved her with his chest, which propelled her into Luci, who then banged into the closed dining car door.

"Ow!" Luci yelled. "Roch, why did you do that?"

Roch grunted.

Emilia studied Luci's face. No tears. She still asked, "Are you hurt?"

Luci shook her head.

"Apologize, Roch," came from the lawman.

Emilia looked over her shoulder at him. How did he know her brother's name?

The man leveled a hard glare on Roch.

"I'm sorry, Luce," her brother answered with none of the sullenness he'd exhibited over the past three days.

The train whistled.

"Excuse me," the porter said. "Can you folks make way for boarding passengers?"

The man pulled out his lapel to show the porter his badge—the badge Emilia couldn't take her gaze from.

Sheriff?

"Give us a minute." He turned back to Emilia and again held the tickets and coin purse in front of her face. "Trust me. You need to take these and go back to your seats."

Emilia shook her head. "Not until you tell me who you are and what this is all about."

"I'm the county sheriff, and you can't get off this train."

"I most certainly can," she snapped back. "I'm meeting my husband."

Tears pooled in his bloodshot eyes. He hunched his shoulder and rubbed his bristled chin against his lapel. After a long moment, he met her gaze, his tears gone and voice hard. "Finn is dead."

Mac thrust one hand inside his pants pocket and swallowed down the remnants of his humiliating, unchecked grief. "Sorry. Shouldn't have been so blunt." No use covering up the truth, though. Finn's pretty little bride needed a hard dose of reality. She and her siblings needed to go home for their own good. Whoever had killed Finn—his breath hitched at the pain—could still be in town. "These tickets"—he held them under her nose—"will take you to San Francisco. Trade them in at the next stop for ones back to Chicago."

"What? What did you say?" Her obtuseness annoyed him. How much clearer could he be? But she stared up at him, her caramel eyes wide, like she was waiting for a reasonable explanation to something so unfathomable. "Did you say Finn is dead? Finn Collins? He can't be dead. He . . . he sent me a telegram four days ago."

He should go easy on her. On all three of them. Their rumpled clothes, the three battered bags clutched in the boy's hands, the lack of claim tickets for any other luggage, the way Miss Luci gripped an empty basket in one hand and an apple core in the other, the look of perpetual hunger in all three pairs of eyes . . . everything about them should command his pity.

But Finn's death was too recent. Mac's emotions too raw. He shook off the images of finding his friend shot through the heart, his eyes open and mouth agape, and the telegram announcing when to expect the Stanek siblings lying on the kitchen table, the yellow paper stained with bloody fingerprints. Had the telegram been what the killer was after, or was it simply another nuisance like the clothes, canned goods, and bedding tossed about like rubbish?

Mac didn't know. The whole scene made no sense, raising question after question with no answers. The only thing he was clear on was keeping this woman from stepping off the train.

"I'm sorry, ma'am, but it's true. You and your family need to go back home."

Miss Stanek blinked and took two rapid breaths. "Go back home?"

Did she have to repeat everything he said?

Mac rubbed the corner of his lip to keep from scowling and scaring her more. His voice was harsh from lack of sleep, so he swallowed and worked at softening his tone. "Yes, ma'am."

She put her hand on top of the black hat barely keeping her head covered. Brown curls hung around her face. The two sisters looked like twins except for Miss Luci's slightly smaller frame and coffee-brown eyes, as opposed to her elder's coffee-with-cream eyes. At least Miss Stanek had been honest about how she looked in her letters to Finn.

I'm small for my age. No one believes I'm twenty-one. Most people think I look more like a fifteen-year-old, and it has caused me more than my fair share of trouble at work. People keep asking to speak to the customer service manager and won't believe me when I say I'm the manager.

Mac had read every one of the woman's letters in the last four hours, searching them for clues and coming up empty. He knew Miss Emilia Stanek and her siblings as well as Finn had.

And, based on the bloody fingerprints on the letters, so did Finn's killer.

Mac leaned deeper into the vestibule, determined to hide the trio from anyone else looking for them, and held out the tickets again. "Trust me. You need to take them." They'd cost him a pretty penny. Money he'd been saving to get his mother out of Helena, though the last time he'd broached the subject she'd told him—in brash, vulgar terms—to mind his own business instead of hers.

Roch shook his head, as if to say, *I knew this whole thing was a dumb idea.*

Miss Luci started to reach for the tickets, her fingers trembling.

"No!" Miss Stanek pulled her sister tight, trapping her arm from reaching any higher. "We are staying. We are not changing plans again. Especially when I have no idea if *this man* is even telling me the truth."

This man?

Mac gritted his teeth. How dare she question him! *She* was the one who'd written a lonely bachelor, convinced him to marry her, and preyed on his orphaned past to convince him to let her drag two siblings into a slapdash marriage. Mac had warned Finn not to send for a mail-order bride. People could say whatever they wanted in letters. Didn't make it true.

Same way people could live a lie right in front of you.

Take Finn, for example. He'd never said a word about continuing to court a bride. Mac discovered that little tidbit after plucking Miss Stanek's letters out of the piles of rubbish cluttering Finn's cabin, putting them in date order, and reading every last one of them for clues. Had Finn's murderer tossed the letters out of frustration or because he'd found what he needed and wanted to make it harder for others to figure out? Was he here waiting for the Stanek family?

Mac gripped the vestibule handrails, arched his back, and scanned the thinning crowd on the platform. He'd gotten to the station almost an hour early to watch for suspicious people or activity. He'd seen nothing then and he saw nothing now.

I need clues!

If he could find something—anything—solid to follow, maybe the churning in his gut would ease up. From the moment Isaak Gunderson slammed through the office door yesterday morning and shouted "Finn's dead!" Mac hadn't stopped. Hadn't eaten. Hadn't slept.

Who would kill his friend? Was Finn the innocent victim of random violence? Mac wanted to believe that, but he'd been a lawman too long to ignore how Finn suddenly had enough money to buy alfalfa seed and livestock when he'd been flat broke a month before. And why did he have greasepaint and a bandanna in his kitchen cupboard?

Finn had been a horse thief at one time. Years ago. He'd made a clean break, even tracked folks down to repay them for their losses. So why would he keep the tools of his thieving trade so close at hand? What was he hiding? Other than a mail-order bride! They'd discussed it and decided it was a dumb idea.

What had changed Finn's mind?

Everything about his murder felt . . . off. Like a clock that ticked and tocked in separate rhythms.

"Sheriff?" The porter interrupted from behind. "These people need to get out of the way so others can board."

Mac returned his attention to Miss Stanek. How was she reacting to him being called sheriff? She continued to glare at him, eyebrows pinched, like he'd asked for her virtue instead of her cooperation. He leaned backward to demand another minute, but he was so tired he stumbled down the steps and onto the platform. The Stanek trio descended before he could right himself.

The porter, his neck veins pulsing and skin mottled red, stepped behind the Staneks, preventing them from reboarding. As the porter helped passengers into the vestibule, Mac thought about ways to make an arrest. None were viable, of course, but it didn't stop him from imagining slapping handcuffs over the man's pudgy wrists and hauling him to jail.

Miss Stanek tilted her chin up at him. "Could you direct me to Mr. Hale Adams, please?"

"No." Recalled to the immediate threat, Mac pointed his finger at the chit's nose. "Stay here." He turned on his heel and headed for the ticket office. The next train heading east was in six hours, and the Staneks were going to be on it even if he had to lock them in a jail cell between now and then.

"Am I under arrest?"

Mac whirled around. Instead of doing as she was told, Miss Stanek had followed him across the platform. "I told you to stay put."

"And I asked if I was under arrest."

The jut of her chin and militant gleam in her eye exasperated what was left of Mac's patience. "Not yet, but I can arrange it."

Behind her, the brother crossed his arms and smirked.

"You think this is funny, young man?" Mac took one step, grabbed the boy by his collar, and pulled him close. "Finn Collins is"—his stomach flipped upside down and grief clawed his throat—"*was* my friend. My good friend. Do you understand me?"

The boy's eyes stretched wide and shifted to his sister.

Assuming the woman would make some sort of protest,

Mac pointed his left finger in her direction. "Stay out of this." He waited until Roch's attention returned to him. Mac lowered his brows at the boy. "I need to get your sisters out of this town for their own safety. I assume you aren't keen on finding them dead on the floor some morning despite whatever differences of opinion you might have."

Roch's eyes were about to fall out of their sockets. "Yes, sir. I mean, no. Sir."

"Then stay here and watch over them while I get your train tickets exchanged."

"Yes, sir."

Mac let go of Roch's collar. He swung his gaze to Miss Stanek and her little sister. "Don't move. Don't talk to anyone. Do you hear me?"

Miss Luci bounced her head up and down, but Miss Stanek glared. "You have no authority to—"

"Don't. Just don't." Mac spun around and left.

As soon as he marched across the threshold into the train depot, he looked to the right. The door to the telegraph office stood wide open, a line of people waiting for Yancey Palmer to clack out messages for them. He marked *Keep Yancey from discovering Miss Stanek's arrival* off his invisible list. Because she'd stood in as the proxy bride—another shocking discovery—Yancey would no doubt know about Miss Stanek's arrival and want to meet her.

One thing at a time.

Get the Staneks out of town first, then explain to Yancey why it was necessary and why she needed to keep it secret.

He rubbed his cheek, the bristles scratching into his palm sniping at him that Miss Stanek might have reason to doubt he was the county sheriff. Helena's leaders had advertised far and wide that the city had more millionaires per capita than any other in the world—an exaggeration designed to help make Helena the state capital once Montana was admitted to the union—which meant a sheriff was expected to live up to the reputation.

Though he despised the deception, Mac straightened the badge on his lapel and the one on his pinstriped vest. A sheriff needed to look respectable and trustworthy whether his town was a mere watering hole or the finest city on earth. Without respect, people would disobey his authority, and that would lead to all kinds of trouble.

He got in the back of the short line waiting for the train ticketing agent. A few odd looks came his way. Too bad he couldn't fix his bloodshot eyes and stubbled cheeks as easily as his badges.

Madame Lestraude emerged from the telegraph office. As was her custom, she wore some shade of red. The color papered the walls of her parlor house, draped its windows, and identified her girls. Men who saw them around town knew by the wine-colored bows tied above small, cameo brooches which brothel to frequent if they wanted a night with one of the beauties. Most men couldn't afford it. Those who could were treated to a luxurious illusion of romance and, sometimes, a quick exit. Prostitution had become a criminal misdemeanor a little over a year before. All the madams in town changed their business practices to hide the true purpose of their newly renamed music halls, luxury hotels, or vaudeville theaters, but they were thin disguises.

Unfortunately, the punishment for a misdemeanor was nothing more than a fine, and judging by Madame Lestraude's new, fashionable velvet dress trimmed with satin, one she could afford to pay.

She passed Mac, tipping her regal head to acknowledge his presence. Not one of her dyed blond curls fell out of place. He dipped his chin. She continued on without the smallest acknowledgment to show she was past her anger at him over the interview in the *Daily Independent* endorsing the law criminalizing prostitution.

"Next."

The line in front of him had disappeared. The ticket agent behind the barred window beckoned Mac forward with a swirling wrist.

Before stepping up to exchange the tickets from the morning westbound train to the evening eastbound one, Mac checked to see that Miss Stanek and her siblings were obeying his instructions to stay put and not talk to anyone. So far, so good, although judging by the pointing fingers and red faces, they were having a rousing argument among themselves. He turned his attention to the ticket agent. He should have gotten Hale or another friend to make the exchange. Buying and then returning tickets in the same hour was too memorable.

He needed sleep before he made any more mistakes.

But the agent didn't make any comments or otherwise indicate he cared that Mac wanted to exchange the tickets. With methodical precision, the man behind the window wrote out three bills of sale to Chicago and counted out the change due.

Mac pocketed the coins, said thank you, and pivoted to rejoin his charges.

The Staneks were nowhere to be seen.

He inhaled so fast, he choked on his own spit. Where were they? He paced his steps to the depot door. If they had moved to get out of the wind, he would look foolish—not to mention draw unwanted attention—rushing outside in a panic.

The door resisted. Mac shoved it. A gust of wind caught the swinging wood and slammed it against the wood-slat exterior. He stepped outside and looked left and right while closing the door behind him to shut out nosy observers.

Miss Stanek and her siblings weren't on the platform.

He jogged toward the baggage claim area in case he was wrong about the three bulging bags containing all their possessions. Yancey looked out her office window as he passed, smiling in greeting. Mac ignored her. He couldn't see anything but Finn's face, frozen for all time in horror. Couldn't hear anything but the drums inside his ears beating in time with his heart.

Were his eyes so bleary from lack of sleep that he'd missed seeing Finn's killer?

There was no unclaimed trunk, no attendant waiting to assist passengers, no trio of siblings.

Mac worked his way around the depot, crossing in front this time as he scanned the street for Miss Stanek's pink dress, but even though the streets were sparsely populated with townsfolk going about their Thursday morning business, he saw no sign of her.

He turned the corner of the depot, hoping to find them there, bickering.

A lone tree swayed in the breeze, its bare branches not yet ready for spring, its long shadows lacerating the ground with gnarled fingers.

The Staneks were gone.

Chapter Four

Jackson Street and Sixth Avenue

Emilia stopped in front of the narrow, two-story building wedged precariously between a bank and a red-bricked, partially constructed building at the top of the hill. Her legs trembled from the lengthy trek from the depot. She studied the law office, more to give herself time to catch her breath. Mr. Hale's wooden building seemed to have received a recent whitewashing. Were the eight-foot shutters on either side of the arched windows for protection from wind? Or from vandals? Save for the shingle carved with the words HALE ADAMS, ATTORNEY AT LAW, the structure, with potted flowers and rocking chairs on the second-floor balcony, looked more like a home than a business.

"Luci, you can wait with Roch in the parlor while I speak to Finn's lawyer." Emilia opened the door and a bell jingled. She waited for them to enter before closing the door.

To the left of the foyer was a parlor, sparsely decorated with a Persian rug and blue-and-white curtains, both looking eerily similar to those Spiegel had imported last year from the Mediterranean. The room smelled of oil soap. From the floors? Emilia looked down. Rough-sawn planks were nailed down, like the ones Finn had described in his cabin. A telephone rang, and Emilia turned toward the sound. To the right of the parlor was a set of open double doors with a blond, studious-looking man standing on the threshold.

Emilia pointed to his office. "I don't mind waiting if you need to"—she lowered her shaking hand—"to, um, answer the call."

He drew his spectacles down to the tip of his nose and stared at her as if contemplating a mathematical equation. "How may I help you?" Like his expression, his tone held a decided lack of emotion.

"I'm here to see Mr. Hale Adams."

The telephone continued to ring, and he continued to seem disinclined to answer it. "I am he."

While he wasn't near in age to the elderly man she'd expected, she guessed he was several years older than she was.

Emilia forced a smile to cover her inner nerves. "Sir, it seems there was some confusion at the depot. My husband, Phineas Collins—"

His brown eyes lost their blank mien. "Miss Stanek? Emilia Stanek?"

"Yes, I—"

The telephone stopped ringing.

"You two, sit." He pointed to the parlor.

To Emilia's surprise, Roch quietly followed Luci to a button-tufted sofa centered on the rug and facing the foyer. Luci smiled contently. Roch leaned back, folded his arms across his chest, and closed his eyes, clearly without a care as to how his behavior would look to a man in a fancy three-piece suit worth more than Da earned in a year.

A little snort of air came from Mr. Adams.

Yet when Emilia met his gaze, the indiscernible expression was back.

"Miss Stanek, this way," he said gravely.

Emilia followed him into his office. Books filled the wall of shelves behind his ornate mahogany desk. Where there weren't books on the floor, there were stacks of files and a couple of unhung paintings half-wrapped in butcher paper. Two wooden Windsor armchairs sat in front of the desk. One, though, held a stack of unopened packages.

Mr. Adams closed the doors. "Have a seat."

As he wove around stacks of books, Emilia removed her haversack from around her neck. She then took her place in the empty chair, bag in lap.

Mr. Adams settled behind his desk. He pushed his spectacles back up his nose, then collected a pencil and a notepad. "Miss Stanek, please elaborate on what occurred at the depot."

The black cast-iron telephone on his desk rang again.

Emilia waited for him to answer it. Never in her life had she seen such a fancy telephone, not even in the Speigel catalog.

But he didn't answer the call.

His gaze leveled on hers. "Go on."

"When I was attempting to disembark the train, the county sheriff blocked my path. He said my husband is"—her throat tightened—"dead. Is this true?"

He nodded. "Sheriff McCall found the body yesterday morning."

Emilia sucked in a breath. Finn couldn't be dead. He'd sent Da a telegram four days ago. "What happened to him?"

The telephone stopped ringing.

Mr. Adams laid his pencil on the desk. "It looks as if he was murdered."

"Murdered?" Emilia stared at him, waiting for him to correct himself. To say something else besides *murdered*. He did nothing of the sort. He regarded her with a complete lack of guile, which she suspected was true to character. It was no wonder Finn had hired him. In one of his first letters, Finn had remarked that he preferred to be told the truth, even if it was unsettling.

My dear Emilia, I have learned trust, once lost, is harder to regain than forgiveness is to give.

She remembered his words because that had been the first time he'd call her his dear Emilia. The first of many. Until she became *my love*. And now she would never hear him speak his affection. Never hear him say—

Emilia held herself still, blinking rapidly, waiting for the rush of emotion to abate. She released the breath she held. "Who, uh . . ." She cleared her throat. In a stronger voice, she asked, "Who killed him? Who could have any reason to kill him? Finn was an honorable man."

"The investigation is confidential and ongoing."

"Confidential and ongoing?"

He nodded again. "Mac will find Finn's killer. It may take time, but you can trust him to do his job. Finn was his friend."

Emilia turned her gaze to the window, to the bright afternoon light streaming in. When they'd buried Mama, it had been raining. It had rained all week.

"Miss Stanek, there is nothing for you in Helena. You should go home."

Emilia clutched the haversack to her chest. Go home? She was never returning to Chicago. Helena was her home now. In three months Da would join them. She couldn't leave. She had her siblings to care for, to keep safe. She had the ranch. She owed it to Finn to do right by him. She owed it to him to make his ranch a success.

She returned her gaze to Mr. Adams. "When will the funeral be?"

"We buried him yesterday."

Already?

At the prick of tears, Emilia blinked rapidly to rid herself of them before they fell. "Where is he buried? I should pay my respects."

"You can't."

"I can't?" she said suddenly. "Why can't I?"

"You can," he corrected himself. "You *shouldn't*." He leaned forward, his elbows resting on the desk's edge. "Miss Stanek, as Phineas Collins's lawyer, I advise you not to file the power of attorney legalizing the marriage."

"But won't that cause an issue for the judge who performed the proxy marriage, trusting that I'd bring this"—Emilia tapped her haversack, where she'd kept the power of attorney the entire journey—"with me to file when I arrived?"

"My uncle is the judge who performed the ceremony. He'll have no problem smoothing things over should anyone complain." Hale smiled in a fatherly way. "Be wise and return to Chicago on the next available train."

"I don't understand why you and the sheriff are so intent on me leaving."

For several moments he seemed lost in thought. Then his head shook, almost as if he were dislodging an argument. He looked at her intently. "Not only is the man you married by proxy dead, he was in debt."

"In debt? How much?"

"One-hundred-seventy-nine dollars and thirteen cents."

Emilia collapsed against the spindles of her chair. It couldn't be true. Finn had said the ranch was improving. He'd made arrangements to recoup the losses from the hard winter. He'd ordered alfalfa seed. He'd ordered fencing and a plow. He'd bought a bull and breeding cows.

She blinked. Wait a second . . .

He'd bought cows. And cows cost money. Seed and fencing did, too. She slowly nodded, everything making sense. It wasn't the same as the way credit worked at Spiegel, but she understood why Finn had borrowed money to buy seed, fencing, a plow, and cows. It was an investment in the future. Their future.

"Miss Stanek," came the lawyer's voice, drawing her attention. "Any beneficiaries of Phineas Collins's estate will be liable for his debts. It is in your best interest to leave town before filing the power of attorney legalizing the proxy marriage. Until then, you have no obligation either legally or morally to the Circle C Ranch. Do you understand?"

Debts she understood.

That the man she'd married was dead she also understood.

Were she to leave Helena before anyone discovered she was Finn's beneficiary, she could escape his debts. She would also forfeit her claim to his ranch. She needed the ranch. Ever since reading *A Lady's Life on a Farm in Manitoba*, she'd dreamed of life on the western frontier. She couldn't give it up now, not when she was so close. Working the ranch would be hard, especially without Finn there to guide her—

"Yes," she said firmly. "I do."

"Good." He shuffled through the papers on his desk. "You have about an hour before the next train arrives heading east. Your trunks should still be at the depot."

"We don't have any trunks."

He looked up, his eyes wide. "Where are the rest of your belongings?"

Emilia gave a sad shake of her head. He had no idea what it was like to live in a disease-infested tenement. To have one set of clothes for church, one for day wear, and one for work. To go to bed without dinner because there was no money even to buy a basket of moldy vegetables. To be buried with nothing but your name. He had no idea what it was like to yearn for more than the life he'd been born to. He had no idea.

Finn knew. He understood her life, her fears, and her dreams.

She understood him.

Which was why she took a deep breath, straightened her shoulders, and said, "Sir, while working in Spiegel's customer service department, I heard myriad excuses from people trying to wiggle out of their debts. I swore I never would. Paying off Finn's debts is the right thing to do." She eased forward in the chair. "If Finn hadn't died, when were his creditors expecting payment?"

Mr. Adams gave her a strange look. "In the fall, after the cattle go to market."

"As long as I plant the seed, put up the fencing, and care for the cattle, as Finn would have done, then his creditors will be paid." She offered a bit of a smile. "All will be well, right?"

"One likes to hope," he muttered.

"Then if you would be so kind as to—"

The front door opened, then slammed closed, rattling the doors to the office.

Emilia grimaced. It was him: Luci's Mr. Romeo. It had to be. She never should have asked the sheriff for directions to Mr. Adams's office. Nothing the man could say or do would entice her to leave Helena. Her family's future was here. Her future was here.

Sure enough, the double doors jerked open.

The sheriff strolled in with the ease of a man used to doing what he wanted, when he wanted. His livid glare shifted from her to the armchair next to hers . . . or, more precisely, to the stack of packages taking residence. He stood next to the desk.

"I have the tickets." Said in a manner of one expecting applause to follow.

A number of retorts danced on Emilia's tongue. She studied Mr. Adams. While she hadn't retained him as *her* counsel, something told her to let him speak on her behalf.

He leaned back in his chair. Even though there was a mantel clock above the fireplace, he withdrew his pocket watch and checked the time. "She isn't leaving."

The sheriff muttered something under his breath. He looked ready to tear someone's head off. Or, to be more gentlemanly, toss that said someone on her backside into jail.

Emilia eased to the side of the chair, putting as much additional space between them without being overtly rude as possible. "Mr. Adams, if you would be so kind as to provide a list of my husband's debts and his creditors, I would be mighty appreciative. Once I explain the situation, I am sure they will be willing to wait for repayment."

"You can't," the sheriff ground out. He stepped forward and gripped the arms of her chair, his face inches from hers. "You have to go home."

Emilia said nothing. More than one Proverb warned against arguing with a fool.

"Mac." Mr. Adams's quiet voice was filled with reproof and a bit of compassion.

The sheriff jerked straight with a huff.

Mr. Adams opened the folder on the center of his desk. "Here's the list." He withdrew a piece of paper and stood, offering it to her. “I advise you to inventory everything at the ranch.”

The sheriff crossed his arms. It was enough of a response for Emilia to know his thoughts and feelings on the matter.

She stood and took the paper. A list of businesses and numbers were typed in a column. “Thank you, for this and for all you did for Finn.”

Mr. Adams gave a wistful smile. “When you are ready, I can assist with the sale of his estate.”

Emilia slid the paper into her haversack. “Oh, I won’t be selling.”

Mac swiped his index finger under his nose. Did the woman have no sense at all? About self-preservation *or* business?

Hale stood the moment Miss Irrational rose from the chair. “Miss Stanek, I don’t know where your determination to succeed here comes from, but let me assure you, my friends and I will assist you in any way we can.”

Mac grunted his disagreement.

“And Sheriff McCall”—Hale continued in his smooth, lawyerly tone though he cut a stern glance at Mac—“will escort you to City Hall before taking you out to Finn’s . . . to your ranch.”

What did Hale think? That Mac was such a cad he’d leave the chit unprotected? He’d accompany her and her siblings. Keep them safe. But he didn’t have to be happy about it. Not when she was making a foolish mistake.

Miss Stanek shot a glare at Mac. It lasted a mere moment, but it struck him like a slap across the face. She feared him . . . or at least didn’t trust him. How could she? She’d only known him a few minutes. Trust required respect, and he hadn’t earned it yet. Hadn’t had the time for it. A tactical error he would have recognized if only he wasn't so tired. So churned up inside over his friend's death and the deep sense he was missing critical pieces of information—things right in front of him that he saw but couldn't make fit because none of it made sense.

". . . excuse us, I'd like a word with my friend." Hale's voice penetrated Mac's thoughts.

"Of course." Miss Stanek slid between her chair and Mac to escape the room while clutching that beat-up bag of hers like armor.

Mac watched her shut the double doors behind her before he turned to Hale. "This is a mistake."

Hale nodded. "But it's hers to make, and you can't keep her from it."

How many times had the two of them rehashed this same argument, only with different names and situations?

"Besides"—Hale tipped his head toward the double doors leading to his waiting area—"you have no idea what's motivating her insistence on staying. We've been operating under the assumption she'd be better off going back to Chicago. What if it isn't true?"

"Anything is better than dead."

"Says the man who's never tasted hunger." At Mac's glare, Hale raised his hands as though warding off further argument. "I know, neither have I, but it doesn't invalidate my point. Have you looked at the three of them? Really looked? At their luggage? The threadbare hems, stitched spots, and small patches on their clothes? Or how their cheekbones and chins are too pronounced because their flesh is stretched tight with malnourishment?"

Mac closed his eyes and rubbed at the headache pounding in his temples. Of course he'd noticed, but none of it changed his conviction that they were better off going home than living on a remote ranch with no one to protect them.

"How's a city girl going to run a ranch? Her brother looks like he'll hop the next train without our help just to be anywhere but here, and the sister is about as hardy as a dandelion seed." He huffed and opened his eyes again. "Trust me, this is a huge mistake."

The knowing grin on Hale's face—the one saying, *Glad we've come to the end of this discussion*—did little to soothe Mac's ruffled sense of unease. Yes, most of their arguments over letting people make their own choices ended this way, but it was different this time.

This time it was about Finn.

Mac's closest friend . . . the one who'd become more like a brother. But how could it be true when investigating his death had turned up so many secrets?

Mac lowered his voice so the trio in the parlor couldn't hear. "Did you figure out how Finn afforded the seed and fencing?"

Hale shook his head. "Everything on the list of creditors I gave Miss Stanek is from last fall. It includes every major feed store in town, so my best guess is Finn bought his new supplies from someone outside Helena."

"What about the new cows and bull? Who did he buy them from? Where did he get the money?" More pieces not fitting.

"As to where he bought the livestock, my guess is from one of those big ranches that went bankrupt." Hale sat and pulled out his pocket watch again, popping the cover open and shutting it in a steady rhythm. "You counted eleven new cows and a bull. There's no way to know how much Finn paid because the price would have depended on how desperate the seller was, but I'm estimating ten dollars a head."

"What about the alfalfa seed and fencing costs?"

"Likely another eighty to a hundred dollars, but it's only a guess."

Where did a man without two pennies to rub together in February come into that much money in March? The easy answer was that Finn had donned his thieving disguise again, except no bank robberies had occurred within a hundred-mile radius of Helena in the past two months.

Pieces and more pieces.

Mac rolled his neck to ease the tension in his muscles. "Did you mention those things to Miss Stanek?"

Hale snapped his pocket watch closed and stuffed it in his pocket again. "I couldn't substantiate the debt, so no."

Mac eyed his friend. "Leaves you with the hollow feeling that somewhere down the road—likely the worst possible moment—it's going to rise up and bite you, doesn't it?"

Hale grinned wryly. "I know."

The admission soothed one tiny spot in Mac's soul. "So what do you suggest?"

"Give an inch. Help her out. Show her what she's up against before she files the proxy." Hale ticked each point off on the fingers of his left hand.

Not a bad plan. The moment Miss Emilia Stanek laid eyes on Finn's tiny cabin and the sorry condition of his cattle, she'd beg to take advantage of the train tickets he had stuffed in his vest pocket and take her siblings back where they belonged. "I'd better get going." He shook his friend's hand and left the office before he changed his mind.

The three Staneks occupied a sofa meant for two. Miss Stanek had an arm around her sleeping sister while Roch sat with his arms crossed and face turned toward the wall.

"You ready?" The question came out gruffer than Mac intended. Lack of sleep was ravaging his voice as well as his ability to think.

"Yes." Miss Stanek roused her sister while ignoring her brother. "We're ready."

Mac held the door open. As soon as the girls left the

parlor, Roch huffed, retrieved the wicker basket and three pitiful bags, and marched outside. He clearly felt this whole ranching thing was a big mistake. That made him Mac's ally in a way, same as the hard truth was.

As soon as Mac stepped outside, Miss Stanek said, "I do need to send a telegram to our father, letting him know we arrived safely. Should I do it before or after going to City Hall?" Purple tinged the skin under her eyes. Same for Luci.

What they needed was food and rest—Hale's suggested inch of help.

"After, but . . ." Mac flicked his gaze to Luci, who was practically asleep leaning against her sister's shoulder.

The hostility in Miss Stanek's pretty face eased. "What did you have in mind?"

"A deal. A friend lives nearby, to the west of the gulch. She'll be happy to feed you lunch while I hitch up her husband's surrey to take you to the ranch. After that, if you still want to file your proxy marriage certificate, I'll take you to City Hall myself. It doesn't close until five, but it's on the far side of the gulch and the hills are steep. We can borrow their surrey and stop at the telegraph office before returning to the ranch." Mac waited for a nod or some indication she thought it a good plan.

She continued to stare up at him, distrust lingering in the hard set of her lips and wary pinching around her eyes. "I accept your deal, but I'd prefer not to be beholden to strangers. Is there a restaurant—"

"We accept, sir," Roch interrupted, the jut of his chin announcing he'd had enough.

Miss Stanek twisted her head so Mac couldn't see her reaction to Roch putting his foot down. Her silence was enough of an agreement for now.

Mac nodded at the boy. "This way."

Roch fell into step with Mac, his sisters following.

The Palmer family lived four blocks away. Since Yancey already knew about the proxy marriage, taking the Staneks to her family home only widened the circle of who knew about the trio's arrival to her mother and father who—like their daughter—could be trusted to keep a secret. Mrs. Palmer always had plenty of food for friends, neighbors, and strangers available in her kitchen. Plus, one look at the exhausted girls and the Palmers' new surrey would be Mac's for the asking.

As they walked up the incline, Mac rested his gaze on every person they passed, categorizing each. Mr. Lombard sitting on the front porch of the hardware store: harmless and lazy. Mrs. Hollenbeck emerging from the bank: pillar of society and good friends with Mrs. Palmer. Judge Forsythe on the opposite side of Sixth Avenue: didn't know he was back in town; check to see if he brought back any WANTED posters from around the territory. Braden Terry lowering his head to look left and right under the brim of his black hat: shifty and suspicious; did he have an alibi for the night Finn was killed? Roy Bennett carrying a couple of brown boxes wrapped with twine: good man; ask him for a balloon ascent to see if any clues to Finn's murder could be viewed from the air.

Roch grunted when Luci stepped between him and Mac.

A small hand fitted itself into Mac's. Luci leaned her head on his bicep. "Is it much farther?"

Two Staneks were already trusting him. Only one to go.

"No, Luci. We're almost there."

Chapter Five

Two hours later

The surrey bumped as the wheels found what had to be the fortieth hole in the dirt-hardened road. Emilia clamped her jaw tight to fight the yawn struggling to escape. The meal Mrs. Palmer had provided went beyond what Emilia would ever define as lunch. A hunk of bread and a wedge of cheese would have sufficed. Except in Mrs. W. H. Palmer's estimation, lunch consisted of pickled beets, shepherd's pie, raisin scones, and cider.

What they didn't eat was packed in the tin bucket Emilia held in her lap.

As the surrey jostled and swayed, Emilia glanced back. Luci rested against Roch's shoulder, while his head lay against the back of the seat. How could they fall asleep so quickly? They'd only left the Palmers' house twenty minutes earlier.

She faced forward, bumping her arm against the sheriff's.

He gave her a slant-eyed look, which she interpreted to mean *sit still.* His gaze then shifted back to the road leading them northwest of Helena. The town's main street had been wider, more hilly, and more crooked than any in Chicago. Great mountain peaks stood like sentries around the town—about halfway around, from what she could tell. While mountains actually encircled Helena, in the north and east they were miles away across a valley. A valley that included Finn's land.

The surrey hit another hole.

The sheriff grunted at the same moment she did, and she couldn't help but look at him. He had finally stopped glaring in her direction, a pleasant change from the expression he'd worn since meeting her at the depot. He looked exhausted. Other than a few words to Mrs. Palmer, he had said little more than "Surrey's ready," "About a mile," "Shall we?" and "Humph."

He scratched his bristly jaw. It wasn't the first time he'd done it. She'd wager he was the type of man who shaved every morning. Finn's death must have—

She took an unexpected breath, her chest feeling as if it had been punched.

"You all right?" came the words, in such a gentle voice she almost believed a fifth person was in the surrey, that it hadn't been the sheriff speaking.

Emilia blinked away the hot tears. She didn't need his compassion right now. She barely had the flap of her haversack lifted when a white handkerchief appeared in her line of sight. "Thank you," she muttered, taking it from him. "I am usually not . . ." She sniffed and dabbed her eyes.

"I understand," he said quietly.

Emilia nodded. He couldn't understand. Not really. He had only lost a friend. She had lost a friend and a husband. She'd lost someone to help carry the load, to shoulder her burdens, to tell her she didn't have to be the strong one all the time. Finn was the man who was to sweep her into his arms. Finn loved her. She loved him. And now she had no one.

The sheriff's loss wasn't the same.

He pointed to the right. "That road leads to the fairgrounds."

"Finn wrote about last year's Harvest Festival," she said, happy to make conversation. "He said a teacher was fired because of the hot-air balloon race. Whatever happened?"

"She'll tell you all about it."

"She lives in town?"

"She served you tea."

"Mrs. Palmer's daughter, Luanne? She's so kind and friendly. I can't imagine why the school would want to fire her."

"Luanne fell in love with the wrong man." A muscle at his jaw twitched. "According to some folks."

Emilia studied him for a moment. He seemed serious. "I don't understand. How could falling in love with the wrong man cost her her job?"

He gave her a you'll-have-to-ask-her look.

He turned the surrey onto a narrowed road, following the ruts framed with brush taller than Emilia was. Once they crested the hill, the brush cleared.

Emilia drew in a breath.

The Circle C Ranch.

To the right was the field Finn had plowed. To the left was a green pasture with two dozen cows, two goats roaming free, and a prime view of Mount Helena. Straight ahead was—

She blinked a few times until the cabin with a covered front porch came into focus. Her heart sank. Good heavens, it was smaller than a tenement building. Much smaller. The afternoon sun glinted off the roof. Tin?

"Surprised?" His tone held no laughter, yet she heard the smug satisfaction of a man knowing his point had been proven.

In actuality, Finn's description had been fair and true. He'd said he lived in a two-story log cabin nestled in the foothills and surrounded by fertile pastures. He'd said he could admire the sunrise and the sunset with the simple turn of his rocker.

What *she* had imagined his log cabin to be wasn't . . . this. The building couldn't be more than ten by twelve feet in size and had one glass window to the side of the front door and one in the center of the pitched roof. Two stories? If anything, it was a one-and-a-half-story cabin. Even with her petite height, she doubted she could stand without hitting the ceiling of the second floor. But in three months, Da would be here to help. Until then, no matter what came her way, she would manage.

Emilia moistened her lips. "It's . . . um, it's the way he described it. Finn never lied to me."

The sheriff snorted. "He did to me."

She ignored him as she looked around. There, by the cabin, near the well, was a pen for the goats. Off to the left was a coop with five chickens pecking at the ground. Stacks of wood posts and rolls of barbed wire rested against the arch-roofed barn, double the size of the cabin. Inside had to be Finn's horse and wagon.

She certainly could make this work.

Emilia jerked around on the bench, bumping the sheriff again. She patted Roch's leg and then Luci's. "Wake up, wake up. We're home. And it's beautiful!"

A strange sound came from the sheriff.

Emilia whipped her head around to face him, expecting to see a return of his sour mien. His stricken—stricken!—gaze was on the house. His jaw clenched, lips pursed tight.

He drew the surrey to a halt. He didn't say anything. Maybe he couldn't. It had to be hard on him, seeing his friend's home.

Emilia swallowed nervously. "Thank you for escorting us here. I know you have duties to attend to, so don't feel you need to stay for our sakes." He grimaced, yet said nothing, so she continued with, "When I am ready to return to Helena, Finn's wagon . . . his horse . . . um, I—we can manage from here."

Sheriff McCall gave her a skeptical look. "You ever driven a horse and cart before?"

No, and she knew full well that book learning was a far cry from practical experience, but she wasn't about to admit it to the sheriff. "We'll manage," she repeated, then nodded at Roch and Luci. "Tell him thank you."

Luci leaned forward, wrapping her arms around the sheriff's neck, knocking his cowboy hat forward. He caught it before it hit his lap.

Sheriff McCall settled his hat snugly back on his head. He scratched his jaw again.

Roch didn't speak. Didn't move.

Emilia released a weary sigh. He'd been taught manners. He'd do the right thing. Eventually. Without waiting for the sheriff to help her out of the surrey, she grabbed the tin bucket off her lap, jumped out, and headed to the cabin. She had a journal with notes she'd made on ranching. She had every letter Finn had written to her. Among those and with a healthy amount of common sense and persistence—and more than a few visits to the Helena library—she could make Finn's ranch a success.

She stepped onto the small covered porch. Gripping the iron door handle, she tugged. Nothing. "It's locked."

"Try pushing," Luci suggested.

Oh. Cheeks warm, Emilia pushed. The door creaked open. She stepped inside, turning as she eyed the stream of sunlight through the front window and the back. Clothing, cans, and she didn't know what all else littered the floor.

Her gaze fell to the odd discoloration on the pine planks. Brown. With smatters ebbing from one blot. A strange feeling crept up her spine. Her vision blurred. Grip lessened on the tin bucket. Ground shifted and—

"I've got her . . ."

Mac lifted Miss Stanek into his arms. She weighed close to nothing—even with her ever-present haversack looped across her body. He peeked inside the cabin to see what caused her to faint. Finn's blood. He'd forgotten all about it. When he and the Gunderson twins buried Finn yesterday morning, they'd cleaned up the worst of it to keep wild animals away. That'd been good enough to cross it off Mac's list of things to do because he logically assumed the Staneks would head back to Chicago.

However, Miss Emilia Stanek and logic appeared to be strangers.

Careful not to hurt the woman in his arms, he stepped back and turned around, keeping his body between the cabin door and Miss Stanek's siblings to block their vision.

Luci gripped Mac's forearm with both hands and stared into her sister's white face. "Is Emme all right?"

"She's fine, Luci, but maybe you could help me get her hat off." A rocking chair made of scraped pine logs sat on the porch near the front door. Mac used his foot to scoot it closer and leaned down to deposit Miss Stanek into it.

While Luci untied her sister's hat and pulled it loose to use as a fan, Roch slipped inside the cabin. "Is that blood?"

Blast! Turning so he could grip the boy's arm, Mac whispered, "Yes, but I'd prefer we at least protect Luci from seeing it." He pulled Roch out of the cabin and shut the door.

The young man glowered, as if the next words out of his mouth would be, *Who are you to tell me what to do?*

Were all the Staneks stubborn to a fault? Mac raised his eyebrows and dipped his chin lower.

Roch huffed, dropped the wicker basket and bags onto the porch like they were lucky he'd put up with them this long, and leaned against the doorjamb.

Up to now, the boy's attitude had been tolerable because it was another reason for Miss Stanek to decide the odds stacked against her were too high. But if he so much as twitched the wrong way and caused his sister more heartache, the temptation to wallop the boy might prove overpowering.

Mac shifted his gaze to find Miss Stanek staring at him with big eyes. "Thank you."

For catching her when she fainted or for dealing with Roch? Either worked, even if his plan for earning her trust hadn't included holding her in his arms. "You're welcome."

Luci rushed over and wrapped her arms around Mac's waist. "I'm so glad you're our friend."

Mac tensed, unsure how to respond to both her declaration and her hug. Trust was one thing; friendship he couldn't afford. Not when he was so close to getting them back on the train and home to safety.

Luci pulled back and looked up at him with the same big but slightly darker brown eyes as her sister like she was waiting for him to say something . . . or do something. But what?

"I'm sorry." She returned to her sister's side.

The frown on Miss Stanek's face said he'd offended the younger girl. How? Why?

Miss Stanek tucked her sister under her arm and kissed her forehead. "It's all right, sweetie."

Mac opened his mouth to apologize on general principle but was interrupted when Roch snorted. Whatever the sound signified, it made Luci tear up and Miss Stanek frown. Mac twisted his torso to glare at the boy. "Your sister has seen enough. Get those bags back in the surrey, and I'll take you back to town so you can catch the—"

"—the city clerk," Miss Stanek spoke atop Mac's voice. "I want to file my proxy marriage certificate and visit Finn's creditors before everyone goes home for the day."

What? After food, rest, and viewing the harsh conditions she was up against? The woman was impossible! Mac spun on his heel and marched down the porch steps.

Wood thudding and a swish of fabric announced she'd followed him. "Do you intend to honor your promise to take me to City Hall?"

He whirled around. "What is wrong with you? How can you possibly look at"—he pointed at the cabin where Finn's blood had made her faint—"*that* and decide it's wise to stay? Don't you care about your brother and sister?"

Her nostrils flared. "Don't you dare question how much I care about my brother and sister! You have no idea—*none*—what I've sacrificed to get us here. You think you have us all figured out, but you don't know the first thing about us."

"Wrong." He slid a finger under the shoulder strap of her haversack. "This tells me your father was a courier in the Union Army in the war. Any man smart enough to survive the war is smart enough to know—no matter how bad you think you have it back home—you're better off there with him than out here alone."

She pushed him away with both hands. "Wrong again, oh mighty sheriff. My father was the one who—despite my protests—arranged the proxy marriage so Roch, Luci, and I could come here without him precisely *because* we are safer here."

"Not when the bridegroom turns up murdered!"

She pursed her lips and looked away. For a minute, the

only conversation was between the mooing cattle and a bleating goat.

Mac rubbed his left eye with the heel of his hand. Between his exhaustion and this woman's stubborn adherence to a plan she claimed wasn't hers, his mind felt like it was in ten different places, none of them on the most important thing: solving his friend's murder. At least knowing the proxy marriage wasn't her idea explained why the letters he'd read never mentioned changing the agreed-upon arrival date in July, followed by a month of courtship, to this hasty wedding. One mystery surrounding Finn's murder solved . . . only about a hundred left.

"Finn wrote once about a friend of his who was always sure he was right because he *almost* always was." Miss Stanek's soft, wistful words—when she'd been shouting a moment ago—took him aback. "You're *that* friend."

Mac moved his head a smidgen in acknowledgment.

She lifted her face and pierced him with clear caramel eyes. "You said Finn lied to you. Did he? Or did he just not tell you the whole truth?"

Mac crossed his arms over his chest.

"Finn said his friend tried to talk him out of marrying a mail-order bride so many times, he stopped talking about it. He believed you'd come around once I was here." She looked away again. "At least he hoped you would. He didn't want to lose a friend who was closer than a brother."

The phrase slammed into his gut.

"I'm staying, Sheriff McCall. This is my home now, and I hope one day—for Finn's sake—you'll forgive him for marrying me." She took a few steps toward the house before turning around to address him again. "Next time my sister offers you a hug, be the hero she thinks you are and return it."

Ouch!

He'd never meant to hurt Luci. Of the three Staneks, she

was the only one he *didn't* want to strangle. He owed her an apology and a big hug, but before he gave them, he needed to cool off.

Mac trudged to the water pump, removed his hat and suit coat, leaned down, and ruthlessly pumped icy water over his head. He scooped some over his face and into his mouth to wash away road dust. The shocking cold cleared his brain of stupor. Finn. Just last week he'd said, *"The problem with you, Mac, is that it takes you so long to warm up to folks, they've long since written you off as a cold, unfeeling loner. You might try being a little nicer—maybe even smile—when you first make someone's acquaintance."*

Maybe.

But being nicer just backfired.

Mac shook the water from his hair and stood straight. Rivulets trickled down his neck, soaking his shirt collar and raising gooseflesh on his chest and arms. It wasn't as good as getting a few hours of sleep, but it would suffice. After straightening the tin star on his vest, he retrieved his coat and hat. A mirror and razor would be welcome. For now, they'd have to wait.

A sheriff, even a scruffy one, should project calm. Maintain a sense of decorum. Inspire reasonable thinking. He shouldn't let a woman provoke him into anger no matter how illogical she was.

He walked to the cabin. If Emilia Stanek insisted on staying in Helena, there were a few things she and her siblings needed to know before he left them to face the consequences of her decision. With any luck, a night of trying to sleep through howling coyotes would force the city-bred chit to face up to the dangers of Montana Territory, but she'd been amazingly resistant to common sense so far.

The Staneks were inside, the girls busy in the kitchen while Roch righted the overturned table. All of them avoided looking at the bloodstain.

"Miss Stanek, may I have a moment of your time?" Mac held the door open, indicating he wanted to speak to her privately.

With a resigned huff, she wiped her hands on a towel. She tossed it on the yellow cupboard, then whispered something in Luci's ear before giving Roch a look to warn him that he'd better not slack off when she didn't have her eye on him. The boy pounded the four legs of a chair into the floorboards.

Mac wasn't the only one who needed to learn a new way of dealing with people.

Miss Stanek scooted past to join him on the porch. "Yes, Sheriff?"

He closed the door and motioned to the rocking chair. After she sat, he crossed the porch to lean against the support pillar so they faced each other. "Would you agree we both want to keep Roch and Luci safe?"

She nodded, but her eyes remained wary.

"Have you dealt with many bears, cougars, or wolves?"

"Only the human kind."

It took him a moment to remember she'd worked as a customer service manager at a large department store in Chicago. Her letters to Finn had described some of her more harrowing encounters. For someone as petite and young-looking, managing irritated customers required spunk.

Mac removed his hat and swiped a hand through his damp hair. "Do you or your siblings know how to shoot a gun?"

"No. However, Finn said we'd all need to learn."

In her letters, she'd written something about being willing to learn whatever was necessary. Was it in response to shooting a gun? "And you agreed with him?"

"Of course."

Good. Maybe she had some common sense after all. Mac

slipped his hat on before raising his gaze to hers again. "I'd like to start today with Roch."

Miss Stanek studied him for a long moment.

Mac leaned forward. "Whether or not I'm right to be concerned about Finn's murderer returning here, I *am* right about the threat of wild animals."

Whatever she read in his eyes, it convinced her enough to nod.

Now for the part she wasn't going to like. "I'll be sleeping on the front porch tonight to keep guard."

"You should go home to your family."

"I don't have a family."

"Oh. You still should go home." Miss Stanek pressed her hands into her thighs. "You're about to drop with exhaustion. You can't—"

"Which is why I need help. Even if Roch takes to shooting, I can't leave him alone to stand guard while I sleep."

Apparently admitting he needed help stunned her into silence.

"A man I know is working on his family's ranch about a mile back. I'll take Finn's horse, bring him back here, and then we can all eat and sleep before any more decisions are made. I'll be gone about an hour, so before I leave, I need to teach Roch the basics of how to keep all three of you safe."

Please let her be reasonable for once.

For the second time in ten minutes, Mac was pleasantly surprised. Not only had Miss Stanek agreed to his plan, Roch hadn't argued about learning to shoot.

Mac half-expected the boy to put up a fuss out of sheer orneriness.

Before leaving the cabin, he lifted his friend's rifle off the pegs holding it over the front door. He showed Roch how to hold it—butt under arm, barrel to the ground—while walking.

Mac grabbed his hat. "Let's go outside for the next lesson."

Roch put on Finn's black Stetson. "I found it in the barn. Do you think Finn would mind?"

Mac swallowed the emotion clogging his throat. The hat matched his own, something he and Finn had jokingly decided made them twins much like the Gunderson brothers. "I'm sure he thinks it looks fine on you." Although why Finn had left his hat in the barn when whatever business got him killed happened in the cabin remained a mystery.

Roch tucked the gun under his arm.

Once they reached the back of the barn, Mac stopped.

Roch looked confused. "Don't we need to go farther out so we don't scare the animals with our shooting?" He glanced to where the pregnant sow rutted in the dirt.

"Good thinking, Roch, but we aren't going to shoot anything right now."

The mulish twist of the boy's mouth conveyed his sentiments. "Then why did we come out here?"

Mac reached into his coat pocket and withdrew the yellow, bloodstained telegram from his coat pocket. He held it open for Roch to read. "What does this tell you?"

Roch lifted his face, his brown eyes reflecting shock. "Someone with blood on his hands knows Finn was expecting my sister to arrive on this morning's train. You think the man who killed your friend . . . you think these are his fingerprints?"

"Uh-huh."

Roch scrubbed the back of his head like he was trying to get past his skull to his brain. "But it doesn't necessarily mean he's after us, does it?"

"I'm not willing to risk he's not." Mac dug the train

tickets out of his coat. "Your sister wouldn't take these, so I'm giving them to you because my job involves lots of travel. If this guy shows up again, trade these in and get your sisters out of town fast."

Roch took the tickets and stuffed them in his pants pocket.

"Tonight, I need to go get my friend to help guard your sisters."

"Not if you teach me how to shoot."

Mac leaned against the barn and folded his arms across his chest. "Taking care of womenfolk is a man's job, and all I've seen from you today is a sulky child."

The play of emotions across Roch's face ended with shame. "Yes, sir, and I'm sorry about that."

"Good."

"But my father charged me with looking after my sisters before we left Chicago, and I aim to do just that." The tilt of Roch's chin said he meant it.

Even better. "I'll teach you a little today, but we aren't shooting for a couple of reasons. First, I don't want to frighten animals or leave the sightline of your sisters. Second, I don't want to waste ammunition."

"In case I need it later, you mean." The boy was smart. A good sign.

"You understand how shooting an animal and shooting a man are different things." Mac waited for Roch to nod his understanding. "We need to keep watch tonight in case he"—Mac held up the telegram with the bloody fingerprints—"comes back. I don't trust myself to join you because I've been awake going on thirty-two hours now. I need to get Finn's neighbor to help us both, but before I go, I need to show you enough to make you dangerous."

The prospect put a smile on Roch's face. "Yes, sir."

For the next twenty minutes, Mac showed Roch how to clean, load, and aim Finn's Winchester Model 1873 rifle.

"When it comes to animals, shoot high. The noise will scare most predators." Mac put a hand on Roch's shoulder. "Aiming a gun at a man takes a steady hand and a steely eye. You have to make him believe you'll shoot him where he stands. Make him back down."

Roch's Adam's apple bobbed. "What if he keeps comin'?"

Mac looked Roch straight in the eye. "Then you pull the trigger."

Chapter Six

"It's been an hour," Luci said suddenly. "Should we go looking for him?"

Emilia looked from her ranching research journal to Luci, sitting on the other side of the rickety table. "Sheriff McCall told us to stay put. Stay put is what we will do."

Luci seemed to ponder that, her frown growing. "But what if someone attacked him?"

"No one attacks sheriffs," Emilia explained. "They're the law."

Besides, the last person who would ever ask for *her* help would be Sheriff McCall. His dislike for her was apparent. Then again, he undoubtedly would feel the same toward any other woman who arrived in town as Finn's mail-order bride only to discover the groom was dead. She ought not to take his dislike personally. He was merely acting in what he felt was their best interest.

She'd always believed Da was the most determined-he-knew-what-was-best man in the world. Who would have thought she'd met someone worse? Yet for all Sheriff McCall's confidence in his opinion, he *had* reasoned sense into Roch. And he *had* finally given up trying to convince her not to file the proxy and leave Helena. He'd also apologized to Luci. He'd given her a lengthy hug and encouraged them to attend Sunday church services, where he promised to introduce Luci to some girls and boys her age. He even knew some Roch's age. Finn wouldn't have considered the sheriff his closest friend if the man didn't have more virtues than flaws.

Emilia returned her attention to her notes on tending chickens. She resumed reading aloud. "'In addition to feeding and watering, they need to be culled regularly.'"

"Culled?" Luci echoed.

"It means we remove the sick, injured, or inferior."

"What do we do with them?"

"We kill—"

Her vision blurred, chest tightening. Not now. Emilia blinked repeatedly until she could see clearly. She had to gain control. She had to be strong. She had to think about . . . eggs. The coop would be full of them, she was sure. Finn had boasted about his hens all being excellent egg producers. *Her* hens now. And if part of owning a ranch meant culling her small flock, she would do it.

Please, Lord, let there not be any sick, injured, or inferior hens.

Discovering Finn had a pregnant sow had been bad enough. Why a pig? She'd been very clear with Finn about how much she despised the smell of them. Perhaps she could barter it for something useful—a problem to manage tomorrow.

She searched the page for where she'd left off reading. What to look for in a nonproducing hen . . .

"Let's see." Emilia found her spot. "'Dirty feathers are a sign of a healthy chicken. Scaly and pale combs and wattles are bad. Vents should be large, oval, and moist. To examine the vent, lift the hen's tail feathers and—'" She slapped her journal closed. "That's enough for today." Until a hen stopped producing, its feathers were staying unlifted. "Sheriff McCall said to cook more than we think will be enough. Even with the beans and the leftovers from Mrs. Palmer, we should boil some eggs. Would you like to check the coop with me?"

"I don't know," Luci replied with a shrug.

"They won't bite."

"So you say." Luci walked to the kettle of beans cooking on the cast-iron stove. She lifted the lid. "Someone should definitely watch these."

Emilia tilted her head and studied her sister. Luci had always been the one to shy away from animals; strange, considering how easily she took to people. Chickens weren't dogs. Chickens didn't have fangs. Once Luci settled into the ranch, she would realize the chickens were no threat. She'd thank Emilia for teaching her not to fear animals. Eventually.

For now, Luci could enjoy the safety of the cabin.

Emilia eyed the solid interior shutters, which could cover the front window. The only door could be latched shut. Whoever had built the cabin had taken care to build it securely. But how could Finn possibly have viewed this little building as normal-sized? When he'd described his living room and kitchen, she'd imagined two separate spaces. What he'd considered a private bedroom was a loft. No door. Certainly no privacy. She'd had to send Roch to the barn so she and Luci could change out of their Sunday dresses and into their gray work ones. Where had Finn planned on Luci, Roch, and Da sleeping? The barn?

No wonder Roch had looked at the cabin in revulsion. It was smaller than the tenement apartment they'd left back in Chicago. Yet here they had no need to whisper to keep any neighbors from hearing through the paper-thin walls. Nor did they have to share an outhouse. Or listen to gunshots. Or have to step preciously around the sewage in the streets. In time, they'd all forget about the bloodstained pine boards under the makeshift rug. Thank God they'd found several tatted blankets in Finn's covered wagon to place over the spot. Until she could afford a proper rug, these would do.

"Luce," she called over her shoulder, "where did Roch put the wicker basket?"

"You should ask him," Luci suggested.

Emilia looked at the door she'd left open to allow in fresh air. From this angle she could see Roch's legs and his right hand clenching the rifle lying across his lap. Loading and unloading the gun twice made him no expert. Watching Sheriff McCall saddle Finn's horse and being able to repeat the actions on his own made him no expert. Roch shouldn't have to stand guard. He shouldn't have to fear someone coming back to the cabin to attack them.

They'd made it to Helena. They were supposed to be safe.

"Are you going to sit there all day," Luci asked, "or collect eggs?"

"Eggs." Emilia strolled forward, only to stop the moment Roch jumped to his feet.

"It's the sheriff," he said, sounding pleased. Apparently a gun, a horse, and matching black hats were enough to bond them as friends. Not that she'd complain. Not now that Sheriff McCall had improved Roch's disposition.

Emilia stepped to the edge of the covered porch, shielding her eyes from the late-afternoon sun. Over the ridge came Sheriff McCall on Finn's brown horse. From here, it looked like the other horse was white with leopardlike dark spots. And the huge man riding it . . .

She dashed to the henhouse. There weren't going to be enough beans and leftovers to feed them all.

* * *

She didn't mind sharing a meal with two practical strangers. She didn't mind sharing a spoon and tin plate of beans, fried egg, and leftover shepherd's pie with Luci. But permitting a guest to wash the dirty dishes . . .

Emilia stood firm and refused to release the blue enamel mug to the man with as strong a grip on it. "Please, Mr. Gunderson, I can—"

"Jakob," he insisted with the same twinkle in his blue eyes that he'd had since the moment he'd slid off his odd-colored horse and introduced himself as *Jakob Gunderson, but please call me Jakob. Mr. Gunderson is my brother.* He tugged on the mug. "I like to help, and I'll show Luci how to make coffee."

"We don't have any grounds."

"I always carry some in my saddlebag."

"Just let him do it," Roch yelled from where he sat on the hearth. He returned to watching the sheriff demonstrate how to clean the rifle.

The sheriff, Emilia noted, never looked away from the gun.

She released the mug. Not because she no longer minded Mr. Gunder—Jakob—cleaning the dinner table and washing dishes. No, this was nothing more than a decision based on pain and suffering. Her neck verily ached from looking up at him. She'd thought Sheriff McCall was tall until Jakob had dismounted his spotted horse. Four, maybe, five inches over six feet. Good heavens, the tip of her head barely reached the middle of his chest, and her boots had inch heels! He'd had to duck and turn sideways to enter the cabin because of the breadth of his shoulders. She'd seen a few stockmen his size. What did he spend his days lifting? Cows? Never had she felt more petite . . . or more tired of arguing her point.

No, she was flat-out tired. Period. Unlike Luci, she hadn't

had a nap. With what little sleep she'd had on the train, the thought of climbing the ladder to the loft tempted her.

Jakob gave Luci the mug. She smiled, muttered her thanks, and intently watched him roll up the sleeves of his blue shirt. Emilia didn't have to hear her sister sigh to know she'd done so. And to think he had a twin . . .

Emilia looked at the chair she'd occupied before Jakob had started piling three tin plates upon the one he'd used. An hour or so before nightfall, she could sit here to work on her notes for tomorrow . . . and risk falling asleep for all to see. The cabin afforded zero privacy. Before the sheriff returned with Finn's nearest neighbor, the cabin had felt cozy. Now it felt invaded.

One too many persons crowded.

Emilia grabbed her haversack from the wall hook next to the door. Jakob and Luci could wash the dishes. The sheriff and Roch could clean the gun. She strolled onto the porch. And grimaced. The rocking chair was inside. Fine. She could manage without it. Happy for a moment to herself, she sat on the tree stump Finn had used as a table. If she turned her head, she could easily see through the window into the cabin. From here, though, she also had a prime view of the setting sun above the black mountains.

Orange faded to gold to green and into blue. Magnificent streaks of light with nary a cloud for as far as she could see. The expanse of the sky . . . a distance she could not fathom. And she'd thought Jakob made her feel tiny.

How had Finn felt when he'd surveyed the horizon? Awe at God's handiwork? Insignificant and alone?

Who am I that God is mindful of such a sinner as me?

He'd written that question twice in his letters. She'd planned on asking what he'd meant, but now? She sniffed and blinked rapidly to dry her eyes. Now was not a time to cry. Now was not the time to grieve. She had work to do. She dug through her haversack to find journal number three and a pencil. The tip?—sharp enough. She rested her haversack against the stump, only to have it fall over, spilling the contents.

Would this day ever end?

She turned to the list of possessions she'd compiled while Sheriff McCall had been fetching Jakob. Barely enough to fill a single column running down the page. More than they'd had in Chicago. Mr. Adams had suggested she sell some things. Once she learned how to make goat cheese, she could barter it and half the weekly production of eggs. Come harvest, she'd have alfalfa and a few cattle to take to auction. Of course, by then she'd know if any were breeding. How long was a cow's gestational period?

She snatched her ranching journal from the ground. Flipped through the pages. Calving cycles . . . it was here somewhere. She'd copied the information out of *The Book of the Farm.*

A set of scuffed work boots entered her peripheral vision.

Emilia turned another page. If she ignored Jakob, he'd go away. Ah, here . . .

Cows may be ascertained to be in calf between the fifth and sixth month of gestation, she'd written. She put an asterisk next to the sentence. Since calving occurred in the spring, if any of Finn's cows were carrying, then—She counted on her fingers April, May, June, July, August. So September, then, would be the earliest she'd know if the herd was growing.

The boots hadn't moved from the threshold.

She tossed journal number two onto journal number one, then returned her attention to her list of estate items.

Harness. Plow. Shovel and rake. Covered wagon. Even though it was a third the size of a Conestoga, she'd need a stool to climb up to the driver's bench. Every morning she'd have to harness the horse. She'd never be able to do it on her own. Roch would have to help. Unless . . .

She nipped at her bottom lip. If she didn't need the wagon for the ranch's sake, it'd be prudent to sell and purchase something more manageable. She drew a question mark behind *covered wagon.*

"What's in the journals?"

Emilia looked to Jakob, trying to discern his motive for asking. He seemed genuinely curious. Not that she cared if Jakob Gunderson knew what was in her journals. She didn't. She had nothing to hide. No secrets. If she said anything, he'd join her out on the porch and they'd have a conversation. He'd tell an amusing story to get her to laugh. When she didn't, he'd offer a joke. He'd done it enough times during the meal for her to wonder if he felt compelled to set people at ease. More than once, she'd noticed him looking at her as if he sensed she was on the precipice of tears, and his obligation—no, duty—was to rescue her from grief.

Was it such a bad thing?

She glanced through the window. Luci had moved to the living area and was sitting at the sheriff's feet, her head resting against his knee. His attention, though, was on whatever Roch was saying. If anyone needed coffee, Sheriff McCall did. No, more than coffee; the haggard man needed sleep . . . and time to grieve his friend's death.

Emilia pointed at the two journals on the ground. "The top one has notes about things I figured I'd need to know as a rancher's wife. The other contains historical research I shared with two stockmen while we rode the trolley on the way home from work. They only had a few years of schooling."

Jakob leaned against the doorframe, his palm resting casually on the hilt of his revolver. "Did you ever think of becoming a teacher?"

"It never interested me," she said in honesty. "I like—I *liked* working at the department store. Things arrived from all over the world. When I saw Byzantine textiles, I wanted to know where they came from, so I went to the library to research them."

He gave her a strange look. Not strange; more like he suddenly saw her in a new light. "Did you find out?"

"Byzantium was the earliest name for Istanbul, Turkey." She paused as he sat next to her, using the cabin wall as a back support. "Istanbul was founded more than six hundred years before the Common Era. In fact, the country is partially in Europe and partially in Asia."

"Whoa." He drew his legs up to his chest, wrapping his arms around them. "I could never figure out what separated Europe and Asia. North America and South America make sense to me because there's a narrow strip of land almost separating the continents."

"The Isthmus of Panama."

He dipped his head just enough to acknowledge he knew what she was talking about.

Emilia tapped her pencil against the journal on her lap. "Because of the sideways *S* bend, the Isthmus of Panama is the only place in the world where one can see the sun set in the Atlantic and rises in the Pacific."

"I'd like to see that." Then his gaze shifted, focusing absently on nothing in particular, a frown growing.

"What is it?" she asked.

"I just realized the farthest south I've ever been was Denver."

"I'd never been out of Chicago until three days ago."

He was watching her with a curious expression, saying *why did you leave the only town you knew for a man you'd never met?* His voice was soft. "I'm sorry about Finn."

Vision blurring, she gave him a weak smile. "Me, too." She paused until she'd gained control over her emotions. "Thank you."

"For?"

"Tonight. It was kind of you."

"Finn would have—" He cleared his throat, then stretched his legs, resting one ankle atop the other. "What's the dividing line between Europe and Asia?"

"It's—oh."

"Oh?"

"I have no idea. I can't believe I never looked that up." She grabbed her historical journal, turned to the page she'd last written on, and underneath *Burma* wrote *What divides Europe and Asia?*

Luci's laughter drew Emilia's gaze to the window. From Roch's spot there on the hearth, he shrugged yet smiled and continued speaking. The sheriff sat, left arm crossed over his chest, gripping his right arm at the elbow, his fisted right hand partially covering his smile. Someone with gray bags under his eyes should be in bed, not engaging in conversation. Why didn't he have a wife and children? Surely there was a girl he was courting. Someone he escorted to the theater. Someone he sat next to at church.

His head turned to the window, to where she was sitting. His brow furrowed; his smile died. *What are you and Jakob discussing?*

Emilia jerked her gaze back to the journal in her lap. She did *not* know what the sheriff was thinking. He could be wondering nothing. Or anything. Or something more likely to be, *Why isn't she sitting in a fit of tears or laying prostrate on Finn's grave or packing to return to Chicago?* To be sure, he wished for the latter.

She sighed. He could hope whatever he wanted. She wasn't leaving.

"What's in the third journal?" Jakob asked, his voice lighthearted yet intent on getting the information he wanted.

Emilia picked a piece of lint off her gray sleeve. "It's a calendar of sorts. A schedule of what I need to do and when I need to have it done by. It also helps me keep track of my finances. Upon Mr. Adams's advice, I've listed every item in Finn's estate." She felt a crease growing between her brows. "How much is Finn's covered wagon worth?"

"I'd say thirty-five. He bought it last summer." He leaned toward the threshold. "Hey, Mac, how much you say Finn's wagon is worth?"

Sheriff McCall stepped onto the threshold. "About twenty-five. He didn't buy it new."

Emilia wrote *25* next to *wagon*. "How difficult is it to drive?"

Jakob and Sheriff McCall exchanged glances before Jakob asked her, "Where are you planning to drive it?"

"Into Helena." Good heavens, where did they think she was going? She'd wager the sheriff was hoping back to Chicago. "Finn had debts. As his wife, I am obligated to see them paid."

The sheriff's lips pursed, as if he was holding back words.

"You can't handle a wagon," Jakob insisted.

"Why can't she?" Luci stood next to Sheriff McCall, with Roch right behind her. Her fingers curled around the sheriff's left hand. "Emme can do anything."

Roch snorted. "She's too wea—" The *k* at the end of the word died under Sheriff McCall's gaze.

Strangely enough, Luci didn't counter Roch's words. Likely she knew he was right. Emilia was too weak to do what she needed to here on the ranch. Today she was. In time, she would be capable of doing more.

She looked to Jakob. "Is it necessary for me to have a vehicle this large, or can I accomplish ranch things with a more manageable wagon? Maybe a buckboard?"

"You'll need something big enough to haul alfalfa to market." Jakob turned to the sheriff, who gave a shake of his head. He turned back to Emilia. "Sell the wagon and borrow one when you have a need."

Borrow? Better to learn how to drive what she owned than put herself at the mercy of others.

"How am I supposed to get into Helena if I don't have a vehicle?" Emilia held up a hand. "Shh. The question was meant to be rhetorical." On the line with *covered wagon*, she wrote, *haul alfalfa*. The tip of her pencil lingered on the end of the word, something niggling at her mind, something not making sense.

She and Finn had begun exchanging letters last summer. At the time, he'd had three hundred head of free-range cattle. Then came the hard winter. Finn had bemoaned not having hay and not having built corrals.

She looked at Jakob. "Why would Finn buy a wagon last summer for the purpose of hauling alfalfa when he didn't buy alfalfa seed until last month?" When Jakob didn't answer, she looked at the sheriff. "What has he been using the wagon for?"

"What a day." Luci's announcement broke the silence in the dark cabin.

"Shh," Emilia said without opening her eyes. "Go to sleep."

"I can't."

Emilia released a frustrated breath and rolled over on the featherbed. Never in her life had she slept on something so soft. Moonlight streaming through the tiny loft window brightened her sister's face, making it almost as pale as their cotton nightgowns.

"Why can't you sleep?" she whispered.

Luci sighed. "He's so beautiful."

"The sheriff?"

Luci gave her a strange look. "No, Jakob Gunderson."

Emilia blinked. Jakob? Why would Luci be thinking about him, considering she'd spent most of the evening latched onto Sheriff McCall? Any words she'd exchanged with Jakob had been minimal. No matter how many times Emilia had caught Luci staring at the man and given her a silent command to stop, Luci had gone back to doing it again. Even if Jakob were bathed, shaved, and smelled nothing of sweat and manure, Emilia wouldn't describe him as beautiful. To be fair, he was handsome, charming, nice to talk to, and, considering the way he'd insisted upon washing the dishes, gallant.

Impressive, Jakob was.

Beautiful?

What hung in the gallery across the street from Spiegel was beautiful. Landscapes. Portraits. Fruit. Flowers. How many lunch breaks had she sacrificed to spend twenty minutes in the gallery? Too many. Not enough.

Emilia rubbed her tired eyes. "Beauty is not enough reason to marry someone."

Silence lingered inside the cabin. But outside—

She turned her head toward the sound. The voices were too faint for her to discern who spoke. They'd all still be trying to figure out why Finn had bought the covered wagon last summer if the sheriff hadn't ordered everyone to bed. Was he trying to hide something? What did he know about Finn that he wasn't telling her? There had to be something. She had not imagined the look of dread on his face after she'd first asked what Finn had been using the wagon for.

Just when she'd started to believe—hope, really—that her sister had fallen asleep, Luci said, "What is?"

Emilia looked at her sister. "What is what?"

"What is enough of a reason to marry someone?"

"Strength of character. Common values." She shivered, then adjusted the quilt to recover them. Tomorrow night it might be wiser to move the featherbed and straw mattress in front of the hearth. "Oh, and love," she hastened to add. It ought to have been the first reason she'd given; it was why their parents had married.

Luci's brow furrowed. "Only three reasons?"

Emilia released a tired breath. There were more reasons, some less desperate than others, but it was late, it'd been a long day, and more than anything she wanted to sleep. "Can we talk about this tomorrow?"

"I suppose." Luci rolled onto her back. She stared at the ceiling, her eyes not closing, and released a loud sigh that clearly conveyed *I'll do what you asked, but that doesn't mean I'm going to be happy doing it.*

Emilia softly chuckled. "Thank you." She rolled onto her back, closed her eyes, and adjusted the quilt, drawing it and the luxurious sheets up to her chin. How had Finn afforded such nice bedding?

Between what little remained in the cupboard and the root cellar, they had a week's worth of food. Then they'd have to live on eggs and goat milk and whatever her seven dollars could buy. Considering the amount of milk the goats produced, she ought to try making cheese. And butter. The Helena library should have a recipe book. Or she could ask

Mrs. Palmer when she returned the tin lunch pail. Yes, that was what she'd do tomorrow after attending to the proxy and the list of creditors. Of course, in the morning, before she left for City Hall, she needed to feed the sow and the goats and let out the chickens to graze. Roch could check on the herd and—

"Emme?"

"Yes?"

"You told Da you were marrying Finn because it was convenient." Luci paused. "If convenience was enough of a reason to marry him, you should marry Sheriff McCall. He said that, out here, a good woman was worth more than her weight in gold."

Emilia turned her head just enough to see her sister was studying her face. "Are you being serious?"

Luci nodded vigorously. "You're not much of a widow, so you shouldn't have to wait a year before marrying again like Mrs. Palmer said you did."

Mrs. Palmer's exact words had been, *You should not feel obligated to wait a year before marrying again*. Not that Emilia would correct her sister's memory. "Sheriff McCall was Finn's closest friend."

"I don't think that stops him from thinking you're awfully pretty."

Emilia stared at the ceiling beams. Every time she'd looked Sheriff McCall's way, he'd looked at her. Did he think she was pretty? Men leering at her—*that* she was quite familiar with. She'd never allowed their actions to bother her. Eventually, because she'd give them no encouragement, they'd stop. She'd hoped, the moment she'd stepped off the train, to see a man looking at her with such blatant admiration and love—like she was a precious treasure. It was what she'd expected to see in Finn's eyes.

Instead, she saw anger in Sheriff McCall's weary, suspicious eyes. Not only had his good friend been murdered, but now he had the mess of managing his dead friend's mail-order wife. No wonder he wanted her gone. She was an unnecessary and unwanted burden. Luci was right—she wasn't much of a widow.

A hot tear slid down her cheek.

And then another.

She rolled to her side to keep Luci from seeing her tears.

She hadn't married Finn because of the strength of his character or because they shared values . . . or for love. She'd married him to escape the sewage called Chicago. She'd married him for the hope of a better life. She married him because he'd promised her love.

If marrying another stranger—regardless of whether he thought she was pretty or not—was what she had to do for her family's sake, she would do it. Love didn't feed a family. Love didn't keep a body warm. Love—

Emilia brushed away her tears. Love wasn't enough.

Not for her.

Why would Finn buy a wagon last summer for the purpose of hauling alfalfa when he didn't buy alfalfa seed until last month? What has he been using the wagon for?

Mac couldn't get Miss Stanek's questions out of his brain, but he was so tired a reasonable answer eluded him. He strolled through the dark toward the surrey while Roch and Jakob sat on the front porch discussing who would take first watch. Too bad Jakob's brother, Isaak, hadn't been the twin tasked with cleaning up the family ranch for new tenants. Though they weren't identical, it was impossible to tell which blond-headed giant was which from afar.

Isaak was the responsible one, the serious one—although he could be wickedly funny if you were standing close enough to hear some of his asides. Jakob, on the other hand, seemed more interested in charming Miss Stanek than protecting her. Washing dishes. Helping her make lists. Telling her to call him Jakob. It was almost enough to make Mac regret asking for his help.

Yawning, he retrieved his rifle and bedroll from beneath the backseat. Hopefully, Jakob was sticking to the plan to make Roch think he'd be taking a shift on his own tonight. Hardly. But Mac could be diplomatic when necessary, despite what some people might think.

Why would Finn buy a wagon last summer? What has he been using the wagon for? The answers were important. Mac knew it in the place he'd learned to trust over his seven years as a lawman. If only he could think past the headache pounding behind his eyes. How many hours without sleep was he up to now? Thirty-five? Thirty-six? It felt like he'd been out riding for a week.

Out riding. Why did the thought spark the vague sense he was close to answering Miss Stanek's questions? Or was it just because he had to take prisoners down to Deer Lodge Penitentiary tomorrow afternoon? If Miss Stanek didn't change her mind about filing the proxy in the morning, he'd be cutting it close to get her around to Finn's creditors before it was time to leave. Was that why he felt a warning in his soul?

Mac breathed air in through his nose and let it out with a huff. He'd never figure it out without sleep. Tucking the bedroll under one arm and the rifle under the other, he returned to the porch. His eyes stung and another yawn stretched his jaw.

"That's legal?" Jakob's voice carried in the night air.

Mac blinked and focused on Roch. "What's this?"

"I was just telling Mr. Gunderson about how our landlord back in Chicago told us we had to come up with thirty dollars for repairs or he'd evict us."

Jakob frowned. "You ever heard of such a thing?"

Mac shook his head. Was that what Miss Stanek had meant when she said they didn't have a home anymore? "There are laws against requiring tenants to pay for their own repairs."

"Yeah . . . well, what the law says and what a landlord can get away with aren't always the same thing." Roch tapped his index finger against the long-barreled rifle.

You have no idea what's motivating her insistence on staying. We've been operating under the assumption she'd be better off going back to Chicago. What if it isn't true? Hale's words chased away thoughts of Finn's wagon.

Mac handed his rifle to Roch. "In case you need another one. It works just like Finn's."

"Is it loaded?" Good. The boy was learning.

"No. Have Jakob help you." Leaving Roch and Jakob to work together to check the rifle's readiness—at least Jakob was responsible enough for that—Mac found a spot to sleep at the bottom of the porch. He kicked pebbles and branches aside before laying out his bedroll. If trouble came, he was close enough to boot awake.

"Where's your father now?" Jakob kept up a steady flow of questions.

Mac revised his earlier opinion. If Roch was going to stay awake tonight, he'd need someone to keep him talking. Jakob, not Isaak, was the man for that job.

Mac assumed, once he stretched out on the bedroll, he'd fall asleep regardless of the conversation going on. He was wrong. Only it wasn't Roch's voice keeping him awake . . . it was his sister's.

Why would Finn buy a wagon?

The question, combined with all the other puzzle pieces, swirled through Mac's brain.

The hat in the barn when Finn was discovered in the cabin.

His belongings tossed about but nothing of value missing.

The bandanna and greasepaint.

Bloody fingerprints on the telegram and letters.

A secret marriage.

Five creditors, none of which accounted for the new cattle, fencing, alfalfa seed, or plow.

Mac shifted to his side, tucking one arm under his head as a pillow. The pieces fit together. All of them. Somehow.

Would they fit if he started supposing Finn wasn't innocent but guilty?

Chapter Seven

West Main Street

"What took so long?" Sheriff McCall opened the door to City Hall, bracing it with his right arm, as Emilia crossed the empty foyer. He gave her a bit of a look—brows raised a fraction, mouth indented in one corner. Not a smile. Not an I've-been-anxiously-awaiting-your-return look. Neither, though, was it a scowl. She'd take it.

"After the judge verified the proxy and declared the marriage legal, this other man knocked on his office door. Mr. Fisk offered to buy the ranch," she said in awe. "The price was what you said the land was worth. To the penny. Judge Forsythe also said the offer was fair."

Sheriff McCall gave a nod. "Expect multiple offers."

The moment she stepped over the threshold, his left hand rested against her back. Politely guiding her outside? Or nudging to speed her along her way? Regardless, a tingle raced up her spine. She didn't need him to think she was pretty. She certainly didn't want him to suspect she had any matrimonial aspirations toward him, because she didn't. She wouldn't. He was Finn's closest friend.

Emilia lifted her skirts and hurried to the planked sidewalk to put space between them. She headed to the surrey.

"Wrong way." His palm pressed into her back again, long enough for her to know in exactly which direction he wanted her to go. This time it wasn't toward the surrey. "Cannon's is just up the road."

Emilia fell into step with him. "I saw the door labeled Office of the Sheriff. Why didn't you tell me you worked in City Hall?"

"Hadn't been relevant to any conversation."

True, so she didn't argue. "I presume you talked with your deputies while I was upstairs with the judge."

He nodded.

Emilia glanced back and forth, from him to the uninviting row of wooden buildings stretching along the street, nearly all with sham fronts. The back of her neck ached as she stared up at him. As she waited for words to follow his nod. Drawing words from him rivaled drawing (usually unsuccessfully) words from her brother.

None came, so she said, "There must be more pressing duties demanding your attention than escorting me about town."

His gaze stayed on the road ahead.

"Please don't think I'm not appreciative, but—" She pursed her lips. There had to be a polite way to say, *Please return to your job and ignore me.* "I'm indebted to you for the extra mile you've walked on our behalf, but there's no need to walk two extra. Even Finn would agree you've done more than necessary."

His head slowly turned in her direction, just enough for her to see his narrowed gaze and pinched lips. And then he returned his attention forward. Emilia couldn't help but sigh in frustration. The man had the conversational talents of a ten-year-old.

Only a starry-eyed romantic like Luci would ever suppose this man thought Emilia was pretty. Although she'd believe he thought her pretty annoying.

They stopped at an intersection and waited for a buggy and two wagons to roll past.

"There's no need to do more," she said because he was clearly pondering her words and realizing she was right. "I can manage from here on out." She pointed over her shoulder in the direction of City Hall. "I shall meet you at your office when I'm finished."

He rubbed his heavily bristled jaw, then started up another steeply inclined street. Emilia hurried to keep pace with his long-legged stride, despite the burning in her legs. What she'd give to sit for a moment on one of the benches lining the sidewalk's street-side curb. Nothing about his demeanor indicated he felt the need to fill the awkward silence. For goodness sake, the forty-five-minute drive from the ranch to Helena would have been unbearable had she not initiated conversation . . . and figured out how to deduce his nonverbal responses. He wasn't a complicated man. Nor did he seem one given to subterfuge.

Thank you for showing Roch how to use a gun.

A you're-welcome nod.

I appreciate your asking Jakob to help stand guard.

The I-appreciate-your-appreciation tilt of his chin.

Roch and Luci seemed taken with him.

Silence because he needed a moment to think about how Luci and Roch had interacted with Jakob . . . and then, after realizing she was right, a people-usually-are-taken-with-Jakob shrug.

Weeks on end of managing disgruntled customers had truly tuned her ability to interpret what a person was thinking by expressions and body movements, sighs, and groans. Based on Sheriff McCall's clamped jaw, he was evaluating how to convince her to accept Mr. Fisk's offer, use the funds to pay Finn's debts, and then leave Helena. She ought to be amused by her uncanny ability to understand him.

They stopped under the wooden awning of a dressmaker's shop.

"Why should I—" Emilia asked at the same time as he said, "You should sell."

He gave her a sideways look, a silent, *I'll listen to your reason for not selling, but I won't change my mind about you leaving Helena.*

Emilia sighed. "Why should I expect multiple offers for the ranch?"

His brow flickered with surprise. Clearly not the question he'd anticipated.

"Helena has had nine additions to the town site." His gaze stayed fixed ahead as they resumed walking, now passing a quiet and orderly saloon. "Finn's land is just north of the fairgrounds and Helena has grown to over ten thousand people in the last five years. A forward-thinking man will see the value in buying those forty acres, figuring on dividing them up into housing lots as soon as the city spreads farther." He shot Emilia a quick yet telling glare: *It's in your best interest to sell.*

Maybe it was. After paying the debts, she'd have enough funds to start over somewhere new, away from Helena, away from danger, away from being known as a murdered man's widow. She couldn't sell. This was their home now. Her home. The land of milk and honey. This was where they'd prosper. She couldn't give up without trying. She owed it to Finn.

She owed it to herself.

Emilia pointed at the brick building ahead, with the words CANNON'S GENERAL STORE painted in black above the awning. "There's Cannon's."

He grabbed her arm, stopping her. "Miss Stanek—"

"Collins." She looked up at him and said in a firm voice, "I'm Mrs. Collins now. And I have business to attend to. Private business. I'll meet you back at the surrey by eleven."

He appeared not to know what to say.

Emilia glanced about the street. Several pedestrians had, like them, stopped on the boardwalk, looking their way. A wagon rolled past, the driver's head cocked in their direction. Word that she was Finn's widow couldn't have traveled this quickly. No, more likely all were curious as to who their sheriff was speaking to. A new woman in town, even a town like Helena with ten thousand people, was sure to attract attention, even if her pink dress and black bonnet weren't the height of fashion.

He stepped closer. "You need to understand something."

Emilia looked up at him and waited.

Even though no one was nearby, he spoke softly. "Hale and I don't have a full accounting of Finn's debts. These creditors are the only ones who've come forward so far. The new cattle, alfalfa seed, plow, and fencing—we don't know where the money for them came from."

"Do you think Finn was doing something shady?"

He shook his head.

She sucked in a breath, stunned at his admission. He shook his head not because he was saying he didn't think so. He was saying he didn't know, and the doubt—the confusion—could only mean he suspected and maybe even feared the worst of Finn. She refused to believe the worst.

When in doubt, trust what you know. Finn was a good man. She knew his character. However he'd found money to buy cattle, seed, plow, and fencing, he'd done it legally.

"Sheriff McCall! Mac!"

Emilia looked left, toward the dapper man waving his gray derby in the air, dashing across the street, taking care to dodge piles of manure.

The sheriff muttered something under his breath. Then he shifted his stance, his right hand casually resting on the hilt of his revolver. "Morning, Hendry," he said as the blond man, who looked to be around the sheriff's age, drew up next to them.

"Morning." Mr. Hendry nodded at Emilia, muttered, "Ma'am," then plopped his hat back on his head. He released a steadying breath. "Mac, you aren't an easy person to find. I heard a crazy rumor yesterday and—uh, can I have a word?" His gaze flickered to Emilia to imply *privately*.

"If it's about Chicago Joe, she's going legit." Said in a monotonous voice she hadn't heard from Sheriff McCall until now.

Mr. Hendry looked surprised . . . and skeptical. "This isn't about her. And it can't wait until tomorrow's meeting."

Sheriff McCall breathed deep. "Two o'clock. My office."

A smile brightened Mr. Hendry's face. "I'll be there." He turned to Emilia and stuck out his hand. "Joseph Hendry, reporter for the *Daily Independent*."

Emilia shook his hand. "Mrs. Phineas Collins."

Pause. Then—"I didn't know Finn had gotten married."

"Proxy" was all Sheriff McCall answered.

"Hm." This from Mr. Hendry. Had his face colored or was she imaging it?

Emilia gripped the haversack strap across her chest. "It was nice meeting you, Mr. Hendry. You look like you have something else to say, so I shall leave you two to talk. Sheriff McCall, I'll meet you at the surrey at eleven."

Without waiting for a response from either man, she resumed the trek to the general store. She couldn't fault anyone for being shocked at learning Finn had married by proxy. Nor would she allow anyone to make her feel ashamed for being a mail-order bride. She'd done it for her family. She'd do it again if necessary.

A long bench sat out front, under the large display window.

She stopped and drew in a steadying breath, withdrawing a journal from her haversack. The grocer was no different from a Spiegel customer. She straightened her shoulders. *Be gracious. Be firm. Be willing to lose a battle in order to win the war.*

Emilia followed the dirt-tracked footprints inside the dark, damp building. Bagged, boxed, and canned goods—along with hats, guns, crockery, and pans—lined the shelves around every wall and up to the ceiling. Nothing near as organized or upscale as Spiegel, but a person could find anything she needed here. A coffin stood against a stack of crates. Boxes and barrels crammed the floor. Tables piled high with bolts of cloth. Spices. Baking powder. Oats. Flour, sugar, honey, and molasses. Bins and bins of coffee beans. Bagged tea leaves. Yet the musky smell of cigars and tobacco overpowered it all.

She made her way past the potbellied stove and a table with a chess set. On one side of the counter was a coffee grinder and scales. On the other side, the cash register.

"Hello," she called out.

A red-faced, hearty man wearing a white apron exited the back room. Sleeves rolled up, he crossed his arms and leaned over the counter. "What can I help you with?"

Emilia opened her notebook and double-checked the list

of creditors for the correct name. She smiled at the man. "I'm looking for Mr. Charles Cannon."

He grinned. "You found him."

"Excellent." Emilia stretched out her hand and he shook it. "I'm Mrs. Phineas Collins, and I'm here to pay his debt."

His mouth gaped for a second. "Uh, you don't look old enough to be married. What are you fifteen? Sixteen?"

"I assure you, I'm twenty-one."

He whistled. "Well, I'll be. I heard his ranch was going up in a sheriff's sale." He looked past her. "You know about her and Finn?"

Emilia looked heavenward. The sheriff was worse than a stray dog. He was a flea . . . which meant she was the stray dog he'd attached himself to, not any more pleasant of a thought. With a grumble under her breath, she turned around. Sheriff McCall leaned against the seed cabinet, all casual and calm. As if he had nothing better to do than stand there. No wonder the man wasn't married.

She gave him an obvious please-leave look.

Something flickered in his eyes. If he dared laugh, dared show the least bit of amusement, why, she would—

He looked at the grocer. "The land belongs to his surviving heir."

"I see," muttered Mr. Cannon, his disappointment evident.

Emilia waited for Sheriff McCall to look her way. His gaze stayed on the merchant. Fine. She could ignore him.

Putting the sheriff out of her mind, she turned and rested her journal on the counter. She flipped to the page with the payment schedule. "Sir, to show my good faith, I would like to begin with bartering eggs and goat cheese to you"—she rotated the notebook so he could see her estimates of high and low production numbers—"while I spend the next nine weeks providing bartered labor to the other creditors to eliminate the smaller debts. After setting aside the eighth through the nineteenth of June to focus on sowing alfalfa and putting in a garden, I will barter labor to you."

She paused to give him an opening to respond.

He studied her numbers, clearly lost in his own thoughts.

She continued. "Now, if we add a fair dollar-a-day wage for an unskilled laborer to the lowest bartered egg-and-cheese numbers of four dollars and fifty cents, the debt will be eliminated by mid-November. Give or take a week."

Of course once Da arrived in July, he would insist on helping her reduce the debt. Not that Mr. Cannon needed to know about Da. Or Roch and Luci . . .

"November, you say?" Mr. Cannon drummed his fingers on the counter.

"I know it seems a long time from now," she reasoned. "Wisdom says to eliminate the smallest debts first, then attack the largest one with a vengeance. Bartering eggs and cheese is the most I can offer at this time." Unless she offered a piglet or two. That would have to wait until the sow delivered, which had better be soon because she couldn't bear the smell.

His gaze flickered to the sheriff before settling on hers. "I like your grit, Mrs. Collins. Can't say this about everyone I meet. How about you sell me the ranch for two hundred and I'll balance out Finn's line of credit?" Before Emilia could respond, he added, "You won't get a better offer."

"She will," the sheriff said dryly.

Mr. Cannon didn't seem to care for the sheriff's response. His gaze shifted back to Emilia. "Two-fifty, debt erased, and I'll buy any eggs, cheese, or vegetables you have to sell."

Emilia looked down at her notes. Mr. Fisk had offered four hundred, the top price for forty acres of improved farmland, which he said Finn's land was. The thought of selling the ranch soured her stomach. As unimpressive as Finn's cabin was, it was their home. Her home.

She couldn't help but smile.

"Mr. Cannon," she said to him, "I appreciate your offer. The most prudent course of action for me at this time is to make a go of the ranch. I realize the imposition I am placing upon your generous nature. If you would be willing to agree to my payment plan, I promise I'll work hard and finish in a timely manner."

He didn't look convinced, yet he nodded.

Emilia reached inside her haversack and withdrew her precious fountain pen. She offered it to him. "If you would be so kind as to sign." As he took the pen and wrote his name, she glanced around the store for a witness. No one else was shopping. Which meant her only option was—"Sheriff McCall, it would be best for us to have a witness."

He took his leisure in stepping forward. *L. McCall* was all he wrote.

Once the payment schedule had all three signatures, she purchased three-dollars' worth of dry goods and a yard of cheesecloth. "I'll be back by noon to collect these."

Mr. Cannon shook her hand again. "It's a pleasure doing business with you."

"Thank you, sir." Emilia returned the pen and journal to her haversack.

Sheriff McCall followed her to Dr. Abernathy, the dentist, where she arranged to work every other Friday until debt paid . . . and then to the bootmaker, a Mr. Zeb Inger, who preferred a quicker payback. Every Thursday, plus the Fridays she wasn't working for the dentist. The sheriff, availing himself as witness to the agreed-upon payment schedules, made his presence a fraction more tolerable.

A minuscule fraction.

After leaving the bootmaker's shop, Emilia consulted the map Jakob had roughly drawn, including the names of the main streets, the locations for each creditor, the church,

Mr. Adams's law office, and Luci's school. Granted she could have asked the sheriff for directions. The man seemed content to stand beside her and say nothing. Having gained her bearings, she headed north, with the sheriff dutifully keeping pace. If he was content to walk in silence, she would be, too.

She breathed in the midmorning air. Clean, even with an occasional dust cloud from passing traffic. This was what Da's lungs needed. Everything would work out perfectly. She tapped her notebook against her palm as she turned onto Lawrence Street. Three days a week was all she had left to offer, with two creditors left to visit. If both asked for a quicker payback—

Emilia worried her bottom lip. *Please, Lord, let them be reasonable.*

She stepped at the intersection with Last Chance Gulch, then turned right.

Sheriff McCall's hand rested on her back again. "This way." He nudged her left.

"You don't have to escort me to every creditor," she insisted. "I'm fully capable of managing this myself. I'm not your responsibility."

The corners of his mouth indented.

Emilia growled. He was worse than a flea. A blight of locusts. A plague.

Chapter Eight

They continued north toward a two-story, triangular-shaped brick building twice the size of the general store. Emilia eyed the building. In black-painted letters near the flat roof, THE RESALE CO. lined both edges. At the intersection of three roads, they crossed to the other side of Last Chance Gulch. Then they crossed again.

Sheriff McCall motioned to the right. "Helena Avenue will take you to the depot."

Emilia held a retort.

He stopped at a propped-open door underneath a cloth awning.

Sheriff McCall motioned for her to enter first.

She tucked her notebook under her arm. Then she slid past him, withdrawing her fountain pen from her haversack as she walked. As in the general store, shelves lined the walls of the secondhand store to the ceiling. Unlike in the general store, a set of wood and iron stairs led to a loft with shelves of books and other home goods. Furniture stacked on furniture. Twine-bound rolls of rugs. Lamps. Paintings. Baskets and blankets hung from the ceiling beams. And candles. Lots of candles and soaps, which must be what fragranced the shop with such a welcoming scent. A sleeping tabby cat—either pregnant or merely well fed—lay inside an open cupboard. Despite the urge to pet it, Emilia continued on to a white-painted counter taller than the one she used to stand behind at Spiegel.

Sheriff McCall stopped next to her and tapped on the bell.

Emilia leaned close to whisper, "I don't need your assistance."

"Humph," he muttered.

"Mac!" a deep voice bellowed. "I wasn't sure I'd see you before we left." An older man with an impressive handlebar mustache that rivaled his silvery shoulder-length hair, strolled around a stack of crates, carrying a box overflowing with doorknobs. "How are you holding—" His surprised gaze narrowed on Emilia. "Miss, I'll, uh, be with you in a moment," he said before looking back at the sheriff. He set the box on the counter. "What brings you by?"

Before the sheriff could say anything, Emilia stretched out her hand to the man she assumed was the proprietor. "He's with me." *Unfortunately.* "I'm Mrs. Phineas Collins," she said, shaking his hand. Like the previous creditors, he stared at her with a when-did-Finn-get-married expression. Once again, she felt disinclined to explain. "Are you Mr. David Pawlikowski, the owner of this fine establishment?"

"I am."

"Excellent." She rested her journal on the counter, then flipped to the page with her payment schedule for the secondhand store. "You extended my husband the credit of twenty-five dollars and forty-three cents. I would like to—"

"He bought a cookstove."

Emilia looked up. "Excuse me?"

Mr. Pawlikowski's gaze flickered to the sheriff before settling back on her. This time, though, he had a twinkle in his dark eyes. "Was a month back. Said he needed to get his home in order. He bought some fancy linens and the nicest featherbed I had. Some Englishman used to own them." He rested his elbow on the counter and leaned forward. "The first time my wife sat on a featherbed she vowed she was never leaving." He gave her a cheeky grin. "It's best not to argue with a woman when she's with child. Or when she's not."

Emilia's face warmed.

To the sheriff's credit, all he did was look heavenward . . . and grin somewhat.

She returned her attention to her payment plan. "Sir, I would like to barter labor against the debt." She turned the notebook to face him, using her fountain pen to point to the numbers. "According to my calculations, if I work two days a week at a dollar-a-day wage, I can retire the debt by the end of June."

Mr. Pawlikowski studied her instead of her calculations.

Emilia held his gaze. He looked suspicious. Why? She was being sincere. If he would give her a chance, she'd prove she was trustworthy, a hard worker, and worth the two dollars per day she'd been offered to stay at Spiegel.

"Prior to arriving in Helena," she rushed on, "I worked at Spiegel Department Store in Chicago for almost four years. I delivered catalogs and oversaw the register. My most recent, and longest position, was as customer service department manager. I handled returns, credits, and complaints. And gift wrapping." Occasionally, she also attended to a lost child.

He slowly nodded. "Impressive accomplishment for someone your age."

"I'm twenty-one."

He gave her a dubious stare.

She forced a smile. "My height does me no favors."

He acknowledged this with a brief nod.

"I can request a reference," she offered, "if you need one."

The sheriff crossed his arm and muttered, "Humph," drawing Mr. Pawlikowski's attention. Neither said anything, yet something had been communicated.

"No need," answered Mr. Pawlikowski. "I trust your word."

He looked down at the notebook, his mouth tightening into a thin line. He abruptly turned back a page. Emilia opened her mouth to question what he was looking for. He kept turning pages until he reached her list of what was on the ranch, with question marks next to items she wondered about selling and the list of things she hoped to buy. She gripped her fountain pen with both hands to keep from snatching her notebook away. His imposing behavior didn't justify rudeness on her part. She had no shame at what was on those pages. It all testified to how hard she intended to work. If he'd give her a chance, she'd prove it. She could do this.

And yet she shifted her weight uncomfortably. It wasn't as if she'd expected to keep the debts a secret. Word would travel. News would spread about how she was bartering labor against debt. Creditors would talk to creditors. Reading her notebook allowed him to reach the truth quicker. She was in debt: $179.13.

In her haversack, she had $3.94 to make last until Da arrived in July . . . or until she could find another way to earn money. The man she'd married by proxy was dead. She was responsible for two siblings, two goats, five chickens, twenty-two cows, a bull, and a rank-smelling, pregnant sow.

I can make this work.

Mr. Pawlikowski regarded her coolly. "I'll give you three

seventy-five for the ranch. Land and cabin only. You can keep or sell everything else."

"I'm not interested in selling."

"It would be in your best interest, Mrs. Collins."

"She knows," muttered the sheriff.

Emilia pressed her lips together to keep from saying something impolite to both men.

Maybe it was because Mr. Pawlikowski was near Da's age. Maybe it was because both men had dark brown eyes she'd swear could see into her soul. Maybe she was being fanciful due to exhaustion and hunger and grief. But when she looked into Mr. Pawlikowski's eyes, she saw disappointment. With her. How could that be? He didn't know her.

Nothing in the notebook testified to what she'd sacrificed.

It only showed how hard she was willing to work.

"May I?" Mr. Pawlikowski motioned to her fountain pen.

Emilia handed it to him.

He flipped the pages to where she'd written *The Resale Co., David Pawlikowski, proprietor.*

He drew a line through her payment schedule, then wrote, *A dollar a day until debt is paid.* He signed his name. "Mrs. Collins, you may work at your convenience. I leave this Saturday to take my wife on a year-long and quite belated honeymoon. As long as the debt is paid by the time I return, I'll be satisfied. Because my sons, Isaak and Jakob, will be splitting their time between the store and readying our ranch for new tenants, you can work the front counter."

Ranch for new tenants? That sounded like—

"Is Jakob Gunderson your son?" Why hadn't he said anything last night?

Mr. Pawlikowski and the sheriff exchanged glances again.

"He is." Mr. Pawlikowski offered Emilia her pen. "How do you know Jakob?"

She couldn't look away. While he looked distinguished with his silvery mane and mustache, and he was a taller man, she couldn't find any physical similarity to his son—or, she presumed, his step-son in light of their different last names. "Sheriff McCall asked him to help stand guard last night," she finally answered. "He's teaching my brother and sister to catch and clean fish."

"Not surprising," he muttered. "You be sure to tell Jakob his mother expects him home for dinner."

"Certainly."

She signed her name next to his, then handed the pen to the sheriff for him to sign. This time, though, he only wrote *Mac.* He laid the pen in the center of the notebook.

She shook Mr. Pawlikowski's hand. "Thank you, sir. I'll start Monday. Nine A.M. Enjoy the holiday with your wife."

"I will." He cocked his head to the side, his brow furrowing with concern. "I'm sorry for your loss. Finn was a good man. Be patient and know God will lead Mac to whoever killed your husband and why."

Emilia swallowed. Her chest tightening, she moistened her lips and tried to form words. Nothing came out. It hurt to think about Finn. To think that she'd never see what he looked like. To never hear his voice.

Mr. Pawlikowski gave her a gentle smile. "May I give you a piece of advice?"

She nodded.

"That land of yours will draw men—some good, some not. Don't marry the first man who proposes. Like my wife was, you can afford to be choosy." He twisted his silver wedding band, his expression growing solemn. "And then choose wisely."

Unsure of what to say, she merely nodded.

Then he clasped the sheriff's shoulder. "How are you holding up?"

Silence.

Emilia snatched her notebook and pen and hurried to the front door. This wasn't a conversation she needed to overhear.

She stepped out into the warm morning sun and, despite the way her hands shook, deposited her pen and notebook into her haversack. Resting her hands over her heart, she breathed deep. And choked back a sob. This wasn't the moment to break down. It wasn't. Tears blurred her eyes. *Don't do it. Don't cry.* There were too many people on the street to see. *Head up.*

Emilia raised her chin. She blinked rapidly to clear her eyes. After another steadying breath, she checked her map. To the right was Main Street. To the left, Helena Avenue. So if she headed south on Main Street, the first intersection should be Eleventh. She started forward.

A group of Indians, wearing their blankets like togas and with the dignity of old Roman senators, strode slowly along the other side of the street. The squaws, all but two with papooses on their backs, peered into the windows of the businesses. Indians. Chinamen. Buffalo soldiers. Miners. Mountain men. Top-hatted men with gold pocket watches. Grand barouches. Mule-pulled carts. Since arriving in Helena, she'd seen more skin tones and social levels than she'd seen her whole life in Chicago.

She turned left onto Eleventh and looked around for a HESS BLACKSMITHY sign. The blacksmithy had to be around here somewhere. She smelled smoke, but it could be from anywhere, including the bakery across the street. Her stomach growled. Once she visited the blacksmith, she could return to Cannon's General Store to collect her purchases. With the cornmeal she'd bought, she could make—

A hand tightened around her arm, pulling her to a halt. "We need to talk about Samuel Hess."

"We don't." Emilia jerked free of Sheriff McCall's grasp. She looked side to side to see if anyone had noticed them. Wagons and riders continued past. "Sheriff McCall, I am quite capable of negotiating with the blacksmith on my own."

"You don't know him."

"Of course not. I don't know anyone in this town," she reminded him. "And I won't know anyone until I speak with them. Talking is how people make friends."

He glowered down at her. "Trust me. There are people here you shouldn't talk to. People who don't have your best interest at heart."

"And you do?"

His eyes narrowed.

She coughed a breath. "We have known each other for a day, and a good eight hours of it we were both asleep. And yet you expect me to trust you because you say you were my husband's closest friend and because you wear a badge."

He looked at her as if she'd suddenly sprouted horns.

Emilia ignored him. "I'm not some burden you have to cart from place to place. I'm not your responsibility. I don't need your protection." She resumed her trek toward Warren Street. She hadn't taken three steps when he spoke again.

"Mrs. Collins," he said in a tight voice, "until I discover who killed your husband, you do."

Mac opened the door to the blacksmith's shop. Miss—no, Mrs. Collins; he had to get the change into his head—

shot him another of her I-don't-need-you glares before easing past him.

The vindictive part of his soul wanted to leave her to her own devices. The comment about not trusting him hurt—especially after all he'd done to earn it last night and by signing for her repayments this morning. If she were dealing with any other merchant, he'd march to his office and let her fend for herself. But not with Hess. Even though the man looked like a painted postcard of St. Nicholas, he was nothing but a crudity. Why had Finn done business here when there was a good blacksmith with identical rates two blocks away?

Mac released the door and stepped inside. Heat blasted his skin even though the barn doors at the opposite end of the shop were open. Should he have been specific about Hess's character with Mrs. Collins? Exposed her to such embarrassment? No. Surely the blacksmith would be on his best behavior with the county sheriff on hand. Mac opened his coat, adjusting the lapel so both his tin stars were visible.

"Mr. Hess?" Mrs. Collins repeated her call five times before Hess stopped pounding on the horseshoe hooked over his anvil and thrust it into the water barrel to hiss.

"What do you want?"

She remained unflinchingly courteous in the face of Hess's scowl. "I'm Mrs. Phineas Collins." She opened her journal. "According to my records, I owe you twenty-seven dollars and nine cents."

Hess looked at her as if she were an oddity in a traveling circus.

"I would like to work out some sort of arrangement—"

"Not interested." The blacksmith wiped a rag across his damp forehead, swiping soot from one side to the other.

Mac took a step closer to Mrs. Collins. He didn't want

her spending a second longer in the blacksmithy than necessary, so he didn't give Hess the same you-will-hire-her glare he'd given the other shopkeepers—not that Pawlikowski had needed it. The hard winter had changed everything. Men who might otherwise be moved by a widow in desperate need of credit had been bombarded by tales of woe for the last two months. Mac's silent intercession on behalf of Finn's widow closed the deals as surely as his signature witnessing them had. Hess was a different matter, but Mac was behind Finn's widow—both literally and figuratively—as far as Hess would know.

"Ain't nothin' you can do for me." Hess raked his lecherous gaze over Emilia. "At least not here."

It took all Mac's resolve not to plant a fist in the man's jowls. The naïve city girl couldn't know Hess was a frequent customer of some of the cheaper brothels in town. Mac swept aside his long coat to finger the gun handle strapped against his right thigh. One more filthy look at the widow and he would haul the worm to jail on some pretext.

Mrs. Collins tapped her journal against her palm. "Mr. Hess, I'm willing to consider any *honorable* offer you have."

Good for her! Mac compressed his lips to hide a grin.

The blacksmith's face lost its leer. He crossed beefy arms over his chest, the sooty rag dangling like a flag of truce. "Finn still have the wagon I sold him last September?"

Mac tensed. "What's your interest in it?"

Mrs. Collins twisted to throw another of her useless glares at him.

He kept his eyes trained on Hess. September. What else happened last September? The Harvest Festival and the hot-air balloon race. That wasn't it. What had his tired brain been unable to connect last night? What was it trying to tell him now?

Hess swiped his rag along his jawline. "Might be interested in trading it for a two-wheel cart I've got out back."

Mrs. Collins jerked her attention back to the blacksmith. "We might be able to work something out, but I'd like to see the cart you're offering first."

Was the wagon purchase another piece of the puzzle Mac needed to fit into Finn's murder? Or was it insignificant? What else happened last September . . . a brothel girl ran away! Or so Big Jane had said, but the brothel owner employed two bouncers to keep undesirable men out and her girls in. How had one slipped away? Mac and several other men in town had tracked her for several days but never found a body or other physical evidence aside from a blue scarf.

"Sheriff!"

Mac snapped his focus back to Mrs. Collins. "What?"

"Would you come take a look at this cart Mr. Hess is offering to trade? I'd like to know if you feel it's something I can drive."

How many times had the woman said she didn't need him today? Ten? Twelve? Was this one of those times when Hale would advise that any mistake she made was hers to make and Mac needed to stay out of it?

Nah.

Besides, she'd filed the proxy. No fixing that now. Keeping her and her siblings safe—making sure they succeeded—was his new priority, even if she didn't think him trustworthy.

Yet.

He followed them outside to where a cheap but functional cart sat. Mac gave her a nod to say it was a manageable size and another one when Hess said it was worth about eight dollars. While she asked questions, tugged on the wheel, and bartered with Hess about how she'd pay off the remaining twenty-dollar balance, Mac thought through every bit of evidence related to Finn's murder. Time to pay a visit to Madame Lestraude. If anyone knew what was going on inside Big Jane's house, it would be another brothel owner.

And maybe if Mac solved the mystery of Finn's murder, he could get rid of the yawning hole in his chest.

Chapter Nine

Helena Avenue and Main Street
April 11

Mac pulled Lightning's reins too quickly, and the horse snorted. "Sorry, boy." He patted the gray's neck. "Didn't mean to startle you."

Like the sight of forty or fifty people lined up outside The Resale Co. at ten o'clock on a Monday morning had startled Mac. Had they heard Finn's widow was working there?

During the four days he'd been escorting prisoners down to Deer Lodge Penitentiary, Emilia Stanek—Collins!—must have become a celebrity in town. Isaak Gunderson had to be pleased. The store hadn't seen so much business on one day since . . . since Mac moved to Helena. At least the crowd meant she was alive. But if the last four days proved anything, it was that Mac needed to figure out a way to make sure the little family was protected so he could sleep at night.

One thing at a time. First he needed to pay a visit to his mother to ask if there was any chatter among the brothel owners about how a fifteen-year-old girl escaped Big Jane's house last September.

Because, after days of trying to fit puzzle pieces together—everything from real possibilities to wild speculation—the only thing he knew for sure was that Finn had bought a covered wagon he didn't really need, and a few months later, a brothel girl went missing. Were the two things connected? Or mere coincidence?

Mac turned Lightning toward home. A change of clothes and a decent shave were in order before he visited Madame Lestraude's *Maison de Joie*.

Oh, how he hated the name of her brothel. He saw nothing joyful—nothing even charming—about the place even though his mother insisted it epitomized the height of the profession. It was nothing more than three stories of flesh trade euphemistically called a luxury hotel dressed up in French fashion, silk draperies, suffocating perfume, and smiles that never reached the young women's ancient eyes.

But Madame Lestraude—Mary Lester to those who knew her before she ran away from home—insisted she cared for her girls. Mac huffed. Giving the girls lessons in deportment, reading, writing, and sums hardly counted as caring for them. Not when she charged her girls room rent and demanded they dress in the latest fashion at their own expense. Not when she rotated girls in and out every six months with other high-end brothels in Nevada and Wyoming to keep her clientele interested and to keep her girls and the clientele from forming attachments. Not when . . .

Mac rubbed a hand over his unshaven cheeks. Going over the list of reasons did no good. He'd argued all of them a hundred times before. Nothing worked. Madame Lestraude had no desire to become plain old Mary Lester again—not even for her only son, who wanted to give her a real home. He was ready to leave at a moment's notice. He'd accumulated plenty of money to start over anywhere his mother agreed to go.

If she would agree to leave.

Mac rode into the alley behind his two-story home. The town supplied the county sheriff with a house built for a family. Painted sky blue with white gingerbread trim, it boasted a large front porch, a cupola, and enough space to mislead a woman into believing life inside its walls would be safe and comfortable. Not for Mrs. Simpson. Six weeks after her husband's frozen body was found, she'd been forced to vacate it for the newly promoted sheriff.

Him.

He'd only been in the house five weeks, but if history repeated itself, the lovely home would be no more than a place to stable his horses, eat his meals, and keep his clothes. Was it time to plant roots in Helena? To give up thinking he could save his mother from the life she'd chosen over him?

He slid off Lightning, settled him in his stall next to Thunder, gave both horses a good rub down and some oats, then headed toward the house, past the fenced-off garden that had once been Mrs. Simpson's. How Finn used to tease about Mac's determination to grow a decent tomato. Just one. It wasn't a lofty goal, but he'd never managed it when he lived in the boardinghouse and tried to grow tomatoes in pots on the balcony.

Mac swung open the screen door and stopped cold.

What if Sheriff Simpson had been after another runaway brothel girl? Or helping one escape! A logical explanation for why he'd gone alone instead of with a posse. But then, wouldn't one of the madams or crib owners have reported a missing girl? Maybe not. One escaped girl was bad enough. If word got out that another one had successfully run away, it could start an epidemic in the red-light district. But why would anyone choose February for an escape when the threat of more snow loomed in the air? The only way it made sense was if you could get someone out fast and under protection from the elements.

Like the thick tarp over Finn's wagon.

A man who lived next to the railroad.

Finn once boasted that, back in his thieving days, he could sneak onto a train faster than a mouse.

Mac shoved the door open. Too many things plagued him about Finn's death. Were the clues that contradictory, or had he lost all perspective? Grief did that. He knew it might. Of course he knew. But knowing it and experiencing the heaviness that permeated his mind, heart, and spirit like they were trapped inside a dark cave were two different things. Maybe that was why custom dictated black curtains over windows to lament a family member's passing. The shadowed rooms tinged in gray mimicked in the physical realm a soul's mourning.

Tonight, after he'd crossed off all the items on his list of things to do, he'd lose himself in the poetry of Walt Whitman. The man shaped words to capture emotions, something Mac envied. His talents lay elsewhere, but every once in a while, he longed to seize the right words, tie them together, and compel them to express the longings of his heart.

Maybe if he could just put the right words together, he'd finally get through to his mother. After all, her letters—the ones she'd written to her sister—had sent him to Helena to find her in the first place.

Mac stumbled and righted himself against the kitchen table. Finn had understood. His friend, his brother, the one man who knew how it felt to be the son of a woman who'd slept with so many men she didn't even know who had sired you. Never again would they share a cup of coffee while watching the sun set in a blaze of glory. Never discuss the deeper meaning behind a passage of scripture or why certain hymns tightened their throats with gratitude. Never pound each other's backs in greeting.

Mac pressed both hands against the table and squeezed every muscle in his face. Hot tears bled from his eyes. He gripped a chair, yanked it back, and fell into the seat. In the seven days since Finn's death, Mac hadn't stopped. Had kept his focus on things to accomplish. Pressed on. Dammed up his sorrow, anger, and disbelief.

Now it poured out in throbbing torment.

Why, God? Why him? Why him and not me?

No answer. No comfort. Just pulsating grief and the watery promise of heaven. Mac needed something to hold, to touch, to strike. Heaven—though he knew it was as real as the pine-wood table supporting his crossed arms and bowed head—felt too insubstantial and slippery to prop up such heavy anguish.

He pounded the table with one fist. Again. And again.

Why, God? Why?

Someone once told him that questioning God was a sin. The way he figured it, God didn't mind the questions so much as those who tried to make up their own answers. So he prayed for all the things he knew were true—but weren't offering consolation yet—to permeate his soul, clear his mind, and bring him peace.

After the tears slowed, he sat up and wiped his face. Blubbering like a child wasn't going to bring his friend back. Neither would solving his murder, but one thing was more productive than the other. A wash, a shave, and then it would be time to get some answers.

Wood and Joliet Streets

Half an hour later, Mac tied Thunder's reins to the hitching post outside Maison de Joie. He went in the front door and dipped his chin at the huge bodyguard. The title implied the man kept the girls inside safe. Hardly. Mr. Lui protected them from drunk clients so they could keep making money for their madam.

Mac knocked on the door of her office.

Moments later, she pulled aside the peephole cover before unbolting the locks and letting him in. Dressed in her traditional burgundy, blond hair curled and pinned up, she looked like she was about to step out for a night at the theater. "Mac, this is an unexpected pleasure." She backed away from the door. "Please come in."

Mac removed his hat and stepped into the richly appointed room. As always, a large bouquet of hothouse roses sat on the edge of her desk, their elegance and fragrance masking the ugly work they oversaw. The urge to topple them with a swipe of his hand, to spill water over her ledger so the ink ran until the dollar figures were no longer distinguishable, made Mac grip his hat brim with both hands. "I won't take up much of your time."

"There's no rush. The girls are sleeping." She extended a white hand toward the overstuffed wingback chair opposite her mahogany desk. "And Mr. Green was just here, so there's not even a lump beneath the cushion."

Madame Lestraude hid money in various places around her office for her assistant to find, like some twisted game of hide and seek. As long as Green kept turning in every penny of larger and larger bags of cash, she continued to trust him. Mac had stumbled—or, more accurately, sat on—the secret over a year before. The game was as ridiculous as it was manipulative, and he'd given up trying to make sense of it.

He settled into the chair and tossed his hat on the desk. It bumped the vase of roses, making the petals shiver. "How much did you tempt Green with this time?"

Madame Lestraude's painted lips twitched. "In other words, how much more do you need to come up with to tempt me out of my life of sin?" She lowered herself into her ladder-back chair. "Never mind. I won't tease you today. You look like—never mind. What can I do for you?"

Nice of her to refrain from vulgarity for him. "Remember that brothel girl who went missing last September?"

"Of course." She picked a fountain pen from the middle of her ledger and closed the book. "Why do you ask?"

"I wondered if there were any new rumors circulating about her . . . or any others. Maybe about a runaway in February?" Mac didn't blink to ensure he caught every nuance of her expression.

Other than a slight pinching around her eyes—which could either be suspicion or curiosity—her features remained placid. "Nothing I've heard."

"Anything you suspect?"

She twirled the pen between her fingers. "Meaning?"

He held his facial muscles in check. Suspicions and rumors were dangerous. If word got around that Finn had helped runaway brothel girls get out of Helena, whether it was true or not, affected business owners might decide to make up their losses with Emilia Collins or Luci Stanek. Although Madame Lestraude would never do such a thing—she only employed women who entered the sisterhood by choice because she could charge a premium for the illusion of romance that was as phony as her French name—she'd never cross owners who employed different recruitment tactics.

Mac leaned forward. "Meaning you know as much about what goes on in . . . here"—he couldn't bring himself to call this place her house—"as you do about what goes on around town."

"I'm flattered you think so highly of me, but I'm afraid

I don't know anything more than what the newspapers are reporting."

Unlikely, but if that was the game she wanted to play, so be it.

"And speaking of the papers, you might want to drop a friendly word in that sensationalistic reporter's ear. Joseph Something-or-other."

As if she didn't know the full name of the man who'd been single-handedly waging war on prostitution since the day he stepped foot in town. After his exposé of Chinese opium joints, decrying them as "a threat to young white womanhood," the newly elected city council had authorized a police raid. That raid, and the subsequent press approval, resulted in the establishment of quarterly license fees. There wasn't a person in Helena Madame Lestraude resented more than the reporter who'd started the ball rolling.

"You mean Joseph Hendry?" Mac put emphasis on the last name.

"That's the one." Her tone was light, friendly, even disinterested—which meant she was paying close attention indeed. "He's making some strong enemies with this campaign of his to shut down the red-light district."

Mac hoped it worked. About time the rest of the legal system started enforcing the territorial laws against prostitution.

She stood. "If I hear anything else, I'll be sure to share."

So much for having lots of time—not that he wanted to stay a minute longer than necessary. He retrieved his hat from beside the roses. "Thank you."

He crossed to the door, pausing before touching the handle when she called, "I've heard you've become quite the champion to Mr. Collins's widow."

Champion? Spending a morning helping Mrs. Collins

file a proxy and ensuring the creditors cooperated with her repayment plan didn't make him her champion.

Mac swallowed and turned around. "Finn was my friend. I made a promise to look out for his family, as he did for mine."

Cynical laughter greeted the pronouncement. "So . . . let me get this straight. If something happened to you, Finn Collins was supposed to woo me out of my life of sin?"

"Something like that."

Her practiced smile revealed lines around her mouth and beside her eyes. Didn't used to. She used to look younger than her years; now all forty-two were etched in her face. "Be that as it may, the best thing you can do for your friend's widow is to let her fail."

Four days ago he would've agreed. Once the proxy was filed, however, the best way to fulfill his promise to Finn was to help her succeed. "That's up to Mrs. Collins, not me."

"Mrs. Collins, is it? Interesting." Madame Lestraude's voice, at least, had recovered its brashness.

What else was he supposed to call her? Collins was her name now. He was going to regret this, but—"What do you mean?"

"I find your labels interesting, that's all." She shrugged, a secret smile tugging at her lips. "For instance, I'm Madame Lestraude whenever we discuss business or you're upset with me. I'm your mother when you want me to give all this up"—she waved a hand to indicate her business—"so we can start somewhere fresh. So I must wonder why your best friend's widow is Mrs. Collins to you and not Emilia. Such a pretty name, Emilia. Just rolls off the tongue."

"I don't have time for this." Mac shoved on his hat and headed out the door.

Her voice followed him into the hallway. "Is she Mrs. Collins to keep her distant or to keep her close?"

* * *

Instead of going back to his office, Mac headed straight to Hale's to see if any new creditors had staked a claim against Finn's estate—particularly ones who would explain away the troubling purchases.

Judge Forsythe was coming out of the door. "Here to see my nephew?"

"Yes, sir." Which was pretty obvious, but Mac refrained from saying so. "You still trying to get Hale to come back to work for you?"

The judge waved a dismissive hand. "Not this visit. I want him to run for mayor so, when the time comes, he'll be ready to run for judge."

Mac raised his brows in surprise. Territory judges didn't run for office; they were appointed by the President of the United States. Only full-fledged states held elections for judges.

"I realize Montana hasn't achieved statehood yet, but it takes him"—the judge tipped his head toward Hale's window—"time to change streams. The folks I'm talking to think we're a year or two away from becoming a state. If he's elected mayor of what's sure to be the capital city of Montana, he'll be ready to run for judge the moment statehood happens."

"Hale will make the right decision." Mac started to move past, but Judge Forsythe kept talking.

"I lack your confidence." He tapped his gold-handled cane against the wooden sidewalk. "You and I both know there are men who can be bought for the right price."

True enough. The current mayor of Helena being a prime example.

"My nephew—though I disagree with some of the choices he's made—is not for sale. Montana needs that kind of integrity in our courts." The glint in the judge's eyes dared Mac to disagree with him.

He didn't. Even though Mac's jurisdiction kept him out of Mayor Kendrick's sphere of influence, Helena deserved better. Hale would never run, though. Even if he probably should.

"Then add your voice to mine." The judge's tone was one he used when passing sentence, one that brooked no argument. "You are planning to run for sheriff next year, correct?"

Mac nodded. As undersheriff, he'd been appointed to the position of sheriff after Simpson's death. Staying in the position would require being elected, which—even as the son of Madame Lestraude—was pretty much a sure thing.

"It's in your best interests to convince Hale to run, too." Forsythe pointed a finger at Mac's chest. "An honest sheriff and an honest judge will make quite a team for the state of Montana."

In a few years. "Yes, sir."

A sheepish grin relieved the stark lines around Judge Forsythe's mouth, taking years off his face. "I'm up on my high horse again, aren't I?"

"It doesn't make you wrong."

Judge Forsythe nodded. "Then convince Hale." He looked at a spot over Mac's shoulder and waved at someone. "I'm off. Lots of people to see before I head out next week." He turned on his heel, tapping his cane in a steady rhythm as he retreated. As a territory judge, he spent more time outside of Helena than he did in it. Mac's responsibilities only took him around the county. What did Mrs. Forsythe think of her husband's constant travel?

Mac reined in that line of thought. It might lead him back to his mother's comment about a certain woman who would remain nameless—although a picture of her piquant face and light brown eyes jumped into his mind readily enough.

He found Hale sifting through the books, folders, and loose papers piled on the second chair. "Met your uncle outside."

"I saw through the window." Hale looked over his wire-rimmed glasses. "I presume he filled you in on this nonsense about me running for mayor so I can be a judge someday."

"Not the worst idea I've ever heard." Mac leaned against the wall and crossed his arms over his chest.

"Did he tell you that he also advises me to get a wife?"

So that accounted for the red face. "Yancey Palmer would oblige."

"Not funny, Mac."

Debatable.

Hale dug through the catastrophe of files and books strewn across the entire surface of his desk. "If you're here to see if any more creditors have shown up, they haven't. At least not ones to account for the rash of purchases we both find so perplexing. But your upcoming trip reminded me to check at City Hall to see if Finn paid his property taxes. As you can imagine, they've been overwhelmed this year and said I'd need to wait for the delinquent list to be posted." He plucked a piece of paper from one of the files and held it out. "This bill, however, did show up."

Mac took the paper, his brain latching onto Hale's meaning at the letterhead. "Red Star Saloon?"

"Precisely."

Finn had sworn off drinking when he gave up thieving. At least that was the story he'd told. Had he lied about that, too?

"Twenty-five cents is an odd amount." Hale voiced Mac's thought. "My questions are: first, why would Vincent Humphries create a tab for a man without two bits; second, what was Finn drinking; and third, why was he there in the first place?"

Mac checked the date on the bill. Three weeks ago. Odd. And why the Red Star Saloon? Like his mother's hotel, the saloon was a front for prostitution, except it catered to a lower-class clientele. The serving girls cost little more than the drinks. Mac folded the paper and tucked it into the pocket of his waistcoat. He'd check at the saloon for more information as soon as he finished here. He retrieved some loose change. No way he was bothering Emilia Collins with this debt.

Emilia.

Hmm.

Hale waved off the coins. "I already paid it, but . . ."

It wasn't like him to leave a sentence unfinished. "Whatever it is you don't want to say, I've probably already thought it."

"Mrs. Collins may still need your protection, whether she wants it or not." Hale pushed his wire-rimmed glasses into place with a finger. "Only you'd have to do it without getting her hackles up."

"I'm open to suggestions."

Hale grinned. "As it happens, I've been feeding a stray dog."

Chapter Ten

Later that day

"Uh, Emme, what's that on the porch?"

Luci's panicked question drew Emilia's gaze away from the new barbed wire fencing lining the dirt road. She looked to the cabin in the distance. "What are you talking about? I don't see any—oh." Unless her eyes were deceiving her, something white and furry sat in the rocking chair. Certainly not something human. It stood, circled, and then sat again.

The cart hit a hole in the road and bumped. Emilia glanced over her shoulder to check the wooden crate. None of the vegetable seedlings from Mrs. Hollenbeck had spilled over. With a sigh of relief, she adjusted her grip on the reins as best she could despite how much larger Finn's leather gloves were than her hands. Based on the size of the animal compared to the rocking chair, it had to be—

"It's a cat," she said in her most hopeful voice.

Luci didn't respond.

Emilia turned her head enough to study her sister, whose gaze had narrowed on the porch. Cats were tolerable, in Luci's estimation, because they minded their own business until a human lured them with a *Here, kitty, kitty*. Three words Luci had never uttered—nor likely would ever utter. The best way to avoid interaction with a cat was to ignore it. As Luci had done today after school with Mr. Pawlikowski's well-fed feline.

"It looks friendly," Emilia suggested, craning her neck for a better view. "Mr. Pawlikowski's cat is friendly and gentle, and if you would just pet—"

"That thing on our porch is *not* a cat," Luci ground out.

"It's certainly not a mountain lion, if you're thinking that."

Her worried gaze flicked on Emilia before returning to study the porch again. "I wasn't, but now I am. Please don't lie to me to make me feel better. From this distance, it's impossible to tell if it's friendly. Are, um, baby mountain lions white?"

"I don't know." Emilia shielded the left side of her face to block the late afternoon sun. The nearer they came to the cabin, the more she knew their porch guest wasn't feline. "You're right, it's not a cat. The tail looks too short. It's a baby goat. See how the hair is sticking up? Someone must have brought it," she said and sighed in annoyance.

Another gift of sympathy. Another person to thank. Her financial journal already had a page filled with the names of people who'd visited the ranch and expressed their heartfelt sympathies over Finn's passing. The cards wouldn't have to be responded to, but the gifts?

Emilia, proper etiquette dictates that when someone gives us a gift, we must give something back in return.

Her mother had drilled that into her up until the day she died, likely in case anyone brought condolence food to her funeral. How was Emilia to give in return when she had barely four dollars to her name? The only solution was to find an additional means of employment for when she wasn't bartering labor. But what? She couldn't carry a tune or play a musical instrument or even dance. Her cooking skills were marginal. Other than housekeeping, she had no other serviceable skills. Not to mention she had no more days to work with Saturday spent tending to the ranch and Sunday being the Sabbath after all.

She clicked her tongue, then flicked the reins to spur the horse into a trot. No sense in delaying the inevitable. They might as well see if there was any other unexpected gift, besides the goat, to add to their weekend bounty.

Dried fruit. Fresh fruit. Four Mason jars of bread-and-butter pickles. A potted orchid. Two books of poetry. Dozens of cards in condolence. Thanks to Judge and Mrs. Forsythe's generosity, an entire leg of lamb! That would last them a good week. All were lovely gifts, but to barter any of them to any of Finn's creditors would be bad form. The food they'd eat. The seedlings from Mrs. Hollenbeck they'd plant. The orchid she'd have to figure out how to tend. The books of poetry could be read . . . if she found time. Luci may like them.

The goat, however, was another matter.

Of course, it *could* be part of another marriage proposal.

Emilia cringed as images from her first day at work came to the forefront of her mind. What kind of man proposes to a woman right after he introduces himself? Worse, what kind of man proposes after three men before him proposed and received a resounding *no*? For all that she'd sold today at The Resale Co., a fair portion had to be purchases made in hopes of impressing her. Then again, maybe Montana miners liked china tea sets, Jane Austen novels, and white-painted terrariums.

Please, Lord, anything but another proposal.

If it was a welcome-to-Helena gift . . .

"It had better be male," she muttered.

"Why?"

"We can breed him with our two—"

The goat jumped out of the rocker and onto the porch, barking rapidly. With every yip, its whole body bounced. Luci screamed and scrambled onto the back of the cart's wooden seat, almost knocking Emilia off the bench.

Her knees pressed against Emilia as she held tight. "Go back to Helena. Go! Go now!"

Emilia drew the cart to a halt in front of the cabin. "Calm down."

"I can't!"

She loosened Luci's grip around her neck, yet her sister's hands continued to tremble, her dark eyes wide with alarm. "It's just a dog, Luce. Look, he's not much bigger than our hens."

"I don't care," Luci roared. "Take me to Sheriff McCall. Now!"

"Why?"

"He promised he will always keep us safe." She growled. "Just go. Please."

Emilia clenched her jaw. A promise like that—one that couldn't be kept no matter how well intentioned—meant nothing. They didn't need the sheriff to protect them.

"Listen, we don't even know if Sheriff McCall is back in town," she said to help Luci be reasonable. "Jakob and Roch will be back soon. We can sit here and wait, all right?" She waited for Luci to settle back down on the bench. "See, you'll be fine. The dog can't reach you up here."

Her ashen face regained a bit of color. "I suppose that's true." Her petrified gaze shifted to the dog. "Why won't it stop?"

Emilia looked at the dog barking and bouncing on the porch, its snowy white hair sticking out like needles. Why did it stay on the porch instead of charging at them? Customers used to walk through Spiegel with leashed dogs. Not once had there been a dog attack or a dog run loose. Each dog had known what its owner expected. Good behavior.

No . . . *trained* behavior.

A thought sparking, she removed Finn's gloves, then tossed them onto the floorboard. She slid off the cart before Luci could stop her.

"Emme, don't! Da said not to go near strays."

She ignored her sister, pointed at the dog, and commanded, "Sit."

It did.

Tongue hanging out, it gasped for breath.

Emilia looked over her shoulder. "Did you see that? It must belong to someone."

Luci shifted on the bench, not looking scared so much as nervous. Or maybe puzzled, like Emilia was, as to why a house pet was this far from town.

"Then how did it get out here?" she asked.

Emilia shrugged. "The Gunderson ranch is our closest neighbor." She glanced around. The railroad ran along the southern boundary of Finn's land. "Maybe its owners live closer to the mountains. It couldn't have traveled far. It doesn't look starved." She looked back at the dog, sitting and breathing heavily. What a feisty little breed! Furry and bouncy and impressively obedient. A little cute even.

"Don't," Luci warned.

"Don't what?"

"Don't go near it. Put your hand down."

Emilia looked at her right palm, turned up as Da had taught them all to do before approaching a dog. Without giving it another thought, she started toward the porch. "Hey there," she said softly. The dog's tail wagged. She sat on the porch step, and the dog licked her upturned palm. "Where did you come from?" she murmured. Glancing around, she could see no card or letter. Something could have been left inside the house.

Emilia stood and untied her bonnet strings. She headed to the door, the dog following. Once inside the cabin, she hung her hat on a wall peg, then looked around for any correspondence. Nothing. Everything was in the same spot as it had been in when she and Luci had left for Helena that morning.

She looked down at the dog, sitting next to her, its fur touching her gray skirt. The thing was too friendly to be a stray. It was used to human interaction. "I don't think you're part of a marriage proposal," she said, watching it watch her. "You're someone's pet, aren't you?"

Its tail wagged.

"I'm taking that as affirmation."

It looked to the opened door, its ears twisted, then took off running, barking as frantically as it had earlier. Emilia hurried after it. She stepped out onto the porch to see Jakob and Roch riding down the lane, dust clouds behind them. Jakob waved. She waved back. They drew up next to the cart with Luci perched on the bench seat.

"Shh. Sit," she commanded.

Again the dog obeyed.

She scooped the dog into her arms, tucking it under her left arm. Definitely a little bigger than a chicken. Heavier, too.

Jakob and Roch walked their horses to the porch.

"Where did you find that?" Roch asked, eyeing the dog warily.

"He was here on the porch when we arrived." She looked to Jakob. "Who does it belong to? For all the noise it makes, it's pretty tame."

He tipped the front brim of his hat. His brow furrowed. "I've never seen it before. Several large ranches around here went belly up after the hard winter. Ranchers who wintered in California never returned, and others who'd endured the winter skedaddled as soon as the snow cleared. Only a fraction of cattle on this side of Montana survived." He stepped forward to pet the dog. "This little feller looks mighty fancy to be a stray. Someone has been feeding it. Hey, Luci, come see—"

"No," Emilia and Roch blurted out in unison.

Jakob's bemused gaze shifted between them.

"She's petrified of dogs," whispered Roch. He tipped up his hat just like Jakob had. "One bit her arm when she was little. All animals make her wary." He turned to Emilia, as if looking for approval that he hadn't shared something he shouldn't have.

She gave him a soft smile. While his words to her of late tended to be sparse and tense, they always found common ground with Luci. "What do you think we should do about the dog?" she asked Roch. "It can't stay here."

He shrugged.

They both looked to Jakob.

He laughed, holding up his hands. "Whoa. I'm not taking the critter," he said and yet took the dog from Emilia; it immediately started licking his hand. He scratched under its chin. "I'll wager someone from Helena felt sorry for you three being out here all alone. For all this one's size, he"—he checked its belly—"she has a mean bark. No one could sneak up on you without Dog with Needles for Hair hearing it."

Roch chuckled. "Dog with Needles for Hair. I like that."

Emilia looked over at Luci, sitting on the cart bench, her silent pleas evident. Why did she feel the immediate need to go to Sheriff McCall? He could make all the promises in the world to keep them safe, but promises didn't bolt the door at night. Promises couldn't protect them against an attacker. Promises—

Someone from Helena felt sorry for you three being out here all alone.

"He did this," she muttered.

"Who?" Jakob asked.

"Sheriff McCall." And then, because she didn't want Jakob to think she thought ill of a man he clearly admired, she added, "He wouldn't have done it if he'd known about Luci's fear. His intentions were honorable."

Roch gave her a bemused look. "It could have been anyone."

"You're right. It could have been anyone," she admitted. "I *know* it was him."

"Do you?" he bit off. "Or do you want it to be him?"

Emilia tensed. What had she said or done to make her brother think she had feelings for the sheriff? "What's that supposed to mean?"

His eyes narrowed. "Your husband's been dead a week. Stop, all right?" He untied Finn's horse and led it to the barn.

Jakob sighed. "Emilia, Roch didn't intend—"

"Yes, he did."

Everything she'd done was to make sure her family had a better life. But Roch didn't see it. After she'd started exchanging letters with Finn, Roch had pushed her out of his life. He'd built a wall between them, and no matter how many times she'd reminded him that she was doing this for him—for all of them—he was too angry to notice anything but how she no longer had the time to be his substitute mother.

Emilia turned to Jakob. "He thinks I'm on the hunt for another husband. I'm not, but Roch is happy to think the worst of me."

They were silent for a moment.

She scratched the dog's neck. "I'll take this little one back to Sheriff McCall in the morning."

"Why? It's not his." Jakob grimaced. "At least I've never known him to own a dog, but I wouldn't put it past him to pick up a stray and bring it out . . ." He left the sentence unfinished, implying that Sheriff McCall's kindness extended to both the dog and the Staneks.

"Regardless, the dog can't stay here. Not when my sister is terrified of him."

Jakob tipped his head, gazing over to where Luci sat. A crease deepened between his brows. "Emilia, go inside." Said in a hard tone unlike anything she'd heard from him before.

"Why?" she asked.

"She'll never learn to be brave with you hovering over her."

She glanced from him to Luci and back again, realization of his intention dawning.

She opened her mouth to argue, but his jaw clenched. This was her sister they were talking about. Hers. In time, Luci would grow out of her fear, just as Emilia had grown out of hers of unfamiliar animals. What she needed to do was find Luci a book about dogs. Knowledge chased away fear. Forcing a child to confront her fear by petting a dog?

"I don't think—"

Jakob turned to face her with such a don't-argue-with-me expression, the rest of her argument died in her throat. She swiveled around and strolled, shoulders high, into the cabin. Regardless of what happened, tomorrow she was taking the dog back to Sheriff McCall and letting him know they didn't need his interference in their lives.

Because she needed to.

She certainly had no interest in seeing him.

* * *

Say what she had to say and leave.

Emilia drew in a breath, yet the action did little to calm the butterflies in her stomach. Agitated butterflies. Not excited-about-seeing-the-sheriff ones. The last time she'd stood outside the door to City Hall, Sheriff McCall had opened it for her so she could enter and file the proxy. Five days ago. Things had ended peacefully between them. No reason to fret that he'd retained any anger at her for filing the proxy, for staying in Helena, for not doing what he'd wanted her to do. No man held his anger for five days. Sheriff McCall was like every other man she'd ever dealt with.

Except he made her feel jittery.

Just thinking about seeing him again made her feel jittery.

Knowing what she had to say to him made her even more jittery.

Oh dear, she hadn't felt this inner turmoil when she'd resigned from Spiegel. What was wrong with her? No reason to feel nervous. No reason to dawdle either. Mr. Gunderson was expecting her back to work by one and she needed time to eat her lunch—not that she'd need more than a few minutes for a wedge of cheese and two pickles. She'd need another ten minutes minimum to walk back to The Resale Co. Better plan for fifteen in case another person stopped to welcome her to Helena, to ask if he could take her to dinner or lunch or the theater or—

Stop dawdling!

Emilia jerked open the door and stepped inside. For all that the building housed—city marshal, police court, fire department, jail, city council, and, temporarily until the new county jail was built, the office of the sheriff—it was quite unpretentious. The door closed behind her, causing an echo in the foyer, despite the dozen or so people milling about.

"Mrs. Collins," the city clerk called out. "It's so good to see you again." Smiling, Mr. Dunfree motioned her over to his counter. "How can I help you today?"

Every person in the foyer looked her way.

Emilia hurried to the counter before anyone decided to engage her in conversation. "Good morning, Mr. Dunfree. I'm looking for the sheriff," she said softly. "Is he busy?"

"Yes—no." His face scrunched as he thought about it. "Come to think of it, I don't know. Mac's been in and out all morning. He's got a hanging over in Marysville. I could take a message for you."

"I'd prefer to speak in person."

He looked offended, as if she'd insulted his ability to be discreet. "Then how about you come back tomorrow? Between nine and ten. After that, he has a trial. Could last all day."

She glanced at the door to the office of the sheriff. "I can't come back at that time. I have work." At the sound of sudden laughter, she looked to her right.

A trio of firemen descended the stairs. They turned to their left and opened a door, revealing a water wagon. The door closed.

She looked back at the clerk. "Mr. Gunderson said this was Sheriff McCall's lunch hour. Surely this would be a convenient time, if he's in the building."

He stared at her, clearly knowing something she didn't. He leaned on the counter. "I know everyone in this building. I'm sure I can find someone to help with your need."

Emilia just smiled. "Thank you, but I need to speak with Sheriff McCall."

The door to the city marshal's office opened. A ginger-haired man leaned out, scowling. "Dunfree, I'm tired of waiting! Get me the d—" His gaze settled on Emilia, his face blanching. "Uh, I need those liquor licenses I asked for," he said in a more genteel tone. "Ma'am."

She tipped her head to acknowledge him.

He closed his door.

Leaving the clerk to find the forms the city marshal so desperately needed, Emilia maneuvered through the crowd to reach the door with Office of the Sheriff etched into the glass. She softly rapped on the glass pane, waited, and after deciding no one was going to answer, opened the door. Four men stood around a desk, all talking over one another. None looked like the steely-eyed gunslingers she'd expected to see, despite the guns strapped to their thighs. Each wore a vest over his white shirt, although Sheriff McCall's gold damask was the fanciest. Considering the stuffiness of the room despite two windows being open, she wasn't surprised all had discarded their coats and rolled up their sleeves.

She stepped inside, then gently closed the door, yet the moment it latched, all four turned her way. Their gazes shifted from noticing her bonnetless head to her gloveless hands, their disapproval evident. Sheriff McCall looked downright angry. Why? Because she stood before him in a tattered black dress with a white apron, a clear reminder she was a clerk and a cleaning woman all because of his friend's debts?

Or because she was a visible reminder that his closest friend was dead?

Emilia raised her chin. "Sheriff McCall, I have a situation I'd like to discuss with you."

His grip tightened on the papers he held.

"Is this a good time?" she said with all the confidence she could maintain under the intensity of his gaze. "Or should I come back later?"

He slapped the papers against the chest of the deputy

next to him. "Keenan, get these juror summons delivered. We can talk about the trial when you get back. O'Mara, go with him. If you see Yin Sing, tell him to get in here and pay his taxes before Friday, or we'll have no choice but to arrest him this time."

"What about Timberline?" asked the third deputy, the shortest of the four men. "I have two eyewitness accounts that she's selling opium out of her laundry shop."

"Ask Forsythe for a search warrant." Sheriff McCall snatched a file off the desk. "Mrs. Collins," was all he said before walking into his office.

The two summons bearers grabbed their hats and suit coats, then left.

"Ma'am?"

Emilia looked to the third deputy. His shoulders were eye level with hers, a pleasant change from having to crank her neck backward to meet a man's gaze. Now that he stood closer she could see his skin was a light toffee color; he had some mixed heritage.

"Yes?" she said with a smile.

He shook her hand. "I'm Deputy Nick Alderson."

"Nice to meet you."

"I'm sorry about your husband. Finn was a good man."

Based on the number of people who had said the same, Finn had been mightily respected in this community. No wonder merchants had no qualms at extending him credit.

"Thank you," she said before casting a nervous glance at the opened door to the sheriff's office. She swallowed. "I suppose I shouldn't keep him waiting."

Deputy Alderson's voice lowered. "Be careful. Mac's in a short temper. He's always like this when we have to do a hanging."

Emilia nodded, although she didn't know why. She didn't know Sheriff McCall well enough to understand his moods or why a hanging would anger him so. That she should be careful around him she understood.

"Duly noted," she whispered back.

"If you will excuse me, I need to see the judge."

"Oh, of course." She started toward the sheriff's office.

She stopped just over the threshold. The file Sheriff McCall had grabbed lay on his desk, the papers strewn from where they'd fallen when he'd clearly tossed the file down. He was standing at the window, his hand braced against the wall, staring outside, his expression stony. A man had to be strong—as much on the inside as the out—to enforce the law, especially when the consequences resulted in the loss of life. He shouldn't have to bear the burden alone. No lawman should.

No man should.

She looked down at his desk. Where to begin?

Emilia clenched her hands together, then breathed deep.

"I'm not angry." She cringed. That probably hadn't been the best way to start this conversation. It might make him think she *was* angry . . . and she wasn't. She was nervous.

He gave no indication he'd heard her. Or, more plausibly, that he needed to respond . . . yet. In the two days they'd spent together, she'd learned he was a man of few words. Was that by nature or by choice? Or did he merely not care enough about her feelings to be bothered if she was angry at him or not? She was a person. A woman who cared and loved and wanted to be loved. She had feelings.

She felt. She hurt. Regardless if he cared or didn't. But why shouldn't he be nonchalant toward her?

I think he thinks you're awfully pretty. Luci clearly had favorably—and faultily—interpreted the man's looks in Emilia's direction.

She was nothing to him but Finn's widow.

Emilia stepped farther into the office. "When I realized it

was you, I wasn't angry either. I know your intentions were honorable. You couldn't have known about Luci. You were only with us for two days, and then we didn't see you for another four."

He continued to say nothing.

So she trudged on. "Jakob talked with Luci. She adores him, although not so much as she does you. It's a different kind of adoration." Emilia grimaced. A different kind of adoration? He was going to think she'd gone mad. "Jakob worked a miracle—well, maybe *miracle* is too strong a word. Luci needs time to be completely comfortable with Needles, but she's less fearful now. What I'm trying to say is thank you for thinking of us, but . . . uh . . . please don't do anything like that again without talking to me first."

He turned and looked at her, a weary lavender under his narrowed eyes. "What are you talking about?"

"The dog. The stray," she corrected.

He stared blankly.

"Don't pretend you don't know about it."

"I'm not."

She watched as his right hand rested on the hilt of his revolver, an action he often did. Consciously? She cocked her head, studying him. Some men would do it to intimidate. Could it be less about intimidation and more of a reminder of his duty to uphold the law? Surely he didn't doubt he was an honorable man. A good man. A man any woman would be honored to love and cherish.

I'd take the one right there if I were you.

Emilia shook her head to rid it of Luci's words. Yes, he was attractive. But for heaven's sake, he was her husband's closest friend. Dead husband but still . . . "I don't know where you found the stray," she said to break the awkward silence. When he still didn't respond, she added, "Jakob says it isn't yours. Is it?"

He shook his head.

"But it's not wild. It's been raised in a home. I was thinking about putting up flyers or buying an advertisement in the paper. Someone around here should know who the dog belongs to. Or, if not, maybe someone will want to take it."

"You can't afford flyers," he snapped. "Or an advertisement."

Emilia felt her jaw drop. Of course she couldn't afford either. She couldn't afford to feed a dog. Her husband was dead. She had two siblings to care for. She owed five creditors and was obligated by propriety to do something nice in return for every person who'd brought condolence gifts—gifts she'd never asked for! The debts continue to pile up. Plus she never knew when to expect another embarrassing marriage proposal or request to court her. And now she had a dog she didn't want, didn't need, and couldn't afford to feed or find its owner. To top it off, she was wasting her lunch break to listen to a man—a man who cared nothing about her feelings—impolitely point out her impoverished state.

She stomped over to him. "I *know* I can't afford flyers."

He gave her a look as if to say, *Then what's the problem?*

"You." She poked his arm. "The dog I can deal with. You, Mr. McCall, I can't!"

He walked to his desk and returned the strewn papers to the folder. "Good day, Mrs. Collins."

Emilia didn't move. Surely this wasn't the end of the conversation, yet the second the telephone on his desk rang, he snatched it up and responded. As the person on the other end of the line spoke, he sat at his desk, grabbed a notepad, and began to write.

Of all the inconsiderate, insufferable—

She whirled around. Three steps out of his office, she stopped.

Deputy Alderson stood next to the door to the hall, a look of disappointment on his face. She didn't have to ask to know he'd heard everything. Not that she faulted him for listening.

She continued forward, taking care not to meet his gaze. "I could have handled that better," she admitted.

"Finn was his friend."

Instant tears blurred her vision. "Don't you think I know? He's done nothing but remind me since I arrived." She reached for the door handle, but he blocked it with his hand. She looked up, fearing she'd see condemnation but finding nothing but pity instead. "Deputy Alderson, is this your way of telling me I should go back and apologize?"

He wiped the tear that trailed down her cheek. "Do you want to, ma'am?"

If she went back to Sheriff McCall's office and apologized—well, she wouldn't be able to do it without crying. The man did nothing but bring out the worst in her. If she apologized now, he would either sit there in stony silence, staring at her as if she were a broken spout, or, even worse, draw her into his arms and hold her as she cried. She couldn't risk either happening. Her heart hurt enough as it was. Her brother wasn't showing her any compassion, the man she'd pinned all her hopes and dreams on was dead, she had no friends, and Sheriff McCall? The man made her horribly uncomfortable.

If building a wall between the two of them was what it took to convince him to leave them alone, so be it.

Deputy Alderson released his hold on the door. "The choice is yours."

And so she left. Doing so was best for both of them.

Chapter Eleven

Wednesday, May 4
7:59 A.M.

"Morning, Sheriff."

Mac dipped his chin to acknowledge the city clerk. "Mr. Dunfree."

"Haven't seen you in, what? Two weeks?"

"Three." In no mood to chitchat with a man who made it his business to know everyone else's, Mac weaved through the crowd to the opposite side of the hallway on the way to his office. The overabundance of people almost made him miss the solitude of riding the long, oddly shaped Lewis and Clark County with nothing but a quartet of horses and a deputy county assessor who liked the silence more than Mac did. Helena sat in the bottom corner of the county, so covering the entire landscape was long and arduous. Or maybe it was just the grim work this year.

Every March, the county sheriff and an assessor went out to the remote areas around Helena to collect property taxes. This year, because of the late thaw and the weeks when every able-bodied man was needed to dispose of livestock carcasses, the annual tax collecting rounds had been postponed. The month-long reprieve mattered little to those left devastated by the hard winter. Not surprisingly, the big operations suffered the most. Some of them were selling cattle for as little as two dollars a head. If Finn ran into an outfit selling off that cheap, maybe he didn't owe as much as Hale suspected.

"Sheriff, when you have a minute, we need to go over the new list of delinquent taxes," Deputy O'Mara called from behind a stack of papers piled a foot high on his desk.

"Give me five minutes." Mac stepped into his office, hung his hat and coat on the peg behind the door, and settled in behind his desk. The mound of messages was more than double the usual for a three-week absence. By the time he read *Luci Stanek at 3:40 P.M.* for the tenth time, he figured she'd popped over every day after school for the past two weeks. The route between Central School and City Hall took her through the heart of the red-light district. For her own safety, she either needed to take a circumspect route or walk five blocks in the opposite direction straight from school to The Resale Co.

"Sheriff, you got a minute to talk about the Collins case?"

Mac looked up at Undersheriff Keenan's voice. As second in command, he'd been put in charge of investigating Finn's murder. "Sure."

Keenan closed the door before sitting down. "I ran down that lead from the Red Star Saloon."

Mac sat forward. "And?"

"I'm afraid it raises more questions than it answers."

Of course it did.

Keenan reached inside his vest. He withdrew a small notebook and opened it to a dog-eared page. "According to the bartender who was on duty on April 2, Finn arrived around seven thirty in the evening and ordered a shot of whiskey. Bartender, a guy named"—he checked his notes—"Vincent Humphries, remembers that some sort of fight broke out that required him to come out from behind the counter. In the commotion, he never got Finn's payment, so he put it down as a tab."

Sounded reasonable . . . except for Finn ordering whiskey and being at a saloon in the first place.

"Here's where it gets odd." Keenan pointed to the words in his journal. "Bartender says Finn had been into the saloon at least two, maybe three other times, all of them months apart. Every time, he sat at the end of the bar and nursed his one drink for a good hour, then downed the whole thing and left. But in April, Finn disappeared during the fight. When Humphries got back to the counter, Finn's shot of whiskey was still full."

Mac rubbed his chin. "What do you make of it?"

Keenan closed his notebook. "Given that you said Finn Collins swore off drinking, I asked Humphries if he ever actually saw Finn down his whiskey."

"Good question."

"Humphries said he couldn't say for sure." Keenan grinned. "And guess what's at the end of the bar where Finn always sat?"

"Not in the mood for guessing."

The undersheriff smiled bigger. "A spittoon."

Mac sat back and crossed his arms over his chest. "So Finn could have dumped his whiskey while no one was watching."

"Exactly. After nursing it along for an hour to blend in while he did whatever it was he'd actually come to do."

"Which was?"

Keenan shrugged. "No idea, and I decided against asking pointed questions like we discussed."

Before leaving town, Mac had shared his suspicions about Finn helping girls escape prostitution with his undersheriff. Keenan said he'd be discreet while investigating, and that he'd keep a sharp eye on Mrs. Collins and Luci Stanek in case anyone came looking for revenge on Finn through them. "Good work. Let me know if you see or hear anything else."

"Yes, sir." Keenan scooted out of the chair and left the office.

O'Mara was waiting to come in with his list of tax delinquencies. "Now, or do you need another five?"

"Now's fine."

As expected, the list of those who couldn't pay their property taxes had grown by at least twenty. Mac exhaled his relief when he passed the surnames that started with *C* without finding Mr. Phineas Collins. One bright spot in a bleak landscape. He filled O'Mara in on his trip with the county assessor. "Mr. Wiggins has the list of those we visited who were unable to pay. He'll bring it over as soon as he's registered the names at the county assessor's office."

"Bad?"

Mac nodded. "At least five places were abandoned, so we tacked notices on the doors that payment was due in ten days or the places would be sold at auction."

O'Mara handed over a beautifully penned letter on thick vellum. "From Lord Hugh Bradley. Short version is he's not returning to Montana to assess his damages. We're welcome to sell off what we can to pay his taxes."

"Nice of him to let us know, I guess." Mac set down the letter. "Big crowd outside. I'm assuming you posted notices of local properties going up for auction."

"First thing this morning. I'm not sure if people came to see the list because they were interested in bidding or grateful not to be on it."

"Maybe."

"Auction is going to be bloody."

Every year, when properties were sold to pay tax debts, people with money snatched up land, homes, and even household possessions for pennies on the dollar. Isaak Gunderson would be bidding on items for The Resale Co.; Judge Forsythe, Charles Cannon, and J. P. Fisk would no doubt get into another shouting match in their rivalry to outbid one another on various properties; and Chicago Joe, Madame Lestraude, and Big Jane—the most successful brothel owners—would buy up places either to expand their flesh trade or diversify with legitimate businesses. This year there would be enough property to satiate all of them.

After Deputy O'Mara finished detailing the owners who needed to be notified to either pay their full tax bill or vacate, he left the office. A steady stream of other visitors followed. It was a quarter past noon when Mac left the office for lunch. Deciding to get a little work done while everyone else was out, he walked across West Main Street to The Last Chance Café and ordered a turkey sandwich to go.

Hale Adams sat alone at a corner table reading a newspaper.

Mac weaved through the crowded tables. "Mind if I join you for a minute?"

Hale lowered the paper. "When did you get back in town?"

"Last night." Mac pulled out the second chair and sat. "Remind me again why I agreed to be sheriff."

"This was your first time collecting property taxes from the outlying areas, wasn't it?"

"Yes."

"Rough year for your initiation." Hale folded his newspaper in half and laid it beside a half-eaten ham and cheese sandwich. "But I don't think you came here for my sympathy."

Mac leaned his elbows on the table. "I have some news we'll need to discuss later, but first tell me how Mrs. Collins and her siblings are doing."

"Fine." Hale took a sip of his coffee.

For the first time in his life, Mac understood why people got exasperated with his short answers. "Just fine?"

A quizzical expression pinched Hale's eyebrows together. "She goes to work, they all go to church, no one has died or even been severely injured."

Mac huffed with exasperation. "Fine."

"That's what I said."

Itching to shake more details out of his friend, Mac leaned closer to Hale to quietly inform him that he had news about Finn. When someone came too close to their table, Mac spoke louder. "Collins property isn't delinquent on taxes."

Hale nodded.

Needing a new topic of conversation, Mac dropped his gaze to the paper. "Anything interesting while I've been gone?"

"Actually, yes." Hale turned the paper and tapped his finger at a headline. "Joseph Hendry is making more noise."

"My mother warned me he was making enemies."

"Sheriff McCall!"

Mac turned to see the counter clerk holding up a paper bag. "My lunch is ready. Are you available for dinner tonight?"

"Sure. Gibbon's Steak House?" Hale named his favorite restaurant in town.

Mac stood. “No. I’ll bring something to your office tonight.”

Hale opened his mouth, likely to protest because he preferred much richer dinners than Mac.

“We’ll be able to have a private word then,” Mac added to make sure the purpose of dinner in the office was clear. After Hale nodded his understanding, Mac weaved around people to the lunch counter, grabbed the bag with a large sandwich protruding from one end, and returned to City Hall to catch up after his three weeks away.

“You’re back!” Luci Stanek burst into Mac’s office two hours later. She’d gained some weight and appeared happy. Mac barely had time to stand before she wrapped her arms around his waist and hugged him tight. “I’ve missed you!”

Mac patted her back. “I’ve missed you, too.”

“You wouldn’t believe everything that’s happened since you’ve been gone.” She pulled away, a look of scolding in her chocolate-brown eyes. “You said you’d be gone two weeks.”

“Two or three.”

“No, you said two.” An impish smile lit her face. “But I forgive you. Now sit down and let me tell you what’s been going on.”

“Yes, ma’am.” He saluted for good measure, a grin threatening to spoil his mock subservience.

Instead of sitting across from him, she paced back and forth, her hand doing as much talking as her mouth. She was full of Roch and Jakob, Jakob and Roch, Emme and Jakob, me and Jakob, until Mac was sick to death of Jakob. But at least it sounded like Roch had taken responsibility for the ranch chores by getting the barbed wire fencing up and beginning a corral.

"You should have seen Roch and Jakob when they first started plowing. Oh . . . it was so funny." Luci's laughter was hard to resist. "One would handle the reins while the other pushed the plow into the soil. They fell over so many times and their rows were so uneven and Needles kept barking and barking, which made the horse even harder to control."

Mac chuckled at the picture she painted. "Sounds like you should have charged admission."

"But I shouldn't laugh so much, at least not at Jakob. He's been kind about getting me over my fear of dogs."

Mac cringed. "I'm sorry about that, Luci."

"It's all right." And off she went on a new topic: the wonderful Jakob Gunderson and Needles.

According to Luci's story, Gunderson deserved a medal—one Mac wanted to pin straight into the man's massive chest. Just how much time had Jakob spent with the Staneks? With Em—Mrs. Collins? Was there a reason she'd accepted Gunderson's help but given Mac the evil eye whenever he offered? Jealousy aside—because the green-eyed monster gripped his insides whenever he thought of Jakob and Finn's widow together—Needles was Mac's problem. *He* should have fixed it. Instead, he'd left town a couple of days later, and someone else had to clean up his mess. Not exactly the best way to earn Mrs. Collins's respect, even if she had said she forgave him. He should have apologized to her the instant she told him, but between the hanging and her convoluted explanation, his patience was exhausted by the time he untangled who Needles was and why Luci was afraid of her.

". . . funny thing in the barn."

Mac jerked his attention back to Luci. "What thing?"

"I don't know. Emme found it last week. She said we should show it to you in case it was a clue." Luci's face sobered. "Do you think it could be . . . a clue?"

"I don't know. Can you describe this thing for me?"

"Uh-huh." She held her thumb and index finger about an inch-and-a-half apart. "It's about this big and it's shiny and it has a swirly-thing coming out of it."

Not exactly helpful. But Mac couldn't dismiss anything at this point.

"I can ask if I can bring it to school tomorrow, then I can come visit you again." Anxiety filled her young face. She needed a friend, not a sheriff.

"Miss Luci"—Mac leaned forward in his chair and took her hands in his—"you can come visit me any time. You don't need an excuse. But I need you to promise me you'll take Broadway to Main Street. Don't walk down Joliet after you reach Broadway. Ever."

"I promise!" She beamed and threw her arms around his neck. "Thank you, Sheriff Mac."

"Just plain Mac, if you please." He held her close for a minute before pulling back. "I need to ask you a quick question."

"All right."

"Do you think your sister would mind me coming out to the ranch so I can see where she found the funny thing?" Would she mind? Would he mind if she minded? He shouldn't, but there was no denying how his pulse pounded at the idea of seeing her again . . . or how he dreaded the idea that she might not want to see him, too.

Luci tilted her head. "Emme was furious at you. About Needles."

As she should be, and next chance he got, he'd offer her

a full apology. Would that make her not mind seeing him again?

Land's sake! Wondering what Emilia Collins thought or wanted or needed frayed his edges.

"But she's better now."

"Whew, that's good." Mac wiped his brow with dramatic flair for Luci's benefit, but he was careful to catch the actual beads of sweat collecting at his temple.

Luci giggled. "She brought the funny thing to work with her. Do you want to go see it?"

Chapter Twelve

The poor man was no salesman.

With a chuckle under her breath, Emilia stepped around a pair of grandfather clocks standing back-to-back to reach the table of oil lamps. Dusting furniture, though, paled in comparison to the theatrics playing out in the store this afternoon. Isaak Gunderson may be Jakob's twin, but the Goliath had none of his brother's easygoing charm, nor any of his stepfather's renowned salesmanship, which drew customers from Missoula, Cheyenne, and even Denver. He must take after his mother. Not that Emilia would know, because Mrs. Pawlikowski had left Helena before they could meet. For all the twins shared about their mother, how could she not imagine Mrs. Pawlikowski to be anything but a saint?

Much could be said about a man who sang his mother's praises.

Emilia tucked her duster under an arm, then stood on her tiptoes to look inside a glass chimney. How did that lint get in there? She pulled it out and dropped it onto the floor to be swept up later. After a glance to where Mr. Gunderson and Yancey Palmer stood talking, she resumed dusting, moving around the table as she worked.

The twins were both affable enough fellows. Dutiful sons. Hard workers. Faithful in church attendance. Well read. So how was it that a pair of twenty-one-year-old men as handsome and financially secure as the Gunderson twins weren't married? Or even courting?

All right, how was it *Jakob* didn't have a girl?

Young women flocked around him at church. Even Miss Palmer, Jakob's closest friend, had admitted she'd had no luck matchmaking Jakob to one of his plethora of admirers. Jakob should have a girl yet strangely didn't, even though he'd told Luci there was a lady he favored. Mr. Gunderson should have a girl, too, but the reason for his static bachelorhood was clear.

Despite how much she admired Isaak Gunderson's organizational skills and his this-is-what-must-be-done-and-this-is-the-best-way-to-do-it attitude, the man was too serious. Like Sheriff McCall, he needed to smile more . . . well, smile. Even a smirk would do. And laugh. If only she could teach her employer how to be charming and complimentary without being a flatterer. She had to help him. Had to. He and Yancey Palmer were quite suited. If Miss Palmer would give him a chance, Mr. Gunderson would prove to be a devoted husband. Emilia was sure of it.

"Isaaaaaaak," Miss Palmer said, elongating his name until it was more like a groan.

Emilia stopped dusting and looked their way.

"Are you not listening to me?" Miss Palmer asked. "Luanne and Roy don't need matching daggers. Stop showing me knives."

He said nothing for a long moment. Then—"So you *don't* want these?"

"I already said I didn't."

He fiddled with his loosened tie, which seemed to annoy

him, like the button at his collar that never stayed buttoned. "You do know every married couple needs knives?"

"Hopefully not after their first fight."

Emilia snickered.

Miss Palmer took the knives from Mr. Gunderson and laid them back on the counter. Emilia couldn't see Miss Palmer's face because of the exquisite feathered derby she wore, but she could imagine the expression: pained tolerance.

"Isaak," Miss Palmer said, "why do I even come in here on the days you're working?"

"When am I not working for you to come in and *not* see me?" Mr. Gunderson stared at Miss Palmer, his face devoid of any emotion. When Miss Palmer didn't answer, he added, "Nothing says love like a good set of cutlery."

Miss Palmer drew in a breath and released it loudly. "Silverware says *I love you both and wish you well on your nuptials.* Matching daggers say *rethink this marriage*. I need the perfect wedding gift . . . and under five dollars. I'm not made of gold."

Mr. Gunderson looked around. He strode around a stack of trunks, then said, "Here's something perfect." His muscles bulging in his rolled-up shirtsleeves, he lifted an intricate metal headboard as if it weighed nothing. "Italian cast iron with mother-of-pearl inlaid. The footboard matches."

Emilia moved around a cupboard for a better view of the pair.

Miss Palmer studied the frame. Then she looked up—not so much as Emilia had to—at Mr. Gunderson and gave him the most quizzical look. "This is a twin bed," she said matter-of-factly.

"Yes, ma'am, it is."

"For Luanne *and* Roy?"

"That would be ridiculous, to say the least," he said with a frown. "Unless their home in Denver is the size of a boxcar, they will need beds for the multiple rooms they have. While a bed frame is not the most romantic gift, it is practical. And considerate. If not now, eventually they will appreciate your foresight. Children need beds, too."

Miss Palmer just looked at him.

He stared back, unflinching under her intense gaze.

Emilia nodded even though neither were looking her way. His point had merit. What Isaak Gunderson lacked in charm, he excelled in confidence, not that Miss Palmer found that as attractive as Emilia did. She should probably mind her own business and stay out of matchmaking. At least until Mr. Gunderson was no longer her employer.

With a sigh, she resumed dusting.

"Oh, this is new." Miss Palmer picked up a peacock-shaped lamp, the satin shade swinging. "Luanne likes fringe." She checked the price tag as Mr. Gunderson rested the headboard against the footboard. "Only four dollars! I'll take it."

"Because every bride wants a wedding gift that says males are prettier than females," he muttered.

"Your cynicism is not appreciated."

A slow smile spread across his face. "And yet I am right."

Emilia blinked, her mouth agape. Mr. Gunderson was smiling. An honest-to-goodness smile. What else had she presumed wrong about him?

Miss Palmer laughed and handed him the lamp. "Oh, Isaak, I'm not the flibbertigibbet you think I am," she said, following him to the counter. "Is this why you refuse to court Miss Rigney despite her overt interest? You're prettier than she is."

He grimaced. "I do nothing to encourage her interest because Deputy Alderson favors her."

"Good. I want you to be the first one to ask me to dance at Luanne's wedding, and then you will flirt with me."

He gave her a dubious look. "Why?"

"To make Hale jealous. Why else?" she asked as if the answer was obvious.

Emilia froze mid-swipe. Hale? As in Hale Adams, Finn's lawyer?

Miss Palmer suddenly gasped aloud, eyes wide, backing up from the counter, grimacing. "Isaak David Gunderson, you don't think I want . . . you . . . us?" She looked like she was about to lose her lunch.

"I had to be sure." His gaze shifted to Emilia, and she immediately resumed dusting. He turned back to Miss Palmer. "Why don't you ask Jakob?"

"I love Jakob, love him dearly. He—" She exhaled. "He is the dearest friend a girl can have, you know?"

"No, I don't, but go on."

"It's just . . ." She shook her head. "I loathe complimenting you."

He nodded. "I don't take it personally."

"You wouldn't," she admitted. "It's not in your character. For all that I adore about Jakob, you are the twin Hale most admires. That's why he suggested you run for mayor. You know everyone in town. People respect you because your word is your bond. You're an honest man, just like Hale."

"Jakob is honest, too," he said absently.

"True. Please, Isaak," Miss Palmer begged. "Two dances, that's all I ask. No, let's do three for good measure."

Emilia inched around the table to get a better look at Mr. Gunderson's face. His brow furrowed, his mouth in a straight line as he eyed Miss Palmer.

"I'll dance with you," he finally said. "But I will not flirt."

Miss Palmer beamed. "You've made my day. Twice."

He rang up her purchase. "Would you like this boxed up and delivered?"

"That would be helpful." Miss Palmer opened her beaded reticule. "Mother gave me a list of items to pick up at Cannon's." She withdrew four dollars and gave them to Mr. Gunderson. "Because you were wondering . . . this Saturday we're having morning tea in honor of the bride."

"Yancey, I have yet to wonder about anything you do. Thank you for your business." He handed her the receipt. "Mrs. Collins?"

Emilia hurried over. "Yes, sir?"

"Record Yancey's purchase in the sales log. I'll box the lamp." He grabbed the lamp and headed to the workroom in the back of the shop, calling out, "Yancey, I'll do my best not to be here the next time you pay a visit."

She yelled back, "Much appreciated."

Emilia withdrew the heavy leather book from beneath the bar-height counter. She plopped it down, then stepped on the wooden stool Mr. Gunderson had found for her so she would be able to reach the cash register. Yancey stood there as she recorded the purchase.

"Mrs. Collins?"

Emilia paused writing and looked up. "Yes?"

"Mother and Luanne requested I invite you to the tea." She laid her hand over Emilia's and gave it a little squeeze. "Please come. Most of the ladies there will be ones from church. We'll be taking turns sewing pearls on Luanne's veil. You don't have to bring anything."

To attend the bride's tea would mean losing an hour and a half in travel to and from Helena. She liked the Palmer family. Miss Palmer's older sister, Luanne, had been in the shop numerous times to look at books. She'd even recommended several, including *The Angora Goat: Its Culture, Origins, and Products,* which Mr. Gunderson had graciously allowed Emilia to read on her lunch breaks. She'd planned on spending Saturday attempting once again to make goat cheese.

"Please," Yancey begged. "You're welcome to bring your sister. Mrs. Truett will be there with her daughter, Melrose."

Emilia nipped her lower lip. Since Sunday, Luci had been begging to spend a day with her new friend, Melrose. With the ranch being so far from town, she couldn't in good conscience have the Truetts bring their daughter out for a visit. The bride's tea was a reasonable compromise. Besides, Yancey had graciously stood in as Emilia's proxy, so attending the party upon her request would mean they were even.

"Yes," she said with as much contrived delight as she could muster, "we would be honored to attend."

Miss Palmer grinned. "It begins at ten. Mother and parties—I suggest coming with an empty stomach."

Before Miss Palmer even stepped outside, Emilia returned to dusting, a seemingly unending task. Three customers came by. Two made purchases. One examined everything he touched. Yet when she asked him if she could help him find anything, he shook his head and muttered that he was just looking.

Emilia continued dusting. Every so often, she'd look up and catch the man looking at her.

"Mrs. Collins?"

She turned to the familiar voice.

Mr. Gunderson walked out of his office. "Would you mind bringing me the—" His gaze shifted from her to the perusing customer. "Afternoon, Ulman. Can I help you find something?"

"Just looking."

"For anything in particular?" When Mr. Ulman didn't respond, Mr. Gunderson strolled past Emilia to the counter. He withdrew the sales log, then looked to Emilia, then back to Mr. Ulman. After tucking the log book under his arm, he walked up to Mr. Ulman. He draped an arm around the man's lean shoulders and turned him away from the table of oil lamps. Together, they walked to the door. Whatever Mr. Gunderson spoke was too soft for Emilia to hear.

Mr. Ulman left the shop without a backward glance.

Mr. Gunderson returned to his office without saying a word.

Emilia stopped dusting in order to pet the cat sleeping in its favorite cupboard. What she'd give to have a day when she had nothing to do but sleep. "Your favorite twin stopped that man from inviting me to supper."

The cat's tail flicked back and forth. It stretched its neck to give her better access.

Emilia sighed. "I'd be honored, if I didn't suspect that every man asking to pay suit was interested more in my land than in me."

The cat continued to flick its tail.

And so Emilia resumed dusting. As the minutes passed, she finished the last of the bookshelves on the second floor. She glanced at the nearest grandfather clock down below. Almost closing time.

"Emme!" Luci dashed through the propped-open front door. Two steps behind her was Sheriff McCall, wearing a modish black suit. Emilia's breath caught. Good heavens, the man was more handsome than she'd remembered. He immediately removed his Stetson, his dark hair longer, shaggier, yet neat. His gaze shifted around the shop and looked to the stairs, to where she was descending.

Her heart increased its beat.

He smiled. At her. As if he was happy to see her again. As if he missed her. As if he knew she'd thought of him at least once a day since she'd left him in his office because he'd thought of her as much. What? Why would she think that? She didn't like him. She was, though, obviously drawn to him. Which was foolish. She didn't need to feel anything for him. She was a widow. Not so much a widow, but still the widow of his closest friend. Besides, he didn't like her.

Maybe he liked her.

But he didn't *like* her. Not that she wanted him to.

Unless he did.

She couldn't exactly forbid him from liking her. And even if she did forbid him, he would like whoever he wanted to like, which could be her. Unless it wasn't her.

She stumbled on the bottom step.

"Emme, are you all right?" Luci asked. "You look a bit flushed."

"No," she croaked. "Um, no," she said in a normal voice, "I'm fine. It was hot up . . ." She motioned at nothing in particular.

Feeling her cheeks warm, Emilia brushed the front of her apron for no logical reason except to give herself a moment to catch her breath. Then she smiled and walked to where her sister stood next to the red cupboard, close enough to pet the cat if she wanted, but not close enough to dart out of the way should the cat lunge.

"How was school?" she asked.

Luci shrugged. "It was fun. Guess who's back?"

Emilia did her best to block out Sheriff McCall, but how could she? Instead of wandering the store as she'd hoped, he stood next to her. Right next to her. He smelled of bergamot and cedar, a scent similar to one of the eaux de cologne the shop sold. Her skin tingled. She gave her head a little shake, but it did nothing to deaden the pounding of her pulse. It'd been a long day. She'd sniffed too many perfumes earlier, that was all.

She forced a smile, then looked up at him and said,

"Sheriff McCall, it's good to see you again." Not a lie, but neither the complete truth.

"Good to see you, too, Mrs. Collins." He gripped his hat with both hands. "Luci said you found something in the barn?"

Emilia nodded.

He cocked his head to the side.

How strange. And fascinating. She'd never noticed his brown eyes had flecks of gold, almost the exact color as the fur of their goats. Quite lovely actually.

He gave her a curious look. "Something wrong?"

Emilia released a nervous chuckle. "No, I was just, um, thinking how much I enjoy"—*looking at you.* "Um, I was thinking about our goats. I've not been successful yet at making cheese. I thought the problem was vinegar." Oh dear, now she was rambling. "Never mind. What brings you by?"

"The barn," he answered with a hint of exasperation in his tone.

She looked to Luci for answers.

"That funny thing we found on Saturday," Luci returned, along with a what-has-gotten-into-you look.

"Oh, that! Wait here."

Emilia hurried to the back office. After explaining the situation to Mr. Gunderson, she found the odd thingamajig inside her haversack. She stepped into the hall where Mr. Gunderson couldn't see her and held her hand over her heart as she breathed slowly. By the eighth breath, the frantic pounding in her chest abated into a normal rhythm.

"Lord, help me," she whispered.

Her heartbeat steady, she returned to the store.

She stepped around a stack of trunks, then stopped at the sudden laughter. Luci and Sheriff McCall were examining a croquet set. Whatever Luci had said had made the sheriff laugh. Too often, Emilia had returned home from work to find Luci and Da laughing. She hadn't been jealous. When had she had time to curl up on the sofa with Da and listen to him read a book? She never had time after Mama died. Someone had to ensure they had food. Had to pay the bills on time. Had to see that Da visited the doctor. He couldn't care for his health if he was caring for the three of them.

With work and her duties at home, her school friendships had fallen by the wayside. She had too many responsibilities to play games. Or to be silly, like Luci was being with the sheriff. Or to learn to ride a horse for the sheer fun of it.

It didn't matter anyway. What was more important was Luci finding someone to fill the void caused by Da's absence. Once Da arrived, everything would return to normal. And Sheriff McCall would no longer feel the need—*obligation*—to protect them. He could find a girl to court. Emilia could find a suitor. They could go their separate ways.

Not him with her. It would never be him.

Because she'd married his friend first.

Ignoring the strange ache in her heart, Emilia started forward. "I went by your office on Monday during my lunch break. Your deputies didn't know when you'd be back," she said and stopped in front of them, "so I thought I'd wait until I'd heard you'd returned." She handed him the scratched metal oval with a long screw in its center. "I found this when we were cleaning the side of the barn with only two stalls. It was buried under some hay. It's not the same type of metal as anything else on the ranch. Jakob says it was probably left by the people from whom Finn bought the ranch. Six and a half years is a long time for it to be in a barn and not be rusted, don't you think?"

"What do you think it is, huh, Mac?" Luci asked, leaning against his arm to study it, too.

Mac? Her sister's use of his first—wait, Mac wasn't his first name. He'd signed the agreements with the creditors as L. McCall. Mac was his nickname per se.

"Miss Luci, that's a good question." He looked to Emilia. "Mind if I take this?"

She shook her head. "I have no use for it. You could come out to the ranch this evening, and I'll show you where we found it."

"How about Saturday morning?" Something in her expression must have prompted him to add, "Better daylight."

"I won't be there," she said as he slid the thingamajig into the inner pocket of his frocked coat. He looked up sharply, a question of *Where will you be?* clear in his eyes. So she explained, "The Palmers invited me and Luci to a bride's tea, and I thought it would be polite—"

A stylish and oddly familiar brunette wearing a feathered hat entered the shop, a covered basket looped over her arm. Oh! She was the woman who sat with her family on the left-side middle pew at church.

Her bright blue eyes settled on Emilia. "Mrs. Collins! I hurried over, praying I'd make it here before the shop closed. I made it with a minute to spare."

Emilia stepped around Sheriff McCall and met the woman at the counter. She stepped up on the stool. "I'm sorry. I don't believe we've met."

The woman held out a gloved hand, the white kidskin with exquisite floral embroidery. "Mrs. Kate Watson. My husband is the chairman of the board of trustees for the Helena Public Schools."

Emilia shook her hand, hoping her dirty hand hadn't soiled Mrs. Watson's expensive glove. "It's nice to meet you. Is there something in particular you're looking for? Mr. Pawlikowski sent a shipment of silk parasols, shawls, and fans from San Francisco."

For a second, Mrs. Watson looked mortified, and then her smile returned. "I'm not here to shop. I'm here to see you." Her gaze shifted to something behind Emilia. "Hello, Sheriff."

"Mrs. Watson" was all he said.

She set the basket on the counter. "My dear Mrs. Collins, please accept my apology for not paying a call sooner. Our youngest has had the croup."

"I'm sorry to hear that."

"He is much improved." She waved at nothing in particular. "But enough about me. I have heard such wonderful praise of you for how you are managing the unexpected debts your husband left behind. Other women of lesser character would have succumbed to—to a less strenuous means of financial security. The Good Lord always blesses the wise choices we make."

"Thank you" was all Emilia could think of to say in response to words that sounded like a compliment but felt like an insult.

Mrs. Watson motioned for Emilia to walk around the counter. Once she did, the woman, who looked to be someone in her thirties, took both of her hands in hers. Was it intentional that two cupboards blocked Luci and Sheriff McCall's view?

Mrs. Watson spoke softly enough that Emilia doubted anyone could hear but her. "I imagine there are nights you don't feel so blessed. Ranch living can break more than our backs. It can break our spirits." Her eyes grew teary. "I know because I watched that happen to my mother. Please know if the ranch and these debts you should never have had to inherit ever become a burden too heavy to bear, the amount my husband would pay for your land would enable you to buy a nice home here in Helena. You could marry again. Start a family."

"Thank you," Emilia whispered back and was pleased her tone sounded sincere. "I'll keep that in mind."

Mrs. Watson sighed. "When I look at you, I see so much of myself. Hard to believe it's been ten years since I left the ranch." After one final squeeze of Emilia's hand, she turned and walked to the door.

"You forgot your basket."

"It's for you. Apple pie. Welcome to Helena!"

Emilia stared at the door long after Mrs. Watson was out of sight.

Luci appeared from around the cupboards. "That woman seemed creepy to me. What did she whisper to you?"

"I think, a sales spiel."

"Humph."

At the sound, Emilia turned to Sheriff McCall, standing at Luci's side. Something wasn't right. Something raised an inner alarm, something she hadn't felt since Mr. Deegan had informed her of the debt they owed for the tenement repairs. For the last two Sundays Mrs. Watson could have walked over and introduced herself. Instead, she and her husband skedaddled out of the church after the last amen. Everyone knew women bearing apples shouldn't be trusted—at least in the Bible and in fairy tales. Was that why Emilia felt wary?

She gave some thought to the exact wording, rolling the question in her mind until she knew exactly what she wanted to ask.

She refocused on Sheriff McCall. "Considering the number of Helena businessmen who have offered to buy the ranch, and the eight marriage proposals I've received in the last three weeks, do you think it's possible someone was willing to kill Finn for his land?"

Chapter Thirteen

"That, ma'am, is why I wanted you to stay on the train."

Emilia stared at Sheriff McCall, rendered speechless by his admission. His brusqueness, his irritation at her for not accepting the tickets, his insistence on guarding the cabin that first night—it all made sense. Now. If someone had killed Finn for his land, his wife became the next target. *She* became the next target. Although a man didn't need to kill her to gain possession of her land. Marriage would do that. And it would eliminate the risk of losing the land in a sheriff's sale to a higher bidder.

"Why didn't you tell me—" She fell silent as his gaze shifted to the store's opened door. Anyone could walk in and overhear. She touched her sister's arm. "Luci, would you go tell Mr. Gunderson that I'm locking up?"

Luci gave her a look that clearly said, *We're going to talk later.* And then she nodded and headed to the back office, trailing her fingers on anything she could touch.

Emilia hurried to the front door. She moved the brick keeping it propped open. Once it was bolted, she turned around . . . and gasped. Sheriff McCall stood there. She could barely catch her breath looking up at him.

He was staring at her most intently, his gaze soft.

Contrite. "I should have told you. The day you arrived, not twenty-four hours earlier, I'd buried the man who was a brother to me."

Who was also *her* husband.

But it wasn't the same. She'd only known Finn through letters. She never experienced the sound of his voice or his laughter. He had. Even if Sheriff McCall had shared with her the degree of his loss that first day, she would have stepped off the train. She had to. She couldn't go back to Chicago. Her future was here. Even without Finn.

Sheriff McCall's future was here, too.

Without Finn.

She reached out and curled her hand around his. "I have failed to express how sorry I am for *your* loss," she said softly. "I'm sorry I didn't realize the extent of it the day I arrived." The movement was small—a flinch perhaps—but she felt it. "You shouldn't have had to deal with us that day. Or any day. We're nothing but a reminder of Finn. For that I am also sorry."

He looked to where their hands joined, his expression pained.

Emilia's cheeks warmed. She released his hand. How could she have been so bold and imposing when she knew how uncomfortable he'd first been when Luci hugged him? The man didn't like to be touched.

"I'm sorry," he muttered, studying her face. "I had no idea Luci was afraid of dogs. I figured you needed something to raise an alarm, if necessary."

"You had the right intentions."

He swallowed. "To think what could have happened to—"

"Nothing did," she rushed to say. He was making himself the villain, she could see that. But he shouldn't. "Luci adores Needles as much as the dog adores her now. Jakob worked a miracle."

A muscle under his eye flinched. "It should have been me."

Something nudged at her to ask *why do you care?* But her heart was pounding again, her stomach in knots. Why did he care so deeply? In no way had he inherited Luci or any of them by way of his friendship to Finn. He wasn't bound to them. Except . . .

He believed they were.

As long as she remained Finn's widow, that was what they would be to him. The only solution was to marry someone else in town. But what man would want a woman who came with the burden of family and debts? A man who cared.

Or one who wanted her land.

Her land of milk and honey. Her albatross.

His gaze shifted from her to something—to nothing in particular. He looked tired. And lonely. Did he have anyone to confide in now that Finn was gone?

"I'm sorry, too," she said, drawing his attention.

His brows rose in a silent question—*for what?*

"Your deputy warned me you were in a dark mood." Emilia released a breath, the action ebbing the tension in her shoulders. "I should have waited and I'm sorry I didn't. It wasn't the best moment to have that—any—conversation with you."

"I'm sorry I was terse."

"I'm sorry I—" Emilia chuckled. "We're quite a sorry pair, aren't we?"

He grinned. "Indeed, ma'am, we are."

Emilia didn't respond. Not yet. This—a camaraderie between them—was too nice not to pause and enjoy the feeling. She nipped at her bottom lip. "I have a couple of things to finish here before I can leave. You're welcome to follow us home. Jakob likes to help Roch catch some fish before he returns to Helena. You can eat with us, and then I can show you where I found the—"

"Can't," he cut in. "I have work to catch up on."

"Tomorrow would be fine."

"How about Saturday midmorning?" he suggested.

"Could you come earlier? Around eight instead? The Palmers invited me to the bride's tea," Emilia reminded him. "Is there a reason you look surprised?"

He shook his head. "Eight marriage proposals. Jakob helping at the ranch. You attending a tea. A lot has happened while I was away."

Emilia didn't reply. She couldn't tell by his voice if he was bothered or merely remarking upon facts, so she said, "Because Finn's creditors agreed to the payment schedule, I didn't feel a hasty marriage was a needed solution to—"

"Emme! Emme!" Luci dashed through the shop. "Mr. Gunderson said I could borrow a croquet set and bring it back Monday." She stopped next to the wooden box she'd been examining with Sheriff McCall. "I don't know which one to pick."

"Excuse me, Sheriff." Emilia stepped around him. They didn't need a croquet set. None of them knew how to play. Nor did they have time to waste playing. She stopped next to Luci, placing her palm against the wooden box, stopping her from picking it up. "We can't borrow anything from Mr. Gunderson."

"Why not?"

"You know why."

Luci's lips pinched. "Fine."

"How about if I buy it for you?" offered Sheriff McCall.

"Thank you," Emilia put in before her sister could accept, "but please don't. I know you mean well. I do. But I need you to stop trying to fix our problems."

His confused gaze shifted from her to Luci, then back to

her. "Understood." He gave Luci's arm a gentle squeeze. "Come by my office whenever you like." He slid his hat back on his head, muttered, "Ma'am" in Emilia's direction, and headed to Mr. Gunderson's office, presumably to use the building's back exit.

"Emme?" Luci's voice was soft.

She turned to her sister. "Yes?"

"I don't think Mr. Gunderson expected anything in return for letting us borrow the croquet set."

"Not immediately," she explained, because Luci needed to hear the truth Mama had drilled into her, the truth confirmed every day she'd worked at Spiegel. "One day he will need a favor and he will remind us of when he loaned us the croquet set. Until then, we owe him and, in a way, that means he owns us. Best not to place ourselves under any debt."

"Can't people do things just to be nice?"

Emilia opened her mouth to say *of course not*, then stopped, the denial dying in her throat. Maybe, in the world somewhere, there were people who did nice things and never expected anything in return. Maybe. She'd never met anyone like that. No one was *that* kind.

Were they?

Mac arrived at the ranch bright and early on Saturday morning. As soon as he dismounted to tie Thunder's reins to the porch beam, two things greeted him: zealous barking and the scent of fresh-baked biscuits.

His stomach rumbled despite the steak-and-egg breakfast he'd consumed before leaving town. Assuming Emilia Collins was like most women, she'd offer him something to eat within a few minutes of his arrival and—after seeing how much weight she'd lost during his three-week trip—there was no way he was taking food off her table. Given that Luci appeared to have gained all the weight her sister had lost, it seemed there was enough of that going on out here. Was the woman giving her siblings larger servings?

Mac stepped onto the porch and raised his hand to knock.

The door flew open. "Mac!" Luci launched herself into a hug.

He wrapped his arms around her shoulders, looking over her head to see an approving smile on her sister's beautiful face.

His stomach did another roll—only this time from attraction rather than pretend hunger. Other women had smiled at him, some going so far as flirting, but none ever twisted his insides.

Mac nodded at her. "Mrs. Collins."

"Sheriff McCall." She bent to pick up the frenzied Needles. "Quiet!"

The dog stopped yapping but continued to voice his distrust of the intruder with low growls.

"Seems your dog doesn't like me." Mac eyed the white ball of fur wriggling in her arms.

Mrs. Collins's lips twitched. "Serves you right, I'd say."

A chuckle bubbled in his chest at her sass before he caught himself. This was his best friend's widow. A woman he found far too appealing and who invaded his thoughts often enough without their bonding over shared jokes. If he'd thought of her once, he'd thought of her a thousand times in the last two days, wondering who the eight men who'd offered proposals were and wanting to shoot every last one of them for daring to bother her when she still loved Finn.

Luci pulled away from the hug, grabbing Mac's arm to tug him inside. "Do you want some biscuits? Emme and I baked them this morning. They're delicious."

Wait! Was marrying Finn a repayment of sorts?

Mac recalled a line from one of her letters, the ones he'd read and reread looking for clues to solve Finn's murder. *I'm so grateful we are equally matched.* Mac had thought she meant in personality and scoffed. No one knew someone's true character through correspondence. But what if she'd meant equal in what they brought to the marriage? Finn's wide-open ranch got her out of a squalid tenement that stank of butchered pigs—the ones she'd written about in so many of her letters—and she eased Finn's loneliness by providing him with not just a wife but a whole family.

No indebtedness, because they were even.

"Are you coming inside?" Emilia—Mrs. Collins poked her head out of the barn.

"Yes. Give me a minute." Mac pulled in a deep breath. Time to focus on facts. The barn, the nickel-plated oval screw, the hat. What story did they tell? He closed his eyes to picture how the barn looked on the day of the murder.

Floor swept.

Hat on a nail hook on the right side about halfway back.

A pile of dirty hay near the door, rake and broom propped beside it.

Wheel tracks in the mud outside.

Wagon with fresh mud on the wheels inside.

With the picture in his mind, he stepped into the barn.

Emilia waved him closer to one of the horse stalls on the left side. "Here's where I found it." She bent down to point at the base of the door. "It was covered with hay."

Mac knelt to get a better look. He pictured the swept floor again.

Why swept? Why not just raked? And if Finn was going to be fastidious enough to sweep a dirt floor, why would he leave stray piles of hay along each side of the barn's center aisle?

Mac pivoted and scrutinized the dirt floor. Nothing he could see, but it wasn't as clean as it had been that day. Standing, he looked where the broom had been. It wasn't there. Just the rake. "Where's the broom?"

"I needed it in the house."

Right. Finn always kept it propped against the yellow cupboard. So why, on the day he was murdered, was it out here along with his hat? Mac's skin prickled. He was on to something. He turned to face her. "Would you get it for me?"

"Why? What are you thinking?"

"Not sure yet. I promise to tell you what I find."

She shook her head. "You'll promise to tell me what you're *thinking*."

Hmm. Might be more than she bargained for. "Deal."

After a quick nod, she picked up her skirts and raced out the open barn door, looking more like a twelve-year-old girl than a twenty-one-year-old woman.

Twenty-one. Same age as Isaak and Jakob Gunderson.

Now why did that make his skin prickle, too?

Mac pushed the thought aside and wandered around the barn, looking for any clues he'd missed. Four nail hooks offered a place to hang a hat, two by the big door, one in the middle on the right, and one in the back. So . . . whatever Finn had been doing was most likely near the center of the building. He wandered to the exact middle. What happened here? Was Finn's murder a straight-up land grab?

If so, Charles Cannon fit the bill. His latest get-rich-quick scheme was buying property—like Finn's forty acres—on the edges of Helena's boundaries, putting up cheap houses, and lobbying the city council to expand the city limits. But the ranch was too far outside Helena, and Cannon was hardly the type to murder someone. Nor would J. P. Fisk. Right? And while at least five men and Chicago

Joe had offered to buy the ranch, it was Watson's wife who'd made Emilia suspicious.

Emilia.

He shouldn't be thinking of her by her given name. She needed to stay Mrs. Collins. His heart needed her to. Because she was Finn's widow. Because she had made friends with Jakob and Isaak Gunderson, who would champion her. Because, no matter how much Mac hated the thought, she was doing fine without him . . . and he wanted her to need him.

There. He'd admitted it. Now he could get back to being rational.

Pattering footsteps drew near. Face flushed and broom in hand, she sailed through the door, and his heart ignored every lick of common sense by flipping upside down at her return. "Here."

He took the broom from her extended hand—keeping his fingers from touching hers lest she see how her presence affected him—and began gently sweeping away pebbles, hay, and loose dirt from the barn's center.

"Why are you going so slowly?" she whispered, her face inches from his left bicep.

She smelled clean and a little bit of lye, a heady combination that made him think of soap and baths and things best not imagined. "I'm trying to preserve evidence," he whispered back.

"Like what?"

"If I knew that, I wouldn't need this." He angled the broom toward her.

Silence. Then, "Why are we whispering?"

Mac laughed, all his mental instructions to keep himself from finding her adorable flying out the barn door at her nearness. "You started it."

She laughed, too. "I suppose I did. What's that?" Her

full-voiced question sounded like a shout in the quiet barn. She knelt and dug at something white and oval-shaped. When she pulled it free of the compact dirt, she held it up. "See how helpful I am? I found a rock."

He was already a goner, so there was no point in holding back a chuckle at her dry wit. "A truly helpful discovery."

Ten minutes later, the entire floor swept, they'd discovered nothing more helpful. So much for the prickling. Either he was losing his edge, or being near Emilia Collins played havoc with his lawman instincts.

Mac blew out a breath. "I wish I knew what Finn was up to out here."

"What do you mean?" She took the broom and leaned it against the wall.

"I found his hat there." He pointed to the nail hook opposite the stall where Finn had kept his horse. "But he was shot in the cabin."

She scratched the base of her neck. "I don't understand why that's suspicious to you."

"Finn never would have left the barn without his hat. It was either on his head or in his hand."

"Maybe he was distracted and forgot."

"Distracted by what?"

"An animal. A person." She gasped. "What if someone was pointing a gun at him?"

"That's a possibility." Mac leaned against the post behind him. "Every crime is a story. Some of them are simple and straightforward, like *John stole bread because he was hungry and had no money*. Others are complex and interwoven with other stories. Finn's story has too many pieces for it to be simple, so now I have to figure out *why* it's complex and *whose* story interweaves with his."

She nodded. "And what the thingamajig has to do with Finn's murder?"

"More like *if* it's connected. It could be nothing."

She brushed loose hay from her apron. "Thank you for sharing your thoughts, Sheriff McCall."

"Emilia . . ." His mother was right. Her name rolled off his tongue.

She gave him a wary look. "Yes?"

"Would you mind calling me Mac?" When she didn't answer right away, he rushed on. "Most people around here do."

Something mischievous glinted in her eyes. "I suppose I could. On one condition."

He already knew what it was.

"That you tell me what the *L* stands for in your signature."

Not what he'd expected. "All right . . . on one condition."

She took a step toward the open barn door. "What? That I let you help us?" Her teasing grin didn't match the sharp-edged questions.

"No. That you let me tell you a story."

She blinked a couple of times, her mouth falling open in surprise. "All right, Mac." Pink crept into her cheeks, as though saying his name felt as breathtaking to her as hearing it fall from her lips had felt to him. "It better not be too long, though. I need to change clothes for Luanne Palmer's bridal tea. It's a forty-minute drive to Helena."

Mac refrained from asking how she knew the bride well enough to be invited to the tea. It didn't matter. What mattered was whether Emilia would think of the invitation as another debt that courtesy demanded she repay.

He tipped his hat back on his head. "Are you familiar with the Bible story about the paralyzed man lying on a mat who was lowered through a roof so he could be healed?"

"Yes."

"Who brought him to Jesus?"

"His friends."

Mac licked his lips. "Here's the thing. All of us want to be the friends in that story. We want to be the ones helping, the ones lifting the burden for others, but sometimes—if we want deliverance from whatever it is that's crippling our bodies or souls—we have to be willing to lie still on our mat and let others carry us."

She didn't stomp away or throw the nearby rake at his head; she simply stared at him like she was working out a puzzle as perplexing as her late husband's murder. The sound of a door slamming in the distance flicked her attention away from him. "I need to go or I'll be late for the tea."

Mac watched her leave, then bowed his head and prayed the story would take root inside her heart.

Palmer family dining room
Later that morning

"When did you first realize you were in love?"

Emilia stopped stitching a pearl bead onto the tulle bridal veil. She looked at Miss Carline Pope, trying to gauge why she'd ask such a bold question. Despite Miss Pope's twice-a-week shopping trips to The Resale Co., they'd never exchanged more than a few words. Not long after Emilia and Luci arrived at the bride's tea, Miss Pope had shared how she, too, had only been invited because of her friendship with Yancey Palmer, the ever-welcoming maid of honor. With their blond hair, blue eyes, and striking looks, Miss Pope and Yancey ought to have a fair share of gentlemen callers. Yet neither were courting.

"With Finn," Miss Pope added softly. "I think how you met is so romantic."

Yancey smiled at the ladies around the table. "I was Emilia's proxy."

And then she and Miss Pope focused on Emilia in expectation. More like *in desperation* for her to confirm their own struggles with knowing whether they were truly in love. What was she supposed to say? *Yes, Yancey, your feelings for Hale Adams are true, and in time he will reciprocate?* Emilia had no deep insight into love. Nor could she see the future. Of course the object of Miss Pope's affection could be Geddes Palmer. Or one of the Gunderson twins. Or any one of the numerous bachelors who attended their church or lived about town.

Except Mac.

Emilia had never seen Miss Pope speak with Mac for any length of time. She couldn't believe Miss Pope bore tender feelings for him. If she did, and Mac reciprocated, Emilia would be happy for them. She would. But Mac and Miss Pope together seemed wrong. Very wrong. And just the thought of it made her chest hurt.

Someone made a noise. Emilia glanced around the table. The six older women sitting around the tulle-covered table had stopped stitching pearl beads onto the veil's edge. All stared at Emilia.

The cloying scent of a dozen potted lilacs permeated the dining room as the women sat there and stared. And stared.

"I'm not sure," Emilia answered and hoped the conversation would move on. She looked at the bride, desperate for someone else to answer Miss Pope's question. "Luanne, what about you and Mr. Bennett? When did you know you wanted to marry him?"

Miss Alice Rigney, sitting between her mother and Mrs. Hollenbeck, leaned forward on her chair. Her gaze narrowed on Emilia. "How can you *not* be sure?" she said, her voice somewhere between curiosity and impatience. "That doesn't make sense to me. You had to have known you loved Mr. Collins or else you wouldn't have agreed to marry him."

"Alice!" Mrs. Rigney grabbed her daughter's arm, pulling her back. "Don't be impolite."

Emilia's face warmed. Her cheeks surely matched her dress. Hearing chuckles, she looked to where Luci and Melrose were huddled in a corner of the room, but their attention was focused on whatever Melrose was sketching in her journal.

"I apologize, Mrs. Collins," Mrs. Rigney said.

Emilia looked back to see the woman peering around her daughter and Mrs. Hollenbeck.

Mrs. Rigney's chin tipped up. "Alice's views regarding love are a mite . . . idealistic. She is used to speaking directly for the benefit of her sixth graders. I promise she meant no offense."

Miss Rigney opened her mouth and—

Mrs. Hollenbeck held her threadless needle in front of Miss Rigney's face. "Rethread, please."

"And mine, too," Mrs. Forsythe graciously said, stretching her arm across the table.

Mrs. Snowe, Mrs. Truett, and Miss Babcock offered their needles as well.

Miss Rigney sighed, then stuck all but one of the needles in the pin pillow and began her chosen job of rethreading.

Mrs. Palmer stood. She brushed the strands of white thread from her dress. "Perhaps now is a fitting moment to check on the food."

"Excellent idea." With a smile that only enhanced her beauty, Mrs. Forsythe followed Mrs. Palmer into the kitchen, clearly content with acting in Mrs. Pawlikowski's stead because Mrs. Palmer's dearest friend was away on a belated honeymoon.

The friendships among the women participating in the

bride's tea astounded Emilia. Miss Babcock and Miss Rigney taught at Central School and had remained friends with Luanne even after she was fired from teaching. According to Mr. Gunderson, Judge Forsythe had proposed to his mother prior to her marrying Mr. Pawlikowski. Both couples had grown close over the years. While at Spiegel, Emilia had become friendly with several of her fellow shopgirls, but whenever one was fired or ran off and eloped, she never returned to the store, never contacted Emilia, never made any attempt to continue the friendship.

To have a friend like these women had . . .

Miss Luanne Palmer cleared her throat. "To answer your question, Emilia, I knew for certain I was in love with Roy when he gave up his desire to live in Denver."

Emilia stared at her, dumbfounded. "But aren't you moving there after the wedding?"

"Love makes sacrifices." Luanne wove her still-threaded needle into the beaded headdress, then set it on the table. "Roy took a job here because he knew how important my family and friends are to me."

Emilia understood the obligation Luanne was under. Whether she wanted to move to Denver or not, courtesy demanded the gift be returned. "Agreeing to move to Denver after the wedding is your way of repaying his sacrifice."

Luanne's lips quivered into a smile. "I can see how it could seem that way. My father likes to say, *A healthy relationship is when both parties know how to give and take*."

Mrs. Truett, Mrs. Snowe, and Mrs. Hollenbeck all nodded.

Luanne gave her sister a pointed look. "Roy and I have been happy here in Helena," she said, and Emilia realized Luanne's words were meant for her younger sister. "Moving to Denver is what we realized we *both* want to do." She clenched Yancey's hand. "Someday you will understand what it means to put the man you love ahead of your family."

Yancey's eyes grew watery.

Mrs. Hollenbeck stood and clapped her hands twice. "Ladies, I do believe I heard the clink of china. It's time we retire to the parlor." Within moments, the stately woman had everyone out of the dining room . . . except for the Palmer sisters, who clearly needed a private moment.

Emilia stopped at the parlor's threshold as the other ladies found seats. She glanced back toward the dining room. Nothing in Luanne's voice or expression had testified to any falseness in her words. Love sacrificed. Love gave with no expectation of anything in return. If Luanne and Roy could live out what they believed, then it was possible the Palmers had invited Emilia to the bride's tea out of friendship, not pity. By the same token, it was possible Mr. Gunderson had offered to lend them the croquet set out of friendship, not in an attempt to indebt them to him.

To know for sure meant to ask if his offer was still available. To ask meant taking a step of faith. To see if, according to the story Mac had shared earlier, she could allow people to help her, knowing full well they may want something in return, but they may not. They may enjoy doing nice things for others—for her—merely for the sake of doing something nice. Blessed to give, or so she'd heard Mrs. Palmer say.

Since she'd arrived in Helena, Mac had repeatedly helped her and had yet to ask for a returned favor. Was he so convinced people were like that because *he* lived that way?

Emilia's chest ached something strange, something fierce.

When Miss Pope asked what it felt like when Emilia fell in love, the first face that had come to her mind was Mac's. Not Finn's. The anticipation she used to feel before opening one of Finn's letters was the same as she'd felt this morning waiting for Mac to arrive at the ranch. Was *that* what it felt like when one was falling in love? Or was the futile ability to breathe evenly around Mac a prelude to it? Maybe she'd never really been in love with Finn. Maybe she'd fallen in gratitude. How did one know the difference between being in love, infatuation, and passing attraction? She certainly was drawn to Mac. But that didn't necessitate love.

While Mac had been different at the ranch—more relaxed, more engaging—he'd done nothing to suggest he viewed her as anything but his friend's widow.

Of course he could be waiting for a sign that she would welcome his attentions. Some men were like that. But if she did and he wasn't interested—she couldn't be that bold. She couldn't. She wouldn't become another Yancey Palmer.

She refused to fall in love with a man who didn't return her feelings.

Chapter Fourteen

The next morning

Nothing like food and ladies to draw men to church.

Emilia gripped Luci's right hand, then stepped inside the crowded church aisle, the air tinted with cologne and sweat. Surely every pew wasn't filled. Couldn't be. Where were the dozens of people standing going to sit? Not once in the last four Sundays had the building been this full. She bumped into a man in a tweed suit smelling of cigars.

He turned and glared.

"I'm sorry," she offered. "Excuse me."

He nodded and stepped to the right to give her room to pass.

"Hey, there's Mac," Luci said, tugging Emilia's hand.

Emilia looked around for Mac. She found him sitting on the left side of the fourth row, his gaze focused downward. Reading? Praying? If he were Roch, she'd guess sleeping. Thankfully, she didn't feel out of breath or fluttery or *aware* of his presence. She felt at ease. Such a welcome feeling after yesterday.

"Emme, let's sit with him."

Should they? There was space enough for two people

between Mac and an older woman in a straw hat. He couldn't be saving the spots for them. "There isn't room for Roch," Emilia explained. "It's better if we sit over there."

Luci glanced around. "I don't see—"

"Right *there*." Emilia motioned to the pew three rows behind Mac, with enough room for Roch to sit, too. As long as Mac didn't look their way, she could slide into the other pew. That way when—*if*—he noticed her, they'd already be seated and he wouldn't feel obligated to invite them over.

He looked their way. And smiled.

Once again her chest felt all fluttery. Emilia frantically nudged Luci toward the open pew, but Luci wouldn't budge. Eyes narrowed, she seemed preoccupied with studying the family on the pew in front of Mac's.

Mac stepped out into the aisle and waved them over. "Come on. There's room."

Emilia hesitated. True, he looked happy to see them. But her heart pounded fiercely, and her legs felt weighted to the floor. If they sat with him, people might presume things. As kind and innocent as Mac's offer was, she should be wise and not—

"You're so slothy this morning." Luci shoved Emilia forward.

Slothy? Of all the animals in the world that Luci could discover existed during her class's study on South America, she *had* to develop a fascination with the sloth. *You're so slothy* could only mean her sister considered her slow. Or that she hosted moths, beetles, fungi, and algae on her body. Emilia elected to believe the former.

Anyone would be slow if faced with a cold sponge bath on a rainy morning. True, she had wasted time staring into the bucket of well water and thinking about the warm—all right, occasionally warm—tub baths back in the small bathroom they'd shared with three other families. She wanted a real bath. One with scented soap and oils she'd read about in the newspaper. She wanted to take the luxurious bed-sheets she and Luci slept on each night and sew them new Sunday dresses. She wanted what Finn had promised: a partner, a friend, a—

She tripped over someone's foot. "Excuse me," she called out, stumbling forward and hoping the owner of the injured foot heard her. Luci grabbed Emilia's hand and pulled her past the podium, around the front pew, and then back down the aisle.

Mac stood against the wall. He motioned for them to sit.

Luci slid onto the bench, tapping the shoulder of the boy in the pew in front of them. "Hey, Seth. Missed you in class last week."

The dark-haired boy turned around. He looked startled for a moment, as if he was surprised she knew his name. "I had to help Pa build a new chicken coop."

Emilia studied her sister's face as she told Seth about their chickens. The boy kept staring at Luci, in awe that a girl as pretty as her sister would willingly choose to speak to him. Luci didn't look besotted with Seth, but how would Emilia know if Luci was or wasn't? She couldn't read her sister's heart any more than she could judge Mac's. He certainly didn't look besotted when he looked *her* way.

Emilia groaned inwardly. What was wrong with her? She should never have gone to the bride's tea. If she hadn't, she wouldn't have spent yesterday afternoon and last night and this morning thinking about what she did and didn't feel for him. Or what he may or may not feel for her. He hadn't seemed bothered upon hearing of the numerous men who'd asked her to supper or to see a vaudeville performance or to go on a buggy ride. She'd refused flowers, confections, and every attempt at courtship because she'd needed time to grieve Finn's passing.

But what if Mac was the real reason for her refusals?

What if she was falling in love with him?

"I don't know about you," came Mac's soft voice near Emilia's left ear, "but I'd prefer not to stand during the service."

Emilia snapped to attention. She slid onto the pew and heard Luci say—

"Hey, Mac, would you like to play croquet after the lunch auction? Please, please"—Luci pressed her palms together as if in prayer—"pleeeeese."

Emilia groaned under her breath. Playing with Roch had been torture enough. She jerked her gaze to Mac, sitting with a proper space between them, and started to say, "Please don't feel obligated," but stopped. He looked so utterly intrigued—so happy—to be invited.

"Are you looking for a fourth to play teams?" he asked Luci.

Leaning across Emilia, Luci cupped the side of her mouth and whispered, "Some people in my family don't play nicely together. I need an adult to remind them to quiet their . . . uh, disagreements."

"Some of those people are right here," Emilia muttered.

Mac leaned toward Luci and whispered back, "Understood."

Luci squealed with delight. "Emme, can I also invite . . . ?" She nodded toward the boy in front of them. Seth, whose last name Emilia didn't know.

"Next time."

"You're taking the game back tomorrow," Luci grumbled. "There won't be a next time." Her lips clamped in a thin line, and that was when Emilia knew her sister's invitation to Mac had been part of a ploy to have Seth come play croquet with them. More precisely, with Luci.

"Where did you set up the wickets?" Mac asked Luci.

Leaving the pair to talk, Emilia shifted on the pew in order to look around for Roch. Men lined the side aisles and back wall. Even the balcony was filled. Mr. and Mrs. Watson and their three adult children and four younger ones filled a pew. The Fisks sat behind them. The Palmers and Miss Palmer's fiancé sat in their usual spot; so did Mrs. Hollenbeck, who smiled and waved. Emilia waved back. Mr. Gunderson and the bladesmith, Mr. Buchanan, stood like guards on either side of the opened doors. Because of the overflow of churchgoers?

Emilia squinted. Was that—?

She leaned a bit to the left to get a better look through the doors, to where Jakob and Roch stood at the bottom of the church steps. Jakob gripped the back of Roch's collar with one hand and was pointing at him with the other, hand shaking. His words had caused Roch's face to redden. Maybe a stern lecture from a man he looked up to was what Roch needed.

Not to say he wouldn't receive another lecture from her later, once she found out what Roch had done.

Or she could say nothing.

Now that was an intriguing idea. She only lectured Roch because Da never gave him the what for. Roch had no reason to change if he never received any punishment for his actions. What if she didn't ask him or Jakob about what was going on? Roch had spent more time of late with Jakob than with her or Luci. If she could trust Jakob to take Roch with him on a delivery to Fort Missoula and keep him out of trouble during the train ride there and back, then she should extend the same trust now.

"What are you looking at?" Luci asked.

Emilia whirled around. "Nothing." Out of the corner of her eye, she could see Mac giving her an odd look. She grabbed the hymnal and studied the first page. Jakob could handle Roch. He could. And she would enjoy a holiday from having to manage her brother.

"Hold my seat," Mac announced. He was halfway down the aisle before she could tell him to stop. The crowd instantly stepped out of his path. He'd promised not to interfere and she believed him—or at least she was trying to—so what was he about?

Luci stood, resting one knee on the pew and gripping the back. "Where's Roch?"

"He had to put our lunch basket with the others. Jakob's probably with him." Emilia looked over her shoulder in time to see Mac stop and say something to Mr. Buchanan. He patted Mr. Gunderson's arm, then shook his hand.

The second Mac stepped outside, Luci plopped back down on the pew. She grabbed a hymnal and turned the pages, humming to herself. Emilia faced forward, too.

As the organist began to play, the center aisle cleared.

Emilia resisted the urge to turn around again. She was going to trust Mac to honor his promise, even though it didn't look as if he was at the moment.

After a quick prayer, Reverend Neven welcomed everyone. He congratulated Miss Luanne Palmer and Mr. Roy Bennett on their upcoming nuptials next Saturday. And then he opened a hymnal. "Let's stand and turn to hymn 276 'Sweet Hour of Prayer.'"

Emilia turned the pages of the hymnal she held and stood.

Luci stood, too, then gave her hymnal to the lady on her right. "Please, take mine, ma'am. I'll share with my sister."

"Thank you, dearie." The woman looked over Luci's head, a tender look in her eyes. "Mrs. Collins, I was sorry to hear about your husband. Finn was a good man. In March, he helped my husband clear the bloated cattle off our land. We tried to pay him, but he refused to take anything." Her voice caught. "Said God would bless him."

Emilia blinked at the sudden tears in her eyes. A choking feeling in her chest limited her response to a tentative smile. The woman nodded. She then opened the hymnal and turned to share it with her husband. Emilia didn't mind. She was in grave danger of becoming a blubbering mess.

She missed Finn—that *wasn't* the cause of her morning lulls. Of her slothiness. Of her restlessness. Of wishing for more than her lot in life. She wanted respite from having to be the friend—the older sister, the surrogate mother—who lifted and carried another's burden. Was it too much to wish, for once, to lie still on her mat and let someone carry her?

If Finn hadn't died, he would have.

But he *was* dead, and until Da arrived in Helena, she was on her own.

Falling into a fit of tears in the middle of church would do her no good, so Emilia turned her attention to the open hymnal in her hands.

The singing continued for two songs before Mac returned. He slid into the empty spot on the pew. The man behind him patted his back. Mac turned and shook his hand. "Good to see you, Mayor Kendrick." He faced forward. "Did I miss anything?" he whispered to Emilia.

"Not much," she whispered back. "Is everything all right?"

He nodded. "Jakob dealt with it."

As he joined in the singing, Emilia studied him out of the corner of her eye. The more time she spent with Mac, the more she realized he wasn't the type of man not to help. He breathed. He ate. He aided and protected people. So how could he have stood by this time and let Jakob handle Roch? Doing so wasn't in his character.

Because he'd promised her he would stop trying to fix their problems.

Because he was a man of his word and wanted to prove it to her.

Because he put the needs of others before his own.

And maybe, just maybe, because he cared about her as something more to him than his best friend's widow. Could that be? Or was it nothing more than her own wishful thinking? If so, she was asking for heartbreak. He would never court his best friend's widow. Or was she wrong about that as well? She'd never been more confused about anything in her life.

Emilia focused on the hymnal as the chorus drew to an end.

Reverend Neven flipped several pages until he found what he wanted. "Here we go. Hymn 291, 'Jesus Paid It All.'"

The congregation began singing.

Luci hurriedly flipped pages to find 291.

Emilia pulled the hymnal back in front of her. "We have to share with Mac."

"No need," he said. "I know the words."

Luci turned to Emilia. "He knows the words."

"I heard," she responded.

Luci and Mac's voices joined the music, filling the sanctuary.

"'. . . Child of weakness, watch and pray, Find in Me thine all in all.'"

As the chorus began, the singing grew louder.

Emilia glanced around. The eyes of the woman next to Luci were closed, yet, like Mac, she sang every word.

"'Thy grace must make me whole.'"

She frowned. How strange. Finn had written words close to those in several of his letters: God's grace has made me whole. He had to have known this hymn, too. How could a man who believed so strongly that Jesus had paid his debts, indebt himself to so many people? Yet she'd heard *Finn was a good man* from many people, like the couple beside them. All because he'd helped clear their land of bloated cattle.

Emilia drew in a sharp breath, her pulse increasing. What if the couple did something nice for her in recompense for Finn's actions? Good manners dictated they do so. So did the Bible. Do unto others . . . Once this couple did something for her, she'd owe them.

She turned her head just enough to see Mac. He'd stopped singing. Jaw clenched, he blinked rapidly. Slowly drew in a breath.

The chorus rang out.

"'. . . all to Him I owe . . .'"

Exactly! For all God had done for her, she owed Him. She owed Him good works. She owed Him a giving heart. She owed Him tithes and offerings. But faithful attendance in church, right now, was all she had to give. That *and* her basket lunch for the charity auction. Was it enough to pay God back? What if it wasn't?

Her heart pounded frantically. Her lungs tightened. Emilia touched her chest, yet the action did nothing to stop the pressure. What if she could never do enough to pay God back? Obviously she'd be forever in His debt. That wasn't fair.

Or was that God's point?

The high branches of a tall pine tree provided shade while offering a full view of the church grounds. Mac surveyed the scene, keeping an eye out for trouble. Like Christmas and Easter, the basket auction drew people who never darkened the church's door otherwise. And, like any holiday, there were certain trappings and traditions observed: Reverend Neven describing the contents of each basket in mouthwatering terms no matter how horrid he knew it would taste; Hamish VanDerCourt and Thaddeus Mueller—who only came to outbid one another over Widow Johnston—glaring enough hatred to restart the War Between the States; and Jakob Gunderson bidding up anyone who revealed his desire to win a particular lady's basket.

Five years ago, a disgruntled winning bidder demanded his money back after tasting what he'd bought. Four years ago, VanDerCourt and Mueller came to blows that landed both men in the county jail overnight. And two years ago, Jakob overestimated the pocketbook and underestimated the temper of Miss Landing's suitor. Their shouting match ended when Mac threatened that, if either of them caused a ruckus in the future, they'd be treated to an overnight stay in the county jail.

With any luck, Jakob would ignore the warning today. Clearly, he'd taken on the role of father to Roch Stanek, and Emilia allowed it. She'd turned her back on the exchange between her brother and Jakob without even a hint of the stubborn independence she insisted on whenever Mac tried to help. It made his neck itch with jealousy.

Isaak Gunderson sauntered closer, the wooden chest tucked under his left arm looking like a toy. "Good afternoon, Sheriff."

Mac returned the greeting and shook Isaak's hand. "I see you got saddled with the collection box."

"Only reason the elders put me on the Widows and Orphans Committee." He said it with a straight face, discounting hours of volunteer work with either humility or some of his dry wit. "Will you be donating directly again this year?"

Mac pulled out a twenty-dollar bill and slipped it in the rectangular slit at the center of the lid.

"Thank you." Isaak set the box on the ground. "So . . . what was going on between Roch Stanek and my brother earlier?"

"Nothing to worry about. Roch wanted to take a few days off—something about researching planting alfalfa—and Jakob was calling his bluff." Mac settled back against the tree. "Roch has discovered that Sally Blair works at the library."

"Jakob preferring work over play? I'll have to mark today in my calendar so we can celebrate annually."

Mac snorted. "You underestimate him. He's been"—*a little too*—"great with the Staneks."

"I'll admit he's lasted longer than I predicted, but I expect that has more to do with the company he's keeping than the actual work."

Emilia Collins had that effect on men.

"Despite their age difference, they seem to have formed quite a bond." Isaak pointed to his brother.

Mac opened his mouth to ask, *What age difference?* when he realized his mistake. Isaak was talking about Jakob and Roch, not Jakob and Emilia. Mac swept his gaze across the lawn. Emilia and Luci were conversing with Yancey Palmer. Jakob was on the other side of the lawn laughing with friends, breaking off conversation to shout a ten-dollar bid that drew an answering one of ten dollars and two bits.

Was it possible Jakob and Emilia *weren't* forming an attachment?

The urge to arrest Jakob lessened. "Your brother's doing a good job."

Isaak grunted. "Is he? When he can't keep Roch from a flibbertigibbet like Sally Blair?"

"I was talking about the auction." Mac jutted his chin

toward the lawn, where Jakob bid eleven dollars on a huge wicker basket with a yellow fabric bow in the same print as Mollie Fisk's to goad Jefferson Brady up to eleven dollars and two bits.

"I guess, but he's going to need to back down soon if he wants to win Yancey's basket."

Jakob and *Yancey*? Might not be hard to push Hale into running for mayor then judge after all . . . so he could be the justice of the peace to perform the ceremony. "Didn't know Jakob was interested in courting her."

Another grunt. "He's not—at least not any more—but everyone knows Mrs. Palmer supplies the food in Yancey's basket, and he's tired of my cooking."

Mac swiveled to look Isaak square in the eye, possible only because the taller man was downhill.

"Since Ma left, I've taken over the kitchen. Jakob complains that having the same meal on certain days of the week is boring him to death." Isaak shrugged. "Suits me fine."

A round of applause broke out. Mac returned his attention to the auction in time to see Jakob bow to a red-faced Brady as he stomped over to retrieve the basket that probably outweighed him.

Jefferson Brady and Mollie Fisk. Now there was a match made at First National Bank. A new mansion would be going up on Millionaire's Hill soon based on Brady's continued glares at Jakob and Miss Fisk's beaming smile.

"I see Mayor Kendrick showed up today." Isaak crossed his arms over his chest.

"Lots of people here to see his piety." Mac scanned the crowd again, locating the mayor and his wife standing next to Mrs. Hollenbeck. "Good for his reelection bid."

Isaak added a half cough to his grunt. "It'd be nice if the

man was as good at running the city as he is at running his publicity. It never ends with him."

"So run against him next year." Hale wasn't going to do it; someone like Isaak should.

Isaak turned to look Mac in the eye but, before more words were exchanged, Reverend Neven lifted the lid on a small, battered basket with a simple red bow. "Looks like we have some biscuits so light you'll think you're eating a cloud, sweet apple butter, crisp dill pickles, hard-boiled eggs, and four slices of apple pie so juicy you'll need a spoon. Who will give me two bits to start the bidding?"

Luci Stanek let go of her sister's arm to wave at Mac, then point to the basket.

"Apparently, that's Mrs. Collins's basket," Isaak drawled.

He wasn't the only one to notice. Mrs. Watson elbowed her husband, who then grabbed his eldest son's arm and whispered in his ear. A few of the displaced ranch hands pushed through the crowd to get closer to the auctioneer's table.

"Wait a minute. Did he say there's apple butter in that basket?" Isaak took a step forward. "Mrs. Neven delivered some to Jakob and me a couple of weeks ago. Why would Mrs. Collins put that in her basket?" Isaak turned to Mac for an answer.

"Obligation." The word tasted like burned coffee on his tongue. "The apple butter came with an invitation to contribute to the basket auction."

"And she took that as an obligation?" Isaak shook his head. "That's about the dumbest thing I've ever heard. Didn't she understand that the invitation was only to make her feel included?"

Mac chuckled in agreement and frustration. Emilia Collins was a riddle. If every assistance rendered to her resulted in a deeper sense of indebtedness, and if every problem she faced sent him scrambling for a way to fix it, where would they ever find common ground? And they needed to . . . to solve Finn's murder.

Nothing more.

Luci Stanek looked across the church lawn at Mac with disappointment and incredulity. *Why aren't you bidding?* she shouted without words.

Because the women of the church had already noticed him sharing a pew with Emilia this morning and were giving him sheep-eyed looks that just as clearly and just as silently screamed, *When's the wedding?*

Mac tore his gaze from Luci's. If she kept begging him to bid, he might succumb. Because he wanted to bid, wanted to spend the afternoon sharing a meal with Emilia, and then go back to the ranch with her to play croquet like he was part of the family.

But the look on her face when Luci had invited him shouted that Emilia didn't want him to join their game.

Besides, she didn't want him rushing to her rescue. She'd made that clear. And none of the men bidding would dare try anything at a church picnic. Not with her, though they might tear each other apart. Reverend Neven didn't even have to call for new bids because the men were so eager to outdo one another. Volume and tempers grew in direct proportion to the escalating dollar amounts. More than one person in the crowd looked uneasy.

Mac took a step forward, ready in case things got out of hand.

"Twenty dollars!" young Watson shouted, momentarily stunning the crowd into silence.

Isaak raised his hand. "Twenty-one!" He tucked his chin and whispered, "We need to get Mrs. Collins out of this fix. Are you going to help or not?"

Before Mac thought of a suitable reply, the bid was at twenty-five.

"Twenty-six!" Isaak again.

Reverend Neven lifted his gavel. "Going, going, g—"

"Twenty-seven!" from young Watson.

"Twenty-eight!" Isaak stepped closer to Mac. "What are you waiting for?"

"Going, go—"

"Thirty-four dollars, twelve cents!" from one of the men Mac recognized as a displaced ranch hand. Did he think to woo himself into a new job over lunch?

Young Watson scrambled back toward his father. The three other men huddled together, apparently pooling their money.

"Are you bidding or not?" Isaak lowered his brows.

He couldn't. Emilia didn't want his help.

"Going once . . ."

Shouldn't. Not after sitting next to her this morning and being invited to the Circle C later. Too many people would pair them up, something Emilia didn't want.

"Going twice . . ."

Wouldn't. Even though it took every ounce of resolve to remain silent.

"Not," he answered.

"Suit yourself." Isaak raised his hand. "Fifty!"

The crowd gasped. The other five bidders stopped what they were doing to shoot nasty glares up the hill.

"Going, going, gone!" Reverend Neven shouted before anyone recovered, pounding his gavel with a resounding crack for emphasis.

Isaak lifted the collection box and tucked it under his arm. "Mac, I have the utmost respect for you . . ."

"But?"

"Since when did you turn into a dunderhead?" Isaak

tipped his head toward where Mrs. Collins waited for him by the auctioneer's table. "I've seen how you look at her. Doesn't take a trained lawman to put the clues together."

Mac gripped his left arm at the elbow. "She's my best friend's widow."

Isaak rested his right hand on Mac's shoulder. "Yes, she is. But a widow before she was a wife, and—much as we all loved Finn—he isn't coming back for her."

Circle C Ranch
Later that afternoon

"You impress me."

Emilia looked up from the croquet set's rule book to see Mac standing in front of her, smiling and blocking her view of the makeshift course they'd staked out in the field on the other side of the new corral. She leaned a bit to the right to see around him. Still on his turn, Roch knelt in front of his orange ball, his mallet stretched out, as he calculated the trajectory to the first center wicket. Luci stood next to him. Mallet in hand, she was saying something. The westerly breeze carried her words away from where Emilia stood.

Emilia nipped her bottom lip, feeling odd under Mac's serious gaze. She didn't mind profound conversations, but not now. This afternoon she wanted to be merry because she'd promised Mr. Gunderson during lunch that she would worry less and have fun more. Why not? She wanted to throw caution to the wind because no one was around to cast judgment upon her or upon Mac.

"Shouldn't you be helping your partner?" she asked.

"Roch listens well."

Emilia slid a blade of grass in the rule book to hold her place. "Are you implying I don't listen well?"

His lips curved in the tiniest of smiles, part *I know something and you don't,* part *I can't wait to let you in on the joke*. The man she'd met at the train depot was a shadow in comparison. If she could travel back in time, before Finn's death, she knew this was the Mac that Finn had described in his letters. His amused gaze flickered to the rule book, then resettled on her—a subtle *you are the one who keeps rereading the rules instead of enjoying the game.*

She gave him an overly sweet smile. "I like to read rule books."

"You read it yesterday." He leaned in, just far enough for her to catch a pleasant whiff of his bergamot and cedar cologne . . . and to send her pulse into slow acceleration. "I'll wager three times minimum."

"You think you know me that well?"

"I do," he said in a soft voice. And despite the reasonable distance between them, she felt as if he was touching her. As if he was holding her close. Just the two of them. Her skin began to prick and shiver. His brown eyes with those lovely flecks of gold were no longer looking into her eyes. They had dropped to her mouth. His lips parted as if he was about to kiss her and—

Emilia blurted out, "Mr. Gunderson said this is an unusually warm May. I can't imagine how hot it will be once summer hits. Don't you think it's warm?"

He looked decidedly uncomfortable. "I think—yes, it is." He dropped his mallet and then wiggled the rule book from her grip.

Emilia watched as he walked to where his horse was tied. He removed his suit coat, laid it and the book over Roch's coat draped over the saddle, then just stood there, his eyes closed. Emilia looked from him to her siblings, who were counting footsteps from Roch's ball to the center wicket and then back to Mac. He breathed deep. Finally, he sauntered back, rolling up his sleeves in the process.

He stopped in front of her, still looking tense. "What were we talking about?"

Emilia kept her face blank as she said, "You've yet to tell me why I impress you. I could list the ways, but compliments are always nicer coming from others."

And with that the tension in his face abated.

"I like how you say what you mean."

"I also tend to mean what I say."

"That you do." He tipped the brim of his hat, easing it back on his head. "I know Finn didn't own a mower, and yet the prairie grass has been trimmed evenly." He gazed at her warmly. "That leads me to presume Isaak loaned one to you from The Resale Company, along with the croquet set."

"He did. Yesterday," she added, lest he think they'd hastily mowed in anticipation of his arrival. She hadn't done anything after returning home from sharing lunch with Mr. Gunderson except change out of her good Sunday dress and into her gray one. "Mowing a quarter of an acre isn't all that impressive. I managed it in a couple of hours."

He looked stunned. He was quiet for a moment, and then he said, "Roch and Jakob didn't do it?"

"They were building the corral." Emilia looked to her siblings. Roch was waving at Luci to back up. She did, until her shadow reached the distance from the center wicket to where Roch's orange ball lay. Roch stood. She turned back to Mac. "Moving the imbedded rocks was the worst part. Luci helped me fill in the holes. Why are you looking at me like that?"

"Once you've made your mind up, nothing stops you, does it?"

Emilia started to deny the compliment, but he was right about her. She never gave up pursuing what she wanted.

Instead, she tipped her chin and proudly said, "No, I don't. It's an excellent trait to have."

"I agree."

She chuckled. "That's because *you* are as afflicted, Mr. McCall."

"We're quite a pair."

"Indeed, we are."

He smiled, and she smiled, too. Goodness, she shouldn't be flirting with him, but she couldn't help it. During lunch, Mr. Gunderson had remarked that often a little flirting was all a woman needed to do to motivate a man into action, and she'd thought of little else ever since. Something about Mac today made her feel different. Free of burdens.

And free to flirt.

"Did you really mow this all by yourself?" he asked.

Emilia lifted her palms for him to see the five calluses that had developed. His right hand rose, as if to touch her palm. But then he shifted his mallet handle from his left hand to his right.

He cleared his throat. "Why did you do it by yourself?"

"Luci had schoolwork. I figured if the game was ready to be played, Roch would agree to play."

He glanced out to where Roch still was practicing his swing. His brow furrowed. "You did this for him, even after the way he's treated you."

His words weren't a question, so she didn't answer.

Eventually, Roch would realize she still loved him, had never stopped loving him. Marrying Finn and moving their family out here was as much for Roch as for herself, Luci, and Da. Anyone looking at him could see living in Montana was good for him.

"Emilia," Mac said softly, "you impress me because after what you shared yesterday about repaying acts of kindness, that you willingly accepted Isaak's offer to borrow the croquet set and mower—"

Whack.

Thunk.

"Roch!" Luci yelled. "After all the time you took to aim, why did you hit my ball?" She pointed at the wicket. "That's your goal. Not"—she pointed to where her blue ball now was—"that!" As Roch laughed, she growled, threw her mallet, and stomped the ground. "I'm never going to win now."

Mac looked sideways at Emilia. "Should we intervene?"

She thought for a moment. "We're the adults, but on one condition. I manage my partner and you manage yours."

He laughed. "Is this why you insisted upon girls against boys?"

"That could be the reason. Or it could be because I know you're easier to distract than my siblings are."

Emilia hadn't taken two steps when she heard him mutter, "How right you are."

Chapter Fifteen

Millionaire's Hill
May 14, 5:04 P.M.

Small, private wedding. Grandiose reception.

From her spot at an empty table, Emilia glanced around the expansive lawn behind Mrs. Hollenbeck's three-story mansion. A string quartet on the patio. Ladies in dresses of every color in the rainbow. Men in three-piece suits. Twelve white cloth-draped tables set with china cups and saucers clustered under the afternoon shade provided by the stately pines. And nary a rain cloud in sight. Was it common out west to host a Saturday morning wedding followed by an afternoon tea to introduce the new couple, dancing, a banquet, and more dancing? Emilia had never seen anything like it.

The only wedding she'd ever attended lasted eight minutes, and the bride and groom had darted from the courthouse as soon as Emilia finished signing her name as witness.

For all practical purposes, she hadn't attended her own wedding. She'd signed the proxy wearing the same pink dress, black bonnet, and boots she had on now. A bride . . . and then a widow three days later. Six weeks ago.

Yet it felt like a proverbial lifetime.

Finn's debts were slowly being paid. Managing the ranch was becoming easier. Luci and Needles adored each other. Roch continued to like everyone but her.

And then there was Mac.

She had no idea where she stood with him. Other than an amiable greeting when she'd arrived at Mrs. Hollenbeck's, he'd maintained his distance. Just as he had maintained his distance all week. Because he felt awkward about almost kissing her during the croquet match?

Or had she misinterpreted that?

Her cheeks warmed in embarrassment. She shouldn't have flirted with him. Doing so clearly ruined the friendship they'd started building.

As the string quartet changed tunes, Emilia eyed the line of reception guests, including Roch and Luci, at the serving tables. The Palmers weren't one of the wealthier families in Helena, so the bulk of the expense must have been borne by the groom's parents. Why, the cost of the tea party alone—she couldn't fathom. But if this was the *minor* reception event of the day, no telling what the Palmers and the Bennetts had planned to feed a hundred guests for supper. Prime rib, she'd overheard someone say. Goodness, the expense!

Mr. Geddes Palmer, best man and brother of the bride, stood. He tapped the edge of his teacup with a spoon, quieting the crowd and the musicians. "To Luanne and Roy, the best sister and best friend a man could ask for. Beautiful. Charming. Compassionate. Witty. Generous to their cores. Their philanthropy knows no bounds. If anyone has a need, they are the ones to go to for help. In fact, they even wrote this speech for me."

The crowd laughed.

"Lu, Roy"—Mr. Palmer raised his teacup—"may our Lord bless your marriage today, tomorrow, and always."

Emilia joined in the applause as Mr. Palmer sat down.

Mr. Roy Bennett, a handsome, bearded man who smiled as easily as Jakob did, stood. He touched his bride's cheek. "Six months ago I was ready to leave this beautiful woman behind to pursue my life as I saw it. How fortunate I am that my father-in-law talked sense into me. Sir"—he lifted his teacup to Mr. W. H. Palmer—"your wisdom has proven true. I promise I will live it and share it with others."

Emilia doubted a man could look as pleased as Mr. Palmer was with his new son-in-law.

Mr. Bennett turned to the guests sitting at the tea tables. "Luanne and I are in awe at the overwhelming support and generosity you've bestowed as we prepare to begin our future in Denver. Thank you for being our friends. Thank you for celebrating this day with us. Thank you for how you've blessed our lives. Of course . . . a celebration should always include food." He motioned to the serving table. "Enjoy!"

Applause broke out.

The string quartet resumed playing.

Emilia watched the guests move down the serving table. Others, content like her to wait until the line lessened, stayed in their seats. Three white-gloved footmen with silver teakettles filled the china cups of those sitting.

"My dear Mrs. Collins, you look like you could use a friend." Mrs. Hollenbeck slid onto a chair next to Emilia. She placed her plate, with a gigantic slice of cake, on the table. "That was an impressive bidding war last Sunday for your basket lunch."

"Miss Pope's basket sold four times what mine brought."

"Considering Carline Pope stands to inherit ten million

from her uncle, her basket should have sold for twice what it did."

Emilia felt her mouth gap. Ten million? Why, then, was Miss Pope shopping at The Resale Co.? Just last Monday she'd purchased a pair of secondhand gloves.

With a "humph," Mrs. Hollenbeck laid her napkin across the lap of her amethyst gown. "I intend on having a word with Mr. Buchanan over not bidding on her basket."

"The bladesmith?"

"Indeed. Have you two met?"

Emilia shook her head. Buchanan Smithy was next to The Resale Co. Despite seeing Mr. Buchanan every Sunday in church, sitting on the second row, right side, she had yet to exchange a word with him. Dark. Brooding. Scary. The literal opposite in every way from Miss Pope. That the older widow desired to match the pair—well, why? Anyone could see vivacious Miss Pope was much better suited with . . . anyone. The pair was no more compatible than Yancey Palmer and Hale Adams.

Mrs. Hollenbeck motioned for a footman. The man hurried over to fill her teacup and Emilia's. He then moved the cream and sugar dishes from the center of the table to in front of Mrs. Hollenbeck, who dutifully made use of them.

Emilia glanced back to the serving table. What in the—? Roch and Luci held plates loaded with enough cake, scones, sandwiches, and tarts for a dozen people. She couldn't tell them to put most of it back, but she could remind them about proper behavior.

She placed her hand on the table, in the space between herself and Mrs. Hollenbeck. "If you would excuse me, I need to—"

"Nonsense!" Mrs. Hollenbeck patted Emilia's hand. "Sit. Mac is attending to your siblings. Let them eat to their heart's content."

Mortification warmed Emilia's cheeks. So that was why they'd been invited to the wedding of a couple they barely knew. To eat to their heart's content. Not because there needed to be an equal number of young unmarried ladies and bachelors, as Mrs. Palmer had insisted at the bride's tea.

Emilia scanned the crowd. Instead of heading to the table she had been saving, Mac led the pair to the table where Mr. Adams sat talking to Judge Forsythe and his wife. "I'm so sorry," she murmured, sitting. "They know better."

"Don't fault them. They're hungry children and the food is good. Especially the wedding cake." Mrs. Hollenbeck slid her plate in front of Emilia. "Enjoy."

"I couldn't—"

"I insist."

Mrs. Hollenbeck gave Emilia a pointed look, and so Emilia picked up a fork and took a bite. Oh my. She'd never eaten anything so rich and tasty. The icing seemed to be flavored with real limes.

Mrs. Hollenbeck looked out over the crowd and casually sipped her tea. "People aren't always what they present themselves to be," she remarked. She turned to Emilia and smiled. "Case in point, Mr. Buchanan."

Emilia nodded, having no other response.

"Underneath all that"—Mrs. Hollenbeck's hand waved alongside her head—"and the"—she waved up and down in front of her chest—"he's a good man."

Emilia almost snorted with disbelief. Instead, she took another bite of the delicious cake.

"You don't look convinced," Mrs. Hollenbeck mused.

"I would never wish to meet him in a dark alley," Emilia admitted.

Mrs. Hollenbeck's brows rose in surprise. Or maybe in disbelief that anyone couldn't see the diamond in the rough that was Windsor Buchanan. Emilia didn't take offense.

Perhaps after one or ten conversations with the ominous bladesmith she'd feel differently herself.

"However, should I be accosted in a dark alley," she said, in hopes of complimenting a man the older widow favored, "he would be my first thought for a rescuer."

"Interesting." Mrs. Hollenbeck sipped her tea, the corners of her lips indenting. "You wouldn't think of either Gunderson? You seem to be close with the twins."

That gave Emilia pause. Would she have thought of them first? Truth be told, if she were ever in danger, she would think of—

She glanced to where Mac sat with her siblings.

She would think of him.

Unwilling to admit that to anyone, she gave Mrs. Hollenbeck a smug grin. "I consider myself wise enough to avoid dark alleys and thus the need for any rescuer."

Mrs. Hollenbeck studied her thoughtfully. "And yet you married Finn, sight unseen."

"Not because I needed rescuing," Emilia rushed to say.

"Then why did you?"

"For my family."

"I see."

Emilia doubted it. She liked the esteemed widow and appreciated the repeated invitations to join the Ladies' Aid Society. But Mrs. Hollenbeck, with her grand mansion and servants, could never understand the desperate need to escape a prison—a fitting description of tenement life in Chicago.

"Ma'am, I would give my life for my family to have a better one."

Mrs. Hollenbeck slowly nodded. "I imagine that's true. Yet I cannot help but wonder what makes your life less valuable than theirs."

Emilia felt her lips part as she sought to make sense of

Mrs. Hollenbeck's words. Her life wasn't less valuable. Or more valuable. She'd made necessary sacrifices to help her family, to lift their burdens, to deliver them into the promise land. Only that land had come with debts and hardship. Her day began at sunrise and ended long after sunset. In addition to working off Finn's debts, she laundered clothes, mucked stalls, milked goats, culled chickens, and lied in her letters to Da about how wonderful life was in Helena. It wasn't wonderful. It was toilsome. More toilsome than she'd ever expected.

All because someone had murdered her husband.

Was it too much to hope that God would give her a little less than He knew she could handle?

"I don't know," she muttered because she had no other answer. Her heart ached for something different. For something more. With Mac. Since their croquet match, she had begun to imagine what her future could be like with him. And yet he was sitting at one of the farthest tables away from where she sat. She groaned inwardly. She shouldn't have taken Mr. Gunderson's advice to flirt with Mac.

A couple approached the table, but Mrs. Hollenbeck waved them away.

The quartet played on.

Mrs. Hollenbeck sipped her tea.

She rested her teacup on its saucer, then leaned closer to Emilia. "Would you like a little advice from an old lady?"

Emilia nodded, for no other reason than to be polite.

"Be cautious because people aren't always what they present themselves to be. But also be compassionate because people aren't always what they present themselves to be. Finally, be wise enough to know the difference." She laid her napkin on the table. "Pardon me, my dear," she said, standing. "I need to play hostess and ensure the ballroom is ready for dancing."

Emilia nodded again. "Of course."

"And don't forget your dance card."

As Mrs. Hollenbeck walked away, Emilia looked at the ornate fan sitting to the right of her knife and spoon, a little wooden pencil tied to the end. Inside, each fold contained a list of the dances for the first half of the evening—polka, waltz, square, reel, contra, and quadrille—and a space for the dance card owner to record the name of her partner. Even though her first dance had already been requested, her list was blank. Being a widow gave her a perfectly good reason to beg off. No one needed to know she didn't know how to dance.

She stared absently at her half-eaten cake and untouched tea.

Time passed, and the quartet changed tunes once. Twice. A third time.

The bride, groom, and bridal party left the dais and headed into the house, presumably to initiate the dancing. One by one, the tables emptied. Mac walked away, talking to Mr. Adams.

"Emme, you coming?" Luci called out.

Emilia looked to where her sister stood linked arm and arm with Melrose Truett in a dress as grand as Luci's was plain. "Go on. I'll be there in a moment. I'm not done eating."

The two girls darted off.

Emilia picked up her fork and finished the cake. Slowly.

Mac scanned the ballroom again. No Emilia. What was he going to do about her?

Last Sunday, out at the Circle C, something shifted between them. She'd flirted with him, no question about it, and Mac's urge to kiss her almost got the better of him. Only Roch and Luci's presence saved him. Even without kissing her, it had been a magical day filled with laughter and ease.

But then he'd gone home.

To Finn's file on the table next to the salt and pepper shakers. The same table Mac had watered with tears of grief not so long ago. The same file he'd spent hours reading because, as both sheriff and best friend, he owed it to Finn to solve his murder—and to not be distracted by his widow in front of the cabin where his blood still stained the floor.

Except the more Mac avoided being in the same part of town as Emilia, the more she invaded his thoughts, which made for a miserable week.

All morning, while shaving and dressing for the wedding, he'd debated with himself about what to do when he saw her again. If he was too friendly, people in town would talk. Well, talk more. Women were already giving him sly looks, and according to Deputy Alderson, men had placed bets in Doc Abernathy's Book of Wagers on whether Emilia would end up marrying Isaak Gunderson or Mac.

One of these days, he was going to burn that stupid book. After the way it spoiled Nick Alderson's last romance, the young deputy might help set the flame.

Mac checked the ballroom again. Emilia still hadn't appeared. Should he go find her? Or wait. If he remained aloof with her, people would talk about that, too.

Land's sake, he was a mess.

Waltz music filled the room, and the new Mr. and Mrs. Roy Bennett took the floor. Their love for each other radiated in their faces, in the way they held each other as they danced, how she lifted her hand to touch his beard, and when he bent to whisper something private in her ear.

Envy filled Mac's chest. He yearned to have a woman look at him the way Luanne looked at Roy. To have someone trust him enough to put her future in his hands. To love and be loved in return.

In years past, he and Finn would stand together chatting until the dancing started, both of them congratulating themselves on escaping the parson's noose. But Finn was gone. As much as it hurt, as much as it would go on hurting for a long time yet to come, it was time to move forward. What had Isaak said? As much as they all loved Finn, he wasn't coming back for Emilia.

She walked through the door and looked his way. Their eyes met, and Mac pushed away from the wall. He didn't need answers to every question. This was a wedding. People danced. And he wanted to dance with her.

He weaved through the ballroom intent on filling at least three slots on her dance card. A few other men headed her way, which was good. It *was*. If Emilia danced with several different men, Mac's attentions to her would be somewhat shielded. Not that he wanted to keep Emilia guessing, but the feelings between them were too new, too private, to be gossip fodder.

She was facing away from him and speaking to Windsor Buchanan. As Mac approached, he overheard, ". . . as a widow, I believe I shall sit this one out."

He stopped so fast, he almost tripped. Before he made a scene, he veered left and walked away.

Had she also spent the week wondering whether the mild flirtation between them betrayed Finn? What if she decided it did? If so, Mac wouldn't make her uncomfortable by asking her to dance.

He continued making his way through the wedding crowd, pausing to chat or observe the guests. Yancey Palmer was being led out to dance by her brother, Geddes, to join the bridal couple for the remainder of the waltz. She kept glancing over to where Hale and Isaak stood chatting, a look of profound longing on her face. For the first time, Mac felt sorry for her. In her blind devotion to Hale, she'd already rebuffed Jakob Gunderson and, judging by the look on Joseph Hendry's face, was going to lead another man down a miserable road—all for a man who didn't return her affection. Why did loving someone have to be so complicated?

Mac headed over to Hale and Isaak. When he got close enough, he heard Isaak say, ". . . a real asset. I don't know what I'd do without Mrs. Collins, to tell the truth."

Hale dipped his head in acknowledgment of Mac, then said to Isaak, "Doc Abernathy sings her praises."

"As have I in my letters to Father." Isaak loosened his tie, then undid the top button of his shirt. "I just received a return letter from him, and he agreed we should offer Mrs. Collins a full-time position at the shop. With an increase in her salary, she could work for us and have extra to pay Finn's debt at Cannon's General Store."

"Is she going to take it?" Mac slipped between Hale and Isaak so he could observe the whole room.

"I haven't had a chance to speak to her about it yet." Isaak gave Mac a questioning look. "Do you always have your back to the wall?"

"Sheriff," was all Mac said by way of explanation.

Hale chuckled. "Don't believe him. He was doing this long before he became sheriff. You should have seen him at the steak house the other night. We waited an extra half hour for a table in the corner so Mac could keep an eye on the whole room."

Isaak shot a significant look in Emilia's direction. "I can see why that would be important."

Heat filled Mac's cheeks. Time to change the subject. "It seems you've worked something of a miracle, Isaak."

"If you're talking about Yancey pestering me instead of

Hale, I hate to disillusion you. She thinks it will make him jealous."

Hale took out his pocket watch and wound the stem. "A pointless endeavor."

"Says the mouse to the cat." Isaak slapped Hale on the shoulder. "Please marry her and put the rest of us out of our misery."

"I feel no inclination to lay down my life for my friends." After a smirk in Mac's direction, Hale fixed a stare on Isaak. "But you might want to take care that Yancey's flirtations don't scare off Mrs. Collins."

"If you're talking about the basket auction last Sunday, I was merely helping out a friend." Isaak slanted a glance at Mac.

Hale slipped his pocket watch into his vest. "Fifty dollars says you are more than friends, and I've overheard a number of whispers connecting you and the lovely widow."

Mac swept his gaze across the room, turning his head at a steady pace even though his eyes stayed on Emilia longer than anywhere else. She was standing against the wall on the opposite side of the room while Jakob and Roch took turns demanding her attention. Was she refusing to dance with her own brother? Either she was a stickler for social customs or her feelings for Finn forbade it.

Which felt like a kick in the gut.

Mac returned his focus to his friends to find Isaak grinning broadly.

"Until you see my name in the *Daily Independent* announcing my nuptials, I wouldn't believe every rumor you hear." Isaak pressed his thumb and index finger into the corners of his mouth, humor dancing in his green eyes. "Besides, if my heart was captured by anyone last Sunday, it was little Miss Luci, once she moved past her annoyance with me for winning the basket bid instead of Mac, of course. By the meal's end, she decided I was—how did she put it?—'just as beautiful as Jakob, though not as smiley.' It may be the nicest compliment anyone has ever paid me."

"Gentlemen," Mrs. Hollenbeck called out, "the ladies await your attendance. Isaak, Yancey says you have claimed the next dance."

"We'll be right there, ma'am." Hale bowed in the widow's direction before returning his attention to Isaak. "Next dance, huh? Be careful or you'll find your nuptials announced sooner than you think."

"Don't be impertinent, Mr. Lawyer, or I'll tell Yancey how to bait your hook." With that parting shot, Isaak left Hale and Mac to claim his dance partner.

Hale watched as Isaak took Yancey's elbow and led her onto the floor. "They actually make quite a handsome couple, don't you think?"

"Jealous?" Mac meant it as a joke, but Hale took him seriously.

"A little."

"Really?"

At Mac's astonished question, Hale turned his head to look at Mac. "Not of Isaak and Yancey, of course, but of love and marriage in general. Luanne and I would have been well suited, but . . ."

Mac remembered how Yancey had spoiled that romance.

"She"—he looked pointedly at Yancey—"has made it impossible for me to pursue any young lady in Helena. Perhaps I'll take a page out of Finn's book and send away for a mail-order bride. Yancey can't scare off a woman she's never met."

Mac wasn't sure about that.

"Enough about me. What's going on between you and Mrs. Collins?"

"Nothing."

"Mm-hmm." Hale pushed his glasses into place with his index finger. "A whole lot of nothing, from what I've observed. You avoiding her while she's avoiding you."

Mac started toward the dance floor. "Trust me. There's nothing going on."

Unfortunately.

"Mrs. Collins, may I have this dance?"

Emilia stopped, fanning her face with her dance card, and looked up from where she sat to see Mr. Geddes Palmer standing in front of her, his blue eyes sparkling with merriment. "I—ah—" She moistened her lips. "Thank you, but as a widow, I believe I shall sit this one out," she said, repeating what she'd told every other gentleman who'd invited her to dance. "The music is delightful, don't you think?"

"It is." He hesitated. No doubt trying to decide whether he ought to forgo politeness and point out that she wasn't much of a widow really. He motioned to where Luci was lining up with Mac in the middle of the ballroom. "Their group could use one more pair."

Emilia smiled. "It is quite agreeable to watch . . . and to listen to the caller shout out instructions to the dancers. Is this common practice out west?"

"For some dances," he explained. "The waltz never needs—"

Miss Melrose Truett dashed over, her red-gold curls bouncing on her shoulders. "Excuse me, Mrs. Collins," she said to Emilia. Then she grabbed Mr. Palmer's arm. "Geddes, your mother says you must dance with me."

He looked over to where his mother stood, waving him toward the dance floor. He turned back to Melrose. "Mrs. Collins was about to—"

"Please go on without me," Emilia insisted. "Besides, your mother did request."

Mr. Palmer had the good graces to look indecisive.

Melrose tugged on his arm. "The music is starting."

He gave Emilia an apologetic shrug.

"Truly, Mr. Palmer, I don't mind," she persisted.

That convinced him.

He allowed Melrose to pull him to the floor. They lined up across from Mac and Luci, whose smile couldn't get any broader, in a square set with Mr. Gunderson and Yancey Palmer and Mr. Adams and a pretty blond woman who, Emilia thought, taught one of the younger grades at Central School. Luci would know. She seemed to have befriended everyone in her school.

As the music increased in tempo, the caller bellowed instructions.

The ladies turned, their skirts a colorful swirl.

Did Mr. Adams look peeved at the flirtatious glances Miss Palmer was giving Mr. Gunderson? Emilia leaned slightly to the side for a better view. If anything, he looked bored. Mr. Gunderson shook his head at something Miss Palmer said. Like the other three men in the square set, Mac had nimble feet. Luci stumbled, then laughed. Everyone else in their set laughed, too. No matter how many mistakes she made, she never looked frustrated or embarrassed.

Mac's gaze shifted to where Emilia sat. As he waited his turn, he watched her, and she forced herself to breathe. Her heart squeezed harder and harder.

"Promenade left."

He watched her.

"Swing your partner."

He watched her.

Why? Did he feel sorry for her sitting off to the side like a wallflower? She'd been asked to dance numerous times.

He had to have seen. He had to have heard her reason for refusal. She'd spoken with the bride and groom and their respective parents, and anyone else who'd wandered over to her settee beside an opened window. She didn't mind sitting by herself and watching the dancing.

Except he noticed.

By the look on his face, he seemed annoyed. Because she wasn't dancing? She wasn't about to make a fool of herself in front of a hundred people, so if she had to rely on the plausible excuse of being a widow prohibiting her from dancing, she'd use the excuse without shame. Even if he asked her to dance, she would say no, contrary to what her heart desired. If she didn't, people would wonder. If she didn't, he would wonder. And if he wondered, would he realize she was infatuated with him? Not a lot. Just enough to have already made things awkward.

Not once since she arrived at the wedding reception had he seemed mildly interested in her. Until now.

So why now?

Mr. Gunderson smacked Mac's arm and Mac joined the promenade, his gaze shifting to his partner.

Feeling strangely warm, Emilia took the moment to hurry out of the ballroom. She turned right, turned a corner, and passed the hat closet on her way to hide in the washroom. Which was—? She turned in a circle. None of the pictures on the wall were landscapes.

"Humph," she muttered.

After checking four doors, she headed back toward the music escaping the ballroom. She turned a corner and there was Mac, leaning against the wall.

His chin dipped down, and he gave her a sideways look. "You went the wrong way," he said with a smug half grin that made her feel warm to the tips of her toes. "You do that when your mind is distracted."

Emilia said nothing in response. She did have her pride after all. There, to the left of the ballroom entrance, was the landscape painting beside the washroom door. Head held high, she continued on past him.

He fell into step.

Emilia kept walking. "Is there something you wish to say?" she asked, her gaze on the open French doors leading to the back lawn.

"You weren't dancing."

"I'm a widow."

"Mrs. Hollenbeck is a widow."

"Because her husband died after forty years of marriage instead of one day?" Or was it because Mrs. Hollenbeck had become a wife after becoming a bride? Something Emilia hadn't. That she was a widow wasn't why she wasn't dancing. But it was better that was what he believed.

Emilia stopped just outside the patio doors. She looked up at Mac, standing next to her. "You never do anything without a purpose. Is this the beginning of your plan to rescue me from my self-imposed wallflowerdom?"

He regarded her for a moment, long enough so that she felt uncomfortable. "Do you wish to be rescued?" The question was low and even.

The breath left her body.

Yes, she wanted to be rescued. She wanted to be loved. She wanted to feel connected to someone. She wanted to know without a doubt that he would always be there for her, no matter what. Heaven help her, she wanted what she would have had if Finn hadn't died. A friend. A lover. A champion to go to battle for her. What girl didn't?

Easing a step away, she looked beyond the potted plants and trees framing the patio, out to where the lawn had been filled with cloth-covered tables. The empty serving table remained, piles of white cloths on top. A nicely dressed man stood next to it, talking to a maid as she folded a white tablecloth. Every time he tried to assist with the folding, the maid shot him an angry glare. Why? The man was only trying to help.

Be cautious because people aren't always what they present themselves to be. But also be compassionate because people aren't always what they present themselves to be. Finally, be wise enough to know the difference.

Did Mrs. Hollenbeck not think she knew the difference?

Maybe the maid had good reason to refuse the man's help. Maybe the man was pressing his unwanted attentions. Maybe they were a couple having an argument. Maybe the maid was tired and wished to be left alone. Or her dog had died that morning. Or her mother was ill. Or she was afraid of relying on someone else to be there to help because she knew one day he wouldn't be there and she'd be left alone to manage it all.

Just like Da had done.

Just like Finn.

She blinked rapidly to stop tears from forming.

Emilia stepped farther onto the paved patio to put needed space between herself and Mac. He followed. Not that she heard his footsteps. She could feel him. There, standing within arm's reach, not too close to be improper, yet close enough to make her skin tingle, heart pound, and breath—Goodness, she couldn't breathe quite right.

"Please leave," she whispered, hugging her arms to her body, "your presence is needed in the ballroom." *Not here. Not with me.*

She was looking down, looking away, and it took all Mac's strength not to trace the curve of her neck. The air thickened around them, trapping them in an enchanted place where no one and nothing else existed. He wanted to twist the curling tendril of hair falling over her ear around his finger, to take hold of her shoulders and turn her to face him so he could bend his head until their lips met.

Because he'd been wrong.

When he'd danced with Luci, she said Emilia was using her widowed state as an excuse because she didn't know how to dance and would be too embarrassed to show it in front of everyone. So Mac watched her, waiting until she left the crowded ballroom to speak with her alone.

And then she asked if he'd come to rescue her from—how had she described it?—her self-imposed wallflower-dom. It confirmed Luci's statement. More than that, it was another move in this silent dance he and Emilia were engaged in. The flirting, the near kiss, the questioning: two steps together, one step apart.

Now for the twirl.

He swallowed hard and took a step closer so they stood side-by-side. "Emilia? I asked if you wanted to be rescued."

She turned her head and lifted her chin, bringing her gaze to his, a confused look in her caramel-colored eyes. She was so close, he could touch her if he desired.

He desired. So much so his skin burned with it.

She remained rooted to the spot, her eyes narrowing the way they did when she was pondering something. Her head tilted to the side. Her lips moved, as if she were struggling to voice words.

He stepped in front of her—face-to-face—bringing them within an inch of each other . . . so close he felt the heat of her body like a physical touch.

She braced her hand over his heart, not pushing him away but not drawing him toward her either. It was enough.

No woman looked at a man the way Emilia was looking at him if she was still in love with her late husband. "Mac?"

"Yes." Whatever she needed, whatever she asked, whatever she wanted him to be, his answer would always be yes.

And he would always come to her rescue.

"Eli Alderson, would you let go!"

Mac jerked his gaze across the lawn to see Deputy Alderson's younger brother holding tight to a white cloth that Mrs. Hollenbeck's newly hired personal assistant was trying to tug from his grasp. He'd been too focused on Emilia to notice that anyone else was outside.

She dropped her hand and turned to leave. "We shouldn't be alone together."

He put his hand out to block her path and waited for her to look at him again. "We're not alone, and we've done nothing wrong. Besides, those two"—he tilted his head toward the arguing couple—"could use a distraction, and we'll need their help if I'm going to teach you how to dance."

Her mouth gaped for a moment, pink tingeing her cheeks. "Was it that obvious?"

"Not initially." And not without a little help from Luci.

Emilia sighed.

"Em." He tried out a new nickname for her—one he hoped would forge a bond between them that was different from the one she had with her family or anyone else. "May I have this dance?"

"On one condition."

"Anything."

"If I'm an embarrassingly poor dancer, you will give up on me."

"Never." He slipped his hand around hers and led her toward the arguing couple. If he couldn't kiss her, at least he could hold her in his arms.

Chapter Sixteen

Monday, May 16

Mac twirled the thingamajig between his fingers. He was missing something. Something big. And he wasn't sure if it was because he couldn't solve Finn's murder or because he couldn't stop thinking about how Emilia had felt in his arms when they danced. Or how she'd flirted with him while they played croquet. Or how he wanted to kiss her until she melted into him. Or because he couldn't think of a single, logical excuse to go to The Resale Co. other than he wanted to see her.

He pushed back from his desk. One more minute indoors and he'd shoot something.

Eleven in the morning was too early for lunch, but he needed a break. An apple fritter and decent black coffee was in order. And the bakery across from The Resale Co. made the best of both. On his way out of the office, he grabbed his hat from a hook beside the door.

As soon as he stepped outside, the bright sunshine lifted his spirit. He breathed in and exhaled, stretching his neck from side to side to ease the ache in his muscles, and set out at a brisk pace. Flowers in every hue of the rainbow decorated window boxes, hanging baskets, and repurposed barrels in front of shops along West Main Street. The hard winter was over, and people wanted to forget it as soon as possible.

"Yoo-hoo! Sheriff McCall!"

Mac turned around to see Mrs. Halford, the postmistress, waving at him. He walked toward her, his boots echoing against the boardwalk. "What can I do for you?"

"You have a package." She disappeared inside the post office but didn't stop talking. "It came a couple of weeks ago, so I . . ." Whatever she said next was lost when the door closed behind her.

Mac didn't run to catch up. By the time he made it through the post office door, Mrs. Halford would still be talking. He'd mumble an "Uh-huh," or something equally noncommittal, and she'd think he'd heard everything she'd said. Not his most gallant response, but the woman could talk the ears off a dead horse.

She was also one of the busiest of Helena's busybodies.

He slowed. Did she know that he'd gone out to the Circle C last week? That he'd danced with Emilia at the wedding two days ago? If so, his decision *not* to sit with Emilia in church yesterday to protect her from women like Mrs. Halford and her particular brand of nosy had been a futile effort.

After a deep breath to fortify his nerves, he opened the post office door and went inside.

The postmistress was facing away from him. Talking. ". . . didn't want this to get lost in the messages and things that must have piled up for you after three weeks of being gone. Such a terrible business you must have had this year with all the foreclosures." She turned around and thrust a package wrapped in brown paper toward him. "I suspect it's another book. Those seem to be about the only thing you ever have delivered."

"Yes, ma'am." Mac tugged the package from her grasp. *"Uncle Tom's Cabin."*

"I thought you were more of a poetry man." Her eyes went wide, and she pressed her lips into a flat line. Her look of consternation confirmed what he'd long suspected: Mrs. Halford opened packages to see what was inside before sealing them back up for delivery. She leaned sideways to retrieve an envelope stashed below her counter. "This is for Mrs. Collins. Return address is from someone named Stanek in Chicago. A relative, I suspect."

And she'd kept it within reach so, as soon as she got him inside the post office, she could see what he'd do with it.

"I've had it for a few days," Mrs. Halford continued. "She works so hard, you know. It's difficult for her to stop by." She waved the letter like a fan.

It was a test . . . and the whole purpose behind her tracking him down on the sidewalk. If he took the letter, she'd have a juicy tidbit to share with her friends confirming the relationship. If he didn't, she could say there was trouble in Paradise or some such nonsense.

Either way, he wasn't getting out of the post office without inspiring more gossip, so he might as well use the excuse to go see Emilia. It was what he wanted to do anyway.

"I'll see that it gets delivered." Mac took the letter and tucked it inside the string wrapped around his book. He tipped his hat to the postmistress then set off toward The Last Chance Café instead of the bakery. If he was bringing Emilia a letter, he might as well bring her lunch, too.

Gripping a sack lunch and a jug of cider, Mac stepped inside The Resale Co. Emilia was helping a gaggle of women, her back to the door. One of the ladies looked at him and then at the lunch sack. He gave her his most nonchalant nod and headed straight back to the storeroom so she'd assume he was having lunch with Isaak.

At least he hoped that was the assumption she'd make. The less gossip he inspired, the better.

Isaak stood with Martin Wegman who was extolling the virtues of a battered travel trunk that had come overland in a Conestoga wagon back in '69.

"I realize it's an heirloom in your family, sir." Isaak kept his tone polite, but his toe tapped against the floorboards. "That doesn't mean I'm willing to pay more than the cost of a new one. Eleven dollars."

Mac set the lunch bag and jug of cider on a nearby crate. He was no expert, but the trunk didn't look like it would fetch more than seven or eight dollars.

Wegman held himself rigid, staring up at the young man towering over him. "I paid twenty dollars for it, and it's worth every penny of that, ya ken?"

Poor man. He'd worked as a stockman for the Diamond S, one of the big ranches that had reported a loss of fifteen thousand cattle. Much of that was exaggeration. The Diamond S—as well as a large number of the other big ranches—practiced a loose kind of accounting for stock growth. Though they said it was because herds of fifty to seventy thousand were hard to count, Mac suspected it was more about keeping their taxes low. But no matter the reason, the huge number of cattle lost over the past winter resulted in hundreds of men like Wegman losing good-paying jobs.

"All right, twelve dollars. But that's the best I can do." Isaak's tone remained firm.

Wegman nodded and held out a trembling hand. As soon as the older man left, Isaak lifted the heavy trunk and set it beside a six-foot-tall cupboard much like the one in Finn's cabin. "What can I do for you, Mac?"

"I have a letter for Mrs. Collins."

"I see." Isaak stared at the lunch bag and jug of cider. "And you're wondering if I can spare her for half an hour?"

"Something like that." Mac shifted under Isaak's continuing stare. "It's just lunch."

"Mm-hmm." Isaak dug a notebook and pencil from the pocket inside his suit coat. "And I just lost a bidding war."

So all that bartering had been to save Wegman's pride.

"It's just lunch," Mac repeated, which made Isaak smirk. "And she'll want a half hour to read the letter."

"Mm-hmm." There was a definite teasing undertone to the murmur.

Mac deserved it. "I know. I should have done this long ago." He snatched the bag and jug off the crate and headed back to the main store.

A chuckle and, "You owe me fifty dollars," followed him.

The women were gathered around the cash register completing their purchases. Mac waited for them to leave before stepping into view.

Emilia gave him a wary look. "Mac."

He walked closer and set the lunch bag and jug on the counter. "I was passing by the post office when Mrs. Halford flagged me down." He dug the letter from inside the twine binding around his book. "Said she'd been holding on to this for a couple of days and wondered if I could deliver it to you."

Emilia took it from him and gasped. "It's from Da." She pressed it against her heart. "Thank you."

"Mrs. Collins"—Isaak strolled into the main store—"I have an errand to run at one today. Would you mind taking an early lunch?"

"Of course not, Mr. Gunderson." She smiled brightly. "Mac delivered a letter from my father."

"Our good sheriff is all consideration." Isaak's tone remained bland, but the side of his mouth tipped upward. "If you wish to take a little extra time to read your letter, that's fine. I just need you back by one."

Emilia looked at the nearest grandfather clock. "Forty-five minutes is far too—"

"—short for you to re-read your father's letter more than twice."

"I was going to say it was far too long."

Isaak walked behind the extra-tall counter and assisted Emilia down from her stool. "Which is why I cut you off before you could say it."

Emilia chuckled and turned her blinding smile on Mac.

His fingers tightened around the paper sack. Did she have any idea what that smile did to him? Heaven help him if she did. "Would you like to sit in the storeroom?"

"Sure. My feet could use a break."

Mac followed her toward the back of the store without giving Isaak Gunderson the satisfaction of a response to the man's smirk.

They sat on a small bench awaiting a fresh coat of varnish, Mac on the right, Emilia on the left. He set the lunch bag and cider between them. Should he tell her that the two of them were inspiring gossip and bets in Doc's Book of Wagers? No. He didn't want to give her any reason to stop having lunch with him. Besides, she was forthright enough to tell him if the rumors and speculation ever became a problem for her.

He opened the lunch bag. "Help yourself to whatever you want. There's too much for one person in there." He withdrew the book from where he'd tucked it under his arm and picked at the twine wrapping.

Emilia ripped open her letter and read in silence. After a few minutes, she looked inside the bag then withdrew a wedge of cheese.

While she nibbled the cheddar and read, he opened his book to the first chapter. The quiet between them was peaceful. Comfortable. Like a couple who'd been together long enough they didn't need to speak to enjoy each other's company.

"Thank you."

He slanted a grin her way. "You're very welcome."

Her return smile made him grateful they were already sitting down. The woman's lips weakened his knees. She dropped her gaze to his mouth, her smile fading. Pink crept into her cheeks and she looked away.

Ho boy! Was that what he thought it was? Did she spend time wondering how a kiss between them would feel? Because, ever since the croquet game, he'd spent an inordinate amount of time thinking about it himself. His heart swelled and pulsed against his rib cage. Should he declare himself? Say out loud that he'd like permission to court her as though she'd boarded the train to come to him? *Him!* Not Finn.

Mouth dry, Mac picked up the jug of cider and uncorked it. The instant he touched the rim to his lips, he realized his mistake. His breath hitched, sending him into a coughing fit.

"Are you all right?" Emilia pounded his back with a small, ineffectual fist while he hunched over his thighs, hacking.

"Fine," he wheezed, and she stopped hitting his spine.

Cups! He should have borrowed some cups. His deputies never balked at sharing the same jug when they were out on a posse, but it was different for women.

He set the jug between them and pressed his coat sleeve against the corners of his mouth. "Sorry."

"For what?" She picked up the cider and took a drink.

Mac's jaw unhinged. The humiliation squeezing his chest loosened. "Uh . . . nothing."

She gave a little shrug and returned to her letter.

And he'd thought he couldn't find her more adorable than she'd been back in Finn's barn or while whacking away at the croquet ball. Or on too many other occasions when she'd done nothing more than look his way.

Mac cleared his throat to dislodge the last of the cider and opened Harriet Beecher Stowe's acclaimed novel. He was on the second chapter when Emilia set her father's letter in her lap.

"Good news?" he asked.

"Da's found a different job. It's not in the cotton mill, so that's good." She cocked her head to get a better look at his book. "What's that?"

He tilted it so she could read the title. "I read it a few years ago and decided I wanted to own a copy someday."

"Roch was reading it before we left Chicago." With a tentative finger, she touched the gold-embossed lettering on the cover. "It's too bad we had to leave before he finished it. It's the only book I ever borrowed from the library that he asked to read himself."

Mac offered the book to her. "Would you like to borrow it? You can't start a book like this and not finish it."

"On one condition," she repeated his words from that day in the barn. "You put your name in it so we don't forget to return it to you."

"Agreed." He dug a pencil from inside his coat pocket and scrawled his signature on the inside cover.

"Do I finally get to hear what the *L* in your signature stands for?" She turned her hand palm up.

He put the book in it. "Lester."

Emilia set the book in her lap next to the open letter from her father. "You don't look like a Lester."

Whatever that meant. He reached in the bag for a sandwich and held it out to her.

She eyed him for a moment before taking it. "Thank you."

He retrieved the other sandwich, unwrapped it, and took a bite. "What else did your father have to say?"

"Would you like me to read his letter to you?"

"Sure." Happiness wrapped around his heart. He had thirty more minutes. By then he'd figure out a way to ask if she'd like to have lunch with him the following day . . . and the day after that . . .

And the day after that.

Chapter Seventeen

Monday, May 23

"We need to talk, and this can't wait until tomorrow's meeting."

Mac stopped writing mid-word. He lifted his gaze to see Joseph Hendry close the office door. Ever since the reporter arrived in Helena last November, he'd visited the sheriff's office every Tuesday and Friday to crusade against perversion in the city. To ask why twelve establishments continued to operate despite proven ties to prostitution, gambling, and all sorts of morally reprehensible conduct to drag a man's soul to a black death. To complain that, because prostitution was a misdemeanor resulting in a fine, overflowing civic coffers made the sin more palatable.

Mac agreed but was bound by law to uphold the city council's decisions, so the two of them had settled into an odd relationship somewhere between enemies and friends.

Mac laid his pencil on the file and leaned back in his chair. "What's going on?"

Hendry shifted his weight from one foot to the other. "I've been chasing a rumor for ten days now." He cleared his throat. "About Finn Collins."

Mac straightened in his seat. "Go on."

"Before I do, let me say I don't want to compromise our working relationship."

A strange comment in light of their previous conversations.

Hendry sat down in the chair opposite Mac's desk, bringing the two of them eye to eye. "There's a new rumor in the red-light district. I took it to my editor and he agreed it was worth following up. I knew you'd want facts. Yesterday a third source corroborated that Finn Collins was luring women into prostitution. My editor wants to run the story."

"I see." Amazing how calm he managed to sound when he wanted to reach across the desk and rip out the reporter's tongue for daring to slander his friend.

Hendry gripped the armrests of his chair. "Look, Mac, I know how close you and Collins were. If it weren't for our jobs, I figure you and I could be friends in light of our shared values. Because of that, before this story goes to press, I wanted to give you a chance to comment."

Mac had dealt with enough reporters to suspect Hendry's buttery words. He wanted to keep meeting with the county sheriff for inside information on crimes committed outside of Helena. If Mac said he knew nothing and Hendry proved Mac was lying *or* if he hindered Hendry's investigation, he would write an exposé on corruption at the highest level of the sheriff's office . . . and Mac would lose next year's election.

He folded his arms across his chest. "What is the exact rumor?"

"Finn agreed to pose as a rancher looking for a mail-order bride. The plan was to offer marriage, but once she arrived, his intention was to sell her into prostitution." Hendry paused. "Her *and* her younger sister."

Fury gripped Mac's ribs with steel talons. Was it the idea

of Emilia and Luci conscripted into such a life, or that he might have been misled by a man he'd considered his brother? "Name your sources."

"I can't do that."

"I could arrest you."

Hendry shrugged. "It won't be the first time." He leaned forward, his eyes taking on the intensity of a warrior in battle. "My strict promise of anonymity is why people talk to me. As much as I respect you as a lawman, I won't risk losing the trust I've built with my sources. I don't care about lessoning the symptoms of prostitution or increasing the city's coffers. I care about ridding Helena of this disease."

"So do I."

"Do you?"

Mac's jaw set. "What are you implying?"

"It doesn't look good for the county sheriff to be the son of a renowned madam *and* close friends with someone who has been kidnapping women into prostitution."

"Potentially."

Hendry shook his head. "No, not potentially. My sources have said outright they know Finn Collins was abducting women."

"You trust them?"

"As much as I trust you."

Mac winced. "But you have no proof, only sources." Because, if Hendry did, the story would be splashed across the front page with or without a comment from the sheriff. His lack of denial confirmed Mac's suspicion. "You have too much integrity to run a story based on rumors."

Hendry's blue eyes blazed with conviction. "I've even heard of couples who ride the trains looking for mail-order brides to scare them into thinking their grooms are involved in such a scheme, then turn out to be the very ones who perpetuate the crime they've assigned to others. People need to be warned. Women need to be warned."

For whatever reason, Hendry had chosen to crusade against prostitution. If he were abrasive, people in Helena would have dismissed his credentials after his first article. Joseph Hendry's strength lay in his compassion and charm, in his ability to be as shrewd as a serpent and as innocent as a dove. That was why he could convince people to confess things. That was why, with the power of his pen, he could fight a war.

And ruin lives.

Like Emilia's.

Despite the way the town had welcomed and accepted her, there was no telling how people would respond after reading an article slandering Finn. Death precluded him from facing a judge and jury in the court of law. His fate would be decided by public opinion—opinion swayed by an idealistic reporter—and absent a villain to crucify, they might channel their outrage to Emilia.

Mac wasn't about to let that happen, and the best way to protect her was by proving Hendry wrong.

"So"—Hendry dug a notepad and pencil from inside his coat pocket—"what do you have to say about this?"

"I can't comment until I've had time to investigate it with people who don't hide behind anonymity."

"We're running a story on Finn in Wednesday's paper."

Mac gave Hendry a flat stare. "Two days isn't enough time for me to rebut or confirm."

"I'm sorry." Hendry stood. "If this is happening in Helena, it's happening elsewhere. Every paper east of the Mississippi has advertisements from men looking for mail-order brides. Naïve women respond, thinking they've found the answer to their problems. Face it, Mac. Anyone can be anything in a letter."

He knew that truth well. Had argued with Finn at length when he'd first placed the ad for a mail-order bride. Mac stood. "Give me a couple of weeks. I have to leave town on Thursday and won't be back until next Wednesday or Thursday."

Hendry stared at Mac for a long moment. "Saturday is the longest I can delay. Give me a quote before you leave, or the story goes to press saying you refused to comment."

After escorting Hendry to the hallway, Mac made eye contact with Undersheriff Keenan. With a jerk of his head toward his office door, Mac said they needed to talk. Now.

Keenan nodded and, two minutes later, sat in the chair Hendry had just vacated. "Yes, sir?"

Briefly, Mac filled his undersheriff in on the rumor about Finn kidnapping women into prostitution. "Anything in your investigation turn up something about this? Because, even though Finn was my friend, I need to hear it."

Keenan's freckled face held no guile. "No, Mac. I promise you, if I'd so much as sniffed something like that, I'd have brought it straight to you."

"I don't want to believe Finn could do something like that"—Mac leaned back in his chair and crossed his arms—"but I can't ignore evidence to the contrary out of sentimentality."

"Then let's review everything we have. If Hendry's rumor is true, we'll find something to confirm it."

"You get Finn's file. I'll get us coffee."

Once they were both back in Mac's office, they laid out the evidence they'd compiled, no matter how vague or seemingly inconsequential. For ten minutes, Keenan listed known facts on a notepad. He looked up. "What sticks out most to me is the money. I couldn't find a single banker who gave him a loan."

"Or admit to it." Mac sipped his lukewarm coffee.

"What if the money wasn't a loan? What if it was a payment?"

"You think someone paid him for Emilia and Luci?"

"It's a possibility. Fits Hendry's rumor." Keenan held up the notepad. "It's the only thing on this list that does. Like you always say: When in doubt, follow the money."

The exact thing Mac had told Hale would come back to bite them. "The first problem I see is Yancey Palmer's involvement. Why would Finn drag a respectable female into something unsavory when he could have used any woman from the red-light district just as easily?"

Keenan ran his tongue over his top lip. "Maybe he planned to say his wife got cold feet and never showed up. Nice lady like Miss Palmer wouldn't be like to hear the goings-on in the red light."

"Possible." Another thought followed, one Mac hated saying aloud because it put an image in his mind that would make sleep difficult. But this was work, and all options needed to be discussed. "What if the idea was to put them in with the women being rotated out of Helena to the next stop down the line?"

"Hate to say it, but that makes perfect sense."

"That's what I was afraid of." Mac took a sip of coffee, the bitter brew coating the disgust in the back of his throat. "The second problem is that Finn and Emilia started corresponding in August of last year. If Finn was planning on selling them into prostitution, why bother with nine months of courting?"

"Maybe his original intentions had been sincere. The

hard winter changed people. Finn loved that ranch of his. Do you think he'd do anything to keep it?"

Mac finished the last of his coffee. "I still find it implausible that Finn would sell his legal wife into prostitution."

"Wouldn't be the first time." Keenan tossed his notepad on the desk and hurried out of the office.

While he was gone, Mac reviewed the list.

Greasepaint and bandanna: mementos of Finn's past kept close to remind him of what he'd escaped or tools of a trade kept close at hand? Cart: bought before he needed to haul alfalfa or other products to market. Why? Because he got a good price or because he was using it for something—like possibly helping girls out of prostitution? It was a stretch, but if that was what Finn had been doing and he'd been caught, the bloody fingerprints on the telegram and Emilia's letters could mean the killer had found Finn in the barn, forced him into the house, then shot him. The messy cabin making it look like the motive was a robbery could have been a cover. The thingamajig could have been left over from the previous owners. Yancey's involvement and the proxy wedding could be circumstantial, too.

All in all, nothing proved or disproved Hendry's rumor except the money.

The cursed money!

Keenan rushed back into the office, handed Mac an envelope, then settled back in his chair. "When you called me in here, I'd just opened this."

Mac scanned the contents. The commander at Fort Missoula was lifting his restriction allowing only wives access to the post. Although his intention had been to reduce immoral conduct among his men, the result was soldiers "defiling the sanctity of marriage by selling their wives in the most degrading fashion possible."

Mac tossed the letter onto his desk. "Great. Just great."

Keenan picked his notepad up from the desk. "What do you want me to do about this?"

"Give me the list."

Keenan tore the sheet off the notepad and handed it over.

"Ask around." Mac slid the paper into Finn's investigation file. "See if you can nail down who started the rumor and why. Be discreet, but if Hendry's already got enough for an article, chances are it's already too late to keep it quiet."

"Do you want to talk to your mother or should I?"

Mac stood and pulled on his coat. "I'll do it, but first I need to warn Mrs. Collins."

"Yes, sir." Keenan picked up the letter from the commander of Fort Missoula. "What do you want me to do about this?"

"Nothing to do except notify O'Mara, Alderson, and the city marshal's office so they're aware. One more thing." Mac picked his hat off the hook. "What's on your schedule next week? I'm supposed to transport a prisoner from Deer Lodge Penitentiary over to Marysville to testify in a bank robbery case. Can you do it?"

Keenan scratched his right earlobe. "Afraid not. I'm slated to be in Augusta for the foreclosure auction, and Judge Forsythe is due back in town, so O'Mara and Alderson are trading off manning the office here and courtroom security."

Blast. "All right. Thanks." Mac followed Keenan out of his office. Before heading outside, he stopped at Deputy O'Mara's desk to see if the judge had sent word he'd be delayed.

"No, sir." O'Mara held his pen aloft. "But I'll keep an eye on it over the next few days."

"Appreciate it. I'm going over to The Resale Company. I

should be back in an hour. I'll phone if anything changes." Mac slipped on his hat and headed outside.

A light rain fell, and the breeze carried the scents of damp wood and dirt. Mac pushed his hat lower and hurried up West Main Street, avoiding buggies, horses, and the biggest puddle-filled ruts.

Emilia needed to be warned—and questioned. He'd read her letters to Finn but not the ones she'd received. Up to now, Mac had shied away from asking her to reveal their contents, a decision based on sentiment and the presumption of Finn's innocence.

And, potentially, a terrible mistake.

Upon reaching The Resale Co., Mac removed his hat, shook off the excess water, and kicked the mud off his boots. He drew in a settling breath, then stepped inside the store. Emilia was helping a customer, so he headed to the back to find Isaak. His office door was open. As Mac approached, he heard one side of a conversation.

"Sounds good. Thanks for the update. I look forward to Sunday's sermon." After hanging up, Isaak stood and walked around his desk to offer a firm handshake. "To what do I owe the pleasure?"

Mac briefly described his meeting with Hendry and the rumor about Finn.

Isaak's mouth pinched tighter and tighter.

"I can't ignore the ramifications for Emilia and Luci." Even if the rumor proved false.

"None of us can." Isaak leaned against his desk, his fingers gripping the edge. "But it goes against everything I knew . . . or at least thought I knew about Finn."

Nice to hear, especially from someone whose judgment Mac trusted. "I need to warn her. May I borrow your office for a few minutes?"

"Certainly, and tell her she can take the afternoon off if

she's too upset." Isaak rubbed the indent above his chin. "Once that story is printed, she may find other debtors unwilling to employ her. Please assure her that won't happen here." He shuffled some papers together and placed them in a drawer. "Let me know if you hear anything or need anything more from me."

"Will do." Mac headed to the front of the store. Emilia was holding the door open for a woman laden with bags and boxes, so he waited. Through the window he could see the rain had stopped.

She closed the door and turned to face him. "Mac." The genuine pleasure on her face twisted his insides. "You're here early. Lunch isn't for another hour."

"May I speak to you in private? Something has come up that we need to discuss." The words sounded brash and impatient, but it was remarkable they made it through his constricted throat.

"Oh, but I couldn't. Not while Mr. Gunderson is otherwise engaged."

"Don't worry, Mrs. Collins," Isaak called from the background. "Mac and I already discussed this. You can use my office, and I'll mind the store."

She blushed and nipped her lower lip. He dropped his gaze and imagined—oh, how he imagined—the feel of her lips on his.

The pink in her cheeks flamed brighter. She swallowed twice, dropped her head, and hurried toward the back of the store.

Was being alone with her a good idea? Nope. Not even a little bit. However, bad news wouldn't wait, and she wouldn't respect him for withholding the truth.

After a deep breath and an inner chastisement to act like the county sheriff instead of a heartsick suitor, Mac followed Emilia into the office and shut the door behind them.

His throat closed up. In his job, he delivered bad news on a regular basis but never to a woman he was courting.

He took a deep breath and forced words past his reluctance. "There's a reporter named Joseph Hendry who has written a number of articles about what goes on in the red-light district."

"I know him. He asked me to dance at the wedding."

"He says he has three sources who all confirm that Finn agreed to pose as a rancher looking for a mail-order bride. Then, after you arrived, he planned to sell you and Luci into prostitution."

Her eyes widened.

"Hendry says he trusts his sources." Mac tapped his wet hat against his knee and wished his misgivings would drop away like rain droplets and splatter on the wood-planked floor. "But I don't think he has actual proof. I asked him to delay the article for a couple weeks to give me time to track down information myself, but he won't wait that long. The story goes to press on Saturday. I have until Thursday morning, before my trip to Deer Lodge, to disprove it."

Emilia regarded him with the steady gaze he'd come to expect from her. "What do you need from me?"

"Anything you can think of—anything Finn wrote to you—that could shed light on this."

"Finn sent me fifteen letters. I can't remember everything in all of them."

Mac ran a hand through his hair. "Think about the ones from February and March."

She stared at her clenched hands in her lap, then gasped and looked up at him. "He mentioned a job he was doing right around the time he sent the thirty dollars for my train fare."

Mac sat down opposite her, stunned at both a job and another expenditure he hadn't known about. "When was this?"

"In February."

The same month one of the brothel girls went missing and Sheriff Simpson died. Circumstantial evidence or facts?

Mac dropped his hat on the floor and leaned forward in his chair, restraining the urge to close his hands over hers. "Can you remember any other details?"

She shook her head. "I have all his letters at home, though, so I could double-check tonight and we can talk again tomorrow morning."

Mac scratched the corner of his eye. "Any chance I can see the letters now?"

"I—I—uh. Some of them are . . . rather personal."

She blushed again, and misgivings filled his chest. Which was worse? Reading Finn's love letters to Emilia or hers back to him. Mac didn't want to read any of them. Didn't want Emilia rereading them, either. Not when he'd been wooing her for himself.

Which didn't change what needed to be done.

"I'm sorry"—Mac stood and held out a hand to help her up—"but I need to see them now."

Circle C Ranch

Emilia crawled across the loft's feather mattress to reach the spot where she'd wedged the bundle of letters between the mattress and the cabin wall. She freed them, her heart pounding. During the ride out to the ranch—longer than usual because of the muddy roads—Mac had said very little after he'd admitted he'd found her letters to Finn and had read them before meeting her at the train station. But he'd return them promptly, he'd promised. Just as he would with Finn's letters to her.

Promptly returning them meant little in light of the fact

that the man who was now courting her had read every word she'd written to his friend. Every word.

Her hopes. Her fears. Her struggles with Roch, and Da's inability to discipline him. Her heartbreak over losing her mother. Her yearning to be with Finn, to hear his voice, to feel his touch, to be his wife.

Mac had read them all.

Every word.

Every *intimate* word.

Her cheeks warmed. She focused on the pink ribbon holding together Finn's letters to her. What he'd written had been poetic, tender, and not the least improper, but still she hadn't shared them with anyone in her family. His words had been for her eyes only. Now she had to give the entire bundle to Mac to read. Every word. It embarrassed her to have him read these. More so than anyone else. Why?

Truth tugged at her heart. At some point between arguing about Needles, the waltz on Mrs. Hollenbeck's lawn, and this moment, she'd fallen in love with him.

She loved Mac.

This week together had only deepened her feelings. She loved how he'd stop by wherever she was working, conveniently right before her lunch hour. She loved studying paintings with him in The Resale Co. She loved the way he sat with her on the lawn next to the bootmaker's shop and Dr. Abernathy's dentistry, sharing fond memories of Finn and reading Walt Whitman's poetry. She loved being with him. Talking to him. Listening to him.

The way he looked at her as if she were something he couldn't live without—was that his way of saying he loved her, too? She hoped so. She wanted to believe.

She'd loved Finn. But it wasn't the same as this with Mac. Her heart had never felt like it was going to explode when she thought about Finn or read his letters. It did when she was with Mac. And now he was going to read words his friend—his best friend—had written about kissing her.

Emilia fanned her face, but the action did little to cool her embarrassment. Thank heavens Mac couldn't see her from where he stood down below.

"Find them?" he called up.

For no logical reason, Needles barked.

"Yes." Finn had died in April. So most likely any clues could be in the month or two prior. Emilia cleared her throat. "Uh, you only need the ones from February and March, right?"

Silence.

"Considering the situation, it's best I read them all."

Emilia closed her eyes and groaned. "Fine." She slid the bundle of letters into her apron pocket. "I'm coming down."

She crawled back to the angled ladder. Heart pounding, she gathered her gray skirt, then eased her feet around until she felt a rung. She moved down the ladder. Strong hands settled on her waist. And she stopped. She turned her head to the left and met his gaze. He was watching her, without a smile, nothing but tension deepening lines on his face.

"Oh, Mac," she said with a sigh. "Finn didn't do what he's been accused of. You have to know that."

"I'd love nothing more than to believe his innocence, but"—his head shook—"I have to entertain the possibility of his guilt."

"Dozens of people have told me what a good man Finn was." She didn't give him a moment to reply. "I won't—I *refuse* to let one man's wild-goose chase for a story shake my trust."

His hold tightened just a bit on her waist. "I understand your fears. No one wants to discover she's in love with someone who only pretended to love her in return."

She shifted on the ladder, resting her hip on a rung even

though Mac still held on to her. "Is that what you think this is about? That I'm afraid of discovering Finn lied to me?"

He shrugged.

Emilia withdrew the ribbon-tied bundle from her apron. "I do not fear *that*. I know Finn was truthful. These letters"—she held them up—"these precious words from Finn were the first romantic moments in my life. When you read my letters to him, you eavesdropped on a private conversation."

"My friend was murdered. I was looking for clues."

"And now you're asking to eavesdrop again."

He released his hold on her and walked to the hearth, raking a hand through his hair. Then he did it again, this time with both hands. He turned to face her. "You think I want to read what Finn wrote you?"

Emilia turned on the ladder until she could sit on a rung and face him, hooking her heels on a lower one for balance. "That's why we're here. You wanted the letters."

He walked back to her. "Do you think I *want* to read what Finn wrote you?" he repeated, with more emphasis this time. He withdrew the letters from her grasp, then dropped them to the ground. His gaze fell to her lips, and she could feel her cheeks grow warm.

Her heart tightened. Fluttered.

Needles barked.

Mac rested his forehead against hers. He let out a slow breath, then lifted her off the ladder. "It's best if we go sit on the porch."

Emilia nodded, unsure if she was relieved or disappointed. He'd almost kissed her. He hadn't said he loved her. He hadn't mentioned marriage either. A gentleman's duty was to declare first, but *I love you* was what his actions had felt like. Then why hadn't he kissed her? She wanted him, too. They were alone in the cabin. No one would know or see or—Oh.

She touched his cheek. "Thank you for being noble."

He grimaced. "At least one of us is pleased with my self-control."

Emilia laughed. "I never said I was pleased."

He groaned.

As much as she wanted to confess how blissfully wonderful she felt being loved, they had to deal with Finn before they could move forward together. As a couple.

She scooped up the bundle of letters, then motioned to the door. "Shall we?"

Mac grabbed his hat off the wall rack and settled it on his head. He handed Emilia her straw hat. They walked onto the porch. The gray clouds from the morning rainstorm had fled, replaced by a sun unfettered. She placed her hat on her head to shield her eyes from the sun then sat on the porch step, using the wooden post as a back support. Needles lay against Emilia's thigh. The dog crossed one front paw over the other and sighed contently as she usually did when she was on Luci's lap.

Mac sat opposite them. He leaned forward, resting his elbows on his knees and staring at Emilia. For several seconds, she could do nothing but stare back. The frustrated look left his eyes, replaced with something else. Not anger. Maybe pain?

Emilia untied the letter bundle. "In the first February letter, Finn mentioned he'd taken a job from a man he called Mr. S—, but couldn't tell me anymore because the man had sworn him to secrecy until the man's venture was up and running. Whatever the job was, it paid enough for Finn to wire me train fare from Chicago to here."

Mac's brow furrowed. "How much did he send?"

"Thirty dollars."

"He could have been paid more by Mr. S—. Enough to buy cattle, alfalfa seed, a plow, and fencing."

"No." Emilia shuffled through the envelopes, found the one she wanted, and withdrew the contents. She turned to the second page. "Here it is. *Mr. S—promises the second half will be paid once the job is completed.* That's sixty dollars, not hundreds."

His head wagged back and forth. "None of this makes sense."

"How can you say that? We know how he paid for my train fare. That makes sense."

"Did he ever mention completing the job?"

"No. He wrote twice a month, except for March. I never received an April letter." She tossed the February letter aside, then withdrew the last letter in the bundle. Of all Finn's letters, this one was the most intimate. He'd spoken of the anticipation he felt for her July arrival and how he was making the cabin comfortable. He had to have been referring to the cookstove and feather mattress. Emilia hesitantly handed the tattered envelope to Mac. "He says he made arrangements to recoup the losses from the hard winter. He never uses the word *loan*."

Mac took the envelope. "I'm sorry."

"For what?"

His gaze fell on the bundle of letters she held. She understood he was sorry about having to read them, about embarrassing her.

"I know," she said quietly. "These letters may be all we have to prove Finn was the good man we know he was."

He didn't respond.

Emilia stared at him in disbelief. "You don't believe he did what Mr. Hendry is accusing him of, do you?"

There was a pause, and then he said, "My aunt and uncle adopted me when I was a baby. When I was nineteen, they gave me the letters my mother wrote to her sister. They expressed how grateful she was to hear about my first tooth, my first steps, my first day of school, and a whole host of other firsts throughout the years. Ma—my aunt—was dying, so those letters became a balm to my grief."

Emilia understood. She'd lost her mother when she was sixteen. Roch, twelve. Luci, seven. Da, in his grief, had ceased shaving for two years. What she would have given to have letters from her mother, like she had Finn's, to console her.

"Seven years ago," Mac continued in a flat voice, "after Ma died, I told Pa I wanted to find my mother. Her last letter had been postmarked in Helena. Pa insisted she didn't want to be found. I refused to believe him. That's when he told me she was a . . . prostitute." A bitter laugh escaped. "Except the word he used wasn't quite that nice."

"You don't look like the child of a prostitute."

"How is one supposed to look?"

She blinked. Then laughed to cover her embarrassment over her ridiculous remark. "I meant no offense."

"I'm not offended."

How this story related to Finn she couldn't fathom, yet she asked, "What happened next?"

Mac gave her a wry smile. "I accused Pa of lying and a whole pack of other things it shames me to recall. I vowed to save my mother from a life she hadn't chosen. Pa said that if I left Ohio, I'd never come back."

"He disowned you?" she asked, horrified and yet intrigued.

"That's how I heard it at first." His gaze shifted to Needles, contently snoring. "He was making a prediction, not threatening me. He was wrong. Five months after I arrived in Helena, I returned to Ohio for his funeral and to settle his estate."

"Oh, Mac." She moved next to him, resting her head

against his shoulder. "I'm so sorry. Did you ever find your mother?"

"I did." His arm curved around her back. "She wasn't who I thought she was."

"Who had you expected her to be?"

He didn't answer.

She looked up to see his brow had furrowed, his mouth pursed tight. "Mac?" she asked softly. "What did you expect to find?"

"I expected to find the sweet, kind Mary Lester who, by her own words, adored me."

Emilia didn't have to say *but that's not what you found* because she knew it wasn't.

He cleared his throat, then moistened his lips. "Not only did Mary Lester not want to be found, she had no intention of ever surrendering her rather luxurious life. Still doesn't."

"You mean she lives here in Helena?"

He nodded. "Madame Lestraude owns the Maison de Joie and a whole host of other businesses. She's one of the wealthiest madams in the entire city." Mac gripped her hand and gently pulled Emilia until she was standing in front of him. "We need to get back to Helena. School ends in less than an hour."

He was right. They needed to return. As long as she'd been away from The Resale Co., she owed Mr. Gunderson another half day of work. Hopefully, she could convince him to let her do that this Saturday. That way she'd have the last week of May and the first one in June to retire the debts at three creditors before she took two weeks off to focus on sowing the alfalfa.

As Mac gathered the letters, Emilia closed the cabin door and ordered Needles to stay put on the porch. She met Mac at her horse and cart. As if she weighed nothing, he lifted her onto the seat before settling next to her.

"Mac," she said as they started down the road, "what does the story about your mother have to do with Finn?"

He drew her closer to his side, and Emilia went willingly.

"The people we fall in love with," he said, "don't always turn out to be who we think they are."

"Is this your way of warning *me* not to trust *you*?"

His grip tightened around the reins. "Emilia, you should be impressed with the self-control I'm maintaining at this moment because I'm a gentleman and you are a lady."

She looked up to see his gaze focused on her lips. "You want to kiss me?"

"Without a doubt." He winked then refocused on the road. "I love you, too."

Chapter Eighteen

By the time Mac returned Emilia to The Resale Co., it was nearly four in the afternoon. She let him help her out of the cart, allowed him to hold her waist for a moment longer than was proper, and smiled at him with a special sparkle in her caramel-colored eyes. It took uncanny strength not to kiss her in the middle of the street, although considerably less than it had taken not to kiss her back at the Circle C.

Land's sake, but it had taken every shred of decency to keep from crushing her body to his and tasting her lips. She loved him, had trusted him with letters he knew full well she wanted to keep private, and had looked at him with such tenderness, the ragged edges around his heart had smoothed enough to tell her about his mother. The only other person who knew the whole story of why he'd come to Helena was Finn.

And now Emilia.

His precious, beautiful Emilia.

After she walked into the store, Mac mounted Lightning and rode toward City Hall to check in before paying a visit to the Maison de Joie. Business would be picking up at his mother's spurious hotel, so she might not want to spare him any time.

Too bad. Discovering what she knew about Finn was too important.

As Lightning cantered down Main Street, Mac kept an eye out for Luci. School was out but she wasn't at the store. Either she was waiting for him at his office or walking from City Hall to The Resale Co.

If not for Luci, he would have kept Emilia out at the Circle C forever. Unlike when he'd shared his story with Finn, Emilia's response had loosened the vice grip around his heart. For years, he'd shied away from any sort of courtship because, before he could think of marrying a woman, she'd need to hear that he was nothing more than a grown man with a boy's need for his mother's love and approval. Fear had paralyzed him from ever opening himself up to the embarrassment such a risk engendered. But Emilia had been worth the risk—and, after she'd heard his story, she hadn't reviled him. More than that, her acceptance freed him to think about his mother without the longings of his boyish heart coloring his perceptions.

For the past seven years, he'd clung to the idea that his mother was the kind, gentle woman in her letters. What if this harder version—the one who scoffed at him and valued money above all else—was the real her? He'd considered it before and rejected it. As much as he spouted that anyone could be anything in letters, he wanted—desperately wanted—his mother to love him. To let go of that hope would be like burying another parent and mean he'd condemned his father to die alone for nothing.

Mac shifted in the saddle, looking to his left when he crossed Wood Street. His hand jerked on the reins at the sight of his burgundy-clad mother escorting Luci Stanek inside the Maison de Joie.

There were too many pedestrians on the street to gallop, but he touched his heels to Lightning's flanks anyway.

People scattered to either side of the muddy road, shooting him angry glares and calling down curses on his head.

He didn't care. He needed to get to Luci fast!

Two blocks later, he pulled Lightning to a halt and slid off the saddle in one movement, tossing the reins over the hitching bar and whistling a signal to keep the trained horse from wandering off. He ran into the hotel, held up a finger at the huge Chinese man to say, *Don't bother trying to stop me,* and slammed his hand against his mother's office door to keep it from closing. "What do you think you're doing?"

Madame Lestraude swung around, her skin blanching under her paint. "Mac! Oh, you scared me."

He seized Luci by the forearm and jerked her away from his mother. "Wait outside."

"No!" Madame Lestraude grabbed Luci's hand.

Tears pooled in the girl's eyes, so Mac let go. He glared daggers at his mother until she did the same, then he kneeled and turned Luci to face him. "I need you to wait in the hallway. Don't leave the hotel, just sit in the hallway. Can you do that?"

Luci nodded and leaned into a hug. "I'm sorry, Mac."

"You've done nothing wrong." He patted her back, his heart swelling at the feel of her tears on his neck, knowing his rough handling accounted for them. "I'll come get you in a few minutes, and then we'll go see your sister, all right?"

Her chin bounced against his shoulder.

"Good girl." He held her forearms, pushing gently until she faced him. "If anyone tries to bother you, come back in here."

Chin trembling, she nodded.

"All right, go on now." He waited for Luci to shut the door behind her before standing and pivoting to face his mother. "What were you *thinking*?"

"Don't take that high-and-mighty tone with me, Lester McCall. Last time we talked, you asked if I'd heard any rumors. Well, I have. So I went to your office to talk to you and found a little girl wandering around without protection."

"So you brought her *here*? Walked her from my office to *here* past who knows how many people?" He marched forward, and she scrambled behind her massive oak desk. "That's not protection. You've just ruined Luci's reputation." And her sister's.

"Nonsense." Madame Lestraude stood behind her chair, putting more distance between them. "Luci is in no danger from me. Everyone knows my business model doesn't include twelve-year-old girls."

"This isn't funny, Mother." He leaned over her desk with fisted hands. "There's a rumor that Finn married Emilia in order to sell her and Luci into prostitution."

"That's why I wanted to talk to you."

Unease skittered across his neck. "So you could tell me what?"

"That it's true . . . the part about Emilia anyway."

Mac narrowed his eyes, his suspicions rising like a porcupine's quills. "You know this how?"

"Because he offered to sell her to me."

Mac shook his head, couldn't stop shaking it. "No. It's not true."

"Mac, I know you want to believe the best about your friend, but the truth is, Finn Collins owed me four hundred dollars. He needed money to restart his ranch after being nearly wiped out this past winter."

Four hundred dollars.

Oh, dear God in heaven, what had Finn done?

She sat down behind her desk, a businesswoman discussing a business transaction. "I agreed to the loan on the understanding that, should he fail to pay me back in . . . in full, I owned his land or could recoup my losses by employing his mail-order bride until the debt was paid."

What had she been about to say? Why in full? Why not monthly installments? Why would she lend Finn money? How did they even know each other? Question upon question swirled inside his head, popping up and disappearing like some carnival game.

He studied her face. "Where's your proof?"

She managed to look both amused and wounded. "In my safety deposit box at the bank of course."

He grabbed onto the chance to get some solid evidence. "So let's go get it."

"Certainly, although not this moment. I have work to do."

Bile filled the back of Mac's throat. He lowered his head and swallowed it down. "Why tell me this now? Why not seven weeks ago, when Mrs. Collins first showed up in town and was making arrangements with her creditors?"

"I'm not heartless, Son."

His chin jerked upward.

There was a softness in her, the very thing that caused him such confusion. How could she discuss recouping losses by selling a woman's body and not being heartless in almost the same breath?

"I figured I'd give the gal some time to get her feet under her before . . ." She cut a glance at the ledger sitting open on her desk.

He looked away. Focused on the painting adorning the wall next to the window. Roses. Pink ones. In a pale blue vase. "Who else have you told about this?"

"No one." She waited for him to return his attention to her. "Not yet."

"Meaning you will if you don't get something in return?"

"That's right."

"You aren't getting Emilia." He'd die before he let that happen.

"Don't be so dramatic, Mac. What I want is far less scandalous to your puritanical way of thinking." She touched the corner of her red-painted lips. "I simply want you to let Hendry run his story. Don't fight it."

"Who told you about Hendry's story?"

Her scoffing laugh grated across his taut nerves. "Did you think a reporter poking around the red-light district and asking pointed questions would go unnoticed?"

"What are you playing at?" Because Madame Lestraude would never do anything without a good reason—a *very* good reason.

"I've said all I'm going to on the matter. Let Hendry print his article."

"And if I don't?"

"Then I'll show him the deed of trust currently stashed safely away from prying eyes as proof that Finn and I conspired to conscript women into prostitution."

It wasn't true. It *couldn't* be true.

But it explained the money—the incriminating, sickening money.

Mac gripped the handles of the guns strapped to each thigh. "You'll be arrested, and this time—"

"I'll pay a fine just like every other time." She rested back against her chair. "But if you fight me on this, I'll say you knew about my arrangement with Finn all along."

"To paint me as a corrupt sheriff?"

"If I have to, yes."

"Even though it's a lie and will ruin every chance I'd have at winning an election bid next year?" Hendry would have a field day with the scandal, regardless of their heretofore genial relationship.

"I'll do whatever it takes to protect myself and my business." She lifted her chin. "Now get out."

Every hope about saving his mother from herself died in that instant. Whatever she'd once been—whatever her letters had portrayed her to be—she cared for no one but herself, and he was done with her. He whirled around and yanked open the office door.

Luci jerked straight, then scrambled to stand up. "I waited right here, Mac. Just like you told me."

The fear in her voice brought him up short. He wasn't angry at her. He wasn't. He was disgusted and didn't know what to do about it. Forcing a breath in and out of his lungs, he leaned down to put his hands under her armpits and lift her into a hug. "Let's go."

She wrapped her arms around his neck, and he shifted his arms to support her weight as he carried her out of the hotel. He set her on Lightning and mounted up behind her. Not wishing to draw any more attention to the situation, he kept his horse at a plodding walk toward The Resale Co. and Emilia.

Emilia Collins.

The woman he loved, the woman who'd struggled valiantly to pay off debts that weren't hers, the woman who—through no fault of her own—would now lose everything because his mother . . .

Shallow breaths shuddered inside his chest. He wouldn't break down. Not here. Not in the middle of the street, where anyone and everyone would see it. He wasn't some little boy who'd suddenly realized his idol had feet of clay. He'd known it for years.

Except not about Finn.

If only Madame Lestraude's explanation hadn't followed the money. Could Finn have been involved in something he'd sworn disgusted him? Had the hard winter changed him beyond recognition? Or had he pretended friendship to keep Mac from suspecting anything?

If the answers were all *yes*, many of the puzzle pieces fit. Too conveniently. Because if Finn had developed a conscience and decided he no longer wanted to put his mail-order bride up as collateral, Madame Lestraude might have had him killed.

I'll do whatever it takes to protect myself and my business.

Mac believed it. He finally believed it.

And the path forward was clear. His mother—and probably his best friend—had gotten Emilia into this mess, so he'd offer the solution. Marriage would keep her and Luci safe, provide guidance for Roch, and make sure Emilia's creditors would continue working with her as the sheriff's wife.

It was four-twenty. He had forty minutes to get to The Resale Co., convince Emilia to marry him, and get back to City Hall before the clerks closed down for the day. The three-day waiting period between requesting and granting a marriage license pushed them to Thursday night. Mac was supposed to leave for Deer Lodge on Thursday afternoon. If he couldn't get one of his men to cover the trip, he could push it back and leave that night, but no later.

He needed to get to Emilia fast. Then, when the dust settled, he'd find answers to the myriad of questions swirling inside his brain. Something was off.

Something was terribly off.

Before entering The Resale Co., Mac asked Luci to let him tell Emilia about the visit to Maison de Joie.

"I'm not in trouble, am I?" Luci's dark brown eyes hadn't lost their fear on the ride over.

Mac patted her shoulder. "You're not in trouble. I promise."

He opened the door, letting Luci enter first. He was about to propose marriage, and he had no idea if Emilia would say yes despite the way they'd spoken of their love for each other a few hours earlier. What if she got it in her head that he was trying to fix things for her? He wasn't. He wanted to marry her because he *loved* her. This rumor and his mother's proof only sped up the timetable of his proposal. Surely she'd understand.

"Emme? Are you here?" Luci called.

"There you are." Emilia appeared from around a stack of luggage crates, a feather duster in one hand. She smiled at Mac, and thoughts of her lips on his rooted his feet to the floor. A question flitted through her eyes before she dropped her gaze to Luci. "Did you have a nice day at school?"

"It was fine, I guess."

Mac checked his watch. Four thirty-three. He touched Emilia's arm. "I—uh—need to talk to you. In private. Again."

Her eyebrows pinched together, creating a crease between them. "Luci, do you mind asking Mr. Gunderson if we can borrow his office for a moment?"

Luci bobbed her head and ran a couple of steps toward the back of the store before swinging around. "I didn't mean to do anything wrong. Honest." She looked at Mac, then at her sister, and then raced off.

"That sounds ominous." Emilia followed her sister's progress until she disappeared into Isaak's office. "Would you like to tell me what that's about?"

"In a minute." Mac pulled the hat from his head and gripped it with both hands.

Emilia set the feather duster on a nearby shelf. "Did she get in trouble with a teacher?"

"No."

"Another student?"

"In a minute, Em."

She crossed her arms over her chest and glared at him. "Mac?"

The clatter of footsteps announced Luci's return, slower thuds indicating Isaak Gunderson followed at a more sedate pace.

Mac transferred his hat to his left hand and took hold of Emilia's elbow with his right hand. "Let's go."

After exchanging pleasantries with Isaak—and a look that he hopefully interpreted as *we need to talk later*—Mac ushered Emilia into the private office and shut the door. "Have a seat."

She settled into one of the ladder-back chairs, and Mac drew the other one close before sitting down opposite her. He tossed his hat on Isaak's desk, leaned forward, and extended his hands toward her with his palms up. What he wouldn't give to be back at Mrs. Hollenbeck's house with Emilia dancing in his arms. Or out at the ranch sharing their hearts. He wanted to shelter and protect her with his body and soul, not bring her pain.

Once she placed her hands in his, he closed his fingers around hers. "We need to get married."

"What?" Emilia shook her head, as if she was trying to clear her thoughts. "I thought this was about Luci, not us."

"It is." Mac squeezed her hands gently. "We don't have a lot of time for me to explain, so you need to trust me on this. We need to get to City Hall to file for a marriage license before the offices close in"—he checked the wall clock—"twenty-six minutes."

"I don't care how much time it takes because it sounds to

me like you've come up against a problem you think I can't solve by myself and want to fix things again."

Yes, except this time there wasn't any other way.

"My mother took Luci inside the Maison de Joie."

Her brows rose. "Inside? You're saying Luci walked into a brothel with a complete stranger? Or did she know it was your mother?"

"I don't know. I didn't ask"—he clarified when she opened her mouth again—"but that's not the problem."

"Of course it's a problem." Emilia scowled at him. "Luci agreed to avoid the red-light district and to wait inside your office if you weren't there."

"You're missing the point."

"How long was Luci inside the brothel?"

"Again, not the point." And at this rate he was never going to get to it.

"How long?" Her voice pitched higher.

He huffed. "About three or four minutes, but I was inside with her for all but maybe fifteen seconds of that." He checked the wall clock. Twenty-five minutes, twenty-one seconds left.

"Why didn't you say so in the first place?" She pulled one hand away and tucked a strand of hair behind her ear. "Honestly, Mac. If you were with Luci the whole time, why is this an issue?" She stared at him, finally done questioning every word he said. Waiting. Watching. Expectant.

He'd been trying to get to this explanation since walking into the store, and suddenly he wanted to avoid it. Run the other way. Go back to a time when Finn was alive and none of the accusations leveled against him held merit. But this was no time for cowardice. Now was the time for truth.

Mac captured her hand again, heaving a deep breath in and then out of his lungs. "Remember how I said I wanted to track down actual proof about Finn in connection with Hendry's rumor?"

"The one about selling me and Luci into prostitution?"

"Yes. My mother says she has a deed of trust signed by Finn for four hundred dollars. She said she loaned the money to him under the agreement that, if he was unable to pay it back, he either forfeited his land or agreed to let her take payment out of you. Not Luci, just you."

She tried to pull her hands away, but he held tight.

"Let go of me."

He did.

Emilia folded her arms across her chest. "Did you see this so-called deed of trust?"

"No, but—"

"Then how can you possibly believe such *slander*?" Her contempt wasn't because he'd failed his due diligence as a sheriff; it was because he'd failed as Finn's friend.

Did she think he wanted this? How could she have known him this long—listened to him talk about how much he loved his friend, how much he loved the law—to think he'd treat either carelessly? "And when I do see it? What will you say then?"

She didn't respond for a long moment. "Then it's a forgery. Finn never would have agreed to . . . *that*."

Seeing her chin tremble cut Mac to the heart. "I don't want to believe it either, but—"

"But what?"

Mac touched her cheek. "Trust me, Em. I'll get to the bottom of this. I loved Finn, too, and I won't rest until I know exactly what he was into and what got him killed." He checked the wall clock again. Twenty-four minutes until City Hall closed its doors. "But it doesn't fix our immediate problem."

"Our problem?" She shook her head again. "It's not *your* problem."

"Of course it is." He pushed back the chair and kneeled before her. "Marry me. I know it's fast, and I know it isn't under ideal circumstances, but trust me, it's the best plan."

The best plan? Walt Whitman would hang his head in shame if he knew that all the hours Mac had spent reading poetry resulted in such a lame proposal. If he'd had time, he could have composed something—stolen a poet's words, if need be—to explain how her smile transfixed him, dreaming of her kiss made his lips tingle, her nearness was pleasure and pain.

If he'd had time, he could have done it up right, but they didn't have time.

"Hendry will print the article on Saturday. I'll be out of town on sheriff's business. We need to be married by then so I can protect you from whatever backlash the scandal generates."

Her eyes narrowed. "What do you mean by *backlash*? And don't give me the short version. Use full sentences." She pointed at him. "The whole explanation."

Why couldn't she trust him? For once, just put her hand in his and say, *I know you'll do what's best.* Was that too much to ask when he was kneeling before her, a man in love who also happened to be a sheriff wanting to protect her?

Mac pulled himself together. Right now she wanted the sheriff instead of the man, so that's what he'd give her. "A lot of people saw my mother walk Luci into her hotel. I'd like to think they won't fault a twelve-year-old girl for that, but I can't be sure. And, if I can't find something solid to refute Hendry's story, once his article goes to press, there's no telling how people around Helena will react. Some may see you and Luci as victims, others may decide you're tainted with the same brush as Finn, and those who saw

Luci enter my mother's brothel might start whispering. You may lose your jobs." Mac took her hand in his once more, braving rejection for the second time. "If you and I marry, it will at least protect your reputation. Whether we believe Finn is innocent or not, I don't want to see you lose the ranch. If we leave in the next two minutes, we can get to City Hall, register for a marriage license, and get married before I have to leave town on Thursday."

"I can't."

His stomach hardened with dread. "You can't believe Finn would do this or you can't marry me?" *Please let it be the first. Please, God, let it be the first.*

"I can't marry you."

Mac slumped, his heels digging into his backside. "I don't see that you have much choice."

Chapter Nineteen

Emilia knew her mouth was gaping in a most unbecoming manner but—good heavens—he was making a proverbial mountain out of a molehill. Of at least one molehill. The deed of trust, if authentic, was indeed a problem, but not one she couldn't manage. Every problem had a solution. Given time and more than a few prayers, she'd think of one.

"No choice?" she repeated. "I won't be forced into marrying anyone. Even you." If he told her to trust him one more time, she'd scream.

Mac's palm cupped her elbow. "I love you. Let me help with this. Marry me, please. If we leave now—"

"No." She slid out of the chair and moved to the other side of Mr. Gunderson's desk to put needed space between them. She couldn't think with him clinging to her as if she was his anchor. He shot to his feet. She followed his tense gaze to the wall clock, knowing exactly what he was thinking. If they raced on horseback, they could make it to City Hall before it closed. If they left now. If they had a horse.

If . . .

She turned to him. His gaze was serious, his posture stiff. "Stop and think." Realizing she had done this dramatic motion with her hands, she lowered them. "Most people in town know Madame Lestraude is your mother. No reasonable person will think she had nefarious intentions regarding Luci. No reasonable person will think Luci's reputation is forever damaged because she was inside a brothel for all of three minutes. You even admitted you were there for most of that time."

"You don't know how things are here." Mac crossed his arms. "Finn's creditors won't be so forgiving."

"Why do you assume the worst of people?"

His eyes narrowed. "If I'm right—"

"Then I'll figure out a solution."

"I've already figured out one," he insisted. "Marry me!"

"No!" she bellowed back, unable to contain her own frustration. "I'm sick of you trying to solve things for me. Your own prejudice and panic has you—you—" She growled under her breath. She thought he'd changed, thought he'd learned it wasn't his place to interfere in other people's lives.

Emilia rubbed at the tension between her brows. Ten minutes ago she'd been dusting and dreaming of marrying Mac. Now he'd proposed and she'd refused. Why? Wasn't this precisely what she'd wanted from the first moment he'd professed his love? If they hadn't wasted who knows how long, in no rush to return to Helena, they would have been back in time for Mac to have been in his office when Luci arrived to see him.

Emilia felt sick.

This was her fault. Hers. For not being mindful of the time of day. For putting her own desire to spend time with Mac ahead of caring for her sister. Not again. She couldn't permit that to happen again.

She looked to him. "If that deed of trust is authentic—and I don't believe it is—then I'll find a way to retire the debt to Madame Lestraude." It might take months, even years, but she would do it.

His brow furrowed. "You're underestimating the power of Hendry's article."

"That's possible," she admitted. She didn't know enough people in Helena to fairly gauge how the rumor about Finn would be received. "But I choose to believe in the goodness of people, in their ability to think reasonably, in the logic of judging a man by his proven actions and not on the salacious hearsay of others."

"I have to leave town on Thursday." He grabbed his hat off Mr. Gunderson's desk. "I won't be here when the article appears."

"Can't one of your deputies cover for you?"

"I'm the sheriff."

Which was exactly why he could do the heroic thing and task someone else with the job. If he wanted to. Clearly he didn't. He cared more about his job than standing up for her. For Luci. For Finn.

"Well," she said slowly, "are you at least going to give Hendry a comment for the article before you"—*flee*—"go?"

"There's nothing to say."

Emilia stared at him, her mouth gaping *again* in an unladylike manner. Who was this callous man she'd fallen in love with? "You could at least defend your friend," she cried out. "Finn would have. He would have risked his life, his reputation, for someone he loved."

Mac slid his hat on his head and stepped to the door. "I hope you're right about people."

"Me, too, but . . ." She paused until he looked at her over his shoulder. "I'm beginning to believe I'm not as good a judge of people as I thought I was."

Mac stormed out of The Resale Co., mounted Lightning, and touched his spurs to the gray's flanks. The massive horse gave a snort and leaped into a full gallop. One benefit of working for the sheriff's office for the last six years was that people assumed he was on his way to an emergency when he raced through town at reckless speeds.

Did wanting to barricade himself in his office qualify?

You could at least defend your friend.

What more did she want? Fabricated evidence? Lies?

Although he sometimes exaggerated his authority to encourage compliance, Mac wasn't corrupt. He didn't bribe witnesses, hide facts that didn't fit his theory of a case, or let the guilty go free in exchange for favors. Guilt was guilt and innocence was innocence. That was how a lawman built trust in his community.

So why didn't Emilia trust him?

He leaned lower in the saddle, encouraging Lightning to gallop faster the moment they turned onto West Main Street.

After she'd shared her hopes and fears over lunch this past week, after telling him she loved him, why hadn't she believed in him enough to say yes? Was it more of her nonsense about being indebted to anyone who ever wanted to do something nice for her? He'd thought she was past that.

Finn would have risked his life, his reputation, for someone he loved.

No words could wound more. Mac hadn't given up, not for two full months. He'd followed leads, kept his undersheriff working the case when he was out of town, worked his contacts. In short, he'd done everything he could to clear his friend—the one he'd known for six and a half years, not ten months through letters. Why couldn't she see that? Did she think he *wanted* to believe his best friend would agree to let a madam take payment out of his bride, or that his mother was so callous she'd take four hundred dollars out of a respectable woman against her will?

Mac pulled Lightning to a stop, his hands gentle on the reins to keep his rioting emotions from causing the horse pain. After looping the reins over the hitching rail, Mac raced into City Hall, not bothering to return Mr. Dunfree's greeting.

O'Mara and Alderson were just about to lock up when Mac ran in. "My office, both of you."

The deputies followed. Mac filled them in on everything he knew and suspected about Finn's case before three this afternoon, then told them about the deed of trust and Hendry's article.

O'Mara took a pencil and small notebook out of his vest pocket. "What do you need from us, boss?"

"Keenan and I were testing out a theory that Finn was smuggling girls out of prostitution instead of in to it. We were trying to be discreet, but we're past that now. Starting tomorrow, you two are going to hit the streets and check every contact, follow every lead, and turn over every rock to see what you find."

Alderson bobbed his head. "What are you going to do?"

"Same thing, only I'm starting tonight." Work was the only thing that would keep Emilia's rejection from playing over and over in his head.

O'Mara and Alderson looked at each other before facing Mac. "Then so are we."

From Monday night until Thursday morning, Mac and his deputies worked the red-light district in between their other duties, Keenan joining in when he returned from Augusta on Wednesday afternoon. Even though they came up empty, no one—*no one*—could say they hadn't done everything possible to clear Finn's name. Mac checked the clock hanging above the door leading into the hall. He had an hour before his appointment with Joseph Hendry.

Should he stop by The Resale Co. and tell Emilia everything he'd done to restore Finn's name? Would it matter? Mac pinched the bridge of his nose. He'd failed. The article was going to press. And she didn't want his help even if there was something more he could do—something other than marry her.

After thanking his men for all their hard work, Mac headed home, packed a bag with enough supplies for a week just in case the trial in Marysville stretched long, and then headed to the offices of the *Daily Independent*.

Hendry greeted him with a handshake, then ushered him into a small office more cluttered than Hale's. "Sorry about the mess."

Mac squeezed past Hendry into the corner. "Promotion?"

"No. It's a community office we all use, mostly for storage. I just thought we might need some privacy. I know"—Hendry held up a hand—"ironic, all things considered."

"That's one word for it." After all, the man was about to run a shocking article that would drag Emilia's name into homes all across Montana Territory.

With a sheepish grin, Hendry shut the door, muffling the sound of clattering typewriters, a ringing telephone, and clamoring male voices. "My sources say you've been making quite a ruckus in the red-light district, asking if Finn Collins was smuggling girls *out* of prostitution."

Mac tossed his hat on top of the cluttered desk, then rested his right hand on his gun handle. "It was a theory. Didn't pan out."

"I could have told you that." Hendry sat on the edge of the desk and crossed his arms. "I was following the same theory before Finn's murder but could never substantiate it."

"Meaning no offense, but I like to track down my own leads."

Hendry smiled. "No offense taken. In fact, it's why I respect you so much." The reporter used his affability like a weapon, getting people to wag their tongues when they'd have done better to keep quiet.

Mac wasn't falling for it. He tapped his index finger on the gun handle. "You said we needed privacy. Why?"

Smile fading, Hendry pressed the heels of his hands against the desk's edge. "Um . . . here's the thing. I knew, of course, that Mrs. Collins was married by proxy, but . . ." His cheeks stained pink. "I didn't know it was Miss Palmer. I just assumed it was one of the ladies from the district."

So he *was* moon-eyed over Yancey. And the thought of making her a public spectacle was discomforting.

Good. Served him right.

Hendry rubbed the back of his neck. "I'm aware of how hypocritical this is—especially considering your affection for Mrs. Collins and how I'm refusing to back down—but I'd like to keep Miss Palmer's name out of the story."

Mac's jaw loosened. Was he supposed to congratulate the man for being aware? Forgive him because he acknowledged the hypocrisy? And since when did Hendry ask for permission about anything he printed? "The proxy's a matter of public record."

"I know, but people don't check these things. Facts are what the newspaper tells them they are." Hendry had the grace to look chagrined. "Look, I'm asking because I know how unfair this is. You and I have a working relationship based on mutual respect. I don't want to damage that. The thing is, I can't tell the story of Finn's treachery without it touching Mrs. Collins. I *can* without pointing at Miss Palmer. I believe both women are completely innocent, and I promise I'll make that clear in the article."

The logic was sound, although that didn't soften the sting of unfairness. Mac inhaled, taking time to let air fill his lungs before exhaling through pursed lips. "Implicating Yancey serves no purpose."

Hendry closed his eyes for a moment, his posture wilting. "I appreciate this."

Mac pointed a finger at the reporter. "But next time you decide to write a story involving innocents, I hope you'll remember this moment and how you wanted to protect someone you care about from being named in one of your articles."

"I will." Hendry's cheeks went pink again. The sporting thing to do was warn him that Yancey Palmer would never give him a second look because she was so set on Hale Adams.

But Mac had already done the reporter one favor. "Was that all?"

Hendry nodded. "Unless you have a quote for me."

Mac dug his prewritten statement from his coat pocket.

Hendry took the paper and read aloud, "'The investigation into Finn Collins's death is ongoing. Given the time constraints, the county sheriff's office didn't have time to conduct a thorough investigation to confirm or deny these allegations before the story went to press, nor could they confirm or deny whether these allegations played into Mr. Collins's death.'" Hendry gave Mac a look of disgust. "This is boring."

Mac grabbed his hat off the desk. "Glad you like it."

Chapter Twenty

Saturday, May 28

Emilia knelt, broom in one hand, dustpan in the other. She glared at the mound of dirt. When she'd walked inside The Resale Co. this morning, the floor hadn't looked dusty. But in the past two days she'd spent at Mr. Inger's boot shop and cleaning Dr. Abernathy's office, a thin layer of dirt had built up on everything. From the chandeliers and baskets overhead to the pine-planked floor. Worst thing was, no matter how much cleaning she did today, by Monday, the grime would be back. When she returned to the cabin, dust would cover everything there, too.

Her life had come down to cleaning up messes.

One pile at a time.

"Someone has to do it," she muttered before sweeping the pile onto the dustpan. She stood and, at the sound of laughter, looked to the propped-open door. Customers?

Two ladies in elegant walking suits strolled in front of the window. Their behavior—glance inside, huddle close, hurry past—no different than that of other townsfolk who'd walked by without stopping on this cloudy morning.

"Don't mind them."

Emilia turned to her left. Mr. Gunderson stood there, tie askew, suit coat missing, sleeves of his white shirt rolled up. In his hands, the dainty teacups and saucers looked like they were from a child's teaset. He offered her one per his usual midmorning habit when she worked at The Resale Co. According to him, tea was best when enjoyed with a friend.

She set the dustpan on the floor, rested the broom against the counter, and then took the saucer. "Thank you."

He grinned. "My pleasure."

She sipped the Darjeeling tea, prepared the way Mr. Gunderson preferred it. No milk. Lots of sugar. Sweet musky spiciness to delight in. For a man Isaak Gunderson's size, one would think he, like his brother, was a coffee drinker. Or, at the bare minimum, would drink tea out of a hearty clay mug. Not so. He preferred china. White bone. A silver band around the edge. Decorated with tiny flowers.

"The first day I worked here," she said, glancing at the door, "there was a line outside the store. Today not one person has stepped foot over the threshold."

"Not uncommon for a Saturday."

Emilia looked to him and blinked. "One hundred and eight people have walked past, but keep in mind, I didn't start counting until the second hour of work."

The expression on his face indicated he wasn't impressed with her mathematical skills. "It isn't because of you." Said in his usual dry tone.

Emilia raised her brows.

He mimicked her action and then sipped his tea.

Emilia sipped hers.

Thanks to Mr. Hendry's article, the word was out that Madame Lestraude had paid Finn four hundred dollars to conscript Emilia and Luci into prostitution . . . and that the madam had recently attempted to recover her losses with Luci, though her actions had been thwarted by the county sheriff. By Mac. By her son. In case the madam's quotes weren't enough proof, the article included a picture of the deed of trust. When Finn had signed it, he'd agreed to begin making payments within three months. Three months had been Emilia's original arrival date. It had to be coincidental. Finn wouldn't have worked for a madam.

It wasn't his character. It didn't fit his values.

That he'd taken out a loan from her, Emilia agreed. The money had to have come from somewhere. Where was Finn's copy of the deed—the one that didn't include the terms of selling her and Luci into prostitution if he couldn't make payment?

Someone was lying, and she'd stake her life that it wasn't Finn.

"The lack of customers is because of Mr. Hendry's article," she said to break the silence. "Don't say it isn't."

Mr. Gunderson paused, clearly debating his response. "Once the shock is over, everything will go back to normal. The *Independent* publishes stories like this all the time."

"Helena has had more than one deceased rancher swindling women into prostitution?"

He grinned. "Epidemic proportions."

Emilia wanted to smile. She wanted to laugh and not feel as if weight upon weight was being laid on her shoulders, but her mood matched the melancholy sky. So she lifted her cup to her lips, pausing before drinking to say, "And if life doesn't return to normal?"

"You could marry me."

Emilia spit the tea onto his shirt. "I'm sorry." She patted her mouth dry. "I don't know why I . . . That was . . . uh . . . I'm so sorry."

He blinked a few times, looking down at the spatters on his abdomen and then at her. "I have now reached the ranks of Windsor Buchanan. He will be impressed."

"I'm so sorry," she repeated again. Emilia looked around, mortified. What type of woman spits on a man? Mr. Buchanan must have done something to deserve it. Or the woman's spitting had been accidental, like now. Finding nothing to dry Mr. Gunderson's shirt, she set her cup and saucer on the counter and untied the apron over her gray work dress. "Trade?"

He exchanged his cup and saucer for the apron. He patted his abdomen.

"I'll wash it for you," she offered and hastily added, "Your shirt."

"No need."

"I appreciate your attempt to ease my doldrums."

He looked up. Frowned. "My proposal was not meant in jest."

"Dear God, why?" tumbled from her lips before she could stop it.

He neatly folded her apron and offered it back. "Would you be more convinced my intentions are sincere if I got down on one knee?"

Emilia stared at him. He looked sincere. He sounded sincere, too. But so had Mac. Both men genuinely cared about her and about the ruination of her reputation. Because they knew their names could be her shield. She'd married Finn for similar reasons. A shield against the grinding poverty and stench of Chicago rather than her tattered last name.

"I appreciate your offer." She looked to the door. A wagon rolled past. She turned and took back her apron. "It is unfair of people to think less of me for something I didn't do, or to think less of Luci for stepping inside a brothel."

"I agree." The phone rang and he stepped to the counter to answer it. "The Resale Company. How may I—" Pause. "She's here instead of out at the ranch. Luci's spending the day over at the Truetts' house." Pause. "I've read it." Pause. "Jakob, don't—" He growled. "Then grab some for four people and head over." Pause. "That's fine." He rested the headset in the cradle, then said to Emilia, "Jakob and Roch are back from Fort Missoula. They're bringing lunch."

Emilia waited a moment, then said, "All right," because, literally, no other words came to mind.

"If marriage isn't an option for you . . ." Isaak cleared his throat. "My father and I would like to offer you a full-time position. Monday through Friday, a dollar fifty a day, plus an extra fifty cents on Saturday."

"Is this because you think Finn's creditors will refuse to continue to work with me?"

"The decision to offer you the job was made the day before Luanne and Roy's wedding."

"Why didn't you offer it back then?"

"Mac."

Emilia gasped. "He asked you not to?" She wouldn't put it past Mac and his belief that he knew what was best for everyone.

Mr. Gunderson shook his head. "I chose not to say anything because I didn't want to interfere with what was happening between the two of you." Something in her expression must have prompted him to add, "Doc Abernathy likes to gossip. He's had a pool going for weeks now on who and when you'll marry."

Emilia drew back in surprise. "Doctor Abernathy is one of the kindest souls in town."

"He's also a sporting man."

People placed wagers on *when* and *who* someone married? What was next? Betting on when people died?

She hesitated then asked, "Have you ever placed—"

"No." Mr. Gunderson reclaimed his saucer and teacup. "You could start working here full-time after you've sowed the alfalfa. Think about it."

As he sipped his tea, Emilia picked up the dustpan and emptied it in the trash basket beside the counter. She had one day left of work at Mr. Inger's boot shop and Dr. Abernathy's, and five days left at The Resale Co. If she worked here full-time, and at greater pay, she could pay down Finn's debts to Mr. Cannon and Mr. Hess in half the time. With Da not being able to leave Chicago until the end of July instead of the beginning as planned, accepting Mr. Gunderson's offer was the most practical decision.

"I see the merit in your offer," she admitted, "but in good conscience, I could only do this if Misters Cannon and Hess agreed to renegotiate our contracts."

"You go talk to them." He collected her cup and saucer. "I'll go home and change shirts. By the time we return, Jakob and Roch will be here with lunch."

As Emilia neared Cannon's General Store, branches of lightning brightened the sky. *One. Two*—A long, low rumble of thunder cut off her counting. Suddenly dozens of rain droplets hit her. She dashed to take cover under the shop's tin awning, silently praying for Mr. Cannon to be more amiable than Mr. Hess had been. The blacksmith's response—"The next time I see you, I want my money!"—continued to ring in her ears. Emilia caught her breath. She wiped her face and smoothed back the wet hair. First the article, then Mr. Hess's yelling, and now she looked like a drowned rat.

With a weary sigh, she pushed open the door. The bells on it jingled.

A trio of ladies turned from the bolts of cloth. Their eyes widened. The tallest of the three swiveled around, grabbing the other two's arms, huddling them together. Because of her sodden appearance? More likely because they knew she was Finn Collins's widow, the woman he'd all but sold into service to Madame Lestraude.

"Oh, Mrs. Collins. So good to see you again." Mr. Cannon set a box on the service counter. His smile looked kind. "Can I help you find something?"

Emilia walked to him and spoke softly to keep their conversation as private as possible. "I'd like to renegotiate our contract." She withdrew her journal from her haversack and turned to their original contract page, where she'd written notes before leaving The Resale Co. "Of the one hundred and ten dollars and sixty-two cents my husband owed you, I've paid down four dollars and sixty-five cents by bartering eggs. Our current contract accounts for twenty-two weeks of work at five dollars a week, rendering the debt paid by mid-November."

She glanced up to see he was nodding.

"Mr. Gunderson has offered me full-time employment." She pointed to the new figures. "Accounting for the increase in pay, I can retire the debt in mid-September, eight weeks sooner than we originally agreed. Would this revised plan be acceptable to—"

The door slammed open, bells banging against the wood. "You don't have a lick of sense, do you?" Roch yelled. "Why did you turn down Mr. Gunderson's proposal?"

The trio of ladies gasped.

Emilia swung around to see her red-faced, water-drenched brother leaving muddy footprints across the floor. She'd never seen him this angry. "Roch, can we, uh, talk about this at another time?"

He stopped in front of her and jerked off his hat, giving it a good shake to rid it of the water. Right into her face. "I understood why you refused those first eight men who proposed 'cause they only wanted you for the ranch . . ."

She took the kerchief Mr. Cannon offered.

". . . but then you refused Mac's proposal." He looked heavenward and groaned. "Why, Emilia? He's the best you'd ever hope to marry. If that wasn't bad enough, you said no to Isaak Gunderson, too, because you'd rather work for him than be his wife. Why?" he yelled, leaning close. "He could have paid off that stupid mortgage your stupid husband made with that stupid madam. What's wrong with you?"

Emilia nervously glanced about. This was neither the time nor place for this discussion. Their audience had tripled. Where had the customers been hiding when she walked in?

"Calm down." She touched his arm, but he jerked back.

"I promised Da I'd protect you and Luci." He pointed his hat at her. "I'm done helping you. I'm done letting you pull me into another mess. I'm done with you. As soon as Luci can pack, we're going home to Da. Have fun paying Finn's debt to the madam." He slapped his hat on his head and followed his muddy footprints. He opened, then slammed the door.

Silence.

Emilia neatly folded the damp handkerchief. She laid it on the counter, then reclaimed her journal. "Mr. Cannon, if it's all right with you, could we resume the negotiations on Monday?"

His brow furrowed, and then he nodded.

Chin held high, Emilia walked out of the general store and into the pelting rain. Her life couldn't possibly get worse.

Circle C Ranch
Wednesday, June 1

Emilia held her apron over her nose as she tossed the remnants from dinner into the slop bucket. Mama sow snorted twice. "You're welcome," Emilia responded and instantly regretted opening her mouth. She gagged tasting the air. She hooked the bucket onto the pen. Why did Finn buy a pig? And a pregnant one at that? Any day now they'd have piglets. No matter how cute, they stank. Even Needles had enough sense to stay away from the pig pen.

Leaving the sow to eat, Emilia walked around the barn. Roch and Jakob were tying their horses to the hitching post. Needles barked and bounced up and down on the porch in utter delight.

"Evening," Jakob said as Emilia approached.

"Evening. I can't tell which one of you wears more dirt." She looked to Roch. "Did you eat?"

Roch continued on into the cabin without a glance in her direction.

"I fed him." Jakob rested his shoulder against the porch post, giving her a look of concern. "I thought his anger would cool after he had time to think. Since Saturday all he's talked about has been leaving. Today—nothing. Not one peep."

"Luci hasn't spoken either." Emilia wrapped her arm around the other post, then rested her head against the rough wood. "Something happened at school today. Luci went straight to your brother's office without saying a word to me."

One of his brows lifted. "Did she talk to Isaak?"

She shook her head. "Mrs. Truett came by just before he locked up for the day. She was in tears, kept apologizing."

"For what?"

"That's just it." She shrugged. "I'm not sure. From the little bit I could understand, Mrs. Truett said it was best Melrose and Luci had some time apart."

Jakob nodded, then looked to the cabin door. "Think Luci will talk to me about it?"

Emilia sighed. "You're welcome to try. None of my siblings want anything to do with me."

Jakob stretched his hand out to her, in obvious expectation she would grip it. Emilia hesitated. She was grateful to him for all he'd done for her family. If she could have an older brother, she'd want it to be him. And his brother.

Were it not for the Gunderson twins bookending her on the pew, she would have walked out of church last Sunday, after those sanctimonious glares from the Watson family and the cold shoulder from half the congregation, including the mayor and his wife, who had no logical reason to attend. There was no charity event to support and they were members of another church. The Gundersons, the Palmers—save for Yancey, who was feeling under the weather—the Truetts, Mrs. Hollenbeck, Miss Pope, and Reverend and Mrs. Neven were the only ones who'd welcomed them to the service. She supposed she could add Mr. Gunderson's friend, Mr. Buchanan. The bladesmith hadn't spoken a word to her prior to the publication of the article, so she couldn't count his lack of conversation now as shunning.

Emilia gave Jakob a weak smile, then gripped his hand.

He walked with her into the cabin. Roch was up in the loft, whispering to Luci.

"Would you two come down for a minute?" Jakob asked.

The whispering stopped.

Roch looked over the edge. His gaze shifted to where Jakob held Emilia's hand. "Sure," he muttered. "But first Luci and I have something to say."

Jakob gave Emilia's hand a squeeze. She broke free and, while Roch and Luci climbed down the ladder, dragged the rocker in from off the porch. Emilia sat. Jakob pulled out the chair from the table, turned it around, and sat, resting his arms on the backrest. He looked at them expectantly.

Roch leaned close to Luci. "You need to show them."

Her eyes welled with tears. Chin trembled. She turned around, unbuttoned her dress, and lowered the back to expose her chemise. Emilia dashed to her. Four bruises showed through the thin fabric.

"Who did this?" she demanded.

Luci pulled her dress up. "Some older kids."

"She's been bullied all week"—Roch glared at Emilia—"because of you."

"Me?"

"They hit Melrose, too," Luci whispered.

"Why didn't you tell a teacher? Or—or Mr. Tate?" Emilia yelled, her heart pounding against her chest. She was angry, beastly angry. "He's the principal. He should know about things like this happening in his school. He needs to punish the ones who—"

"Emilia, calm down."

She glared at Jakob. This wasn't the time to be calm.

His gaze shifted to Luci, and Emilia turned to see tears streaming down Luci's face.

"Oh, Luce." Emilia hugged her sister. "I'm so sorry. Shh. We'll find out who did this. It'll be all right."

"All right?" Roch roared. "Emilia, are you out of your mind? It's not going to be *all right* as long as we stay here."

Emilia pulled back from Luci. "This is our home now."

"Your home!"

"Fine, mine. I don't want to leave. Luci doesn't want to—"

"Oh, she does," he argued.

She looked at Luci. "Do you?"

Her lips pursed, tightened, shifted. "I want to go home."

"Why?" When Luci didn't respond, Emilia whispered, "It's something else, isn't it? What happened in the brothel?" *Nothing, please say nothing.* "Did Madame Lestraude hurt you?"

Luci stared at the floor. Her head shook. "She saved me."

Emilia turned to Roch, who didn't appear to know any more about what their sister was talking about. Neither did Jakob. He looked confused. Stupefied.

"What do you mean, she *saved* you?" she asked Luci.

Luci gripped the sides of her dress, her gaze still on the floor. "I went to see Mac like I always do, but Mr. Dunfree told me he wasn't there." She cleared her throat. "I just thought—I didn't know—" She twisted her dress. "He was always nice to me whenever I went to see Mac."

Dunfree? The city clerk?

"He said God blessed me with such pretty hair and that it was too lovely to wear in braids. He grabbed one. I couldn't move . . ."

Jakob stood so abruptly the chair tipped over.

". . . but then Madame Lestraude was there," Luci continued, although her voice had weakened. "She—she said he'd better get his sick, da—um, his hands off me or she'd cut—" Luci looked up. "She said lots of bad words. Do I have to repeat them?"

"No," Jakob said in a hoarse voice.

Emilia couldn't speak. Shock—dread—*horror* had ripped all words from her throat. Who—? *Why* hadn't Madame Lestraude said anything? Mac would have understood—no, he would have been grateful she'd come to Luci's rescue before . . . before . . . Good heavens, she couldn't imagine. She didn't *want* to imagine what could have happened to her sister if Mac's mother hadn't gone to City Hall to talk to him.

Emilia studied Jakob, who had yet to speak. He looked torn between heartbreak and rage. "We need to report this to—"

Roch jerked on Emilia's arm. "We're not reporting this to anyone."

"Yes, we are," she shot back. "It's the right thing to do."

"That reporter will hear all about it." Roch's grip tightened on her arm. "Do you want this in the paper, too? Do you want people thinking even worse of Luci?"

"She did nothing wrong!"

Roch shook his head in disgust. "You are so naïve." He released her arm, then hugged Luci. "Don't cry, Luce. I promise I'll keep you safe."

Emilia looked to Jakob and Roch and back again. "Tell him we have to report this."

Jakob stood there, frozen.

"I want Da," came Luci's whispered voice.

Tears pooled in Emilia's eyes. She didn't know what to say. She didn't. They couldn't leave. Finn's debts had to be paid. One dollar here. Ten dollars there. One hundred dollars to Cannon. Then there was the deed of trust Madame Lestraude bandied about, as if it were Holy Scripture giving her ownership of them. How could the woman rescue Luci in one breath and claim she'd *paid* Finn for Luci and Emilia in another? It made no sense.

Jakob broke the silence. "Roch's right. You three should leave Helena."

Emilia could only stare at him.

"I have a plan."

She jerked her gaze to her brother. "*You* have a plan?"

"Mac gave me the train tickets he'd bought."

"When?"

"That first night we were here," he answered, and she could hear a maturity in his voice. "Luci and I are leaving tomorrow morning. Emme, you can come with us or you can stay. I don't care. But we're leaving. If you want to come along, we're doing it *my* way."

Chapter Twenty-One

City Hall
The next morning

The city marshal closed his office door. "Dunfree has yet to make it in this morning," he said, walking to his desk. "Miss Stanek, it would be more helpful if he was here and we could confirm he was the one who"—he sat and cleared his throat—"er, offered you the candy."

Luci shifted in her chair. "I'm all right with not seeing him again."

"He's lucky he's not here," Roch put in. "If I see him, I'll kill him."

"And I might just help," Emilia added. With a deep breath, she gripped her haversack close to her chest. "Is there anything else we need to do? Maybe ask Madame Lestraude to confirm Luci's account of the incident?"

The city marshal shook his head. "No, ma'am. I'll bring her in for questioning."

Emilia stood and he jumped to his feet. She shook his hand. "Thank you, sir, for listening. Has Sheriff McCall returned from Marysville?"

"O'Mara said he'd be here on the morning train." He

walked with them to the door. "Let me know if Dunfree bothers you again."

Emilia thanked him. "I'm positive he won't." Unless the creepy clerk followed them to Chicago.

As they left his office, she noticed Luci looking toward Mac's office. No one spoke as they climbed back into the cart and drove up Jackson toward Mr. Adams's office. Off over the mountains, gray clouds hovered. Rain? Emilia hoped not. At least not until they were safely on the train. She pulled the cart into the alley between the law office and the three-story building still under construction. Roch jumped out first. As he tied the horse to the hitching post, she helped Luci gather their belongings. Sans Needles. Thankfully, Jakob had agreed to take her.

Roch opened the door for them.

"Hello," Emilia called out. "Mr. Adams?"

She peeked into his office. As he listened to whoever was on the other end of the telephone, he waved them forward, then pointed to the two Windsor armchairs in front of his desk. Unlike the last time they were here, both chairs were available for seating. Luci took one. Emilia the other. Roch stood behind Luci's chair.

Mr. Adams hung up the phone. "It's a pleasure to see the Stanek family. To what do I owe this honor?"

Emilia shifted in the chair. "I would like to retain your services, but the most I can pay is two dollars."

"What do you need?"

"A typed contract. Six copies. And I would need you to handle the disbursement of items."

His head dipped. He looked over the rims of his glasses. "Disbursement of items?"

"Yes, sir. For the best interests of my family, I've decided to sell the ranch and return to Chicago."

"I see." His tone was flat, conveying none of his thoughts.

Oh what she'd give to know what he was thinking. That she was a coward for fleeing Helena? Perhaps. She could stay. Roch had been clear about his feelings on that matter. As much as she loved the ranch—all right, love was perhaps too strong a word. The pig she could do without. She wasn't too keen on culling chickens or cleaning the stable. Save for those things and the lack of a tub in which to bathe, life on the ranch had been good. Better than good on those mornings when she'd sat on the porch and watched the sun rise. She'd miss the glorious sunsets, too. She'd never get to see the produce from the seedlings she'd planted in the garden. Five calluses. That was how many she'd had after she'd finished mowing the field for their croquet game. Twice that many from preparing the soil for planting. She'd ached for days.

Someone her size wasn't cut out to be a rancher's wife.

She looked down to keep Mr. Adams from seeing the tears in her eyes.

It was good she was leaving. She wouldn't have to pluck and gut a chicken ever again. Roch could stop sleeping on a mattress in front of the hearth and sleep in a real bed. Luci wouldn't have to rise forty-five minutes early because of the daily drive into Helena to school.

She bit her lip and blinked repeatedly until her vision cleared.

Feeling in control of her emotions, she withdrew her financial journal from her haversack. She turned to Roch's plan, with the minor changes Jakob had insisted upon, then looked up to see Mr. Adams's wary gaze. She didn't fault him. While she felt less than confident with Roch's plan, her conscience could live with it.

"'Jakob Gunderson,'" Emilia began reading, "'has offered to purchase the ranch and all thereupon for the agreed price of four hundred fifty dollars. Mr. Hess may have the cart, which will even out that debt. Two dollars are to be left with Mr. Adams to be divided equally between Mr. Inger and Doctor Abernathy.'"

She looked up to see he was writing.

"'From the ranch purchase price,'" she continued, "'four hundred dollars will be paid to Madame Lestraude to satisfy the loan. The final fifty dollars plus an additional fifty dollars from Jakob Gunderson will be given to Mr. Cannon. This leaves me, Emilia Stanek Collins, owing Jakob fifty dollars.'" She closed her journal and looked up. "I think Finn would be proud of what I've done to honor his name."

The tip of Mr. Adams's pencil snapped. He dropped the pencil into a mug filled with other ones, then grabbed a sharpened one.

He looked at her. "What is your plan for repaying Jakob?"

"Before I left Chicago, Mr. Spiegel offered me a job should I return." Emilia slid her journal inside her haversack. "In six months, a time-frame Jakob agreed to, I will wire the full payment."

Mr. Adams finished writing. "Anything you wish me to convey to anyone else?"

Give Mac my love. And tell him I'm sorry.

She reached in her haversack, withdrew the copy of *Uncle Tom's Cabin*, and laid it on his desk. "Give this to Mac." She'd lost him, but she could at least salvage her family. They were stronger when together. "The cart for Hess is tied outside. Jakob said he had some things to take care of this morning in Helena before he heads out to his ranch. He should be by here later for the horse."

"You're planning on walking to the depot?"

"Yes, sir."

"It's too far."

She gave him a light smile. "We walked here from the

depot two months ago. I'm sure we can manage the trek again. Besides, the train doesn't leave for two hours."

He studied her. He had that look her mother used to have before she'd started in on a lengthy lecture, and yet he said, "I have a meeting with my uncle at the top of the hour. Are you comfortable with leaving the cart and horse unattended?"

"Certainly. Feel free to use it, instead of walking down to City Hall."

"Give me a few minutes to type up the contracts." Mr. Adams rolled a sheet of paper into the black typewriter on the side of his desk.

As he typed, Emilia turned in her journal to the contract with Mr. Cannon. She brushed her thumb across Mac's scripted *L. McCall.*

Luci reached over and touched Emilia's arm. "I wish Mac could come with us."

Me, too.

Emilia forced a smile. "We'll have Da and—" Her voice choked. "We'll be all right."

Roch gave her an odd look. He withdrew the handful of bills Mr. Gunderson had paid him for helping Jakob make deliveries to Fort Missoula. Roch laid four dollars on Mr. Hale's desk. And then he walked outside.

Emilia carefully tore out Mr. Cannon's contract, and then the ones for the other creditors. She laid them on the desk. "Mr. Adams, I'd appreciate it if you could also include these with each of these with the typed payment contracts. On the bottom is a short note thanking each of Finn's creditors for their kindness and understanding. Is there anything else you need from me besides my signature on the bill of sale to Jakob?"

He stopped typing. "You've gone above and beyond what

most would do in your situation. Give me thirty minutes and you're free to go."

The clacking of steel on steel reverberated through Mac's bones. He was tired . . . so tired . . . and livid. Once the train pulled into Helena station in a few more minutes, he'd pay visits to his mother and Joseph Hendry. Both were going to get an earful. The only question was which one to confront first.

Hendry's article had circulated around the territory, reaching Marysville by Monday morning, where Mac saw it minutes after he was ordered to keep his prisoner available for questioning through Wednesday afternoon. Instead of defending Emilia as an innocent victim, the article featured quotes from Madame Lestraude confirming her deal with Finn Collins to sell both Emilia *and* Luci into prostitution, an inset picture of the deed of trust providing proof.

Mac's lawman instincts buzzed and prickled, keeping him awake during the over-long trial in Marysville and through the train rides back to Deer Lodge and home to Helena. The major issues making him crazy boiled down to:

1. Madame Lestraude's assertion that, although she didn't employ women against their will or of Luci's age in her personal business, she didn't have a problem selling them to fellow owners who did in Nevada and Wyoming. Mac might have believed it were it not for the addition of Luci. First, it didn't fit. He might question her so-called care for her girls, but he knew for a fact that young girls forced into prostitution enraged her. Second, when he'd talked to her before leaving town, she'd denied Luci played any part in her dubious deal with Finn,

clearly stating it only concerned Emilia. She also implied that the repayment would occur at Maison de Joie. Either she'd lied to Mac to get him out of her office, or she'd lied to Hendry. Who she lied to didn't matter; the real question was why.

2. The terms of the deed of trust made no sense. Finn wasn't stupid. He'd never agree to a three-month loan with payment in full expected long before he had time to plant and harvest an alfalfa crop or breed and sell cattle. Ever since leaving his mother's office ten days earlier, Mac had replayed in his mind her hesitation when she spoke of the loan's repayment terms: ". . . should he fail to pay me back in . . . in full." It had bothered him then; it bedeviled him now.
3. Where was Finn's copy of the deed of trust? Either it was well hidden, never existed, or had been stolen on the day of his murder. Though looking for general evidence as opposed to something specific, Mac had checked everywhere in the cabin—under the mattress, between blankets, in every drawer, even in Finn's clothing while he lay stiff and cold on the floor—and been just as thorough when checking the barn and root cellar. Deputy Alderson had pried at the floorboards while O'Mara knocked on the walls to see if any spots sounded hollow. They'd found no hidden compartments nor any deed in the piles of trash littering the floor. Nothing Hale retrieved from Finn's bank included one either. That left two options: either Madame Lestraude showed Hendry a forged deed, or whoever killed Finn had taken the real one before Mac and his men arrived—which would explain why

the cabin had been ransacked. And if it was the latter, that brought up a fourth concern . . .

4. Had his mother killed Finn? Or—to be more accurate—ordered one of her employees to do it?

Which meant, instead of pounding a fist in Hendry's face as he yearned to do, Mac's first order of business, after letting his deputies know he was back in town, was visiting his mother.

The slowing train shifted into a crawl, blaring its horn to announce its arrival in Helena station. Mac leaned to look out the window. A huge crowd was gathered on the platform, circled around someone he couldn't see. Someone short. Someone connected to Charles Cannon, Doc Abernathy, Samuel Hess, and Zeb Inger.

Someone like Emilia.

Mac grabbed his hat and bag, then hurried toward the exit. The moment his train car was even with the platform, he swung the door open and jumped out. "Hey!" He shoved his hat on as he ran toward the circle of people clustered near the depot door. "Hey! What's going on?"

Heads turned. People peeled back in layers. Mac slowed his pace before he ran into anyone, then started pulling on shoulders and elbowing his way into the center to get to Emilia.

She was standing nose to index finger with a screaming Samuel Hess. "I don't want the cart, you stupid woman! I want my money!"

"Hey!" Mac drew the bully's attention, "You say one more word to Mrs. Collins that isn't polite as a parson's, and I'll toss your sorry hide in jail."

"If anyone's getting arrested, Sheriff, it's her." Inger pushed Hess aside. "She owes me a whole—"

"I've told you three times now, your dollar is with Mr.

Adams." Mac had never heard Emilia sound so frazzled. "Why won't you believe me?"

"So you say." Inger's sneer begged to be wiped off his weasel-like face.

"Are you calling the lady a liar?" Mac fairly itched for the man to say *yes*. If Hendry wasn't getting punched, this vermin would do just as well.

Inger pressed his lips together so tight, the tendons in his neck bulged.

"Well, if he ain't, I am!" Hess reasserted himself.

"Careful, Hess." Mac stepped between the blacksmith and Emilia. "I'm fast losing my patience with you."

Where were Roch and Luci?

Charles Cannon waved his hand over his head. "Sheriff, I can sum up the problem in a more"—he shot a disgusted glare at Hess and Inger—"civilized manner."

"Excellent." Mac turned around to take Emilia's arm and noticed two things simultaneously, both of them bad. First, she was wearing the same pink dress she'd worn when she'd first showed up in Helena, and second, she was gripping a battered bag in both hands.

She was leaving.

Mac absorbed the shock even as he summed up the situation. "Where are Roch and Luci?"

"Inside the telegraph office."

"All right. I need you to trust me for just a second here." *Please say yes. Please, for once in your life, just say yes.*

She eyed him warily. "I'll give you three seconds. No more."

It was progress. Mac fit two fingers in his mouth and whistled, cutting through the shouting and chatter surrounding them. "Quiet!"

Whether out of shock or obedience, the noise ceased.

"Hess, Inger, and Cannon, follow us into the telegraph

office. The rest of you, this is none of your business so move on." Mac stepped sideways and wrapped an arm around Emilia's waist. Was he imagining it, or had she lost weight in the ten days since he'd last seen her? "Let's go."

The depot door opened. Roch and Luci came outside. "Mac!" Luci tossed a familiar basket on the wooden platform and ran toward him.

The crowd between them parted. Mac let go of his bag and dropped to one knee so Luci could run straight into his arms. He lifted her off the ground, holding tight while she sobbed into his shoulder. He captured Emilia's gaze. What on earth?

She shook her head as she picked up his bag.

What did that mean? She didn't want to tell him, she didn't want to talk here, or she didn't know?

As people took note of Luci's sobbing, looks of sympathy and fluttering hankies appeared, the mood shifting from antagonism to curiosity. Mac patted her back while calling, "Move along, folks. Let's go. Move along." Once he reached the depot, he shifted Luci to hold her with one arm, then opened the door and waited for Roch, Emilia, and her creditors to come through before shutting out the busybodies still hovering on the platform.

Inside the telegraph office, Yancey leaned over the empty counter watching the action, a forlorn look on her face.

Where was her usual smile? And her usual mob of customers? "All of you, wait here while I see if Miss Palmer will allow us to use her office." Mac tilted his head to look at Luci. "Do you want to come with me or stay with your sister?"

It took a long moment for her to let go of his neck. "Stay. But you're coming back, right?"

Mac set her down and pointed to the telegraph office.

"I'm just going in there. You'll be able to see me the whole time."

Luci stretched to see for herself. "All right."

Roch took Luci's hand, giving Emilia a glare that reminded Mac of the sullen boy who'd arrived in town nine weeks before. Or was it ten? Forever? Or a minute?

Mac squared his shoulders. Now wasn't the time to get maudlin or take Roch to task or ask what had made Luci so fearful. Now was the time to be the sheriff. "I'll just be a minute." He walked into the telegraph office. "Hey, Yancey. What's going on?"

"Nothing."

A whole lot of nothing, from the looks of things. "Can I use your office for a brief meeting? It shouldn't take more than five or ten minutes."

"That's fine, but"—Yancey shot a nervous glance out the double doors into the depot area—"can I stay in here with you?" Before Mac could say he'd expected her to, she added, "It's easier to pretend people don't have any telegrams to send than that they don't want to talk to me."

"Hendry's article?" It was the only thing that made sense.

She nodded, tears welling in her eyes.

Mac leaned on the counter and put a hand on her forearm, promising himself to exact revenge on Hendry's nose for her sake as well as Emilia's. "Give it another week or so and the inconvenience of avoiding you will wear thin."

Yancey gave him a watery smile. "That's what my father says."

"Smart man." Mac turned and beckoned the six waiting in the depot area to come inside. While they filed into the telegram office, Mac drew the blinds over the windows overlooking the train platform to shut out any gawking stares. "Roch, close the doors, please."

"How come *she* gets to stay?" Hess's thundering voice was loud enough to be heard through windows and doors.

"Are you referring to Miss Palmer?" Mac stepped closer to the burly blacksmith, spreading his feet and planting his fists on his hips. Hess's eyes hardened. He opened his lips, so Mac cut him off by turning to Emilia. "Mrs. Collins, do you have any objection to Miss Palmer's presence?"

"I do not." Her voice was calm, steady, polite. She was back in control.

Mac swung his gaze to Hess. "If the lady has no problem, then you have no problem. Do I make myself clear?"

Hess pinched his lips together.

It wasn't enough for Mac, so he stretched his neck close enough to the blacksmith to smell soot, sweat, and garlic. "I asked you a question, Hess. I'll repeat it in case your limited powers of understanding need help. I said, do I make myself clear?"

Nostrils flaring, Hess dipped his chin.

Good enough. "Mr. Inger, do you have any objections?" After a sullen headshake, Mac looked at the grocer. "Cannon?"

"None at all, Sheriff."

"Excellent. Now, Mrs. Collins, would you like to tell me what's going on, or would you like to hear what these *gentlemen* have to say so you can refute all their arguments at once?"

Emilia's lips tipped into a smile. "I'd like to tell my side of the story first." She explained how she'd spent almost an hour with Hale Adams drawing up contracts that compensated each creditor the remainder of the debt owed.

"And I said I don't want the cart, I want my money!" Hess roared.

Mac stuck a finger under the man's bulbous nose. "One more word from you, and I'll not only throw you out of this room, I'll see to it that you get neither the money nor the cart back. Now sit down and shut up."

Hess plopped onto the wooden bench beneath the shaded windows.

Mac turned to Zeb Inger. "Are you telling me that you're here because Mrs. Collins owes you a measly dollar? After how hard she's worked for you these past two months?"

Inger crossed his arms over his chest. "A dollar's a dollar, Sheriff, and I have just as much right to recover it as Cannon has what's owed him." The man was a stingy rat, but the law was on his side.

Tempted to withdraw his wallet and slap a greenback in the man's scrawny chest, Mac reined in his temper. Emilia would hate him for fixing things, especially because she didn't need it. "It sounds like the lady has already left your funds with Hale Adams, so why are you here hounding her?"

Inger glowered. "'Cause no one can confirm a word of what she says."

Mac twisted his neck to find Yancey. "May we borrow your telephone?"

"Sure."

Not wanting to leave Emilia on this side of the counter while he went around the other one, Mac said, "Roch, ring Hale's office."

"He's not there," Emilia called out. Mac turned his attention to her. "As I've said repeatedly to these fine gentlemen, he was going to his uncle's office."

"I know." Roch stretched the second word with annoyance. He stomped behind the counter, lifted the receiver, and asked to be connected to Judge Forsythe's office.

"Mr. Cannon"—Mac turned to face the grocer—"I believe you're the only one we haven't heard from yet."

Cannon nodded his head. "I received a phone call telling

me Mrs. Collins was skipping town, and I needed to get to the train depot to stop her if I wanted my money. I confess, I arrived a moment before you did, so this is the first I've heard of any arrangements Mrs. Collins has made to pay off the debt."

"And now that you have heard it?"

"I'm reserving judgment until we hear from Mr. Adams, although . . ." Every eye turned toward the grocer. "It looks bad when a woman turns down two marriage proposals that would prop up her financial prospects and her reputation and then suddenly has train tickets for three people all the way back to Chicago."

Two proposals? Who had offered the second? A question for later. Mac looked at Emilia. "Would you like to tell him where you got the tickets or shall I?"

"You can." Her half smile added, *You're doing a fine job.*

Good to know. Even better to see her smile. "I purchased those tickets back in April. I gave them to Mrs. Collins and her siblings so they could leave town at any time in case whoever killed Finn came back and threatened them. As for their reputations, Luci spent less than three minutes in the . . . hotel, and I was with her for most of that."

Cannon frowned. "Why wasn't that information included in the article?"

It would have been, if Mac had given Hendry a decent quote instead of trite drivel.

"It would have gone a long way toward stanching the rumor mill," Cannon continued, piling guilt onto Mac's shoulders.

"Mr. Adams," Roch's voice turned everyone's attention to where he stood holding the telephone, "can you come down to the train station to verify our meeting with you earlier today?" He frowned. "What new problem?" Pause. "Yes, we'll stay right here and wait for you."

Shouting from outside drew Mac to the windows. He lifted a shade to see what was going on, Hess and Inger following suit at the other windows. There were too many bodies between the glass and whatever was happening. Seconds later, the doors to the telegram office swung open. The city marshal and three of his deputies appeared, faces stern.

Mac rushed to meet them. "What's going on, Quinn?"

Quinn Valentine tugged his lapel, drawing attention to his badge. "Stay out of this, Mac."

What an odd and insulting command. As though Mac would interfere with another lawman's duty, especially if he was here for Hess or Inger. Mac followed Quinn as he marched toward . . . Emilia?

"Mrs. Collins and Roch Stanek, you're under arrest for the murder of Edgar Dunfree."

Chapter Twenty-Two

Two hours later

"Thank you for the encouraging words." Emilia slid her hand through the cell's bars. Instead of shaking her hand, Mr. Gunderson gently pulled her forward into the oddest hug she'd ever experienced. Her face pressed against the bars. He patted her back and she breathed in his familiar pine scent. If she'd accepted his proposal, she wouldn't be in this spot.

Then again, if she had accepted Mac's, she wouldn't be either.

Mr. Gunderson stepped back and offered her a sheepish grin. "Windsor has never visited a woman in jail. I have one up on him now."

Emilia chuckled. "Do you feel an incessant need to compete with Mr. Buchanan?"

"Seems I do." He winked, then looked to the door with the four-inch-square peephole. "I ought to go see if Mrs. Hollenbeck has made any headway with Marshal Valentine."

She doubted Mrs. Hollenbeck would have any success. The marshal's office had confiscated the new tickets Roch had exchanged for the old ones. And their bags. How could she leave? She had thirty-four cents in her haversack, which had also been confiscated. On top of all that, because Emilia possessed a train ticket to leave Montana Territory, Judge Forsythe had been compelled to jail her.

She released a weary sigh. "Please tell Mrs. Hollenbeck she doesn't need to post bond for us."

"She can post mine," yelled the miner in the corner cell.

Emilia looked heavenward and shook her head. The city jail wasn't the place to be if one wanted a private conversation. She lowered her voice. "Mac said he'll have us out in a few hours."

In unison came a "Ha!" and "Speak louder, missy, I cain't hear ya!"

Mr. Gunderson's annoyed gaze shifted to Roch, who was lying on a bench, one foot on the ground. Instead of chastising her brother for his outburst, he looked back to Emilia. "If you need anything, let me know."

She nodded, although she had no intention of asking Isaak Gunderson for help. Once Mac and Marshal Valentine interviewed Mr. Adams, the murder charges would be dropped.

As Mr. Gunderson left, Emilia sat on the rickety cot that smelled, ironically, similar to a pig's pen. "What was that *ha!* supposed to mean?"

Roch's head turned her way. His eyes slanted. "As soon as we're outta here, we're leaving. Mac knows that. He's not going to let you leave. We're gonna stay in here until he convinces you to marry him."

Emilia's chest tightened. She wouldn't lie to herself—she hoped he would do that. She yearned for him to kick the door down, stride up to her cell, rip the door off, and carry her home. To his home. To their home. Good heavens, when had she become so melodramatic? In light of the way Mac had looked at her in the depot, Roch could be right. Minus the multiple door destruction.

I need you to trust me for just a second here.

She had trusted Mac, and he'd managed Mr. Hess and Mr. Inger better than she could have. Was that a bad thing? If she loved him, shouldn't she trust him for more than a second? For more than three? Her debts would be paid, save for the last fifty dollars, once Jakob secured a loan. Dunfree was dead and thereby unable to hurt another girl. If she married Mac—if he still wanted to marry her—she and Luci would have the protection of his name. No one at Luci's school would dare bully her. While Da wouldn't have the Circle C to work, he could find a job in Helena.

It would all work out.

Once the city marshal realized his mistake in arresting them.

She had hope. She *had* to have hope.

With a sigh, she untied the strings to her bonnet, then set it on the cot. If they were staying, she may as well get comfortable.

Minutes passed.

Roch stared up at the ceiling, his boot brushing against the floor.

Guttural snores came from the miner's cell.

Emilia waited. And waited . . . and waited some more.

She closed her eyes and—

The jail door creaked. She looked up. In strode Mr. Adams, carrying two paper sacks. He stopped at their cell.

"Mrs. Palmer sent lunch." He stuck the sacks through the bars.

"Oh, we couldn't—"

"Yes, we can!" In one swift movement, Roch was sitting up. "You're in jail, Emilia. Jail!"

Mr. Adams tossed the paper sack hard at Roch's chest. He grunted . . . yet managed to keep the contents from spilling out.

Emilia stepped to the bars. She opened the second sack. Two apples, a meat pastry, and a ham sandwich. "She shouldn't have done this. Taking Luci in was kindness enough."

"I've never known Mrs. Palmer to measure her kindness. She subscribes to the philosophy that you haven't lived today until you've done something for someone who can never repay you." He leaned against the bars. "Judge Gilpatrick refused to grant bail."

"But I thought your uncle was in charge."

Hale shook his blond head. "He issued the original arrest warrant because Marshal Valentine was afraid you'd skip town—his words, not mine—and couldn't find Gilpatrick. He's in authority over the city, while my uncle covers territory business." He adjusted his glasses with two fingers. "To tell the truth, I suspect part of the reason Judge Gilpatrick didn't grant bail, despite Mrs. Hollenbeck's offer to pay whatever it took to get you and Roch out, was because he was indignant that my uncle had usurped his authority."

So she and Roch would sit in jail charged with a crime they hadn't committed because two men were involved in a petty rivalry? "What will happen to Luci?"

"The Palmers will care for her until this is resolved. Mac is reviewing evidence with the city marshal's office. He's doing all he can to help, but"—Hale gave her an apologetic smile—"it looks like you and Roch will be staying through the night."

"I told you," Roch said around a bite of his sandwich.

"Let me talk to Judge Gilpatrick. Once he hears my side of the story, he'll realize we had nothing to do with Mr. Dunfree's death."

"Mrs. Collins," Mr. Adams spoke softly. "I assure you that Mac, Quinn, and I are working hard to prove your innocence."

"I thought a person was innocent until proven guilty?" She released a wry laugh. "Don't mind me. I know you—I *trust* you all are doing the best you can. I do." She reached into the lunch sack from Mrs. Palmer.

You haven't lived today until you've done something for someone who can never repay you.

If Mama were alive, she and Mrs. Palmer would have some heated discussion on kindness and giving. Were their differing views why Mrs. Palmer had smile lines and Mama had had a deep crease between her brows? A life free of burdens. Emilia released a weary breath.

She withdrew the meat pastry and one of the apples, then gave the sack back to Mr. Adams. After a glance at the miner, she whispered, "Please. He could use the food."

Sunday, May 29

"We need to lift our sister up before the Lord."

Mac recognized Mrs. Watson's voice as he walked closer to the gaggle of women clustered in the back corner of the sanctuary on Sunday morning.

"Oh yes." Mollie Fisk placed a hand on her hat to keep it in place as she nodded. "I'm told she had to sleep beside some of them."

Were they talking about Emilia? How last night's raid of the red-light district meant she'd shared a cell with prostitutes until their owners paid the fine to get them out?

"I think we should pray she's able to find a good husband." Mac couldn't tell who had spoken because Miss

Fisk's voluminous hat blocked his view. "Or that the Lord provides her and her siblings a way back home."

Mac's blood heated. They *were* talking about Emilia. Did the bigmouths think they fooled God by calling gossip a prayer need?

"Yes. Let's pray she can go *home* where *no one* knows what happened here and she can start fresh." The words Mrs. Watson chose to emphasize left no doubt that Emilia would not be welcome in church or the community after she was released from jail.

"Shh." Mrs. Hess, a woman as scrawny as her husband was rotund, cast a furtive glance at Mac.

All heads turned his way. "If you ladies are discussing Mrs. Collins, I'm sure she'll find there are plenty of *reasonable* men in Helena who will recognize her complete innocence in all these misfortunes and be perfectly willing to marry such an amiable and beautiful woman."

Applause greeted his speech. Mac twisted around to see Jakob and Isaak Gunderson, Doc Abernathy, and Mrs. Hollenbeck clapping and nodding.

His cheeks heated. "That's enough."

Isaak stepped forward and cuffed Mac on the shoulder. "If I'm not mistaken, that's the longest speech I've ever heard pass your lips."

"Yeah, well, sometimes it's good to use full sentences." Turning his back on the gibbering women, Mac joined his friends.

After exchanging pleasantries, he suggested they find a private place to talk. Reverend Neven agreed to let them use his office as long as they didn't miss the start of service. Mac followed the group of Emilia's friends who were working to set her free into the pastor's office and shut the door. Bookshelves lined three of the four walls and the fourth had two windows overlooking the field where the basket auction had taken place.

Mac opened both to allow a breeze and cut the scent of old leather and decaying paper. "What's the latest?"

Mrs. Hollenbeck's smile wilted. "It's not good on my end. Judge Gilpatrick is holding firm on keeping the poor dears until Monday morning. I don't think he's planning on running for reelection, so my influence is sadly lessened."

Doc Abernathy nodded, his bald head shiny and pale. "Afraid he was quite put out by Judge Forsythe overstepping his bounds in ordering the arrest warrant last Thursday."

"Then he ought to be in his office instead of eating fritters at The Last Chance Café." Jakob's criticism was fair. "I don't see you"—he waved a hand in Mac's general direction—"turning petty over jurisdictional nonsense."

"We must remember, dear"—Mrs. Hollenbeck put a hand on Jakob's forearm—"like Marshal Valentine, Judge Gilpatrick's jurisdiction is the city, while Sheriff McCall and Judge Forsythe's are not."

"Though we don't have to like it." Isaak grinned at whatever it was he found clever in his comment. "Like?" he hinted. "We don't have to *like* that Valentine and Gilpatrick have jurisdiction even though the comparison between . . . never mind. It's not funny if I must explain it." He looked at Mac. "Madame Lestraude continues to refuse to show me her deed of trust. I had to confess that, because Jakob's offer to buy the ranch was for more than our father authorized—"

"Even though he'll be happy to do so once we reach him." Jakob glared at his brother.

"We must confirm the price with him before we can legally submit an offer." Isaak's voice was as cool as Jakob's had been heated. "Until then, I won't be able to pry the deed of trust out of her so we can see whether it was forged."

"Me either." Mac's two attempts had ended with an embarrassing thud when he landed on his backside in the street courtesy of his mother's burly bodyguard. His one consolation was seeing Quinn receive the same treatment—and he'd only wanted her to corroborate Luci's story about Dunfree. Madame Lestraude had yelled out her window that any law officer who wanted to speak with her would have to arrest her.

Quinn was working on it.

"I have something." Doc Abernathy raised his hand as if he were in school. "Marshal Valentine asked me to provide an inventory of my medical supplies. I was hoping you'd know why."

Mac tapped a finger against his lips. "The coroner took Dunfree's body away before I saw it, so I don't know if he was stabbed—"

Mrs. Hollenbeck gasped.

"Sorry, ma'am." Mac took her by the arm and led her to the overstuffed wingback chair behind the pastor's desk.

"I'm allowing you to pamper me only because I worked overlong in my garden yesterday." She snapped open a black lace fan and sank onto the green leather. "Do not feel you must moderate your language too much on my account."

"Yes, ma'am." Mac bent and kissed her cheek. "You're a remarkable woman."

"I am." Her grin was saucy, reminding Mac of how Mr. Hollenbeck used to call her his spitfire. "Now, continue."

Mac saluted her. "All right, then, I don't know how Dunfree was killed. The coroner's report is due tomorrow afternoon. However, if there were no obvious wounds, poison might be the culprit."

"In which case he wants to know if I'm missing any medicine." Doc Abernathy drew his bushy white eyebrows together. "I've never kept a lock on my supplies, but I do keep very accurate records. I'll know if anything is missing."

Faint organ music penetrated the walls.

"Anyone have anything else?" Mac looked around the room.

Jakob, Isaak, and Doc Abernathy shook their heads.

Mrs. Hollenbeck rose from her chair. "You three go on ahead. I need to speak with Sheriff McCall for just a moment." She waited until the two of them were alone in the pastor's office. "You realize your declaration to Mrs. Watson and her little club effectively constitutes a second marriage proposal."

He hadn't thought of it that way. Hadn't thought of anything except defending Emilia.

"A few days ago," Mrs. Hollenbeck continued, "you said Marshal Valentine would either have to come up with some evidence to support holding Roch and Emilia or release them. We both know there is no evidence, so how long before they're released?"

Not soon enough for Mac.

He leaned against the edge of Reverend Neven's desk. "If the coroner says the cause of death is poison, and Doc can account for all his medicine, I'd say tomorrow afternoon."

Mrs. Hollenbeck stepped closer. "Then, my dear boy, you don't have long to come up with a third marriage proposal." She reached up and patted his cheek. "I suggest you make it a good one this time."

Chapter Twenty-Three

The next morning

Mac scooped up the WANTED posters and other notices he planned to use as subterfuge to request a meeting the instant the city marshal's office opened in—he walked out of his office and checked the clock over the door leading into the lobby—four more minutes.

He'd arrived at City Hall almost three hours earlier, stopping at the jail on his way to check on Emilia, both grateful and disappointed to hear she was sleeping. He hadn't come up with his proposal yet, although planning and discarding eight different scenarios had kept him awake for hours last night. He wasn't planning on dropping to one knee in front of steel bars in any case, so his first priority was working on her release.

First, the coroner's report needed to come in. Assuming Dunfree's cause of death was poison instead of something like a heart attack, Doc Abernathy then needed to confirm his medicines were all accounted for. Finally, his mother needed to corroborate Luci Stanek's account of her encounter with Dunfree.

Which should happen in—Mac checked the clock again—three minutes, twenty-four seconds.

Knock, knock, knock. "Mac. You in there? We need to talk."

Hendry. How had he gotten inside City Hall before nine?

Mac swung open the door and stepped into the lobby. A number of people were lining up outside office doors to wait until they were unlocked by the various clerks. Dunfree used to keep everyone out until the stroke of nine. "Not now, Hendry. I'm on my way to a meeting."

"With Marshal Valentine?"

"That's none of your business."

Hendry put a hand on Mac's arm. "Hold up. I know you're mad at me, and considering how things worked out, I can't blame you, but"—he leaned close to Mac's ear—"I have something you need to see."

Mac pulled back. "If it doesn't concern Emilia and Roch, I'm not interested."

"But it does." Hendry raised his brows and shifted his gaze to Mac's office, a clear indication that he wanted to speak in private.

After noting that the city marshal's door was still closed and there were already five people waiting outside, Mac pivoted around to return to his office. "I can give you five minutes. No more."

"That's all I need. What's the latest in the Dunfree case?"

"Funny. I was about to ask you the same question." Mac cut a glance at the reporter.

Amusement sparkled in Hendry's eyes. "I'll make you a deal. I'll tell you what I know and, if it's news to you, you tell me what's in that." He pointed to the stack of papers in Mac's hand.

"Fair enough." Mac stepped to the side to allow Hendry to precede him into the sheriff's office.

"Coroner suspects Dunfree was poisoned."

Mac stopped walking. "His report isn't due out until later today."

"He owed me a favor." Hendry tossed the comment over his shoulder as he walked into Mac's private office.

Shaking his head, Mac followed. Priority number one done, and Doc planned to get to his office early to inventory his medicines. Meaning only the interview with his mother stood between Emilia and freedom. "There are times I want to hate you, and then you do this."

Hendry grinned. "It's part of my charm."

"Here"—Mac dumped the whole stack of papers into Hendry's lap—"enjoy yourself. The short version is six new WANTED posters and—"

"Any for murder?" Hendry licked his index finger, then lifted the corner of the top page.

"Nope." Mac sat down and crossed his arms over his chest.

Hendry looked up. "Go on. You said, 'and . . .'"

"And," Mac repeated, "counterfeit money in Dawson County."

"Again?" Hendry flipped through a few more pages. "Boring."

Mac laughed. "You aren't happy unless it's madness and mayhem, are you?"

"Reporter," he said, in much the same way Mac had said *sheriff* when asked why he always kept his back to the wall. Hendry set the stack of papers on the corner of Mac's desk. "All right. Down to business. Remember when I told you I stopped chasing a rumor that Finn Collins was part of a smuggling ring getting girls *out* of prostitution because I couldn't verify it? I just got proof."

"What?" Mac jerked straight, his hands falling to his thighs.

"Told you you'd like it." Hendry leaned sideways to dig inside his pants pocket. After a brief struggle, he pulled out a crumpled piece of paper and tossed it on the desk between them. "Found this while cleaning out my saddlebag this morning. Don't ask how I missed it or how long it's been there because I don't know."

Mac's neck tingled as he peeled back the edges.

It aint tru. That man tryd to git
girls outta the red lite distrikt.

Mac pressed the back of his hand against his nose and lips. To see his friend and brother vindicated, even in this small way, made his eyes tear up and his nose sting. An unsigned note wasn't actual proof, but it verified what his heart wanted to believe—what Emilia had never stopped believing—about the goodness of Finn Collins.

Mac pulled a handkerchief from his back pocket to blow his nose. He cleared his throat. "Do you think getting girls out of prostitution is what got Finn killed?"

Hendry nodded. "That's what I want to find out, but I don't want to be stupid about it. However, at least I can run a retraction. I think it would go a long way toward clearing the names and reputations of several lovely young ladies around town." The blush that stained Hendry's cheeks said the lovely young lady he was most concerned about was Yancey Palmer.

Mac tucked the handkerchief away. While a retraction would restore some peace to Emilia and her family, they were leaving town once this idiotic arrest was dropped.

Unless he came up with the perfect proposal. Which, based on past performance, wasn't guaranteed. And Emilia had never doubted Finn's character. Seeing him exonerated would be nice but unnecessary. As for Yancey, a few more weeks—maybe less—and she'd be back to her normal, sunny self. "If I were you, I'd let the hubbub in the red-light district die down. You've made enemies over this weekend's raid. Do something boring for a few months"—Mac directed a look at the WANTED posters and news bulletins sitting on the edge of his desk—"then come back to it."

"Yeah . . . you're probably right." Hendry dug through the stack of notices. "How about I take this one?" He pulled out a bulletin and showed it to Mac.

"Nice and boring." He reached for the remaining notices. "You might start by checking down at the train station to see if someone in the telegraph office has any information about counterfeiting."

Hendry stood. "An excellent suggestion, Sheriff." After a handshake, he jogged out.

Mac tucked the notices under his arm and slipped the scrap of paper into his pocket before he hurried over to the city marshal's. He was in time to see a burgundy silk ruffle disappear into Quinn's private office. None of the police officers were at their desks. An oversight on Quinn's part if he meant to keep Mac out of his mother's interrogation. He opened the door and stepped inside.

"Thought you might show up" was the only resistance Quinn offered. "Have a seat. We were just getting started."

Surprised and a little annoyed that he didn't have to put up a fight, Mac sat down. He placed the notices on the floor beside his chair. After greeting his mother, he remained silent while Quinn asked the questions. Every colorless answer confirmed Luci Stanek's account of what happened between her and Edgar Dunfree.

After a few minutes, Officer Jerow interrupted. "Sir, coroner's report just came in. Thought you might want to see it."

Quinn excused himself. "Mac, don't ask your mother any questions while I'm gone."

"I won't." But the moment the door closed, Mac retrieved the scrap of paper Hendry had found and handed it to his mother.

Her eyes widened for the merest instant before the bland expression she'd worn during the entire interview slipped back into place. She rolled the dingy note between her fingers until it was the size of a pea, then she popped it into her mouth.

What did that mean? Had she found the note offensive? Ridiculous? Incriminatory?

While Mac struggled to make sense of her gesture, Quinn returned.

Madame Lestraude rose from her chair with the grace of a princess. "I demand to speak with Emilia Collins."

Emilia sat across from Madame Lestraude and mimicked her clasped hands in her lap, their knees almost touching. Had the woman killed Mr. Dunfree? She didn't look like a murderer. Nor had Mac looked like the son of a prostitute. The similarity was in their eyes—a soft almond shape, thick lashes, chocolate brown. Except Mac's eyes were kind.

"Why?" Emilia asked before the haughty woman could speak.

Madame's arched brows rose. Her eyes shifted to the closed door, behind which they knew both Mac and Marshal Valentine were standing. And listening. Her gaze resettled on Emilia. "Your question could have a million different answers. Which one would you like first?" She spoke at a soft level no one, even with a glass cupped to the door, could hear.

Emilia matched the volume. "Why did you ask to speak to me?"

Madame crossed her legs, then laid one hand on her knee, the other bejeweled hand atop it. "My son is in love with you. Yet you rejected his proposal."

"I've spent the last four days in jail and you wish to give me a motherly lecture?" Emilia stood. "Good day, Miss Lester."

"Sit!"

She'd been gracious in agreeing to meet with Mac's mother. She'd always been respectful to those older than she. No matter how unkind, cruel, or rude the elder was. Proper etiquette dictated it. Etiquette did *not* dictate she divulge her reasons for refusing Mac's proposal to a woman she had met only minutes earlier. Nor did it dictate she obey like a trained pet.

Emilia lifted her chin.

Madame motioned to the chair. She stared up at Emilia for an excruciatingly long moment before speaking in a kind tone, oddly suited to her. "Please, Emilia. Sit."

She needs me. The realization hit Emilia like a slap in the face. She settled back onto the chair and nodded at Madame to continue.

Madame frowned. No, she looked somber, tired, and—was it possible?—afraid. "I wish to ask a simple favor."

"Which is?"

"I forgive the loan, and you"—she waved at nothing in particular—"publicly acknowledge that Finn and I were working together to smuggle girls into prostitution."

Emilia pondered this with a slow nod. "And then we're even?" she asked with a touch of cynicism, because who in their right mind would believe this simple favor was all Madame Lestraude wanted?

"Even. Such an interesting word." She studied Emilia, and Emilia studied her. "I believe we will be . . . even."

"Lies come as easily to you as the truth." Emilia smiled placidly. "You are not that kind."

Madame's painted lips twitched.

Emilia leaned forward. "On *this* we would be even, but I would still owe you."

"For?"

"Rescuing Luci from Mr. Dunfree."

Madame cleared her throat. "You don't believe in kindness?"

Not from you. The words stalled on Emilia's tongue at the flicker of hurt in Madame's eyes. Luci had been adamant about how furious Madame had been at the city clerk. Maybe her actions had been sincere. Kind even. Maybe she had rescued Luci without expecting anything in return. Maybe, in this, Madame had not measured her kindness.

I've never known Mrs. Palmer to measure her kindness.

Mr. Adams fervently believed Mrs. Palmer to be *that* kind. That gracious. That giving.

Emilia moistened her dry lips. "My mother taught that when someone gives us a gift, from a simple favor to a pie to saving a life from a sick man, we must give something back in return."

"I didn't rescue Luci so you would owe me."

"You don't seem the type of woman who does simple favors for anyone without it being a benefit to you."

That seemed to impress her.

Madame rested against the back of her chair and smiled. "Indeed, I'm not."

Emilia took a breath. This conversation was growing tedious. "Have I proven my merit? That I am worthy of your son? This conversation is really about that, isn't it?" She didn't give Madame a chance to respond. "Please leave. Finn was too honorable a man to have worked for you."

Madame leaned forward with a malicious glare. "When all the banks rejected Finn, he came to me asking for a loan. Some would say I was being kind. Others"—her look conveyed *like you*—"would say I did it out of obligation."

Finn asked her for a loan?

Emilia touched her chest, but the action did nothing to slow the pounding. Something in Madame's expression, in her tone, in the fervency of her words had Emilia convinced. Madame wasn't lying. Not about this. How Emilia knew, she wasn't sure, but she knew—*knew*—Madame had given the loan out of obligation.

Glancing at the light slipping through the space under the door, Emilia could see two shadows. Mac and Marshal Valentine couldn't have heard anything.

She turned back to Madame and kept her voice low. "Why did you feel obligated to help Finn? The truth, please."

Madame dipped her head in acknowledgment. "He was helping me smuggle young girls out of prostitution."

Emilia blinked. Swallowed. Stopped breathing.

Not *in* but *out*.

One little word validated all she believed of Finn. If Madame was honest. This woman wore lies as easily as the paint on her face. But were they as easy to take off?

She drew in a breath, then released it.

Madame sat there, looking as one would after saying, *Excellent dinner. Please pass the salt.*

Emilia gathered her whirlwind of *why*s and *how*s and *when*s into one question: "Then why smear his good name?"

"He was already dead and I needed a scapegoat." Madame spoke as though slander was as commonplace as laundry. "I've been helping young girls out of prostitution for as long as I've lived in Helena. It's one of the benefits of being a madam. No one suspects me. The names and faces of those helping me change, but my financier and I have remained constant. And hidden."

She had a financier?

"But then," she continued, "Joseph Hendry arrived in town and stirred up trouble. He caught wind of my scheme. His poking around caused people to wonder aloud if, instead of the girls being runaways, someone was helping them escape. I whispered here and there that Finn was helping me smuggle women into the sisterhood to throw Hendry off the scent. It worked until my righteous son . . ." She shook her head.

"Mac wanted to defend his friend's honor."

"He did it because he loves you." Madame made it sound like a condemnation. "He didn't want your name in the newspaper, so he and his little deputies started shouting their suspicions about girls being smuggled out of prostitution at the top of their lungs."

"So you went to Mr. Hendry and gave him a different story."

"I had no other option."

Emilia stared at Madame. She looked astonishingly casual at admitting her deception. No other option. Lie upon lie. Which could only mean—

"Did you forge the deed of trust you showed Hendry?"

"I did what was necessary."

Several seconds went by.

Madame said nothing, nor did she look as if she felt obliged to break the silence.

Emilia shifted on her chair to ease the numbness in her left thigh. The woman had no shame, no remorse.

"You dragged Luci *literally* and me into the middle of a lie," she said, incredulous.

"Which wouldn't have mattered if you'd said yes when my son asked you to marry him." Her tone of voice adding that Emilia was somewhere in the range of a tree slug for rejecting the offer.

Emilia coughed a breath. "I believe Finn was helping you rescue girls. I can see him doing that. But for all you've done for those rescued girls, your do-what-is-necessary lie hurt my sister. She's twelve years old. Twelve. The kids at school were bullying her. She has bruises on her back from where they pelted her with rocks and called her horrible names. Because of your"—she spoke in a haughty voice—"I-have-no-other-option lie."

Madame went quite still.

"Multiple bruises," Emilia said. "What do you have to say to that?"

"I never meant to drag Luci into this."

"Why did you?"

"If I hadn't, Dunfree would have—" Her gaze shifted to the shadows moving under the door.

In preparation to burst through the door to rescue Emilia from Madame's vile clutches?

Madame rubbed her palms together. "My actions that day were impulsive, regretful, and ones I knew I needed to disguise almost as soon as I'd acted upon them. All the girls I've smuggled out have been under the age of fifteen. The similarities to your sister were too marked. I had no other option but to say Finn had sold her—and you—into service to me."

"If all you have told me is true—" Emilia ignored Madame's raised brows. "If it is, and heaven help me for believing you, then you're asking me, before my God, to willfully lie for you. To perpetuate multiple lies for you."

Madame laughed. "Oh, my dear child, what I ask is much less than what your God asks of you. The Good Book says you are to love your enemies, to do good to them, and lend to them without expectation of being repaid. And you can't even do that."

The words sounded familiar, sounded like something she'd heard in church. "Where—?"

Madame gave a little one-shoulder shrug. "Luke, chapter six, verse 35."

"You demanded this meeting, asked me to lie for you, and now you mock me?"

"I am not the one professing to serve a God who forgives sins."

Emilia swallowed, unsure of how to respond.

"No one will ever write psalms praising my motherly wisdom." Madame leaned forward and gripped Emilia's clenched hands. "But I do know that a true favor is altruistically given, out of the kindness of your heart, not so you can have a mark against the person you were helping. That was how Finn lived. While he was part of my ring, he helped free five young girls from prostitution and refused to take a penny in payment. He said a simple thank-you would do."

Taking payment wouldn't have been in his character.

Emilia leveled her gaze. "Was that why you asked Finn to join your cause . . ."

Madame's brow twitched.

". . . because you recognized him as someone you could use?"

She nodded. Her grip on Emilia's hands tightened. "Finn wasn't the first who sacrificed for my cause. In February, I lost someone else. A few minutes ago, Mac gave me a small note that confirmed my man was killed and the girl we were attempting to rescue that night was returned to Helena." Her tears welled in her eyes. "People have died for this lie,

Emilia. All I'm asking is that you let it stand. If you wish to consider forgiving Finn's loan as a payment for keeping my secret, that's up to you."

"Why did you rescue Luci?" She had to know because it wasn't just about Luci. It was about every girl Madame had rescued, and about every lie she'd told to cover it up. Madame started to draw back, so Emilia gripped her hands. "Please."

Madame held Emilia's gaze. "Because it's what I wish someone had done for me."

Stunned at the admission, Emilia released her hold on Madame, who then stood and walked to Marshal Valentine's bookshelf.

"Have you told your son?"

Madame's chortle was full of bitterness. "He'd never believe me." Pain wrapped around each syllable.

Emilia looked toward the door again. So little and yet so much separated mother and son. "He needs to know."

She smoothed the front of her beautiful, unwrinkled burgundy gown. "You hold my life in your hands. If you are not comfortable with perpetuating the lie about what Finn was doing for me—and I will understand if you aren't—all I ask is that you give me two days to put my affairs in order and leave town. Then you can tell the truth to my son and that Hendry fellow."

Emilia nodded. "Why are you trusting me with this?"

"Instinct," Madame quickly replied. "In my business, you develop a keen sense of who is trustworthy and who isn't. Sometimes I must rely on people without trusting them, but every once in a while I meet a soul I trust within moments of our meeting. You are one. Your husband was another."

But not her son. Unless he was someone she trusted but couldn't rely on.

Madame wiped a corner of her mouth. "The note I spoke of earlier said a man was trying to get girls out of the red-light district. Mac is convinced it refers to Finn. If someone doesn't stop him, his dogged persistence to clear his friend will destroy everything."

Emilia stared at the floor. She pressed a hand over her pounding heart. Honor Finn's name or honor his sacrifice? Which was the right thing to do? Madame did what was necessary. Necessary and right weren't the same thing.

"Emilia, look at me."

She did.

"If you do decide to tell the truth about Finn rescuing those girls, the person who is financing my . . . endeavors will need to be warned."

Emilia nodded again. Naturally there would be consequences to those connected, as there had been to Luci, Yancey Palmer, and herself following Mr. Hendry's article. That article had not put any of their lives in danger, but Madame and the person financing her *endeavors* were. Emilia doubted grace and forgiveness abounded in the red-light district. If Finn were here, what would he advise she do?

Who am I that God is mindful of such a sinner as me?

Finn had written that to her. She'd wondered what he'd meant, but it made sense now. Finn had risked his life to help save those girls because he believed so strongly that Jesus had paid his debts, paid his sins, and made him free. He'd lived out of gratitude, not obligation. Not to even the score. The truth cut deep. Finn lived his faith far more than she ever had hers. If he were here, he would ask one thing of her.

To honor his sacrifice.

Emilia stood. She walked to the door, taking care to ensure her boots sounded loudly against the wooden floor.

The shadows under the door moved. Then she strolled softly to Madame. "If I let the lie stand," she whispered, "would you and your financier continue your endeavors?"

"In time."

Once Finn's reputation had been solidly destroyed.

"Then stay here and keep doing it. However," Emilia said firmly, "I must pay off the loan or else people will be suspicious." Finn's debts would be paid save for the remaining fifty dollars Emilia would owe Jakob, but that she could manage.

Madame's chin rose.

Emilia waited for Madame to offer a counterargument.

"Thank you."

Chapter Twenty-Four

Mac paced between Quinn's office door and a scrupulously clean desk. It bothered him. The desk. How ordered and neat it appeared, while his brain was cluttered with a thousand questions. It felt like those first few hours after Finn's death, when every added detail made the overall picture fuzzier instead of clearer.

This time, the picture was of his mother and, if he thought her behavior contradictory in the past, it was nothing compared to when she'd eaten the note.

She *ate* the note!

About Finn Collins getting girls out of prostitution.

Why? What possible motive did she have for doing something so bizarre? And why had she wanted to speak to Emilia? They'd never met. His mother had never cared two bits about her except as a way to needle him. Did she want to meet the woman he'd proposed to, the surrogate mother of the girl she'd rescued, or the wife of the man she'd lied about in the *Daily Independent*?

Because the one thing he was sure about was that she'd lied. He just didn't know why.

Mac spun around and paced back toward the door. He needed answers. He didn't want them; he *needed* them the way his lungs needed air. He was weary of the questions, weary of the ambiguity, weary of the lies.

Weary of wondering who his mother really was.

Quinn jumped away from his door, rushing to sit on the edge of the annoying desk and appear disinterested.

"Like they don't know you were listening the whole time," Mac whispered.

Quinn glowered, then relaxed into his apathetic pose.

Madame Lestraude appeared first, her painted lips twitching the moment she laid eyes on Quinn. "Marshal, I believe you had a few more questions for me. I imagine they center around whether I had the means or motive to poison Edgar Dunfree."

The astonishment on Quinn's face was worthy of a larger audience—one that paid admission.

"Mr. Dunfree was poisoned?" Emilia followed Madame Lestraude out of Quinn's office and came directly to Mac.

Did she have any idea what the gesture meant to him? To be singled out as the person she wanted to be near? His heart thumped against his rib cage in a painful rhythm. If he fouled up his proposal again, how was he ever going to let her go?

Madame Lestraude addressed Emilia first. "According to the coroner"—she turned to Quinn—"who is a regular client, yes, Mr. Dunfree was poisoned. I, for one, hope it was a slow and painful demise. Now, Marshal, because poison is the culprit and Emilia's only access to medications was at Doc Abernathy's office, I suggest you speak with him. If nothing is missing, I don't see how you can hold her or her brother any longer."

Quinn worked his jaw open and shut.

She faced Emilia. "It was lovely to meet you. I hope you will remain in Helena. If you ever need anything, please don't hesitate to ask."

"Thank you."

Madame Lestraude smiled as though Emilia had passed some kind of test.

What was that about? And did this mean Emilia was staying? More questions instead of answers.

Mac couldn't stand any more. Before his mother disappeared into her hotel again, he needed to know one thing. "Did you kill Finn?"

Emilia's gasp and Quinn's wide eyes barely registered. Mac focused on his mother, intent on reading her every expression so he'd know if she was lying.

She shook her head. Not in denial but in weariness. "Do you know me so little?"

"That's not an answer." Mac took a step closer to his mother, but a small hand on his forearm detained him. He looked at it . . . and then at its owner.

"Don't, Mac." Emilia flicked her gaze at his mother. "Please. Trust me."

The words struck like boxing gloves to his ribs. How many times had he asked her to trust him? He couldn't count them all. And every time she hadn't, he'd been affronted. Angry. Sometimes even disparaging.

He heaved air in and out of his lungs.

What if he said no? What if he denied Emilia the thing he'd always wanted from her? Would she leave instead of stay? Even if he proposed again?

What if he agreed to trust her now? Would it fill her with the same deep pride he'd experienced knowing she trusted him to do what he thought best?

But how could she know what was best in this moment? He'd spent seven years with his mother. She'd spent seven minutes. And yet something had happened between them. Something he couldn't explain but knew in his gut.

Emilia stared up at him, waiting in that patient way of hers.

The questions swirled in his brain. Taunting him. Reviling him. Making him hate himself because he couldn't find the answers no matter how hard he tried. His mother had answers. All the important ones.

Please. Trust me.

Emilia had no idea how much he hated the uncertainty. She couldn't know. Maybe next time he could trust her, but this time he was right to make his mother tell him what she knew.

Finn wrote once about a friend of his who was always sure he was right because he almost *always was.*

Mac jerked his arm from Emilia's grasp. She'd said those words to him the first day they'd met. And her eyes had held the same pain he saw in them now.

He swallowed.

The choice boiled down to pursuing his need for answers from a woman who would never turn into the mother he wanted or honoring the woman he loved by trusting her when he suspected she was wrong.

But perhaps that was the highest level of trust, when you gave it because of *who* was asking, not because of *what* was asked.

Mac held his hand toward Emilia, waiting for her to place her hand in his before turning to face his mother. "If Marshal Valentine has no more questions for you, you're free to go."

Emilia stared out the window of Mac's office. Buildings obstructed most of her view of the mountains. But if she was right about where City Hall sat, if she were a bird, she could fly straight out of this window, across Helena, and to the Circle C. To the promises Finn had made of a home where she could find rest. Where she didn't have to be the one to solve Roch and Luci's problems. Where she could be their sister, not their mother. Where Da could breathe clean air and relish life in Montana Territory.

But she wasn't a bird.

Neither was she in a cage. She'd been set free of the jail, of the debts. She could go anywhere.

"Not without Mac," she murmured.

"What was that?"

Emilia looked over her shoulder at Mac, standing on the threshold and smiling. She turned to face him. "Where's Roch?"

"By now, at the Palmers'." He strolled to his desk, carrying her bonnet, haversack, and the three train tickets Marshal Valentine had confiscated as evidence. "Roch said he wanted to check on Luci, but his stomach growled otherwise." Mac laid her belongings on his desk, then sat on the edge, his arm resting on the hilt of his gun. "You two ever going to make things right?"

Emilia shrugged. "Four days in jail failed to loosen his tongue. I can't force him to talk. I don't know what I did to make him hate me."

"Finn."

The lone word stretched into silence.

Emilia stood there waiting for him to say more. There had to be more. There had to be a reason why Mac had said, *Finn*. Roch had never met Finn. To be sure, she'd shared parts of his letters. Multiple times. She'd talked about Finn constantly because she wanted Da, Roch, and Luci to fall in love with him and the Circle C. They needed to know how wonderful, good, and better their life would be in Montana. With Finn.

And then it hit her. Roch could have interpreted her

words as though she thought their life together—the four of them—wasn't wonderful or good. That they needed Finn to make life better. That they needed Finn because they weren't enough for one another. That Roch wasn't enough. That she didn't need him anymore.

"I blundered," she said to Mac.

"We all do, at times."

One of his deputies laughed. Chairs scraped against the floor, and then a mug shattered. More laughter.

Mac stayed on his desk, never looking away from her, clearly uncaring about the ruckus outside. "What did my mother say to you?"

She gave him a steady look. "That's her secret to tell. It's your job to convince her to trust you with it."

He seemed to consider that. "Where are you headed now?"

Emilia dipped her head toward his desk. "I have a ticket back to Chicago."

"Anything for you there?"

"A good-paying job." She paused. "A man I love—my father."

Mac nodded. "You have a good-paying job here. I heard about the offer," he added. "From Isaak. At Luanne and Roy's wedding. He raved about you . . . your, uh, work ethic. And I'd like to think there's also a man you love here."

"In Helena?"

"I, uh, mean . . . more like in this office."

"You sound nervous."

"My mind's a whirl thinking about how to convince you to stay."

"Oh." Emilia walked to the door he'd left open. She closed it, shutting out the noise his deputies were making. "Does this help you focus?"

His brows rose, and suddenly she could see so much

more of the resemblance to his mother. He withdrew a sheet of paper from the inside of his vest. "I searched through my favorite Walt Whitman poems in hopes of capturing what I wanted to say. I wrote a few things down," he said, unfolding it.

Emilia strolled over to him. "Well?"

He cleared his throat. "'We were together. I forget the rest.' Will you marry me?"

"Interesting."

He looked up from the paper. "That didn't convince you?"

She shook her head.

He read again. "'I discover myself on the verge of a usual mistake.' Will you marry me?"

A burst of air slipped through Emilia's lips. "Is that all?" She snatched the paper from his hand and read what else he'd written. The rest of the paper contained the same three words over and over—*I love you.*

He smiled down at her, a silly half grin that made her thank herself for closing the door.

Emilia tossed the paper onto his desk, noting how perfectly it landed on top of the train tickets. She stepped closer and touched his cheek. "Sheriff McCall, I like your words best."

"Is that a yes?"

She nodded. "But feel free to convince me more."

Epilogue

Spring, 1888

". . . because I fair shudder to think what would have happened to Mrs. McCall and her sweet sister had they fallen into Finn Collins's clutches."

The tidbit of conversation caught his ear from somewhere behind him. He excused himself from the group of people he was with and weaved through the church hall to hear what others were saying. He nodded to acquaintances and kept his ears open. Everyone was full of Finn Collins, his treachery, and how today's wedding between Sheriff McCall and the little widow had put all to rights.

He stopped to greet friends and exchange pleasantries. Duty done, he looked across the room to watch the bride and groom cut a three-tiered wedding cake, and his gaze locked with Madame Lestraude's. She inclined her head, half in polite acknowledgment of his presence and half in recognition of their ongoing stalemate. She knew too much about his secret business, as he did of hers.

What a stroke of luck her recent reconciliation with her son had turned out to be. As long as Sheriff McCall assumed Finn Collins had been killed by one of the brothel owners for helping Madame Lestraude smuggle girls out of prostitution, the real motive for the murder would never come out.

Did their new mother-son relationship threaten his plans for the future in any way? Doubtful. If she knew the real reason for Finn Collins's murder, she'd keep quiet. She might even continue to be helpful—as she had been when informing him of Dunfree's lechery.

A sliver of remorse pierced his heart. Had Dunfree stuck to the plan—and kept his filthy hands off the little girl—neither he nor Collins would be dead now. Incompetence and lechery sealed Dunfree's fate. Finn Collins had deserved better, but best not to dwell on things that couldn't be changed.

Like the need to have Joseph Hendry eliminated. A word here and there had inflamed passions within the red-light district, resulting in the nosy reporter's death. Regrettable, especially because of how it affected the Palmer girl, but at least no blame could be attached to him. It was always wise to have a layer of protection between himself and necessary business—particularly the kind that involved killing.

He noticed what appeared to be a disagreement between the Gunderson twins. Speaking of a problem that needed to be eliminated . . .

He skirted the edges of the crowded room until he drew close enough to hear what Isaak was saying to his brother.

". . . wondered where all your talk about how lucky Mac was that Emilia answered that mail-order advertisement was leading. You've ordered yourself a bride, too. Haven't you?" Isaak Gunderson fairly growled.

"And what if I did?" Jakob tapped fingers to his chest. "Why can't I have my chance at love?"

"Because what happens if"—Isaak's voice lowered to an inaudible level.

"I've been in contact with a matchmaker in Denver." Jakob spoke loud enough to be overheard.

Isaak's eyebrows and his volume rose in response. "And how much did you have to pay this so-called Cupid?"

Jakob clamped his lips shut.

"That much, huh?" Isaak shook his head. "What if this woman shows up and she's entirely unsuitable? You'd better not expect me to clean up after you."

Jakob leaned in and put a finger on Isaak's chest. "And you'd better not pull your big brother act and mess this up for me."

Chuckling, he walked past the brothers before either of them noticed his presence.

Those boys were going to be the death of each other.

DON'T MISS

New beginnings await in Helena,
the Montana Territory's most exciting city—
where faithful hearts stay strong and true
as they pursue their passionate dreams.

COME FLY WITH ME

The first e-novella in the Montana Brides Series,
available wherever eBooks are sold.

Enjoy the following excerpt from
Come Fly With Me. . . .

Central Secondary School
Helena, Montana Territory
September 9, 1886

Please, let him not be here.

As Luanne Palmer climbed the stairs to the second floor, she muttered "please" after "please." She reached the top, then turned the corner and paused. The door at the far end of the hall was closed, but that didn't mean anything. So were all the other doors. She touched her belly, only the action did little to dispel the flutters. Bad enough that she felt them when Roy Bennett looked at her. Now, heaven help her, they started at the mere dread over seeing him. Here. Building a fire in her classroom's potbellied stove. Monday's surprise appearance had shocked her to the point that all she'd been able to do was murmur thanks.

Tuesday—another fire.

Wednesday—one again.

Why? Her sister said it was because he had fond feelings for her, and this was his attempt to show them, to garner her attention. Luanne groaned inwardly. If he had feelings for her, then she must do something to discourage them—like go to her mother and request that her brother's new friend be politely kicked out of the house as a guest. But Mother collected stray people the way some collected stray animals. She would never rescind an offer of hospitality, especially when their guest was still recovering from his broken forearm. No help would come from Father, either. Not when Roy Bennett had done nothing to deserve banishment. He'd been the epitome of politeness. What could Luanne say? That their guest needed to go because she couldn't control her racing heart and fluttering stomach?

No, it was up to Luanne to handle her own emotions and make it clear that she had no interest in a romantic attachment to a man who flew from one place to another to chase adventure. Considering the obvious hints she'd dropped at dinner last night, odds were Roy Bennett wouldn't be here today.

Surely he wouldn't.

Please let him not be.

Her father had understood her hints. Before she left the house this morning, he told her she should outright tell Mr. Roy Bennett to stop building the fires if that's what she wanted.

And it was what she wanted. It *was!*

At the sound of a *squeak*, she cast a nervous glance down the stairs leading to the building's first floor. None of her fellow teachers appeared. Of course, it was a full twenty minutes before she expected any of them to arrive to start the day. No one ever arrived before seven A.M., except for her and the janitor.

And—*this week*—Roy Bennett.

Luanne drew in a breath and started forward, her boots clicking against the floorboards. Logic said he wasn't here. He'd been out late last night ballooning with her brother and hadn't been at breakfast.

But what if he was here?

Roy Bennett in her classroom was a problem. She should have discouraged him from building a morning fire after the first time, but she'd hated the thought of hurting the man's feelings—after all, it hadn't taken her a week of knowing Roy Bennett to realize he enjoyed helping others. Just like she enjoyed being nice. Not only did she like being considerate of others' feelings, she liked living in a town where people knew she was nice . . . or at least knew her by her "Luanne Palmer is such a nice girl" reputation.

Roy Bennett wasn't from around these parts, which was her second problem. He wasn't from anywhere, as far as she could tell. Based off the stories he'd shared about his travels, he drifted into one town and on to the next like one of the hot air balloons he raced. Once the upcoming balloon race was over, he'd leave Helena. He'd made that clear the day her brother, Geddes, brought his new friend back from a balloon race in Butte, Montana, where they'd been competitors. Roy Bennett, his left arm splinted and tied in a sling, promised to be no trouble and to leave as soon as the Helena Fall Festival was over.

Luanne nipped her bottom lip as she neared her classroom. She couldn't smell smoke. Then again, the door was closed. If he was in there—

She stopped just before her classroom door with the familiar TENTH GRADE etched in the glass, beyond where Roy could see her if he looked her way. Her hands clenched together.

She didn't want to see him.

Yet the flutters grew frantic. The flutters made her toes inch forward. The flutters caused her to hope he was in her classroom again.

That was her third problem—and the biggest one of all. She wasn't just attracted to his devastating smile. Or to how his dark beard couldn't disguise the dimples that dented his cheeks. Or to the twinkle in his blue eyes whenever he looked her way. Since Roy Bennett had arrived in Helena six weeks ago, she'd woken every morning in anticipation of seeing him, of listening to stories of his travels, of talking to him about anything and everything.

Even if she could toss away her qualms over problems one and two of why she should not be attracted to Roy Bennett, she couldn't ignore problem four.

Her teaching contract.

For the next school year, she'd agreed not to court any man, not to be alone in a room with one. She'd agreed to remain a spinster. To live according to the Board of Trustees' morality code, regardless of how ridiculously high the standards were. Thus, no matter what feelings she had for Roy Bennett, in light of her contract, they were moot. Her heart needed to accept the fact he was leaving Helena in three weeks. In twenty-five days, to be precise.

Luanne placed one hand on her racing heart and inhaled slowly through her nose in hopes of ebbing her pulse. She exhaled as slowly through an O in her lips. No more secret indulgences. Today she would do the right—and nice—thing and recuse him from building a morning fire for her class. Before she was caught admiring him.

She stepped closer to the door, reaching for the—

"Miss Palmer?" Archibald Tate's nasal voice held a note of censure.

Her heart began a sudden drumming against her chest. Where had he come from?

Luanne squared her shoulders. With an expression she hoped was an appropriate mix of pleasant surprise, quiet authority, and proper humility, she turned to face him. "Good morning, Professor Tate. You're here early."

He dipped his balding head to stare at her over his wire-rimmed glasses. "As are you."

"It's my usual time," she couldn't help clarifying.

After a little *hmmph*, he said, "I hope I'm not interrupting anything . . . ?" He let the sentence dangle with an inflection he considered a subtle attempt to guilt people into confessing their sins.

After nine years of working for the man, Luanne knew better than to take the bait. She'd once overheard him tell a board member that he often left sentences unfinished because how people filled in the thought told him what secrets they were trying to keep. She had no secrets.

Save for one.

From the look in Professor Tate's eyes, he knew about Roy Bennett's unnecessary fires and disapproved of his presence altogether. That, if it were up to him, Mr. Tate would ban Mr. Orey, the janitor, from allowing any unauthorized person access to the school. Such a ban, however, would stop fathers and brothers from building fires later in the year—something the Board of Trustees would never allow because, then, either they would have to help with the fires themselves or pay someone else to do it.

Luanne resisted the urge to glance at her classroom door. From this angle, Mr. Tate couldn't see the potbellied stove in the center of the room. Or Roy.

She gave him her blandest smile. "Of course you aren't interrupting." She motioned to her door. "Would you like to come in and see? Today we are beginning our study on Mendeleev's periodic table of elements."

His pointy chin dipped even lower, his glasses sliding, and his eyebrows lifted higher.

Luanne did her best to maintain her smile under his intense and uncomfortable appraisal.

"No need," he finally said in that usual tone, as uppity as

the cravat he wore with his three-piece suit. "You asked for time to think about my proposal." He eased closer. "It's been eleven days."

Luanne held her ground despite the need to put distance between them. "I've been busy attending to the end of the last school year and preparing for the new one. Of course, once school began . . . you know how much a teacher has to do. I also have my responsibilities at church and with the Ladies' Aid Society."

Her excuses didn't appear to mollify him. "With my wife's unexpected passing, the board deems it in the school's best interest for me to remarry quickly." His gaze shifted to her hands, yet (thankfully) he didn't grab one. "Children are best raised with a mother to give them undivided attention, don't you agree? Women with experience teaching make the best mothers."

"Miss Babcock mentioned at the Independence Day Social how she would like to marry and have children. Perhaps you should discuss this with her."

"Why settle for anyone except the best?"

She didn't respond—not with a smile or a nod or anything that he could misconstrue as her welcoming his attentions. What could she say?

That her one and only marriage proposal had come eleven days ago from the man a mere week after his wife's funeral was humiliating enough. Did he think she was desperate to marry? She didn't feel desperate. Nor did she have any empathetic feelings for the six Tate children, who according to Mr. Tate, desperately needed a new mother to help them overcome their loss. She'd been a coward for not declining his proposal immediately. It seemed best to spare his feelings. Why couldn't her signature on her teaching contract be answer enough to his proposal?

If she married him, she would have to cease teaching.

Professor Tate's children didn't need her as much as her students did. After the tenth grade, there was no more state-required schooling for them. This was her last chance to expand their minds and help the handful of troubled youths she had to see they had employment options besides prostitution and gang involvement.

Luanne motioned to her classroom. "I need to—umm, I have essays to—to read."

Mr. Tate pressed his index finger against the nose bridge of his glasses to ease them up. "I would hate for you to find yourself in a position where both your teaching contract is voided and your reputation is slighted because of the actions of a drifter."

Dread chilled her spine. He *knew* Roy Bennett was in her classroom.

Mr. Tate rested his hand on her shoulder. "Miss Palmer, I'm sure you will soon see the wisdom of a marriage between us. For the benefit of your future here at Central Secondary School. I will be around when you need me." He paused. "Always around." He gave her shoulder a little squeeze before walking away, his footsteps growing fainter as he continued down the long hall.

Luanne dropped her phony smile.

Since his wife's funeral, he'd begun arriving at school even earlier. Had he been the one to open the door this morning instead of the janitor? Had he and Roy Bennett talked this morning? Did Mr. Tate know Roy Bennett had been staying at the Palmer residence for the last six weeks? What a foolish question. Of course he knew. It wasn't a secret. She'd dutifully informed the county superintendent and the Board of Trustees.

She turned back to the door and, thankfully, felt none of the usual flutters at seeing her brother's friend. Nine years ago, on the day she'd taken her teaching certification exam, she vowed to dedicate five years to teaching. After that, her plan was to marry and start a family of her own. It would have come to fruition, too, had it not been for Yancey. Her sister's profession of love for Hale Adams—and declaration in no uncertain terms that Hale was *hers*—had brought an end to that romance . . . and to Luanne's five-year plan. In retrospect, what she felt for Hale was convenience and friendship—and a desire to stick to her schedule. She'd gotten over her disappointed hopes too easily for it to be love. Mr. Tate was suffering under a similar case of misplaced romantic attachment.

I'm sure you will soon see the wisdom of a marriage between us. For the benefit of your future here at Central Secondary School.

What did he mean? That she would lose her job if she didn't marry him? He couldn't mean that. She had to have heard him wrong.

But what if she hadn't?

Luanne blinked and sniffed to keep back tears. A widower with six children was pressuring her to marry him, she would probably lose her job if she didn't, and she had a foolish attraction to a man who had no future here. Not to mention when she cried, it was ugly: wracking sobs, swollen eyes, and globs of snot. She needed Roy Bennett gone as soon as possible—before her tumultuous emotions got the better of her. He was leaving in three weeks. She had a contract to honor. Her commitment to her students came first.

After three fortifying, deep breaths, she yanked open the door, flinging it wide so no one could accuse her of being alone with a man. And, for good measure, she slid the door prop in front to ensure it stayed open.

Roy rose as soon as she took two steps inside the already warm room. "Miss Palmer, what a pleasure to see you this morning."

"Mr. Bennett." She held herself rigid, not daring to move or speak lest her control broke.

"I'll be done here in two shakes of a lamb's tail." He returned his attention to the fire, and she opened her eyes wider, blinking and blinking to keep from tearing up again.

He reached sideways and grabbed a few larger pieces of kindling wood. It stretched the fabric of his white shirt, revealing the bumps and ridges of his muscled arms. He could easily lift her into his arms and carry her down the stairs and not be the least bit labored. Her chest tightened. Flutters—

With a growl under her breath, she looked away.

A *clap-swish, clap-swish* sound drew her attention back to the unwanted man—yes, yes, he was unwanted—standing in the center of the room and tending an unnecessary fire.

He swiped his hands together a few more times, ridding them of lingering dirt and wood. "All set."

Luanne looked heavenward and gave her head a little shake. "Thank you," she muttered.

He drew his eyebrows closer together. "Have I offended in some way, Miss Palmer?"

"Of course not." Luanne waited for him to say more.

He didn't.

They stared at each other for an uncomfortable moment.

She clenched her hands together. "Why . . . uhh . . . why do you ask?"

"You looked put out. And now you are scowling at me."

"No, no, I was—" No matter what her parents said, honesty wasn't always the best policy. Although she had to stop ignoring the fact that she had to tell him in no uncertain terms that his fire-building skills were unneeded.

She met his confused gaze. The poor man was only trying to be helpful. Later. She would talk to him later, when she wasn't distraught over the conversation with Professor

Tate. Yes, that was the wise thing to do. Be calm. Don't cry. Oh, why was this happening to her? Why did Geddes, of all the racers in Butte, have to be the one closest to Roy Bennett when his balloon landed too hard, tossing him from his basket and breaking his arm? And why couldn't Geddes have limited his Good Samaritan instincts to seeing Roy Bennett to the hospital? Why invite him to live in Helena—in the Palmers' house—for two, full months?

Luanne pressed the back of her hand against her nose. She sniffed again.

He picked up his brown tweed coat. He tossed it over his shoulder, one hooked finger keeping it from falling to the floor, and started toward her. "Are you feeling under the weather?"

"I'm fine, thank you." Luanne eased sideways so he could exit through the door. The bustle beneath her navy plaid skirt bent under the pressure of sliding against the chalkboard, but remaining far away from Roy Bennett took precedence over keeping her skirt clean. One sympathetic glance, one expression of concern, and she'd throw herself in his arms with such abandon she'd be fired for sure.

If he didn't believe her insistence that she was fine, Roy Bennett was gentleman enough not to accuse her outright. He stopped on the threshold and offered her one of his sigh-evoking smiles. "I look forward to seeing you this evening at dinner."

Luanne nodded, giving him the same placid grin she'd perfected for dealing with Professor Tate. As soon as he closed the door behind him, her breath caught. The tears she'd held at bay fell. How would this work out?

The wall clock chimed the top of the hour. Seven A.M.

Luanne straightened her shoulders and wiped her face with the back of her hands. A letter would solve this. Two, actually. One to Mr. Tate explaining her refusal. One to Roy Bennett asking him to cease building a fire for her classroom. That was the simplest solution. Starting now, she would avoid him. As much as possible, at any rate. She had her involvement with church, school, and the Ladies' Aid Society to keep her occupied. New plan: be polite but disinterested during family dinner, then disappear for evening charitable causes as soon as the dishes were cleared.

Yes. That's how it would work out.

Books by Bestselling Author
Fern Michaels

__The Jury	0-8217-7878-1	$6.99US/$9.99CAN
__Sweet Revenge	0-8217-7879-X	$6.99US/$9.99CAN
__Lethal Justice	0-8217-7880-3	$6.99US/$9.99CAN
__Free Fall	0-8217-7881-1	$6.99US/$9.99CAN
__Fool Me Once	0-8217-8071-9	$7.99US/$10.99CAN
__Vegas Rich	0-8217-8112-X	$7.99US/$10.99CAN
__Hide and Seek	1-4201-0184-6	$6.99US/$9.99CAN
__Hokus Pokus	1-4201-0185-4	$6.99US/$9.99CAN
__Fast Track	1-4201-0186-2	$6.99US/$9.99CAN
__Collateral Damage	1-4201-0187-0	$6.99US/$9.99CAN
__Final Justice	1-4201-0188-9	$6.99US/$9.99CAN
__Up Close and Personal	0-8217-7956-7	$7.99US/$9.99CAN
__Under the Radar	1-4201-0683-X	$6.99US/$9.99CAN
__Razor Sharp	1-4201-0684-8	$7.99US/$10.99CAN
__Yesterday	1-4201-1494-8	$5.99US/$6.99CAN
__Vanishing Act	1-4201-0685-6	$7.99US/$10.99CAN
__Sara's Song	1-4201-1493-X	$5.99US/$6.99CAN
__Deadly Deals	1-4201-0686-4	$7.99US/$10.99CAN
__Game Over	1-4201-0687-2	$7.99US/$10.99CAN
__Sins of Omission	1-4201-1153-1	$7.99US/$10.99CAN
__Sins of the Flesh	1-4201-1154-X	$7.99US/$10.99CAN
__Cross Roads	1-4201-1192-2	$7.99US/$10.99CAN

Available Wherever Books Are Sold!

Check out our website at **www.kensingtonbooks.com**

More from Bestselling Author

JANET DAILEY

Calder Storm	0-8217-7543-X	$7.99US/$10.99CAN
Close to You	1-4201-1714-9	$5.99US/$6.99CAN
Crazy in Love	1-4201-0303-2	$4.99US/$5.99CAN
Dance With Me	1-4201-2213-4	$5.99US/$6.99CAN
Everything	1-4201-2214-2	$5.99US/$6.99CAN
Forever	1-4201-2215-0	$5.99US/$6.99CAN
Green Calder Grass	0-8217-7222-8	$7.99US/$10.99CAN
Heiress	1-4201-0002-5	$6.99US/$7.99CAN
Lone Calder Star	0-8217-7542-1	$7.99US/$10.99CAN
Lover Man	1-4201-0666-X	$4.99US/$5.99CAN
Masquerade	1-4201-0005-X	$6.99US/$8.99CAN
Mistletoe and Molly	1-4201-0041-6	$6.99US/$9.99CAN
Rivals	1-4201-0003-3	$6.99US/$7.99CAN
Santa in a Stetson	1-4201-0664-3	$6.99US/$9.99CAN
Santa in Montana	1-4201-1474-3	$7.99US/$9.99CAN
Searching for Santa	1-4201-0306-7	$6.99US/$9.99CAN
Something More	0-8217-7544-8	$7.99US/$9.99CAN
Stealing Kisses	1-4201-0304-0	$4.99US/$5.99CAN
Tangled Vines	1-4201-0004-1	$6.99US/$8.99CAN
Texas Kiss	1-4201-0665-1	$4.99US/$5.99CAN
That Loving Feeling	1-4201-1713-0	$5.99US/$6.99CAN
To Santa With Love	1-4201-2073-5	$6.99US/$7.99CAN
When You Kiss Me	1-4201-0667-8	$4.99US/$5.99CAN
Yes, I Do	1-4201-0305-9	$4.99US/$5.99CAN

Available Wherever Books Are Sold!

Check out our website at **www.kensingtonbooks.com.**